BACKSLIDE

Teresa Stores

Spinsters Ink

2008

The following portions of *Backslide* were previously published as short fiction in these journals:

"The Diviner Story, or How I Nearly Got Kilt by a Snake" was adapted as a short story and published in *Oregon Literary Review* 2.1 (Winter/Spring 2007) http://orelitrev.startlogic.com/v2n1/OregonLiteraryReview.htm.

"The Swim Story, or Why Baptists Don't Dance" was adapted as a short story titled "A Time To," published in *Harrington Lesbian Fiction Quarterly* 7.4 (Fall 2006) ISSN 1556-9225.

"Why My Great Aunt Belle Drives a Golf Cart" was adapted as a short story for young adults and published in *Cicada* (January/February 2006) 56-69. ISSN 1097-4008.

A portion of "Sinner" and the "Backslide" portion about the funeral of Virge's brother was adapted as part of a flash fiction story titled "Blue Hole" and published in *Rock & Sling: A Journal of Literature, Art, and Faith* 2.2 (Fall 2006) 78. ISSN 1552-5929.

Spinsters Ink
P.O. Box 242
Midway, Florida 32343

Printed in the United States of America on acid-free paper
First Edition

Editor: Katherine V. Forrest
Cover designer: LA Callaghan

ISBN-10: 1-59493-112-7
ISBN-13: 978-1-59493-112-3

*For Susan, who encouraged me throughout
the very long gestation and birth of this new baby,
now all grown up and finally leaving home.*

Acknowledgments

Thank you to the friends, family and colleagues who have played a role in the creation and publication of this novel. Each contribution of time, child care, kind words, good advice, cheerleading, commentary, reading, editing, feedback and small acts of kindness played a vital role in this long process of writing, rewriting and publishing. The list of folks to whom I am grateful is long: Susan Jarvis, first and always, for a million huge and small acts of love and support, for reading and offering feedback on dozens of drafts, and for simply believing in me and Virge. David Valdes Greenwood in ten years never failed to ask me how the book was coming. Patricia Dunn-Fierstein and Sara Jane Moss helped me to understand and confront the difficult issues that background this material, and my old friends Jenny Hubbard and Dierdre O'Neill helped me survive that toughest of times during which this work was conceived. My colleagues in the Department of English at the University of Hartford had faith that something would come of the work; Bill Stull's enthusiasm, in particular, kept me excited about the project over the long haul. Thank you to my students for their enthusiasm and support throughout; you give me the energy for this work! Susan Jarvis, Katherine

Forrest, Michel Lafantano, Rye Davis and Beneth Sauer were my first readers on various (lengthy) drafts, and their wisdom helped to shape this final version. Peter Elbow offered me sound advice about the narrative voice of my young Virge, advice that also led me to discover her true story. Monona Wali's unflinching eye helped me to untangle the plot and revise when I had nearly lost all perspective on the work, and this final version owes much to her generous feedback. Katherine V. Forrest is, perhaps, the best editor on the planet and her steady hand and warm encouragement have guided me to what I believe is the best novel this book can be. Linda Hill has provided a home, at last, for a book I hope will, in turn, help to solidify the future of the true home of lesbian publishing, Spinsters Ink. The Vermont Arts Council and the National Endowment for the Arts, the Barbara Deming Money for Women Fund, the Richard J. Cardin Faculty Research Fund and a University of Hartford Summer Stipend all provided invaluable monetary support in the form of grants toward the completion of this book. The writers and editors I met at The Community of Writers at Squaw Valley and Breadloaf—and Claire Messud in particular—gave me direction and inspiration at a critical juncture in the revision process. Editors Adam Oldacker, Susan Cowger, Joshua Weber and Charles Deemer, and Judith Stelboum at *Cicada, Rock & Sling, The Oregon Literary Review* and *The Harrington Lesbian Literary Quarterly* (respectively) each offered a much-needed boost by publishing excerpts or chapters from the novel as short stories during the last few years. Donna Galin's help with a million little clerical tasks make her a cherished and indispensable part of my work life, and Juliet Williams and Paula McDonald at the University of Hartford Copy Shoppe put the magic touch on *Backslide* when they snuck a read of the first few pages and complimented the book just before I mailed the manuscript out.

Thank you all. I could not have done this without true believers.

Sinner

"SINNER!"

The white letters against the blood red of the book jacket fill the television screen. I cringe, and the camera cuts to my face. I look guilty. I blink and try to smile, still watching the monitor.

"We're back with Virge Young—" Kora says. I try to relax into the armchair and look at home in the faux living room for the camera. "—the author of this controversial new novel."

I am not a sinner, I remind myself. I don't believe in that stuff anymore. I am not a sinner.

"We've talked a little about the characters in the book," she says, addressing the camera, "the members of this fundamentalist church, each of whom is revealed to be a secret sinner. Why the shifting point of view?" she asks. "And why nineteen-sixty-nine?"

I focus on the audience, resettling after the commercial break. It's just another interview, I tell myself, and it's going fine. A man in the back row—square and blocky, hair very short, neck bulging from his too-tight tie—reminds me of my father. My scalp tingles.

"Virge?" Kora touches my arm.

"Oh." I tear my gaze from the man to meet her eyes. "Yes, sorry." I swallow. I've answered this question before, on my book tour, a hundred times in the last couple of months it seems. The words rush out. "The point of view is an attempt to get at the truth. It seems to me to be ever-shifting, you know? Each character believes in his or her own reality as *the* reality, *the* truth. Christians believe that there is only one truth, one God, one way to God, but I'm trying to show that even for these individual Christians, truth is individual. It comes from inside. It's subjective and fragmented. They profess to believe in this really limited objective truth, but in their individual points of view we see something else."

Kora nods, seeming to agree. "Isn't that what makes them sinners?" she asks.

"Sure," I say. "Partly. Being closed to other points of view makes them sinners."

"Or is it being open to other points of view that makes them sinners?" she asks.

Some of the audience laugh with me, a spattering of chuckles. "Exactly what their belief tells them," I say, smiling. "You can see why these characters are so confused."

Kora leans forward. "How about the setting," she says. "Why set your novel in nineteen-sixty-nine?"

"It was a coming-of-age in American history," I say, repeating the lines I've used in every book talk I've done. "Woodstock, Vietnam, Kent State, right before Watergate. This was an adolescent nation, challenging all the rules, all the authority of the forefathers, the founders. We were testing the limits, pushing the boundaries, even of space." Kora rests her chin on her fist and frowns, listening as I rattle off my little speech. "The old structures fell apart. And the fundamentalist churches were part of that. Old religious ideology was challenged too," I say, trying to raise and lower my voice to make it sound fresh. "That era offered an opportunity to change, to grow, to learn how to keep growing." I'm tired of talking already, rushing it. I hope my voice doesn't betray me. I try to sound upbeat, to frown, to look like I care. "I think a lot of us—the fundamentalists and maybe the country—failed," I say. "We got stuck. We went backward again. We were afraid of the fragmentation that suddenly seemed everywhere—families, generations, churches, politics, races. We were nostalgic for that simpler life that seemed more cohesive. Obviously not so, but it *seemed* so. We backslid, as they would say. They—"

Kora holds up her hand. "Wait a minute," she says.

I close my mouth. *What?*

"If we got stuck back then, or backslid or whatever, why not set the story today, or after that?" Her gaze is serious but her eyes are twinkling. She's asked a good question, one that might make this a real conversation.

I think for a moment. "Hmmm," I stall.

"Maybe we're stuck there after all?" she asks. "Maybe not backsliders yet?"

"Maybe," I say. "Maybe I want to think that we still have that opportunity to change, to embrace this fragmented reality." I laugh suddenly. "Maybe I'm just nostalgic," I say. "Maybe deep down I want to stay there myself, never change."

"Ahhh." Kora smiles, sitting forward. She's caught me. "So this is about you," she says. "Not so much fiction after all."

My face grows warm, but I smile as if this is not a hard question. "It's fiction," I say. "Fiction."

"Some of your critics say not. Some say the book is only a thinly disguised autobiography." I notice that she's got a finger stuck inside her copy of *Sinner.*

My heart beats a little faster. "My truth is in this book, yes," I say. "But life is never this tidy. I could never do the things my characters do, or say the things they say."

Kora tilts her head to the side. "I'd like to read a little passage," she says.

I look down and pick up the water glass from the table next to me. I know what's coming.

"In the opening scene of this book," she explains to the audience, "a young woman comes home to the South from New York to attend the funeral of her younger brother." She glances at me. "Why did you choose this character for the opening point of view?" she asks.

I sip from the glass, wishing I could hold it to my eyelids and forehead to cool off. Kora waits while I swallow. "I wanted to bring a real sinner back in from the outside," I say. "Someone who was one of them, part of the church, but one who had left and gone off to live a life in the world. Someone who is a sinner by their standard."

"And her sin is—?" she asks.

"She's a lesbian," I say. It's not that I'm in the closet, far from it. The reviewers made all parts of my life public. I don't believe in silence either. It's just that my mom will see this, and it's not that big a part of the novel anyway, or it wasn't supposed to be. Only one of a couple dozen characters, one of a dozen points of view. Funny how things turn out.

Kora nods. "As the story unfolds, of course," she fills in, "each chapter is focused from a new character's point of view—different people in the church—each of whom is a sinner of one kind or another." She opens *Sinner* on her lap, looks down, then back to the audience. "At the beginning though, a funeral, a death. Everyone is devastated. The fundamentalist church community Lil grew up in surrounds her—the brother was a deacon in the church, a leader—and at the funeral, someone passes a letter to her." Kora pauses to find her place in the book. With my own words in her voice, I slip back home.

"'Lil couldn't believe that her little brother's big heart had stopped at only thirty-three—just like Jesus. Jesse was the only person back home who knew the truth of her, and now God had taken him.

"'She stood before him in his huge coffin, his nose still sunburned, his skin puffy and cold, his wide shoulders too snug against the blue satin. She felt strange, having just arrived after a thirty-hour train trip from crisp New York autumn into Florida swelter, as if she were swimming in a baptismal pool, everything blurry through green water and glass. I am drowning in home, she thought, in this awful reunion. Papa kept staring at her, mute, and Mama prayed, weeping through closed eyes. "It's better that he died, better than you," she had said at the station. "Better than you." She had paused, but she hadn't said what Lil thought she would. She hadn't accused her of her sin. "I know Jesse's in heaven," Mama had said. Jesse's young widow had wailed, seeing his green eyes in Lil's own, and her little nephews and niece, Jesse's children, wandered through the church now, from adult to adult, looking for their father, trying to understand. Lil's big little brother—witness to her life—was laid out, not breathing, in a box.

"'Lil sat on a hard pew to read the letter passed to her by one of the deacons: *This is your fault. He's warning you. Jesus sayeth, I am the Way, the Truth, and the Life, and no man comes to the Father except by me. Get straight with God, queer. This is your fault.*'"

Kora stops, still looking at the page, and shakes her head, lips pursed. I hear intakes of breath. People who haven't read the book, I guess. They will all get free copies for coming today. Some will burn them. Kora looks at me. "Didn't that really happen to you?" she asks.

The water glass sweats in my hands. I am afraid to look out at the audience. I steel myself. Not my fault. And people need to know. "Yes," I say. "More or less." I take a sip from the glass.

"Not in nineteen-sixty-nine, obviously!" Kora interrupts, and the audience laughs. "You can't be that old!" she says.

I smile. "No, it's fiction," I say, and everyone laughs again.

"It's ugly," Kora says.

I nod. Her brown eyes envelop my own gaze, warm and sympathetic. "Hate is ugly," I say. "They say they love the sinners and hate the sin, but it's not true. They do not act from love. They sin when they hate at all."

"You were once one of them, a Christian fundamentalist?" she asks, not waiting for an answer. "So what does Lil do that is not you?" she asks.

I swallow. Whoa. "It's um—" I stop and start again. "It's fiction," I say. "It's a novel."

"Yes," Kora nods. "And you said that you could never do or say things that your characters do and say." She smiles, having caught me. "So what does Lil do?"

I try not to look guilty. "I'm not so good at confrontation as Lil," I say. "She eventually says what she needs to say directly to her family, to her friends, to her church." I shake my head to clear it of the images of my mother and father and the others. "That's not so easy in real life. It's never so clear. And Lil is still more or less the person she was when she was a girl, before she left the South. I'm not. I've left all my past behind me. I'm completely different."

"Would you say that Lil is a Christian?" Kora asks. She glances at her notes and checks the time while the camera focuses on me.

"Yes," I say. "She would say that she is." I sigh and look off into the lights for an instant. "Nineteen-sixty-nine was different," I continue. "That's another way we're different. I'm a little less afraid of losing my faith in religion or that one particular God, but Lil lives in a time when fewer people were willing to question that God. When it meant something else. She stays safe in her beliefs in God." I pause for a breath. "But you know, maybe she does think a little differently about God than the fundamentalists she grew up with. Like Christian is just one part of who she is."

"A post-modernist Christian then," Kora says, laughing. The

audience laughs too, relieved.

I smile. "Sure," I say, glad for this new direction in the conversation. "I mean, I'm a lesbian and a writer and a mother and a daughter and a teacher and an American and a Democrat and a softball player. We're all so many things—many identities—at once. As writer I try on other people's selves. Which of those selves is most important? Which is the true self? No one self and all of them at the same time."

Hisses erupt from the studio audience, and Kora and I both glance that way. The Christians are here, I think. The protestors that have followed me since the book came out. The man in the shadows at the back stands up, and my neck prickles. He can't be my father; I know he's not my father. He just looks like him.

I swallow and continue. "Christianity—like most official religions—is a human excuse to exclude people—queers, Democrats, softball players—" Laughter. Good. "It's also an excuse to make war, to hate, to make others into the 'true' believer's image, which they will define in very limited terms. Not a god's image, but their own human image, one self that eliminates all the other selves."

Kora frowns. "And so you can be a Christian and a sinner too." She leans forward from the waist.

"Definitely," I say. "Even the fundamentalists agree with that. What matters to them, of course, is whether you are redeemed—saved—from that sin, according to their narrow terms." I don't want to lecture, but here I am. Some big holy nothing. The Antichrist. I sigh. I wish I could go home. Back to the top of the mountain in Vermont, my solid white house with my children and Ruthie under the apple tree. Home.

"The Christians call me a backslider," I continue. "Some say I was never saved—never redeemed from my sins—way back when—" I glide back twenty-five years to the baptismal pool, the wavering blue-green images through the water and glass "—but that is their definition of salvation and their definition of sin. I'm not who I was then." I blink, trying to focus on the here and now and the then and there at the same time. Kora shifts in her chair. "A writer is kind of like God, you know. We get inside characters, inside the skins of other people. Maybe that's a way of trying to understand them. Maybe expose them. Maybe forgive them. Or ourselves . . ." I stop suddenly and laugh.

Kora laughs too. "Does that mean God needs forgiveness too?" she asks.

"Hell yes," I say. "God most of all, at least this one they taught me about in Sunday school all those years when I was little." I feel that old guilt again, that pounding fear in my veins, and swallow it down. "He's a nasty fellow, that old Father with all the rules."

"So what's a sinner then?" she asks, her brown eyes sharp. "What do you think a sinner is if not what the Christians say?"

"A hater," I answer. I don't blink or hesitate. "Sinners shut off love, shut off other people, maybe even shut off parts of themselves. Don't pay attention to their insides. We're just lumps of matter, you know. That's real. That's what we live in." I look into the camera lens. "When we let the rules of religion—any religion—tell us to hate—" I glance toward the man in the shadows "—then we become sinners. That is how the characters in my book are sinners. Love is how they are saved, redeemed. That's how I save them."

Kora nods. "Yes," she says, "well." She lets the silence hang. The audience rustles. Kora looks toward them. "Now I know y'all've been waiting for awhile—" She smiles. "And so I'd like to give some of you a chance to ask some questions too." A couple of the cameras sweep the room. People have lined up at the microphones in the aisles. "Yes." Kora nods at a woman to our right in the front.

She's about twenty. One of a group of gay and lesbian college kids in the front row. "Yes, Kora," she says, blushing. "I just want to thank Virge for this book. It's so right. We've got to be out." She raises her voice. "We've got to be loud and proud to fight the right!" Her friends cheer.

Kora laughs. "Do you have a question for Virge?" she asks.

"Well, um, yeah," the girl says. "What do you think about the gay marriage thing? Don't you think that's just going to make it harder for us to get straight people to accept us? Just politicize something that doesn't really matter?"

I smile and glance over at Ruth, my lover, who is also sitting in the front row, then back at the questioner. "Civil marriage is a state-licensed agreement between two people. If we truly have separation of church and state, and we truly have equal rights for all people, civil marriage shouldn't discriminate between straight and gay couples. Whether it's in a church or not is up to the churches, but the legal union shouldn't be decided upon according to a religious tradition. That does matter."

Hisses and cheers erupt. Kora stands and walks toward the audience. "Okay, okay," she says. "Let's keep it civil." Some people laugh. She smiles. "What about you, Virge?" she asks. "Would you get married if you could?" She is setting up the introduction of Ruthie.

I smile. "I'm a resident of Vermont," I say, "so my partner and I have planned a legal civil union in that state, the same as marriage in Vermont now. A contract between two people recognized by the state to authorize a family. Not the business of the churches." I grin at Ruthie, who is smiling back at me. "That's my partner over there." Ruth's face fills the monitor screen. "We'll have our civil union this coming summer," I say. "In August."

A smattering of applause in the studio audience. The kids in the front row cheer. "And your children?" Kora asks.

"Twins, almost two now. Back at the hotel." I meet Ruthie's eyes. "We were afraid to bring them here." I look at the camera. "We were afraid for our children, you can understand that. We want our children to be safe, to be respected, to have their family honored and respected wherever they go. That matters."

Kora nods, walking toward the other side of the room. "Yes. Children change everything. They raise the stakes, don't they?" She points to the woman standing at the other microphone. "What's your question?"

"Hi Kora," the woman says. She's older, maybe my mom's age, dressed in slacks and a sweater embroidered with a large kitten. "I just love your show!" she gushes.

Kora laughs, reaching her. "Oh thank you," she says and half-hugs the older woman. "Now what did you want to ask Virge?"

The woman dabs her eye, and takes a breath. "Well," she says, "I was just wondering why you didn't write an autobiography instead of a novel since so much of it is true to your life?"

I pretend to think for a minute, even though it's a familiar question. "Well," I say. "I guess I wanted to protect the truth a little, some of the people in my life. Fiction naturally raises the question of whether something really happened or not, so if others in my life want to deny a truth, they can, or if they want to claim a fiction, they can do that too." I pause, thinking of my mother, my father, Ruthie, our children. "The novelist E.M. Forster once said that what separates fiction from reality is that 'fiction is knowable.' In stories, life has a meaning. We can try to know what it means because we can contain it, like a family in a home. But real life is too big, too cluttered to contain—like family—it's too big to truly know." I pause for effect. "And besides, this book *is* fiction." Laughter.

Kora has moved toward the back of the studio. When the lights come up, the man who looks like my father is standing behind the mike. His hands are in his jacket pockets. My ears start to ring.

"Yes sir," says Kora. "Your question."

"I just wanna say that this is an abomination," he says. His voice trembles. Nerves? Anger? I can't tell.

Someone in the back yells, "Tell it, brother!" I slip back again to Free Will Baptist Church, to my childhood, to the drowning sensation of baptism. "Amen!" comes another voice. A small part of me warms at the familiar echo, but then I have to grip my chair to keep from standing up to run away. A row of people near the back stand up, as if on cue, holding signs. The usual stuff: *Adam and Eve, not Adam and Steve. AIDS is God's answer to gays.*

"Do you have a question?" Kora's voice is stern. She doesn't like this. I know she has tried to keep this kind of demonstration from happening, her security people checking at the doors for signs and posters, but they always slip in anyway. I know that from the tour. I'll be glad when it's over.

The man glances at her. His graying eyebrows are bushy, the lines around his mouth deep. "Yeah," he says. "I wanna know why her and her kind aren't afraid of burning in hell? And if her life's so hard, why would she want to bring children into it? Expose them to her filth?" He talks faster, ignoring Kora, who's giving a look to the beefy guys in black T-shirts on the sidelines, out of camera range. "I'll tell you why. These homosexuals are having kids just so they can rape 'em. Bunch of child molesters, that's what they are. Trying to worm their way into our schools so they can get our kids. Adopting kids so they can get 'em. Now havin' their own kids for the same thing. Ought'a be ashamed—"

The beefy guys start moving toward him. "Wait," I say. "Let me respond to that." I look around. "This is hate," I say. I point to the man, then sweep the row of sign-holders with my finger. "This is fear. This is evil. This is sin." I look into the camera. "Fundamentalism is a corruption of Christ, of Christianity, of God, of America. It's nothing but hate. This kind of hate should have died thirty years ago. Don't let them control your minds. Don't let them control your faith, and don't let this religious sect control your country." I look at Kora. "I wrote this book to get people to talking," I say. "Straight people, queer people, Christians, Jews, blacks, plain ordinary people. Anybody who's been silenced or erased or exiled within their own home." I look back at the camera, feeling like a preacher. Why did I ever want to be a preacher? "They are sinners, haters. Don't let them speak without an answer," I say. "Don't let them lead us down a path to the hell that is their invention. Don't let them tell you that this isn't your home too."

People in the audience are standing. The sign wavers are hissing and booing. Some of the kids in the front row are trying to climb over their chairs. Too much Jerry Springer. Kora fills the monitor screen, seeming calm, ignoring the fracas. "We'll be back," she says, cutting to commercial. One of the assistants beckons to me, so I stand, preparing to escape into the wings.

I glance at the scary guy from the back row one last time. His face and neck are red. The security guys are almost to him but distracted by the chaos breaking out all over the room. His right hand comes out of his pocket. He's holding a handgun.

"You're the sinner!" he yells. "Go to hell!"

I hear the shot and feel the sharp shove to my shoulder before the bite of pain registers.

I fall backward, sliding into nothing.

Backslide

I am driving myself home in the old pickup truck. I am going home to the top of the hill.

My home in Vermont looks out over green mountains, and it is warm and big enough to hold my whole life. Sometimes in dreams, I drive up this hill but arrive at my childhood home in Jacksonville, or at my grandparents' home or my grandmother's little single-person house, or at one of the many homes I have inhabited as I've moved around the country, the world, looking for that place I belonged, that person I was supposed to be. No matter where I arrive in those dreams, waiting for me will be all my families, all my people, those now and those past and even those yet to come.

This is like one of those dreams. I think I hear Ruthie. I think I hear the children's voices. My father. My mother. My brother. Others. Maybe it's the wind or the sound of the tires slipping.

The road is icy, the tree limbs bare and etched black with white snow. I recognize Steep Way Road. My truck is sliding on ice. I turn into the skid, downshift and ease the accelerator up, but the tires whirl, unable to grab pavement or gravel, and the upward, homeward momentum slows. Wheels spinning, I begin to slide back.

For that moment, I know I have no control. Time and space and even the me at the wheel slip, glide, whirl. The black limbs and white snow blur into soft grays. I brake. The truck stops. My shoulder throbs. I have no choice. I cannot go home this way.

I turn the wheels and point the vehicle back down the hill. It might take more time, or I might lose time, or I might wander across times as I drive, slipping back into my past and ahead into my future. I know the meandering route on Back Road—a maze of back roads—will take me across boundaries of town and time, through shadowy woods and over light-filled meadows and finally to the top by way of the bottom. I might be a different person along that way. I might be many. I might be both sinner and saved. I might not be either. But I will still arrive at my home at the top of the hill. This is the truth of the backslide.

The Diviner Story, or How I Nearly Got Kilt by a Snake

I turned thirteen in September 1969, but it all started when I nearly got kilt by the snake in August. Or maybe in July when the diviner came to Green Acres to find water for our new home. Or maybe even when I got born again again in June. The stories are all mixed-up together now.

In July, after the astronauts walked on the moon, we left home on Renoir Drive in Jacksonville, Florida, and moved down to our farm, Green Acres, for summer vacation. First Mom made us watch them stake the flag of the United States of America into that whole other place out in space, which seemed kind of like magic, that one small step for man and all those neato no-gravity leaps for mankind. But then we turned off the TV, locked up our squatty concrete-block house in the suburbs, and drove out to the farm through a maze of dirt roads, all us kids in the back of the pickup truck, bouncing into each other over the bumps.

Our farm is called Green Acres on account of that's Dad's favorite TV show, and our place is kind of broke down like that too. At home on Renoir Drive, we watched every week, my little brother, Lee, and me singing along to the chorus about how Green Acres is the place to be. I know the words to the second verse too—about New York being the place where I'd rather be—but I just mumble them, because the hazy city skyline and Eva Gabor's accent and her eyelids painted like Ricki Ann's made me feel funny inside. Dad always used to snort at Arnold-the-Pig jokes and city-slicker Oliver's schemes before he dozed off in his La-Z-Boy lounger, and Mom always came in from doing dishes, drying her hands on her apron, and said, "Ed, that story's so stupid it's funny." But she wouldn't have woke him up—none of us would've—because no telling what he would do.

Our Green Acres has a shack made out of tar paper and tin that we slept in on vacation, and fifteen head of cattle—I gave them names like Bessie, Martha and Karen, pretending that nobody was going to eat them. There are cedar Christmas trees in almost straight rows that Dad planned to sell in town in December and a garden of long lazy watermelons with dark green stripes and pale bellies that he was going to take to the farmer's market. Dad's practically a farmer. When he was a boy he plowed up stones in the mountains at his home on a farm near Birmingham and picked tobacco for pocket money, but now he does regular work like at the docks or on construction crews, except when he's laid off like last summer. Mom's parents are still farmers, bringing us corn and tomatoes, mustard greens, tiny brown field peas, bruised strawberries, squash and okra from their garden in Georgia, especially when Dad's not working. Our white chest freezer is always full of frosty vegetables, dead cows and the frozen pizzas that Mom buys when they're "On Special, 2 for $1." Dad told Mom that Green Acres was an investment, because they're not making any more land, but when we went there in July, us kids riding in the bed of the truck, me bumping into Ricki Ann through the maze of dirt roads, it felt like going backward and forward at once.

I had got saved again just before the astronauts walked on the moon and we went to Green Acres for vacation. I accepted the Lord Jesus Christ into my heart and became a Christian for the second time. I think I heard Him calling me that day in church, I must have. My heart beat fast, sweat rolling down my neck, legs clammy under pantyhose, my stomach empty. When Pastor Bob talked about e-ternal hell and the Lord coming soon to rapture up all His children, I felt scared. I didn't want to be left on earth alone with all the sinners, dope dealers, murderers and Buddhists. Standing there thinking about junior high school in the fall, hanging onto the pew with my hands all cramped up and my eyes squeezed so shut I was seeing stars during the invitation to be saved, I thought I'd explode. I heard my ears ringing. It had to be Jesus calling me up to the front to be saved, even though I thought I was already. So I went. I stepped out into the aisle and just followed my feet down the plush red carpet path, people wailing on the fourth or fifth verse of "Ju-ust as I a-am, with-ou-out one plea . . ." And when Pastor Bob hugged me into his suit, smelling like Dad's Old Spice and dry cleaner chemicals, I told him that I needed to get saved. And he said, "Didn'tcha get saved when you were a little girl?" And I told him I couldn't remember nothing from that time when I was six. "I don't think it took," I said. And he said, "Praise God!" and passed me on to Brother Floyd, who always kind of scared me because he'd get the spirit now and then and start speaking in tongues, which sounded a lot like his mouth was full of marbles, and sometimes even start drooling or foaming and have to be took out. But he was a deacon, like my dad, and he'd led tons of souls to Jesus, so I followed along with him in his Bible and prayed the words he told me to pray—"Lord Jesus, I confess that I am a sinner, and I come to you asking you to forgive me and come into my heart, Amen"—and he hopped up and yelled "Praise Jeeezsus!" And I was saved. Everybody came and shook my hand or hugged me, and Mom cried, and that night I got baptized again. I did remember that from when I was six, because I remember it scared me, like the preacher was pushing me under to drown me. This time I kept my eyes open and I could see all the people in the congregation through the glass front window of the baptismal pool, all blurry and wavy and blue-green from the water, and I knew to hold my breath and how to grab the preacher's arm, and he said the words with a pause when he pushed me under so I could hear them: "Buried in the likeness of His death"—big chlorine breath in, hold it, push down under the water, faces, I hope my robe doesn't float up to show my underwear, then up, breathing in again—"raised up in the likeness of His resurrection." And I was saved. Praise God.

Ricki Ann wasn't saved at all, and I almost didn't want to go to heaven without her. I prayed for her. I didn't want to leave my best friend on earth with the other lost sinners when Jesus came back to rapture us Christians up to heaven. I wanted to be the one to lead her to the Lord, to give my personal testimony about being saved and have that story inspire her to want to get saved too, but I kept getting mixed-up about what to say.

When we got to the shack at Green Acres after the moon walk, Mom sent me and Ricki Ann to the pump out back to fetch water for Kool-Aid and cooking. "Watch out for snakes, Virginia," she yelled like always. We followed the path between blackberry stickers into the cool, dark clearing under oak trees. The pump seemed like an old wizard, all crusty with rust, the dirt around it stamped down black and damp in a circle.

"Cool," Ricki Ann whispered.

I primed the pump by pouring in a coffee can full of water, then push-pulled push-pulled push-pulled on the long handle. It squeaked and groaned, stiff at first, until far away, down inside its throat, some-where deep in the earth, we heard a gurgling. In Florida, water comes from rivers in caverns underground—veins of blue through limestone—the aquifer. We heard something like the catch in your throat before you cough, a kind of voice from underground, and I told Ricki Ann to stick her head under the spout.

"Ye-ow!" she yelled when the water rushed up and out. She jumped back, spluttering. "No way!" she said. "That's too cold."

"Then you pump," I said, and put my face under the stream, so clear and cold it made my head ache. In the summer in Florida, the days get so hot and still you can't hardly move, and the steam hangs over the Bahia grass in mirages, and the cicadas and tree frogs scream one note forever. But through the water rushing up from the aquifer and over my eyes, everything seemed new that day. I looked at Ricki Ann, wavery, pumping the handle, until I finally had to jump back, gasping with the cold myself. The whole world became sharp and clear and cool and light.

That night, Dad unfurled the big blue scrolls of our house plans—two stories, just like Yankee houses in picture books—and we all studied them. We were going to move down to the farm forever someday. The site where Dad was going to build our new home was across the cow pasture and past the tree house, almost in the middle of our sixty acres, far from the shack and the old pump. Dad looked up from the blueprint scroll, his face as serious as when he read from the Bible before Sunday dinner, and said, "We're gonna need a new well." And that's why the diviner came.

"Man, he's old," I said to Ricki Ann, watching the diviner from the tree house. He had a cool old truck and a big yeller dog that sat in the bed with drool dripping off his tongue.

"It's in his hands," said Ricki Ann.

Lying flat on the plywood floor, we spied while the diviner walked down the pasture with my dad. His hands were at his sides, but they were alive, even just hanging there while he talked. He kept his shoulders and his elbows stiff, but his palms twitched out every now and then, like butterfly wings. His hands were pale, not calloused, even though everything else about him was rough: patched overalls, all grimed and dusty; straw hat full of holes, shadowing his face; and his neck was like a plucked chicken's, bones and stringy stuff sticking out under his skin. Ricki Ann was right; his hands were like they belonged to some other kind, the palms so white you could almost see through them.

When I looked over at her, the blue of Ricki Ann's eyes seemed almost washed away, but the eye shadow on her eyelids was dusty and solid. Her blond lashes were like ghost feathers. I pressed my body and my cheek flat to the plywood, as flat as I could get with my stupid new boobs pressing back into my heart. Ricki Ann watched the diviner without blinking. I closed my eyes.

Dad left. I heard his gruff chuckle, the muffled clomp-clomp of his work boots on the dirt path headed toward the far pasture, and the hairs on the back of my neck shivered like always even though I knew he hadn't seen us. And then quiet. Then the swish of Bahia grass, a light step and a pause: the diviner. Something rustled against the floor, a thrum in my ear. I opened my eyes. Ricki Ann's left boob—hers just a swelling, like something trying to break the surface—was beside my face. Maybe it was her heart that thumped.

I looked down again. The diviner cocked his head toward us, listening. We didn't breathe. His fingers fluttered once, like playing a quick scale on the piano, or like the way a snake's tongue tastes the air for movement. He walked to a willow tree, reached into his pocket for a little knife, and cut a branch, the blade glittering and bright. He trimmed the leaves gently, as if undressing something he loved, not at all the way we stripped our Barbies down for their costume changes. I could feel my own fingertips in my damp hand, wanting to twitch, and something cool like leaves between my chest and the wood floor. Ricki Ann breathed a sigh, and I felt her damp air stir the little hairs on my neck.

The diviner closed his eyes up toward the sun through a break in the tree branches, and the shadows made his face all dappled and spotted. The willow branch balanced on his thin papery fingertips, held by his thumbs. His nostrils moved in and out, in and out. Then the wrinkles in his face went flat, smooth in the light. His long legs strode out, and he seemed to slide along behind them, moving fast, pacing like he was measuring the land or being pulled by that branch in his hands.

Me and Ricki Ann choked, trying not to laugh out loud. He looked weird, tromping on those long legs across the flat pasture, right through cow pies and tall grass, between rows of cedar Christmas trees, over rabbit holes and gopher tortoise holes, not caring about Sid the Brahma bull or snakes or anything, with his eyes rolled back in his head, looking up but not seeing the fat clouds in the blue sky. When he got far enough away we scrambled down the tree—the worn-through place in the butt of Ricki Ann's cutoffs leaking clear skin right in my face we were in such a hurry—and skulked along the fence-line, following the diviner.

He stopped. We held our breath. His eyes focused on the tip of the twig. And I saw it. The tip tugged down, the branch straining against his thumbs. Just once, like the end of a fishing pole when you get a nibble. A chill ran up the back of my neck, as if water had splashed up from the dark blue caverns of the aquifer. Ricki Ann's eyes met mine, wide, made wider by her blue eye shadow. She had seen it too.

The diviner tossed the branch away, and Ricki Ann gasped. I felt it too. It was like a lover—like on *All My Children*—abandoned. Wasn't it any good anymore? Was the magic all used up?

The diviner reached in his back pocket for his knife, looked around, and cut a long stake from a sapling, which he poked in the ground. He tied an orange flag on top. All the time I watched the willow twig, cast into the weeds.

The snake happened in August, a couple of weeks after the diviner drove away in his blue truck, the dog bouncing in the bed of the pickup, grinning with the smells and the ride backward into the maze of dirt roads. I think that's another story. Not the diviner story. But they get mixed-up in my head because of the magic. Was it magic that kept me from getting kilt? I want to think it was God, but that doesn't seem right, any more than what the diviner did was God.

Soon as the diviner left, Ricki Ann rushed over and snatched up the willow stick. She closed her eyes and stepped out wide. She walked back and forth, back and forth across the pasture, balancing the twig on her fingertips, just like the diviner. Nothing. Even over the place marked with the orange flag—the place where we'd both seen the stick tugged down by water, cool and damp and deep—nothing.

"Give it," I said, and grabbed the stick from her. I tilted my head way back, the sun making orange halos inside my eyelids, and tried to feel any quiver in the thin twigs between my thumbs and fingertips. I made myself put my feet way out, trying to stride like the diviner had, but I heard Mom's rhymes about snakes in my head—red on yellow; kill a fellow and cotton mouth, black as sin—and stumbled and opened my eyes.

"You cain't look," Ricki Ann said. "Ya gotta feel it." She snatched the twig back and tried again, the blue of her eye shadow twitching on her lids, closed into the white hot sun. She walked with wide swishing steps on short, skinny legs, her thighs brushed by tall green Bahia grass. Her small chin and pointed little boobs poking out through her T-shirt seemed to be leading her down the pasture. I felt dizzy in the heat. I stood very still beside the orange flag, waiting for something to happen.

What happened was the snake. What happened was me flying, flying apart. What happened was me starting to backslide. Now I think maybe the snake was always there, lying silent and cool in the deep swamp below the spring. I think it was there on the day when the diviner came, even though I didn't know it then. I think it was there before I was twelve-going-on-thirteen, before I got saved again. What kept it alive in my head?

Two weeks after the diviner had come and gone, we were lying on the tree house floor on our bellies again. The diviner's stick hung from a stub of a branch on the main tree trunk. I made my Skipper-doll walk back and forth, back and forth. Ricki Ann's Barbie was taking a nap in the sleeping bag she had made out of a sock. It was one of those days when you could hardly move, the air so thick it was like walking through the thin sticky soup that's left after you eat all the noodles.

"Wanna look for rabbits?" I said, trying to think of stuff to do so Ricki Ann wouldn't get bored and want to go home to town.

"Too hot," Ricki Ann said. Her chin rested on the backs of her hands and when she moved her mouth, her head went up and down.

"Lee and Buddy might wanna play Monopoly," I said.

She rolled her eyes. "Ugh," she grunted. "They're sooo stupid."

"Yeah." My brother and his friend were just a year younger, but boys are naturally dumb.

"They'll just cheat anyway," Ricki Ann said.

"Too bad we can't ride Gus," I sighed. Dad said the mule was way too tired for us kids to be riding on him in the heat after he tried to lie down with Lee and Buddy both on her. That was funny though. Lee ended up right in a cow flop, a fresh one too.

Skipper paced back and forth, back and forth. Her hair was almost military short, just shaggy enough in the back to touch her collar. In the Barbie family, Skipper is my favorite. She has almost no boobs at all and her hair is the same brown as mine. Ken's just weird with that smooth bump between his legs, but his clothes are cool for Skipper to wear. Barbie is like this perfect movie star grown-up lady, nobody you can think is real, but Ricki Ann liked messing with her hair and dressing her up in gowns and tiny high-heeled shoes. I only talked her into this camping trip scene by telling her that Ken might show up in his sports car later. The oak leaves whispered a dry scraping sound overhead. Ricki Ann adjusted Barbie's arms so they were outside her sleeping bag. A cow mooed low and sad off in the distance. Skipper hesitated. I don't know what she was thinking standing there beside Barbie, the pasture beyond hazy with heat mirages. It was like my arm was disconnected from me. Like Skipper was part of it but not me. She swooped down and kissed Barbie on the mouth, lying on top of her.

"Yech," said Ricki Ann, and I grabbed Skipper back up, my face hot. What was wrong with her? Ricki Ann looked at me, her eye-shadowed blue lids squinted down over her eyes like she was thinking something hard.

I was blushing, I could feel it. It happened a lot and I hated it. Lee always pointed and laughed and called me "flame face." I sat up. Ricki Ann still looked at me funny, twisted around, lying on her stomach.

"I know," I said, "let's go explore the creek." My brain was humming I was thinking so fast. What had Skipper been doing? The words jumbled out of my mouth; my tongue felt thick. "The creek. Maybe there's treasure. It's like jungle with all those vines and stuff back behind the spring. Like a jungle. Maybe we'll find caves or something. The water has to come from somewhere. Maybe caves where it comes up from the aquifer." I wanted to choke, to drink something cold, to shut up, disappear.

Ricki Ann's eyes slid shut in a slow blink, the water on her eyeball hiding something behind it. After a minute of staring down into the pasture she said, "Least it'll be cool."

When Mom tells the story about me and the snake, she always says, "You girls were white as sin," and her eyes go wide. "Funny," she says, "you could'a died."

Cicadas whirred. The air was still and thick. When we crossed the barbed wire fence, I held the wires apart for Ricki Ann like you're supposed to, stepping down on the lower strand with my sneaker and pulling up on the middle wire to make a space, and she brushed my leg as she passed through. My face flamed again. Barbie and Skipper lay back in the tree house, still and lifeless.

After an hour or maybe a few minutes or maybe forever, we were so deep into the woods that the earth had been swallowed up by the creek, which wasn't a creek anymore, just tea-brown water everywhere. It seemed as if nobody since Adam and Even had been there, at least not since the Indians. There were tracks of deer and coons and something big, maybe a bear. We had to hold onto thick ropes of grapevine for balance and shinny around cypress trees, hugging the soft bark and stepping on the lumps of root they call knees to stay out of the muck. Our sneakers were black with it. There were no caves. The aquifer just seeped up through a mud sieve of swamp, or maybe the swamp seeped down into the aquifer. It was dark and quiet, except for the background scream of tree frogs. I hoped Ricki Ann had forgotten Barbie and Skipper.

"Let's jump across to that bank," I said. "We can go back on the other side."

"Long as we can go back," Ricki Ann said. Her fingertips brushed mine as she rounded the other side of the tree after me. I wanted to look at her eyes but I couldn't.

I bunched my thighs and leapt across a trickle of water, feeling that shiver from her touch travel up my arm like cool water. My feet sank into the sand. "Uhh," I said as I landed. I looked around.

Big and black as a truck tire, loop on top of lazy loop: the snake. It tasted the air, tongue fluttering out like the diviner's fingers, trying to catch my movement, my heat. I saw a white mouth, fangs. Cotton mouth, black as sin; hell's gate, moccasin.

"Ssssnake," I whispered. "Snake." I felt frozen.

Ricki Ann looked at me then the same way she had looked at me in the tree house. Her eyelashes disappeared. Eye shadow streaked blue sweat down the corners of her eyes and across her cheeks.

"Help," I moaned, "get help." My heart swelled into my throat. "Sssnake."

The watery blue of Ricki Ann's eyes thinned, then she opened them wide. She screamed, but I didn't hear anything, just watched her mouth like a pale pink cave, that thing that stuck down in the back of her throat waggling. She turned and ran, aiming for cypress knees, slipping off, her sneakers being sucked down into the mud. Then, when she was gone, I heard her screams echoing like inside a room with water walls, and I heard myself moaning. I felt the snake, heavy, in the small part of my back, in the skin under the collar of my T-shirt, my hands, my thighs, my feet, zinging and numb. I heard my heart thudding like it was waterlogged, moving slow in time.

Now, it's funny, but no matter how hard I try, I can't remember leaping away.

No muscles contracted; I didn't move anything at all. Suddenly I was up in the air—like flying, like maybe the Rapture would feel, no gravity—and the dark water down. I heard a thud in the sand behind me. *Thunk.* I hugged the cypress tree on the other side again, like magic, like nothing had happened.

But when I looked back, the snake lay uncoiled, stretched out in a thick, black line between my footprints—filling with water already—on the other side.

I ran without thinking. I heard only my heart up in my throat saying thunk, thunk, thunk. Snake. Big snake. Footprints. Brown water. I wanted to barf but I kept running. Then Ricki Ann's screaming changed. I heard that. I followed her sound. She wailed, something rushing up and out. *Thunk* said my heart up by my tongue, and I gagged, swallowing it down. *Thunk.* Snake. Big snake. Cotton mouth, black as sin; hell's gate, moccasin.

Ricki Ann hung by her hand, just below the thumb, on the barbed wire fence. A whimpering scream escaped from her open mouth like air out of a tire. She looked at me as if I wasn't real, like I was a ghost, her eyes so wide I couldn't even see the blue on her eyelids. She had no color at all, like the blood was plugged up somewhere inside. I must look like that too, I thought. I grabbed her hand and held it steady. I unhooked her thumb from the wire, lifting the hard, taut metal back and up, feeling her gaze on my face. Both our palms were ice cold. I felt her pulse in her wrist, one hard, sluggish beat. *Thunk.* And then mine. *Thunk.* Something seemed to rustle when the wire slipped out of the base of her thumb, and I watched a big blob of blood well up. As if I was in a trance, I lifted her palm to my mouth. Skin. Sweat. Blood. I tasted the *thunk* of her pulse against my tongue. When I looked up, her eyes were turquoise smooth, like a swimming pool, not blinking.

Dad made me walk back through the swamp with him and his gun and point to the place where I had hugged the cedar tree, jumped, and then flown back like the Rapture. I pointed, my hand shaking and pale. "Dumb," I heard him mutter. Or maybe it was "Damn," but he doesn't cuss. And then, behind me as I stumbled back to the farmhouse, looking for snakes in every twisted vine, the gun had boomed, my heart echoing *thunk.*

Dad hung the snake, cotton-mouthed and black as sin, from the clothesline pole, longer than he was tall and as thick as his arm, a shadow beside him.

"Look at it," he ordered, his one hand locked on my wrist and the other pointing like Moses' after he'd smashed the Ten Commandments. "Don't forget," he said. The snake swayed a little, a thick black line between here and somewhere.

"You'd be dead now," Dad said, and I felt his hand tug, like he was going to push me at the snake. And that's when I fainted, like a girl, sliding backward into darkness.

Ricki Ann wanted to go home after that, so she rode in the cab between Mom and Dad while I bounced alone in the pickup bed watching the maze of dirt roads recede into the dark.

She got saved a week later. She wrote a letter to me, back at the farm: "I took Jesus Christ into my heart as my personal Lord and Savior. Pastor Bob baptized me on Sunday after the tent meeting."

On the last day of our summer vacation, Ricki Ann's letter, all creased and wrinkled from me carrying it around and reading it again and again, lay on the tree house floor next to Skipper, a postcard from Robert E. Lee Junior High School that gave my homeroom number, and the plastic case of blue eye shadow. Some days, when everything was still except the glittering white shimmer of evaporating steam over fields of green Bahia grass, I had taken the diviner's stick down and balanced it on my fingers. Sometimes I had walked over the earth alone trying to feel something move in my hands.

Mom had said "Praise the Lord!" when I told her about what Ricki Ann's letter said, and I'd said "Yeah, praise God" back, but deep down I was just sorry it wasn't me that showed her The Way, The Truth, and The Light.

I dreamed about her baptism, almost like I was underneath the water with her in the blurry blue light. Her hair floated around her face like thin little snakes. She shut her eyes tight. Her robe started to swirl up and I could see her underpants, so I tried to reach out—to pull her robe down, I guess—but my hand smacked into the glass and her eyes opened wide like when I pulled the barbed wire out of her thumb. In my dream, I pressed my face to the glass, and I woke up feeling that cold flatness on my lips.

I wondered if swimming in the caves of the aquifer would be like in the baptismal pool—all blue light and cold and silent.

I hadn't told anybody about my tongue on Ricki Ann's hand and the taste of her blood, not even God in my prayers. It felt like I should say something, but I didn't know how to tell the story. All the stories were mixed-up together. Maybe it was a story that was just beginning.

I laid back on the hard plywood floor of the tree house, the sun almost directly overhead, and closed my eyes to a little slit to look at the moon, which was down low in the east, round and pale in blue sky. I thought I could almost see the little flag the astronaut had staked into it, could almost feel the no-gravity up there in the dark. I opened the eye shadow case Ricki Ann had left and touched the soft powder. It stuck to my fingertips and when I closed my hand it smudged the inside of my palms like bruises. I lifted my legs up and grabbed my bare feet and then they were streaked with blue too. I drew a blue heart on my chest just above the edge of my tank top. I don't know why.

When I rolled onto my side, Skipper was staring dumbly up into the sky. Her hair was shaggy and uneven. I stripped her of Ken's dress shirt and Bermuda shorts and painted her with blue eye shadow all over. The cool plastic of her stupid little nose and her stupid flat chest and her stupid little butt was slick under my fingertip. I hated her. I folded her up, bent her legs as far as they'd go, her nose to her knees, and stood up and stuffed her into the knothole that's hidden on the other side of the oak tree trunk. I put Ricki Ann's letter and the card from junior high school in my pocket and picked up the diviner's stick. The Bahia grass shimmered in the pasture below, and mirages blurred the full moon on the horizon.

Back home on Renoir Drive with junior high only a week away, I kept waking up with that *thunk* in my head, my heart *thunk-thunking* back. Sometimes I thought there were snakes all over my floor and I was afraid to get up to go find Mom, so I just hid under the covers and cried like a stupid baby. Sometimes I tasted blood, like from Ricki Ann's hand. Sometimes I tried to untangle the magic from God, but I kept getting mixed-up, like with the stories. Sometimes I would stick my tongue out, trying to taste the place where the snake waited in the dark like it had tasted the air for me.

Skipper is still there in the tree, I guess. After we got back home, Mom told Dad we were going to have to sell the farm because he was still out of work, and I could almost see inside his head, see how mad he was, like I knew what he was thinking. Nobody but my little brother watched the show called *Green Acres* after that. The new well into the aquifer won't ever get dug. We won't move there. I started junior high. I turned thirteen. I tried to be a good Christian; I went out and gave my testimony about Jesus to strangers. But I was scared. Something inside me was wrong. Different. Bad. Home didn't seem safe anymore. The snake was dead but it was still waiting for me in the dark. I kept sliding back, trying to understand how I flew away from it. Why I'm not dead.

I'm not so sure which way I'm going anymore. I'm not even sure who I am. I still have the diviner's stick here in my room, but when I pick it up, I don't think I'll feel anything magic in my hands.

Backslide

When the truck slides, I turn the wheel and the pain in my shoulder radiates out. My heart thunks. In the blackness, I slide into someone, or they slide into me—Ricki Ann, Lee, my father?

I am a jumble of others, the vehicle keeping us together. Or maybe the pain. Maybe the back roads that will return us home together to the top of the hill. Am I already there?

It is March 2001. I am shot on the Kora Lincoln Show. I am Virge, Virginia Young.

It is August 1969, and I am backsliding ahead through my thirteenth year. But I am not that girl. She's gone. I'm nothing like her.

It is the turn of the millennium, New Year's Eve 1999, and too much is going right. My book will be published. Ruthie and I and our babies are happy and healthy. Our families—save the fathers—have returned us to their folds.

"Why so tense?" Ruthie asks, holding my hand as we watch Dick Clark, sitting on the sofa in our new home on top of the hill.

"It's too good," I say. "Something bad is going to happen. I don't deserve *all this."*

I half-expect the predictions of worldwide computer chaos to begin as the clocks tick down toward zero. War, perhaps. Armageddon.

"You do deserve it," Ruthie says, her fingers squeezing mine. "You've worked hard. You're due."

But I know, somewhere deep inside, that I'm not good enough. The book will flop. God will punish me somehow. I get up to go to the bathroom and stop to make sure the babies are sleeping. To make sure they are still breathing. God will take them from me. Take Ruthie from me. Something is going to go terribly wrong.

Together with my lover in our new house on top of the hill, the seconds tick down: five, four, three, two, one, and the year turns without mishap. Ruthie and I look out onto moonlit snow. We hold hands. We drink a toast to a new age, a new family, and go to bed to make love. But I know, deep inside, that the house will wash away in a flood. My family will die in a bloody crash. God won't let me be this happy.

And it is also the summer of 2001, the end of this book tour. I am on my way to a reunion, to many reunions—my high school class reunion, a family reunion, and our civil union, all in the summer of 2001—but these reunions have not yet happened. It is only March. I have been shot. The terrible thing has happened. I am in the future, the past, the now. How does this happen?

It is March. I am shot on Kora's show. I hear her voice. I feel Ruthie's hand holding mine. Our civil union will be in August, after the book tour ends, after the high school reunion, after the family reunion. But it is August too. I am at Green Acres too. Now. Now. I am Father.

Are we already lost again?

Reunion: Father
August 2001

I'm saved, he will think. Ed will watch the plume of dust kicked up by a vehicle far off down the dirt drive leading in from the road as it blooms toward him. Maybe five minutes till it gets here. He is afraid to move. The snake is gone, but the ache radiating up his arm and into his back and chest feels alive and dangerous, like something moving in the darkness inside his body. His heart *thunks* inside. He tries to breathe evenly.

It will be the diviner, of course. Ed has been expecting him all morning. Some feller named Jayce the guys at the coffee shop had recommended. That was before he'd stopped going to the coffee shop, before they'd started poking at him. He misses his mornings of shooting the breeze with 'em, something to fill up a few of these endless hours of retirement. Her fault. Virge.

His arm flares. Ed chokes. He closes his eyes and tries to breathe evenly. He tries to wipe her out of his mind, tries to leave off from remembering mornings with the guys in the coffee shop. If only she hadn't written that book, hadn't gone on that Kora TV show, hadn't aired her dirty laundry like it was something to be proud of. His face feels warm and cold at the same time, slick with sweat but burning in the sun. No, she doesn't exist. He has no daughter. Just what he'd said to the guys at the coffee shop.

Why is he thinking about her? When he'd said those words to the guys, he'd made it true. She'd been erased, just like that. And here she is again, just when he doesn't need her, making the blood throb in his neck. Begone Satan. Maybe it was seeing that snake, that big cottonmouth, like the one that had almost got her when she was a little girl, back on that first Green Acres. Would've been better if that snake had got her back then. Least she would've been saved, would've been home with Jesus all this time. Wouldn't have made people look at him like that. Now she was gone to the devil. Should've been her that died, not Lee. Ed closes his eyes, his face burning as he remembers Rob snickering, "Maybe I'll be plantin' Kora—uh, corn—this year." And Morrisey answering, "Aw, come on now . . . tell us all about it, Rob, don't hold back." And she isn't even ashamed. She ought'a be ashamed of what she is, not telling the whole world.

Ed had prayed, I'm ready Lord, when he'd first come to and found himself looking up at blue sky, an incongruous full moon pale on the horizon. I've had enough of this old world, he had thought. Nothing but sin here. Why didn't God just wipe the whole place clean with fire? Rapture the Christians up and burn the place down. Forget it. He'd tried to feel ready to die. Take me home, Lord, he'd prayed. Might as well. He'd looked up into the sky and waited for it to open. A turkey vulture had circled in a high lazy loop against the blue. Maybe God had other plans, he thinks now, waiting for the diviner to find him. Maybe God isn't done with him yet. Ed listens to the truck coming closer. Sounds like the clutch is slipping a little, or the tires sliding sideways on the gravel.

Will the diviner, Jayce, see him? Ed considers whether to push himself up to a sit. The concrete slab foundation for the new shop is only about fifty feet away. The plans call for a bathroom with a shower in it, so he can clean up after working in his garden or tending the cows and chickens or tinkering with the engine of the old tractor. If only Mary would move out here to the little farm, he'd build her a brand new house, not so big as the house they'd wanted to build back on that other Green Acres, but something comfortable, a home just right for an old retired couple. "I don't want to be stuck out here away from everyone, Ed," she'd said. "Too far from my people, my friends, the church." So he is building a shop for himself instead. And the slab he'd had poured was where he'd told Jayce to meet him. Ed turns his head to look at it, a white rectangle of rock. Rock of ages, cleft for me, he thinks. His favorite hymn. They'll sing it at his funeral. A safe little cave in the side of God, home.

The ground where he lies is half-hidden from the slab by a stand of scrub oaks. He rolls slowly toward the right, rising up a little against his planted right hand. His left shoulder and side throb. A blue pickup truck shudders to a stop in the dirt yard, the dust billowing up around it in a brown fog. A yellow dog leaps from the bed to sniff the ground, and the truck door creaks open. Through the dust, Ed sees a thin figure, a kid almost, in cutoff jeans, a T-shirt and battered work boots slide out, slam the door, and look around. Familiar to Ed somehow. "Over here," he calls. He wants to wave his arm, but it seems heavy with something thick and dark. His voice sounds soft, weak even. He feels the blackness descending again. Will Jesus take him home this time after all?

When he comes to, the diviner kneels over him, a silhouette against the bright sky, hair cut in that spiky halo younger folks seemed to prefer these days. Almost like a crown of thorns. Ed starts to smile at that crazy thought, then the diviner's hands press warmly on his chest. "I think you might be having a heart attack," the kid says. "I've already called nine-one-one on my cell. I know CPR, but you came around before I started."

Ed looks up, blinking, trying to clear his head again. Heart attack. "I was in a little cave," he says. "In the side of a mountain."

One of the hands, surprisingly strong, grasps Ed's hand and squeezes. "I think you're gonna be fine," the diviner says. "We're just gonna sit here together and wait for the rescue. No need to worry."

Ed blinks. "Yeah," he says. "Okay." He closes his eyes.

The diviner's voice fades in. "Love can make your soul crawl out from its hiding place."

"Huh?" Ed tries to open his eyes. The strong hand squeezes his again.

Backslide

The clutch grinds a little as I try to gain purchase on the slick gravel road. My shoulder throbs as I wrestle the gearshift into four-wheel drive. Where I am? I have slipped backward, then forward, sideways, fishtailing. I am taking the back roads toward home, but I feel a little lost, confused, as if I am a girl again headed for Green Acres, as if I am someone else. I hear voices, fragments, words. "Hate—" "Wait—" "Hurry—"

I hear the echo of gunfire, maybe someone shooting in the woods. But it isn't hunting season, is it? Is Dad killing the cottonmouth again? Is that snake some other snake? Which is story? Which is true? Which snake have I imagined? Which is more lethal?

I hear a trickle of water, feel something wet on my face. My shirt sticks to me as if the weather has turned hot and humid. Maybe I am home in the South again. But these trees are bare. Snow covers the road. My old pickup truck slides on icy roads. I am going home to the top of the hill, the back way, the long way around.

Book tour. Kora. A man with a gun. My father. My father. My father.

"Yeh-low," he says, his usual phone greeting, and my heart lurches at the *sound of his voice. He has not spoken to me in three years. Not since I came out. Not since Lee's funeral.*

"Dad," I say, and there is silence on the other end of the line. "Dad!" I shout. Damn you, I think. Talk to me.

"It's for you," he says, already far away again, and I hear the fumble of the phone being handed off. He's gone just like that. Damn him.

My mother comes on the line, and I tell her the news. "The babies are here. Born at four thirty a.m. Ruthie is fine. The babies are fine." I am a parent—mother? father? other mother?—myself. I cannot stop smiling; I cannot stop the lurching of my heart. I cannot catch my breath.

My mother sounds joyful, as excited as am I. "I'm praying for you all," she says.

The moment I held my daughter in the delivery room, her little mouth sucking my pinkie, the moment my son fell asleep on my chest, his blue eyelids pulsing, I knew that I would never be able to turn away from them. I no longer know my father. And yet I feel myself sliding backward into that old life in the same movement that I slide ahead, into a new story, a new hope, new life. I cannot control this slipping in and out of other selves, other lives, seeing through other eyes. That is what I do when I write. But I cannot imagine a life in which I would deny this love. I think of that other Father who they told me loved the world so much that he could sacrifice a child. They said that God is love. I do not think so. I watch Ruthie and the babies sleep. We are together, all four of us, in a small hospital room, a family now. I allow myself to slide into my own exhaustion.

In my dream on this first day of parenthood—motherhood, fatherhood, something-otherhood—I am at the top of one of the big slides that were popular when I was a girl. I can see the ocean, a maze of highways and roads below. Tiny houses and hotels. Marshes and forests farther inland. Others settle into one of the twenty lanes, then push off, flying down the silver metal slopes, some on their backs, some on their stomachs. Some scream. All are grinning. I am grinning. I remember sitting high in a pine tree on the day I turned thirteen, September 1969. I remember my fear of falling. Did I really think about letting go? Don't let go.

Then I am falling, testing gravity, feeling the earth—or something else, something within me—pull me through air, and the children and Ruthie are encircled by my arms and legs. We are flying together, like magic, not quite out of control, but nearly so. I'm already afraid again, anticipating the contact with earth. It will hurt so much. Don't let go. Don't let go.

Back in my truck, I think I will fly up, like the Rapture, toward home, curving through the woods, the back way. I think I will slide into others, my family always within me. I will slide into other stories, maybe backward or forward or sideways. Snow pelts the truck in soft white clumps, melting into a blur on the glass. I can barely see the road, but I don't stop. I drive slowly along the maze of back roads. I am going home.

The Swim Story, or Why Baptists Don't Dance

Ricki Ann and me always watched *American Bandstand with Dick Clark* together on Saturday afternoon, so when Mom and Dad and me and Lee got back home from the farm in August 1969, I called her up to come spend the night on the last Saturday before junior high started. Even though she'd got saved and baptized and I near about got kilt by a snake, I wanted it to be like nothing had changed. Being back in our regular house on Renoir Drive that looks like every fifth house in Normandy Village made it feel like that. Normal. Except for the bad snake dreams and that postcard from Robert E. Lee Junior High School pinned to my bulletin board next to the diviner's stick. I wanted home to be normal.

"Hi," I said.

"Hi," said Ricki Ann.

"What'cha doin'?"

"Nothin'. You?"

"Nothin'."

"Who'dja get for homeroom?"

"Lonigan. You?"

"Conway." Dang. I had hoped we'd be together, at least in homeroom.

"D'ya think Lonigan is a man or a lady?"

"Sheesh. Who cares? Willy-Jack says you only get homeroom for ten minutes anyway." Willy-Jack is Ricki Ann's brother—she's got five of them, plus a little sister—and he plays electric guitar in a band. He's in ninth grade.

"You think we'll have any classes together?" We would get our schedules in homeroom.

"Maybe. Who knows?"

"Yeah. Who knows." I was trying to sound cool like Ricki Ann, like I didn't care about that stuff, like it was normal, but my stomach was tight.

"Whad'ja get for new school clothes?" she said.

"Oh, you know. Some stuff I can wear to church too. Dresses. But Mom did let me get this groovy pantsuit with a long vest and bell-bottoms and some corduroy jeans."

"Neat. I got two miniskirts and go-go boots and this knitted vest thing and some hip-huggers and a couple of really wild blouses, you know, flowers and pop art kind of designs . . ."

"That shiny smooth polyester stuff?"

"Yeah. Really cool. It's, like wow! 'Sexy,' Leon-Junior says." Leon's another one of Ricki Ann's big brothers. She's next-to-last out of seven kids. Leon's the biggest and he's going off to the army soon.

I swallowed. "Uh, yeah."

"Did'ja get a gym suit?"

I had. It was lying on my bed like some kind of cross between a nurse uniform and a baby's onesy. "Yeah," I said.

"Weird huh?"

"Yeah." I stared at it, all white and starched. I knew I would have to take all my clothes off—no way to do a skirt-shorts, blouse-T-shirt switcheroo because the gym suit was all one piece. I'd have to take all my clothes off in front of all those girls I didn't know, all those girls who were pretty, who were cool, who were all 'no big deal,' who didn't feel like they were inside skin that wasn't theirs. They would all have lots of friends, they wouldn't care about being practically naked in front of all those other girls. What if the gym teachers made us take showers? I felt my face get hot and red even all by myself in my room. I had never really seen much of anybody naked. When God kicked Adam and Eve out of the Garden of Eden, he made them ashamed of being naked, and my mom and dad seemed to agree that that's a good tradition. Nobody's ever naked in our house, at least not so anybody else can see them. I've seen little babies naked, sure, but that's different. And Lee gets to go without a shirt in the summer, but he's a boy, and boys don't have near the rules girls do.

Ricki Ann's voice buzzed through the telephone against my ear, but I wasn't listening. I was still thinking about gym. I would have to get naked in front of everybody twice every day, before gym and after, even when I got my period. I could almost feel the huge pad chafing my thighs, even though it wasn't my period now, and that stupid elastic belt that holds it on itching between my butt; thinking about the blood and powdery Kotex smell made me feel queasy. What if the blood leaked like it does sometimes? What if it got on my panties when I had to change for gym with all those other girls around? What if it got on my pants or a blob on my skirt like happened that time last year? I looked at the gym suit lying on my bed again. Why did the stupid thing have to be white?

"Maybe we'll have gym together," Ricki Ann said.

Something caught in my throat and I swallowed. "Uh, yeah." I coughed. "So, you wanna spend the night tonight?"

Ricki Ann pinched her nose shut, held her other skinny, freckled arm up in the air, and bent her knees pretending to go under water. I crossed my arms over my chest, holding my elbows. I have bad timing for dancing, like the music and my body don't know each other. It made me feel stupid. Ricki Ann wiggled her butt when she went down, in time with the song, and her cheeks bulged out like she was holding her breath, just like the girls on the TV behind her. "Come on," Ricki Ann said. "It's called The Swim. It's easy. Just try."

She reached out and grabbed my nose and started pushing down on my head with her other hand. I choked, gasping air through my mouth and laughing at the same time. I grabbed her nose back, and we tripped and rolled onto the new orange shag carpet giggling so hard we couldn't breathe, trying to keep hold of each others' noses, the TV blaring The Archies' *Sugar Sugar.*

The front door opened, swoosh, a fist of Florida Labor Day weekend heat ramming through the air-conditioning. Dad. I rolled up quick to a stiff sit, away from Ricki Ann, and held still like we weren't doing nothing. He walked over to the TV as if we weren't even there and switched the channel over to the stock car races. "Get me some tea," he yelled to Mom. Ricki Ann rolled her eyes at me and puffed out her cheeks like she was holding her breath again, but I didn't grin back. I was trying not to move because I wasn't sure what kind of mood he was in. What if he saw us dancing? Dad dropped into his La-Z-Boy with the familiar plop and pushed back, whoosh-clunk.

"Hello Mr. Young," Ricki Ann sing-songed. Her voice was too loud. My dad's not like hers, I tried to tell her that before, but she didn't seem to get it. It was like she was doing it on purpose. The stock cars whined on the TV, and his eyes were like chips of granite, not blinking. I felt air rush into my chest and kind of burn there. He reached up and brushed his flattop with his hand, and my palm tickled, remembering the way it bristles, softer than you'd expect. I remembered that from not too long ago, when he still liked me, when I was still allowed to roughhouse with him and Lee, like the day he brought the new shag carpet home from the discount store, two big remnant rolls in the back of the pickup, and me and Lee and him worked all day, rolling it out, cutting it, jamming it under the quarter-round, and taping the seams together so they wouldn't show. We'd ended up by tumbling over the new soft orange floor, all three of us, until Lee had pinned me, straddling my chest, his hands on my shoulders and thumbs jammed in my armpits about to tickle me, and Dad had got this real funny look on his face and said, "That's enough." I remember how he used to scratch my face with his whiskers after work when I was a little girl—maybe last year. I remember how he used to wake me up early on Saturdays back then, and we'd drive down to the farm in the pickup to feed the cows and Gus-the-mule, just him and me, his arm slung along the back of the seat, both of us quiet, listening to the radio and watching the sun pink the sky in streaks. I'd always had to watch him, be careful so when he blew up it wouldn't be at me, but back then at least he'd liked me, at least when I was real quiet and just went along.

I looked over and caught Ricki Ann watching me. I gave her a little nod toward my room down the hall and slid my back up the wall until

I was on my feet. I thought maybe we could slip out. Mom was in the kitchen, stirring the sugar into the iced tea, watching us. Her mouth was turned down and her eyes were soft. Maybe Dad hadn't noticed us. Maybe we could disappear without moving.

But Ricki Ann grinned at me when she stood up, like she was taking a dare. She stepped right between Dad and the TV. "'Bye, Mr. Young," she said, sing-songing, swishing toward my room.

His eyes slid over us, hard as stone. I saw Ricki Ann like he was seeing her: the outline of her bra through the skintight Snoopy for President T-shirt he'd told Mom was unpatriotic; the blue eye shadow and pale pink lip gloss on her freckled face that he'd called "painted like a harlot"; her scrawny legs sticking out of pink hot pants. I stopped breathing. Were my cutoffs too short? Was my bra strap showing out from under my tank top? I heard the leather arm of his chair scrunch when he tightened his hand, and then he looked back at the TV. I started backing out of the room down the hall. We were almost gone, almost out of the room, almost escaped.

"No more dancin'," he said, like he was spitting. He looked at me hard, and I felt like I couldn't move, trapped.

"Ed," Mom started to say.

"Shut up," he spat, and her voice went silent, an empty place in the air. "Sinful," he said, still staring at me. "An ya look dumb anyway."

I grabbed Ricki Ann's thin arm and felt the blood pump below the skin. "Yessir," I said, and led her back down the hall to my room.

Lying in bed that night, we still sang *Sugar Sugar*, but low. Facing each other on the pillow we grinned through the part about being "my candy, girl . . ." Mom had already stopped in once to tell us to quiet down and go to sleep. It sounded weird because we weren't yelling the words like usual, and when I missed the half-beat that started the next phrase, Ricki Ann poked me in the side and we both started giggling so hard we couldn't stop.

"Shhhh, shhh," I said. Ricki Ann wriggled onto her side and squeezed her fingers under my armpit. "Noooo." I felt like I was choking. I fought to keep her from tickling, but I could feel her skinny little fingers working their way into the bare sweaty skin inside the sleeve of my T-shirt. Bubbles of air fizzed in my throat, filling it up. If I let them out, I would collapse into Jell-O, laughing so loud Mom would come back, so I sucked in a deep breath, twisted over and poked my fingers into her sides. She kicked out, trying to defend herself, but I grabbed her leg and tried to reach down for the bottom of her foot. I'm lots bigger than Ricki Ann, but her little fingers snaked into my armpits. I couldn't help it, couldn't breathe. All the air went out of me and I gave up, gasping, so weak that tears ran down my cheeks, trying to quiet the giggles that were choking out of my chest. Ricki Ann rolled on top of me, straddling my chest, her knees pinning my hands to the bed. Her fingers dug into my armpits, and I wheezed, laughing silently, but I stopped struggling. I couldn't move anymore. And then I didn't want to move anymore. It felt good to stop trying, like her weight on top of me—hardly nothing— was making me lighter. It was weird, all backward and mixed-up, maybe like when I flew over the creek without moving when the snake nearly kilt me.

Ricki Ann stopped. I felt her breath on my face. I felt her looking at me. I opened my eyes, sticky with weeping. Ricki Ann frowned, looking down at me. "You think Ronnie Lane'll be at church tomorrow?"

I blinked so hard I heard my eyelids click. Ronnie Lane was in the ninth grade and he'd already got called by God to be a preacher. I thought of him bowing his head after Pastor Bob called on him to offer up thanks to the Lord at the end of the service like he does now and then—a big honor for such a young guy, but then, he's going to be a man of God and he needs the practice and all. His silky black hair hung in heavy bunches over deep brown eyes when he prayed, and he already had wide bushy sideburns that scratched soft against your cheek when he gave you a brotherly hug after church in the vestibule. He liked giving all the women and girls—even the old ladies—brotherly hugs. Men, of course, shake hands with each other, sometimes with all four hands if they're really feeling especially close in the Lord, though my dad don't see the need for all that touching. Ricki Ann was suddenly kind of heavy, weighing down my lungs, but warm. "Um, yeah, probably," I mumbled. "He's most always there on Sunday." I didn't move, even though I could have toppled her off easy. I felt my heart thumping up against her thighs. I didn't want to move, didn't want Ricki Ann to move. Not ever.

Ricki Ann's eyes became blurry. The little frown lines on her forehead smoothed out. She smiled and her freckles twitched. "He's sooo cute," she said. The fingers that had been digging into my armpits relaxed and withdrew, leaving my skin sticky and hot. I felt the indents under my arms, empty. She tucked the long strands of her red-orange hair behind her ears, then fiddled with the bow on her teddy bear nightie. She kept looking down at me, but I don't think she really saw me. The streetlight through my Venetian blinds split with the shadows of leaves and branches moving on the wall behind her head. Her light, bony legs felt sweaty along my sides. She blinked.

"You ever kiss a boy?" she asked.

I couldn't breathe again. No, of course not, I thought. But I couldn't say that out loud. I swallowed. I tried to think what to say, but it didn't matter because she rushed on, her words running together like water over sand: "I only kissed my brother, Joe-Ray, you know, just for practice like he said." A funny look flickered across her face, then she erased it. "It was too gross," she said. "Not like real kissing. You wanna practice?" I must have looked kind of spooked or something, because Ricki Ann kept talking fast, her whispers hissing, soft and warm on my face. "Cuz, you know, going to junior high and all, we should be ready. Guys ask you out and people go steady all the time in junior high. An ya don't wanna look like a little kid, like ya don't know what you're doing or nothing. Cuz boys like girls that know what they're doing. Like they're cool, you know." She stopped. "So you wanna?"

If boys ask me out in junior high, Dad won't ever let me go. Mom said maybe I could date when I hit sixteen, but Dad thinks even that's too young. I had plenty of time to practice.

Ricki Ann looked down at me like she really saw me now, waiting. Her nose was small, and she had these tiny lines beside her eyes from where they crinkled up when she grinned. Her eyelashes were so pale they disappeared in dim light, so her eyes seemed extra blue and dark. She stretched her weight out like a warm cat, small and soft, down the length of my body.

I did want to practice. I shrugged as best I could with my arms pinned under her. "Um, okay."

I had kissed my pillow plenty of times, and my teddy bears, and I had these really great stories I told myself in bed at night with a pillow between my legs, about riding horses bareback—sometimes with cute guys like Bobby Sherman—on the beach or on a ranch out west somewhere. And sometimes they got mixed-up. Weird. But I hadn't ever kissed a real person on the lips before. Mom thinks it's unsanitary, and Dad, well, I guess he thinks only married people are supposed to kiss on the mouth, but he's really old fashioned.

"You got to close your eyes," Ricki Ann ordered. I did. I felt her weight shift just a little and her breath on my upper lip. I puckered. "Noooo," she said. I opened my eyes. "Don't do that! You got to act like it's nothin' different, like your mouth was just hanging around, minding its own business, when these other lips come along outta nowhere." I wanted to laugh, but Ricki Ann looked mad, so I held my breath and felt my grin inside.

"Okay," I said. "Ready." I closed my eyes again and this time I didn't pucker. I tried not to anticipate, but I felt my grin swelling inside my chest. I itched all over, trying to be serious, but warm and jumpy under Ricki Ann's body, trying not to think about letting my lips hang around, minding their own business, or those other lips—Ricki Ann's lips—coming out of nowhere. She moved her arms up onto my chest and her hands pushed down on my lungs. Her skinny little fingers touched my titties. A jolt thudded into my chest. A snort burst out of my mouth. "Plauughh!" Then I laughed, hard, trying to breathe, because that's what it was, I thought, a laugh that needed to come out. I struggled to sit up, and Ricki Ann rolled her eyes at me, holding me down. She had a serious look. Her lips shone in the streetlight.

"You girls!" Mom. In the hall. I was suddenly hot, feeling wrong. Ricki Ann slid off me and we laid still under the sheet. The room smelled funny, like sweat, only sweeter. I suddenly wished I had a lock on my door, like the one Ricki Ann had put on hers.

The door cracked open and my mother's face made a circle shadow against the hall light. "It's after midnight and you have to get up for church in the morning," she said. "Now go to sleep!"

"Yes ma'am," I whispered. Ricki Ann acted like she was asleep.

The door shut and we stayed still, our arms sticky and stiff, side by side.

Ricki Ann fell off to sleep—or kept pretending like she had. I listened to her breathe, thinking about what she had said about how to kiss. I thought about kissing my pillow, the starch and iron flavor of cotton. I thought about kissing my stuffed bear, the cool glass eyes and fur, rough from twelve years of washings. I tried to think of one of the long going-to-sleep stories I usually tell myself about riding bareback on the beach, but instead I remembered how it felt to ride with Ricki Ann behind me on Gus at the farm last summer, the way her arms came around my waist, her hands on my thighs, her chin on my shoulder. I thought about Ronnie Lane and how his fuzzy sideburns felt on my cheek when he hugged me in the vestibule after church. Would boys really want to kiss me in junior high?

I leaned up on one hand and bent over, and I kissed Ricki Ann in the dark. I felt her warm breath tickle the little hairs between my nose and my upper lip. I felt her lips against mine, soft and relaxed, lying there, minding their own business. I didn't want to giggle, but I felt like my breath had been sucked away just the same.

On Sunday, I woke up to Ricki Ann's grin. "I had the grooviest dream last night," she said.

I sat up, blinking.

"Ronnie Lane kissed me!" The little lines around her eyes crinkled. "It was like in the movies. Soft and warm and like no big deal or anything." Her words tumbled out like water trickling. "I think it must be like a sign or something. Like God or something. Like Ronnie's in love with me and he can't tell me so God sent me this dream so I would know."

I was pretty sure that God didn't work that way, but I didn't want to bring Ricki Ann down. She had told me about getting saved at the tent meeting, and how Ronnie Lane had been there helping to counsel the poor lost souls who'd come forward, but that she'd got stuck with some old guy with bad breath. I wanted to ask her if she felt different inside. Had she heard Jesus' voice in her ear? I think I did when I got saved last year, but now it's hard to remember, and sometimes I feel so mixed-up, so wrong, that I'm not sure I really am saved. Maybe I didn't hear God's call at all. But I can't figure out how to ask Ricki Ann all of that. And she'd just said, "Yeah, sure, it's cool," when I'd said "Praise the Lord!" That made me feel kind of embarrassed, even though that's what you're supposed to say when somebody gets saved. She hasn't joined up with a church yet, and I think that if God has anything to do with it at all, Ronnie's more likely kind of like bait.

I rubbed my eyes and yawned like I was just waking up. My cheeks flamed. I had kissed her in the night, but I sure wasn't going to tell her about it.

Ricki Ann twirled around and around in my tiny little room. "He loves me!" she sang.

• • •

When I came back from the shower, Ricki Ann was stretched out on the floor half under my bed. I hadn't dreamed about snakes the night before, maybe for the first time since we had come home from Green Acres. I felt clean and clear. I laid down beside her on the cool tile. "What'cha doin'?" I asked, then I saw. My tongue thickened in my mouth, and I remembered her lips against mine. I breathed in the smell of the black magic marker heart she had drawn. She wrote inside it, *I love R.*

At the end of my first day of junior high school on Tuesday, Mom came into my room, untying her apron. "How'd it go sweetie?" she said. She sat down on the end of my bed and crossed her legs like we were going to have a long talk.

I watched her foot swing. From my desk chair I could just see the black magic marker words on the floor in the dark under my bed: *I love R.* I wanted to go out back and climb to the top of my pine tree and sway in the sunset. I wanted to go up there and never come down.

"How does it feel to be all grown up and in junior high?" she asked.

I thought about the one-way halls and how even though my Civics class was right next door to English, I had to go all the way around the far loop before I could get there so I didn't break the one-way-hall rule, and how I worried the whole time that I'd get stuck behind a bunch of big ninth grade boys who'd get in a fight and I'd be late to Civics. But then I thought about how Mom had to drive all over creation in the Buick on her rounds for the Welfare Department checking up on people to make sure they weren't cheating the government, and how sometimes our old car wouldn't start and she'd be way out in the middle of nowhere with all those poor people she didn't even know, sometimes black people, and it didn't seem right to complain about one-way halls. Then I thought about how my locker was a lower one and the one right over it belonged to this black girl and that I saw that her legs weren't shaved, same as mine, when I was kneeling down trying to make my combination work over and over so many times that I thought sure I was going to be late for my next class, and was about to cry when it finally did open, and how that black girl was wearing panty hose over her hairy legs and it looked really weird, like how I know I look, which is why I will wear my pants to school dirty sometimes since I only have three pairs, and I felt sorry for her, and I wanted to say something to her, but I've never even talked to a black person before, except Tillie who used to come to do our ironing before Dad lost his job that last time. But that didn't seem like something Mom would understand since she has to talk to black people on welfare all the time. So I thought about gym and how I stared straight into the gray box of my locker while I undressed and put on my gym suit as fast as I possibly could—praise Jesus I didn't have my period!—and pretended nobody else was around me, even though all the other girls were laughing and talking to each other, and there's this big window at the end where the women PE teachers can look right into the locker room. But I knew that would be just too embarrassing to say out loud to Mom.

And then I thought about how Ricki Ann wasn't in any of my classes except English, where we aren't allowed to talk and have to sit in alphabetical order so I'm all the way in the back corner behind smelly Hank West. I had sat at the same table as her at lunch, except that by the time I got there almost all the other chairs were taken and I'd had to sit at the very opposite end and she'd looked up right before the bell and saw me like I hadn't been there the whole time and said, "Oh, hi Virginia," like she was one of the teachers who didn't even know that I liked to be called Virge, before she'd hurried off talking to this girl named Michelle who has perfect hair long enough to sit on. But then I saw the magic marker words under my bed on the floor and my ears burned and I didn't think I could say anything about Ricki Ann to Mom either. Maybe not ever again.

Everything seemed upside-down. Maybe it was the diviner or the snake or kissing Ricki Ann in the dark, or the magic marker smell wafting from under my bed, or maybe it was just that I was about to turn thirteen, but something seemed to have pushed me into a spin, or under the water, and I couldn't breathe right, couldn't get my bearings. "It was okay," I said to my mom.

"Do you like your teachers?" she asked.

I shrugged. "I guess so."

"Much homework?"

"Not too much," I said. "I have to write down all the books I've ever read for English. Read some stuff. Do some math."

"Are any of your friends in your classes?"

I hesitated. Ricki Ann was in English, but way on the other side of the room, and she hadn't even looked at me. I shook my head. "Not really."

Mom sighed. Her smile sagged. "Well, you'll make some new friends in no time," she said. She had twisted her hands into the apron she held.

I shrugged again, looking down at my new notebook and the mimeographed papers on my desk. "Welcome Seventh Grade Dance," said the one on top.

"Why don't Baptists dance?" I asked.

Mom blinked and swallowed. "Well. . . um. . . Elvis," she said and stopped.

Elvis, this old fat guy with flesh bulging out of a sequined jumpsuit, all sweaty and hairy-cheeked, squirming around in front of screaming women as old as my mom. "Gross," I said. "I don't get it." The kids on *American Bandstand with Dick Clark* weren't anything like that.

"I know it's confusing, sweetie," she said.

"Some Baptists dance." I heard a hard, strange note in my voice. I didn't care. I wanted Mom to tell me something real, something that made sense. What was I supposed to do?

"The Bible," she said. "When Moses came down off the mountain with the tablets, he saw the children of Israel dancing around the golden calf." Her voice seemed sad, tired. She didn't really believe what she was saying. I watched her face. Her eyes watched her hands in her lap. "He broke the stones with the Ten Commandments on them." She shrugged. "It was a sin."

After she left, I looked in the Concise Concordance at the back of my Bible. There were only a few citations for "dance," mostly in the Old Testament. Jesus didn't talk one way or the other about it; of course, it was dancing that led to John the Baptist losing his head. I looked in Exodus and read the story of Moses and the stone tablets again. I liked the story about the water in the wilderness, especially the part where Moses smites the rock and water comes out of it to prove to the children of Israel that God is with them. I'd like to have seen that myself.

In Ecclesiastes, I read, "To everything there is a season, and a time to every purpose under the heaven: A time to be born, and a time to die; a time to plant, and a time to pluck up that which is planted; a time to kill, and a time to heal; a time to break down, and a time to build up; a time to weep, and a time to laugh; a time to mourn, and a time to dance; a time to cast away stones, and a time to gather stones together;

a time to embrace, and a time to refrain from embracing; a time to get, and a time to lose; a time to keep and a time to cast away; a time to tear, and a time to sew; a time to keep silence, and a time to speak; a time to love, and a time to hate; a time of war, and a time of peace." I guess the Byrds stole their song from the Bible. I hadn't heard the last part before: "He hath made every thing beautiful in its time." I got out a pen and carefully underlined the verses in my Bible in bright red.

I sat back on my bed. I was too tired to climb up into my pine tree and sway with the wind after that first day of junior high. I thought about turning thirteen in a couple of weeks. Would that be my time?

Ricki Ann was at the Welcome Seventh Grade Dance, of course. They were all there: Kathy Zane, Sugar Evans, Jenny Hilliard, the shaggy-haired boys, the black kids from the buses. I had hunched against the wall of the cafeteria. The lights were mostly off. I felt like a spy in the shadows. Safe. The air smelled like old food, dirty mop water, yellow wax. It made me feel sick, or like I was under water.

All the girls wore dresses and skirts that were short and bright and tight on their hips. I was in my pantsuit with the long vest and bell-bottoms and a polyester shirt that itched and rubbed the back of my neck. It was wrong, of course.

"Maybe you should wear a dress," Mom had said. She was pretending that she didn't remember that Dad said "no dancin'." Even Pastor Bob had preached that maybe dancing wasn't always a sin.

I had been reading this book my Aunt Lil had sent for my birthday called *Twixt Twelve and Twenty*, by Pat Boone. The book was a real bore, just an old guy trying to sound hip and young. And that was a lot of years to be all mixed-up.

"Officially a teenager!" Mom had said, drying her hands on a dish towel. "What are you going wear to that big dance after school tomorrow?"

I had just looked at her. I didn't think I was allowed to go to the dance.

"Do you want to wear a dress?" she had asked. "We can go buy a new one."

I bit my lip, thinking. All my skirts had to touch my knees—Dad's orders, Pastor Bob's sermons, God's commandments—and I wasn't allowed to shave my legs yet, so the hairs crinkled up all funny-looking under panty hose. I wished she had remembered that dancing was against the rules.

Because I was the only girl at the dance in pants. Wrong. I unbuttoned my collar and spread the long points of it out wide so it looked like I had cleavage. The pad of folded toilet paper inside the right cup of my bra scratched a little. It was there on account of what Dr. Murchinson had said when Mom took me for my first "female exam" after I started getting my period last year. "You may notice that one breast is smaller than the other one," he'd said. Well, I hadn't noticed till he said it, but it's true. It's like I'm deformed or something. I see it every time I look in a mirror—one huge boob and one tiny one—lopsided like some kind of circus freak. Probably everybody sees it. I hunched my shoulders in like wings. Before the dance, I had gone to the restroom and put on a heavy coat of Chap Stick to make my lips shiny and I kept pinching my cheeks to make them pink, because I'm not allowed to wear makeup. I wished I still had Ricki Ann's eye shadow. But I was the only girl in pants anyway. Wrong. All wrong. I pulled my shoulders in tighter and wedged into a darker spot near the door. I watched the kids moving together on the cafeteria floor. I couldn't dance anyway. My body didn't know how to move to the music, not like that. Nothing had changed, not really, even though I was thirteen now, even after Ricki Ann had stayed over on Labor Day weekend, even after I had been in junior high for almost a whole month, even though everything had changed.

Ricki Ann laughed at something her new best friend, Michelle Mitchell, said. *Sugar, Sugar* started playing, and a tall boy with bangs in his eyes asked her to dance. She grinned, and I remembered how her freckles wrinkled up when she smiled close to my face. She held her nose and pretended to go underwater, doing The Swim. Her miniskirt shifted back and forth across her bottom when she twisted in time to the music, and she grinned and mouthed the words to the song while she danced. I knew the words too. We had sung them together all day that last Saturday when she stayed over. We had sung them together in my bed. Under it was a magic marker heart. *I love R.*

The gym was a darker, brighter place than the cafeteria, where the dance was still going on. Music seeped across the hall, sliding as if on socks across the gleaming wood floor, the lyrics proclaiming *This is the dawning of the age of Aquarius . . .* A few other kids who had escaped the dance were scattered, each alone, around the bleachers doing homework or reading, waiting for the late bus to take us home. Even the woman PE teacher chaperoning the gym area during the dance leaned against the wall by herself. The bleachers creaked as I climbed up and sat beside the concrete block wall near the ceiling. Dust motes waltzed in a narrow beam. I held my knees to my chest. My eyes were closed, my body floated as if I were somewhere else or someone else, turning in water, or dancing with the pine tree. I knew the steps, but my body couldn't follow. I couldn't move. If thirteen wasn't my time to dance, what time was it?

On my birthday, September 20th, I climbed the ladder of rough pitchy limbs up the pine tree in our backyard to the top, nearly forty feet up, where I sat and hugged the trunk, swaying in the hot wind while the sun disappeared over the flat tar roofs of the neighborhood. I felt mixed-up, slipping back to that last night Ricki Ann stayed over on Labor Day weekend, dancing The Swim with her, and forward again to the Welcome Seventh Grade Dance at school. After Labor Day weekend, Ricki Ann didn't come over again, not even for my birthday supper—my favorites, pork chops and a big chocolate cake. Maybe especially not after the big dance. I was thirteen for just one day and already the story was all mixed-up.

The pine tree smelled sweet, and I rubbed the bark with my cheek, swaying in the wind, almost like dancing. The orange streaks of the sky made me think of the new wallpaper in my bedroom below, Mom's birthday present to me. I imagined the popular girls from my homeroom—Kathy Zane, a hippie-type in faded overalls, whose hair was long and straight and blond; Sugar Evans, a cheerleader with long, straight brown hair, who wore a short skirt that revealed matching underpants and muscular thighs; Jenny Hilliard, whose hair was long and straight and black and who was the star of all the school plays and soloist for the school choir—I imagined them coming to a birthday party for me, seeing my newly wallpapered room. I imagined them ooohing and ahh-hing over my hipness, my coolness, my mod, wondering why they had never noticed me behind silver braces, horn-rimmed glasses, and the stringy brown hair that always snarled at the back of my neck; hunching to disguise the fact that I was taller than anyone in the seventh grade, watching them all from the safety of a book. I imagined them in my room, even though they live up in Rolling Hills, even though they were impossibly beautiful for thirteen, even though they danced with assurance, as if their bodies were their own. I imagined them in my room. If the Rolling Hills girls would talk to me, Ricki Ann would too.

The tree creaked, bending, and I bent with it, a part of it. I wondered what it would be like to just let go, to fly, falling, backward, even just for a few seconds. I rubbed my cheek on the bark.

I could see Mom washing dishes in the kitchen, the light behind her. My room was to the right, the window dark. But I could see through the wall, into the dark under my bed. I could see myself there, lying on my belly, unafraid of snakes, feeling the cool tile against my breasts, tracing the black lines, the heart and words written in permanent marker on the floor after I had danced to *American Bandstand* on Labor Day weekend with Ricki Ann, marks made that last summer night before junior high: *I love R.*

Backslide

Time inside the truck slips as do the tires on the muck and ice. I've never had a clock in here, preferring to let my mind wander from past to future while I drive, but now, driving the maze of back roads home, I try to hold on to the present. I've been shot. I was being interviewed by Kora Lincoln about my book. A man who looked like my father told me to go to hell, and then he shot me. Now I'm driving home to the top of the hill by a circuitous route, wandering, it seems, through time and space and even other people. I think I hear Ruthie calling my name. Is this happening now?

"Virge!" Ruthie calls from the sofa. "Telephone!" She holds the receiver out to me as I enter the room.

"Who?" I mouth, but she shrugs, eyebrows raised in a question. She hands the phone over to me and closes her eyes, exhausted from the pregnancy, the twins who roil and churn beneath the skin of her enormous belly. One month to go. One month until we are parents.

"Hello?" I say.

"Hey there Cuz!" The man's voice, the Southern accent, is familiar, but I have been out of touch with my parents' families for years—cousins, aunts, uncles—since my brother's funeral. Since my dad erased me. "It's me, Jeff—Jeffy," he says.

I smile. My cousins are all younger than I, by a year or more, but we are all middle-aged now. I know from my mother that most are parents themselves, as I will be soon. I assume they know I am a lesbian.

"Hey yourself!" I say. As if into a soft chair, I fall back into the Southern accent my tongue remembers. "Wow! How have you been?"

It is an odd conversation, but it is also the fourth such call I've received in the last two months—Aunt Lil, Cousin Ann and Uncle Max, who took us out to dinner when he was nearby on a fishing trip. Now Jeffy, my mother's brother's son. "Yes," I say, "you heard right. Twins. Due in four weeks."

Ruthie opens her eyes and smiles. These four calls from my childhood family don't include the myriad of others—the children of my ex-husband, Ruthie's aunts and cousins, college friends, former roommates, ex-lovers—who have heard the news and phoned. "Coming out of the woodwork," she murmurs.

My cousin, Jeff, says he will visit us in Vermont while he is here on business next week. Little Jeffy is a lawyer now. "I want to make some plans for a reunion," he says. "All our folks are getting older now. We should get together again while we can."

"Yes," I say. "We should." But I cringe inside. What will they be like? How will they treat me now? Some, at least, will be as cruel as my dad. I'm afraid. "We should," I say, "but it's going to be busy around here with the babies for awhile." We discuss dates. There are relatives on the West Coast who will need to plan far in advance, elderly folks who need to prepare for the journey, and most of our generation will have children's school schedules to consider. "I think next summer will be too soon for us," I say, hedging.

Ruthie opens her eyes in question.

"I don't know if Ruthie will want to come," I say.

Jeffy pushes at my excuses. "We need to do it," he says. "Before they all start dying." The old folks, he means, our parents, for our grandparents are already gone. I think of Dad. He won't come. Maybe he'll die before we get around to it. Guilt engulfs me. What if he does come? What if the reunion is the opportunity he needs to speak to me again?

"I have a high school reunion," I say. "Maybe around then, in the summer. I might come home for that anyway."

As we chat, I remember the dinner with my uncle, Max, my father's brother.

"He's wrong, you know," Uncle Max said. "Your dad." He shook his head. *He echoed what all the others have been saying as they reappear in my life: he's crazy, he's mentally unbalanced, he's a fanatic, he's wrong. They all seem sad for me. Sad for him, perhaps.*

Maybe my dad was not the dad I knew. Maybe he was part of us—the family—but different. Who was that little girl they remembered? Not me. Surely not the me I am now.

"You know," Jeffy says, "I wanted to tell you that I don't get your dad. He was always a mean son-of-a-gun, but I don't get how he could be like this to you."

I blink. "Yeah, well." *I thought you all were like him, I want to say. I thought you all were his family, not mine. My family was not like my father. My family was not who I thought they were.*

After I hang up, I snuggle into Ruthie on the sofa. "I love R," whispers in my mind again. The babies bump against my hand on her belly, as if trying to reach out for me. These children, not yet born, not even my own blood, have reopened a pathway to family I thought lost. Ruthie and I have built this new family from nothing, from love. And now it is expanding again, backward and forward. It seems impossible. A miracle. Magic. Like floating backward in space and time and moving forward in the same motion. Unions and reunions from my past meeting those that haven't even happened yet.

The truck slides as I negotiate a curve, pain jolting through my shoulder and down my arm, and I catch my breath. The house on the hill comes into view, white against a winter-blue sky. Home. I'm going home.

Reunion: Ricki Ann

"Why Ricki Ann Purvis, you haven't changed a bit."

Ricki Ann will look at the fat woman in the shiny blue dress—something from Sears, no doubt—thick ankles spilling over high heels, and try to discover something familiar in the padded jowls and mascaraed eyes. She sips her gin and tonic, letting her mind slide back twenty-some years. Nothing. "Hey," she says, her voice neutral. "How have you been?"

A look of disappointment flashes over the woman's face, quickly masked by a smile, the lipstick just slightly too pink. "Oh, you don't recognize me, do you?" She brushes aside her sequined shawl so that her name tag is revealed. "Michelle Mitchell," she chirps. "Michelle Graham now. We were best friends in seventh grade!"

Ricki Ann smiles, because she knows she is supposed to. "Of course, Michelle! I would have known you anywhere! It must be the dim lights in here," she says. The ballroom of the Holiday Inn Westside is indeed dim. Needs to be to hide what twenty-plus years does to you, Ricki Ann thinks. The sign over the stage where a lone DJ—young enough to be her kid if she had any—leans against a stool. A banner behind his equipment reads "Welcome Class of '75!" Why the hell had she come to this?

"Well, well, well, and who's this pretty lady?" Boomer's deep bass resounds just behind her. Idiot. Ricki Ann turns toward him and smiles, but her eyes are narrow. Bid-niss, that's why she's here. For her husband's stupid bid-niss. He looks past her toward Michelle, sticking out a hand. "Boomer Madison," he says, grinning. "And you must'a been the prom queen."

Ricki Ann resists the urge to scowl. Her face hurts with the smile plastered there. "Michelle Graham, my husband, Boomer. Boomer, Michelle." She watches a blush rise up from Michelle's neck as she recognizes Boomer. Her mouth forms a little O and her eyebrows jump.

"I've seen you on TV," Michelle gushes. "Boomer Cadillacs, right?"

Ricki Ann doesn't have to look at him to know that he's beaming. The asshole loves being recognized. He was a football hero at Florida, played a year in the pros, blew out his knee on a slippery field in Detroit, came home to Jacksonville and built a little empire of auto sales, but he still longs for glory. His neck would be bulging at his shirt collar. "Yes," she says to Michelle. "That's right. The dealership is over in Arlington, you know." She sips her drink. "Of course Boomer only does the commercials because he's so well-known. We keep busy traveling a lot these days." Ricki Ann forces herself not to move when his hand touches the small of her back.

"Oh, are you retired?" Michelle asks, cutting her eyes at Ricki Ann so fast she almost doesn't catch the gleam in them.

Bitch. Ricki Ann's face aches as she controls her smile. She doesn't blink, but lets her left hand with the three-caret solitaire toy with the emerald choker around her neck. "Oh no, sweetie," she says blandly. "You don't really retire when you don't exactly have to work for the money, do you?" So what, he's over seventy and an idiot. She makes sure he works out every morning to keep some of that old football player physique, and he plays golf every afternoon so he stays tanned and out of her hair. And she works hard at spending his money. She's earned it. She'd met him five years ago, just before she turned forty and just after he'd turned sixty-five, and let him win one last trophy. She rattles the ice in her glass. Without turning, she says, "Boomer, be a good boy and get me another drink, won't you?"

He reaches over and takes her glass from her hand. "You betcha."

He pulls her close with his other hand at her waist and pats her ass. "Be right back."

Michelle smiles and leans in closer to say something. Ricki Ann prays it won't be a Viagra joke. That stuff ruined everything. But as she watches, Michelle's jaw sags and her eyes go round. "Well I never," she breathes. "Would you look at what just walked in."

Ricki Ann follows Michelle's gaze toward the door. A couple, holding hands, stands in silhouette against the light from the hallway, a woman with long, thick red hair, wearing an elegant green dress, something bought up North, in New York probably, and someone in a dark suit, short bleached blond hair in a spikey halo against a spotlight, another woman. Something about the stark white points of the open collar against the navy suit, the length of woman's neck and tilt of her chin, is familiar.

"Look at her, acting like that . . . that . . . lifestyle is just fine." At the snarling nasty note in Michelle's voice, Ricki Ann suddenly remembers Michelle clearly, remembers seventh grade. Something inside goes very still. "Thinks just because she's all famous, just because she's been on Kora . . ." Michelle's words are drowned out by a sudden blare of dance music, a song Ricki Ann recognizes. The Archies. *Sugar, Sugar.* The tall woman at the door smiles and leads her partner to the dance floor with a crowd of other couples, and when she moves through a spotlight something bubbles in Ricki Ann's throat. Seventh grade. Virge.

Backslide

I slide into her in the bed of the pickup. In my single bed on Renoir Drive. Under the bed as she writes in magic marker.

No. I am driving. And this is someone else. This reunion has not yet happened. Has it?

I'm driving in the dark now. Twilight. Snow. Music plays, something from my past. Sugar, Sugar. *But the truck has no radio. The beat is inside me, throbbing in my arm, thunking in my chest.*

Snow blurs the road. Which way home?

The Witnessing Story, or Seeing Rolling Hills

In October 1969, I stand alone on the corner of Meadowlark Lane watching the red and white church bus—the colors symbolize Christ's blood washing us Christians white as snow—trundle off down Rolling Hills Road in a bellow of black smoke. The "One Way to Heaven" tracts in my left hand are already sweaty and my Bible feels slippery in my right. Brother Carl would be back for me in three hours. By then I am supposed to have knocked on every door down Meadowlark, into the cul-de-sac, around Rambling Rose Way and back up Rolling Hills Road—my "territory." I am going to recite my personal testimony about how I got saved and try to lead poor lost souls to the Lord. I've only been in seventh grade one month, but I'm pretty sure that even if Rolling Hills has some lost souls, none of them are poor.

The kids who live in Rolling Hills—Karen Zane, Sugar Edwards, Jenny Hilliard, Mark Matthews, the cheerleaders and student council

types—are the kids with the coolest clothes, the expensive tennis brace-
lets, and the latest hairstyles, like on *The Brady Bunch* and *The Partridge
Family.* They pass around slam books in homeroom and make lists
of stuff like who's your favorite rock group and do you think David
Cassidy's cuter than Bobby Sherman. They passed one of those surveys
to me on the second day of school back in September. At first I thought
maybe they wanted to be friends. I'm not supposed to listen to rock
'n' roll (even though I try to late at night anyway, with my transistor
radio tuned to the Big Ape, WAPE, under the covers), so I wasn't sure
what to put down for FAVORITE BAND. Sugar Edwards had written
"The Guess Who," so that's what I put too. I really liked The Byrds the
best, but nobody else had written that, and I didn't want to be weird.
All the other girls on the list had put down the Rolling Stones—I knew
from WAPE and by listening to the popular kids that the Rolling Stones
were coming to Jacksonville for a concert, and all the Rolling Hills kids
were going to go—and I liked that Sugar wasn't scared to be different
from everybody else. It turned out it didn't matter what I put. They all
giggled over where they were huddling along the window, glancing over
at me, making my ears and face go all red, and Sugar erased so hard
that the paper ripped and Miss Lonigan called over, "Girls? Girls?" I
wished again that Ricki Ann was in my homeroom. She would've put
something really cool, really wild, on that piece of paper, and nobody
would ever giggle at her.

I wish Ricki Ann were with me now as I go witnessing in Rolling
Hills. She was saved so she has a personal testimony too, I think, and I'd
like to hear it. I'm pretty sure that hers will sound a lot better than mine,
but Ricki Ann got saved down at the revival tent meeting in the Winn-
Dixie parking lot by her house while I was still out at the farm. She still
hasn't joined up in any church. I've been hoping she'll choose ours, Free
Will Baptist, but she sat through the invitation—the part where you can
come up front and get saved or join up or make some other statement of
faith—at the end of the sermon that Sunday just before school started,
staring straight ahead with me poking her hard in the ribs. I had told
her that I'd walk up to the front with her, but Ricki Ann kept ignoring
me. She was mad because she had wanted to sit across the aisle in the
left corner with the teenagers, including Ronnie Lane. But every week at
Sunday dinner Dad growls about "those kids holdin' hands and foolin'
around in the back row," so I was too scared. Besides, we weren't really
in junior high yet that day. And she hasn't come back to our church

since school started. She hasn't talked to me on the phone, and when she passes me in the halls at school she's too busy talking to whoever she's with to even say hi.

The house in front of me on the corner of Rolling Hills Road and Meadowlark Lane is two stories tall, covered in stucco and white siding with a peaked and shingled roof, white pillars like Tara in *Gone With the Wind*, a driveway that curves up between two huge oaks, and a garage door pulled shut nice and tidy. It's like a picture of a house in a book. In my neighborhood all the houses are made of concrete blocks, each one story with a nearly flat tar roof and a short, straight driveway ending in an open carport. There are only five models of houses in Normandy Village, so when you walk into some neighbor's house, sometimes it's like walking in a dream through your own house—only the furniture and pictures on the walls are different. And our neighborhood is flat, like most of Florida, except for the ditches gouged out behind the back-yards so torrents from hurricanes and tropical storms have a place to overflow, where fat black snakes gorge themselves on rats and bullfrogs and the blackberries that grow in thickets. In Rolling Hills there are actually hills, and the trees are old and mossy, like at Grandma's house in Georgia, and all the houses are new and modern-looking, like Yankee houses up North. I bet there aren't many snakes here.

Ricki Ann's house is just on the edge of Normandy Village, an old, wood Florida cracker house that stands up on low posts and has a porch where you can sit and watch all the moms going to Winn-Dixie on Saturday, and all the sailors zipping by, heading away from the navy base toward downtown or the drive-in or the stripper bars for Saturday liberty. Her dad's cab-over semi is usually parked in the side yard when he's home, and the bahia fields for their cows come almost to the house on all four sides. We found a dead snake sticking out of a hay bale up in the loft once, and Ricki Ann's dad wears a .45 pistol in his belt when he mows to shoot snakes. Dad says Ricki Ann's dad has to be doing pretty well, what with truck driving and the price of beef these days, but Mom says that all those kids must take a lot to feed. I mostly get the feeling that Ricki Ann's dad's working toward something bigger—he's hardly ever there—and her mom seems like the kind who pinches pennies till they squeal. Ricki Ann said they're gonna move to a mansion one day, but that was hard to imagine, looking out from her creaky front porch into the yard full of car parts and cows.

The sun has crept up under my nylons and polyester dress while I stand on the sidewalk getting ready to go witnessing, so I'm all damp, standing on a corner in Rolling Hills on a Saturday afternoon. I feel dumb. Sweat beads prickle on my upper lip. I have to do it. It's the most important part of being a good Christian after getting saved. I force my feet to move, the thick heels of my shoes clopping on the sidewalk—a sidewalk! You have to walk in the street or across front yards in Normandy Village. I head toward the aluminum-sided Tara house, going over the Steps-To-Salvation verses in my head. It will feel good if I can stand up later and tell the older teenagers in the youth group that I led souls to Jesus. Maybe Ronnie Lane would give me a special brotherly hug. I breathe my prayer over and over as I climb the hill of the driveway: Jesus, help me. Please help me.

The front door is huge, with frosted glass panels on each side. Jesus, help me. Please help me. I force my finger up and push it into the doorbell. I hold my breath. A deep melodious chime, muffled by thick carpet, rings far away inside. Nothing. I wait, listening and praying. Maybe nobody will come to the door. Maybe nobody is home. Thud! "Fuckin A!" A man's voice, inside. I swallow hard at the cuss word. The doorknob turns. Jesus, help me. Please help me. The door jerks inward, then bounces forward off something and almost shut again. "God dammit!" The door opens.

"Shit! What?" a young guy, about twenty, snarls. Long hair, long mustache, scruffy beard. Dirty. I smell old sweat and something sweet on the air-conditioned breeze that pours out the door. He's sitting in a wheelchair. I blink, hearing my eyelids click inside my head. He stares at me, blue eyes bright and glittering. "What?" He sneers like a dog. "What the fuck do you want?"

I blink again. Of course I hear swear words now that I am in junior high, see them carved in desktops and magic-markered on the backs of the seats on the bus, but I try not to look at them—or the pictures of boys' "things" and naked women either—but sometimes I do turn the words over in my mouth, without sound, just to feel their weight. Some of the rough kids from Marietta even say those words out loud, where no teachers will hear them, at school. But I don't usually hear people actually cuss on purpose, real loud like this guy, and nobody's ever cussed right at me. I take a step backward without thinking.

"Um." I swallow. My Bible feels slippery. I hold out a "One Way to Heaven" tract. "Um—hi!" I say. "I'm Virginia Young from Free Will Baptist Church." I try to look somewhere other than his face, but the only other place my eyes will go are toward the wheelchair. His eyes are bloodshot and yellow in the white parts, and his pupils seem extra dark inside the blue irises. He squints. My jaw feels hinged, and the words come out just like we practiced at the church. "I'd like to share with you my personal relationship with the Lord Jesus Christ."

His bushy eyebrows shoot up. The "One Way to Heaven" tract in my hand shivers in the space between him and me, but I can't reel in my arm. I can't feel it. The guy looks kind of like the pictures of Jesus that were in the middle of the Bible I had when I was little: strands of blond hair over his shoulders and a blond beard. If Jesus came alive in 1969, wearing a T-shirt and blue jeans, he'd probably look like this. Except for the wheelchair. And I don't think Jesus would smell.

"Jesus, huh?" he says.

My heart beats faster. Maybe he's lost. He sure looks like it. Maybe I can lead him to the Lord! Maybe I can help save not just a regular lost person, but a lost wheelchair person!

"Yes sir," I say. I suck in a deep breath. "All of my sins have been washed away because I have accepted Jesus into my heart as my personal Lord and Savior. He gave His life so that all of us might have eternal life in heaven. Would you like me to show you how you can be saved?" My voice sounds kind of like a robot voice, but the words come out just like they're supposed to.

He grins, and my heart feels like it's going to fly out of my chest. Leading souls to Christ is almost easy! Maybe I can be a missionary!

He throws back his head and starts laughing. I can see the underside of his hairy neck and chin turning red as he chokes. He starts weaving from side to side in his chair. "Fuck!" he splutters, still laughing. "Fuck fuck fuck fuck fuck!" He laughs so hard that spit drools out of the side of his mouth and splatters into the air and down his shirt. His chair rolls a little, and I thank Jesus for the threshold, picturing him careening down the hill, laughing out of control.

"Murray?" A woman's voice calls out from inside. I take another step backward. "What's wrong, Murray?" Murray is choking now, the air of his laughter hacking out in short bursts.

"Wait, little girl!" he gasps. I hesitate. "Christ!" he yells. "Come back and let me tell you about gettin' saved, sister! Let me tell you!"

An older woman appears in the doorway and jerks the wheelchair back. "Murray!" she says, looking mad. "What are you doing?"

"I already got saved from hell once, sister," Murray calls. I turn full around and hurry as fast as I can down the sidewalk. "Fuckin' Vietnam! Fuckin' Vietnam!" I glance back. Murray shakes his fist at me then slams it down on the armrest of his chair. "If this is heaven, you high and mighty little bitch, you can have it!" I run.

Panting and heaving, I finally stop and hide behind a wide live oak tree. The tracts in my hand are wrinkled and damp. My Bible is so slippery it's a wonder I hadn't dropped it. I wipe it off on my skirt, then smooth out the tracts as best I can and put them flat inside my Bible. I didn't even give Murray a tract. I want to cry.

Dad was a mechanic in Korea, and Uncle Ralph on Mama's side was in World War II. The pictures in our album make them look neat and clean, their faces young and uniforms creased. And when we were little, my brother and I liked to play with the ribbons and medals in Dad's bureau. I wore his old flight suit last Halloween for my costume. I am too old for Halloween now, but that flight suit was my best costume ever. I've even been thinking I might like to join the navy myself someday. I like those white bell-bottom pants, and Uncle Ralph always says, "No better way to see the world!" And when he talks about "defending freedom" and "protecting the American way," his chin always tilts up kind of proud and his eyes look clearer. You hardly even notice the way his cheeks sag down into jowls.

But Murray. Those yellowed and bloodshot eyes squinting at me. Vietnam. I watch it on TV every night, of course, everybody does. *Huntley-Brinkley* reported the score in our favor, night after night, always something like six hundred Vietcong dead to ninety-two Americans. And we're defending the world from Communism, which is a good thing. But we can't seem to win, which doesn't make sense. Vietnam looks really small on my globe. How many people can it have? And why don't the Vietcong want to be saved from Communism? Dad says that they don't play by the rules of war, and I can see that those little cages they put prisoners in aren't the same as the POW camps like on *Hogan's Heroes*. And maybe it isn't fair the way that they hide in tunnels and plant mines that sound like they're from some weird Chinese torture movie, with flying bamboo stakes and all. But it isn't fair for some big kid to beat up on a little kid, either. The kids in the protests on the *Huntley-Brinkley Report* say that the war is wrong. Dad says they're just cowards, and I can see why you wouldn't want to go and fight in the mud and maybe die, but when your country calls, you're supposed to obey. Aren't you? But the kids on TV say you can't trust the government, that President Johnson, who had looked like a tired old papa when he quit, and Mr. Nixon, with his funny nose and beautiful daughters, aren't telling the truth. But presidents are supposed to be like Lincoln and Jefferson and Washington. Like dads, who know what's right and best and who tell you to do stuff because it's good for you. Like God even. "No respect," Dad growled at the television when it showed kids burning draft cards, and "Yankee hippies," the time the students took over Columbia University, and "Show 'em what this country stands for," when the cops beat up on the kids at the Chicago convention. "One way to get this country back on track," Uncle Ralph said, "enforce the law. Teach those kids a thing or two." But the kids weren't following the law just like the Vietcong aren't following the rules of war. Why? And why was the score so lopsided? Why weren't we winning? And why does Mr. Nixon keep telling us the war is ending when it just keeps getting worse? When there are guys in wheelchairs like Murray?

The next three houses on my route are empty, nobody home, and I dutifully slide "One Way to Jesus" tracts into the doorframes. My clogs are sweaty and my feet slip inside my nylons as I climb the steep drives and descend back to Meadowlark Lane. At the fourth house, after I tumble out, ". . . share with you my personal relationship with the Lord," a very short old lady with a bright red wig and thickly powdered cheeks invites me inside for lemonade.

I hesitate. I've barely gotten started on my territory and a whole half hour has slipped by. Sweat trickles between my shoulder blades. My nylon slip is stuck to my thighs. Maybe she really does want to hear my personal testimony. Even old people can be lost. And they are going to die sooner so it's more important that they hear The Word in time.

She smiles, watching me think. Bright patches of pink rouge on her cheeks, as round as a clown's paint, wrinkle. "Come in, come in," she laughs. "Surely your Lord would not want his missionaries to faint of heatstroke."

I can't help but laugh with her, and so I step inside. The carpet is deep and the drapes drawn shut so that the room is quiet and dark. Air-conditioning sweeps icicles down my back like I'm in a library. I breathe in smells of jasmine perfume, mothballs and cat pee. A TV with the volume turned off flashes black-and-white shadows into the corner of the living room. A cat is sitting on top of it, yellow eyes blinking. The lady leads me on through toward the kitchen, sweeping a fur stole off the seat of a chair to reveal another cat. Soft fur brushes my ankle. My eyes adjust to the dimness and I see cats everywhere: orange cats, black cats, tabby cats, tiger cats, kittens, Persians, cats sitting, cats washing, cats sleeping, cats winding themselves around my legs. There must be dozens of them.

"God forbid you're allergic," she says. Wrapping the stole around the shoulders of her pink polyester pantsuit, the tiny woman opens an enormous, gleaming avocado-colored refrigerator and stands inside the door like an elf at the entryway to some fantastic place. The orange cat lounging atop the fridge stretches out his paw to pat her head, managing to skew her wig a bit.

"Sit down, bubalah," she says. "You look like a wet dishrag. Who knew Florida would be so hot in October?" I pick up the white kitten in the nearest chair and sit, holding it on top of my Bible, where it curls up and begins to purr. "Thank Got for the air conditioner," she says. I think her accent must be German or something. Not American anyway.

Setting a glass of lemonade before me on the kitchen table, she puts her hands on her hips and says, "Miriam Rosenbaum. And who are you with your personal testimony about Jesus?"

I swallow, the lemonade so tart it shrivels the insides of my cheeks. "Virge Young. Virginia."

With a huge thump, a fat cat lands at my left on the table, and I jump. "Oh, don't mind him," Mrs. Rosenbaum says, pulling out a chair. "Falstaff wouldn't harm a hair on your head. You old goot for nothin'," she says, ruffling his fur and chucking him under the chin.

Long hairs cling to her hand as she pets the cat, then drift off into a beam of sunlight, twisting like the strands of DNA those scientists discovered, suspended though, like angels. Mrs. Rosenbaum's pantsuit is covered in cat hair. The skin on her hand is blotched and paper thin, reminding me for a second of the diviner's hands. The way you could see almost through. My grandmother's hands are like that too, and I know the lightness of the bones I see as Mrs. Rosenbaum strokes Falstaff. "Thank you very much for the lemonade, Mrs. Rosenbaum," I say. "It's really good on a hot day like today."

She squints at me and grins. "Such a polite one you are! Yes, yes. Phew. Hot. Too damned hot, that's what I say." I suck in my breath without thinking—I've never heard an old lady curse before. "Florida, Florida," she continues, not noticing. "They all say to me how wonderful, how beautiful is Florida. . . my old friends all down in Miami telling me to move from New York. And my grandson, my grandson the orthodontist . . . What's an orthodontist I say: nothing but a fancy name for a dentist. My grandson the orthodontist said, 'Florida, move to Florida, Gram. Jacksonville is Florida too. I'll buy you a house just across the river from me. A nice neighborhood. Nice people.'" She frowns. "Why not his neighborhood you might ask? Why 'just across the river' in Florida, in this Jacksonville? Why not next door? Why not his grandmother like a mother to him, she died, rest her soul, should live in her grandson the orthodontist's own home?" I shrug, getting interested in spite of myself. I like the rhythm of her words in my ears, like a foreign language, but not quite. "I'll tell you because," Mrs. Rosenbaum says. "I'll tell you!" She leans forward. "Because he's ashamed," she says. "He changed his name. Dr. Rose! Hah! He throws fancy parties for all his rich orthodontist friends and he drives his fancy cars—German cars . . ."

I blink. German cars? Like Volkswagen? Dr. Rose is my orthodontist! My Dr. Rose drives a green Volkswagen Karmen Gia, the neatest car I've ever seen. I open my mouth to say that I know her grandson—though it's weird to think of Dr. Rose with his bushy mutton-chop sideburns and pink-tinted glasses and bell-bottomed hip-huggers as this elf's grandson—but Mrs. Rosenbaum keeps on going, and I close my mouth.

"Those filthy Germans. What they did to young girls. Like you! My daughter was not much older than you—" She stops in mid-sentence. Her pale blue eyes focus somewhere far away. A gurgling sound comes from her open mouth, then she blinks three times fast and sees me again. She grabs my wrist. "See what those pigs did to me?" She pushes up her sleeve. Numbers tattooed into her arm. "And that was not the worst of it!" she hisses. Her eyes are milky and wet, and her hand trembles on my skin.

I gulp, trying not to struggle to get my arm back, trying not to breathe Mrs. Rosenbaum's fishy breath. That tattoo is from a concentration camp! Like Anne Frank! The Nazis killed Anne Frank. The bones of Mrs. Rosenbaum's hand that seemed so fragile a minute before pinch hard around my wrist. It's like I'm handcuffed to her. By her. I can't move.

The kitten on my Bible sits up and yawns, its sharp white teeth clicking in its pink mouth. "Oh what a sweet baby," Mrs. Rosenbaum cries, releasing my wrist to pick up the kitten and hold it to her cheek.

Her blue eyes stare into mine, and then she blinks and sniffs. She blots her tears on the kitten.

"I am sorry," she says. "You are very young and I have frightened you." She places the white kitten on the linoleum table. "Tell me now about your Jesus," she says.

My breath catches in my throat. She's a Jewish person. I've never been this close to a Jewish person before, not that I'd known of—I blink to block out the sudden flash of Dr. Rose's long fingers in my mouth— and here is one asking me to give my personal testimony. Maybe I am going to lead one of the 144,000 Jews who will survive the Last Days and be saved to Jesus! I open my Bible and a "One Way to Heaven" tract on the table between us. Mrs. Rosenbaum tickles the kitten while I talk, her glance straying between me and him.

"Well, as you can see here, the first step to salvation is to recognize that you are lost and a sinner." I flip quickly to Romans 3:23 and read, "For all have sinned and come short of the glory of God."

Mrs. Rosenbaum watches the kitten bat at her finger. Is she listening?

"Do you agree that we are all sinners?" I ask, just like we practiced at Sunday night Training Union. It seems awfully direct here in Mrs. Rosenbaum's kitchen though. I keep my eyes on the kitten and wait, just like we practiced, only when we had practiced, everybody who was pretending to be the sinners immediately said, "Yes, of course," right away. Not Mrs. Rosenbaum.

The silence of Saturday afternoon in Rolling Hills flattens out around us. The hush of the air conditioner muffles the outside, as if we are locked in its hum, the drip of the faucet the only notice of passing time. The kitten extends his claws and curls them around the tip of Mrs. Rosenbaum's finger. She doesn't move.

"Sinners," she finally whispers. "What do you know of sin, little one?" It's almost like she's talking to herself. "It is a sin what the Germans did in the camps. A sin that young girls such as yourself were tortured. Kilt. Worse than kilt." Something passes through her, like a shiver under her skin, a quaver I can only barely see. The tip of the kitten's claw pushes into the flesh of her fingertip, whitening it, about to break through. "What sin had those young girls done?" She is looking at me, I can feel it, but I stare at the kitten. "Grown men, some maybe even with little girls of their own at home—What sin had my little girl done?"

My tongue feels huge, thick against the walls of my cheeks, still shriveled in from the lemonade. I know the answer. We practiced in Training Union. I should flip my Bible open. The Jews killed Jesus. They don't believe that he is the Messiah. But they can still believe. There is still time. And we should not hate them, but love them. The Germans were bad, and they had been wrong. The Jews are wrong not to believe, but the Bible says to love one another. But Mrs. Rosenbaum had been there, in the camps. She could have died like Anne Frank. Maybe her daughter had. My mind weaves, trying to get to the end of my answers. I can't speak.

The kitten's ears tilt forward. A spot of blood wells up around the tip of his claw. Mrs. Rosenbaum doesn't move. The kitten withdraws his paw from her fingertip and sits back, yawning. Mrs. Rosenbaum lifts her fingertip to her mouth and sucks off the blood, then shifts on her chair and laughs suddenly. "What is a sin is to send out young girls into the streets to faint on a hot day such as this," she says. "Have some more lemonade, Virginia Young."

I glance up. She smiles at me, her eyes wrinkling at the corners and the spots of rouge on her cheeks stretched wide. I can't help but smile back.

Back on Meadowlark Lane, I tilt my chin up into the sun and blink, then head down the walk toward the cul-de-sac. Okay, I failed with Mrs. Rosenbaum today, but she told me to come back anytime to talk more about Jesus. I'll get Brother Bob to tell me what to say to win a Jew to Christ and I will come back. Even if I can't get her to accept the Lord Jesus Christ as her personal savior, her stories will be better than Anne Frank, like a real live Anne Frank who doesn't even get killed in the end. More than just hiding in an attic. Escaping! Escaping. The word reverberates somewhere behind my eyes like the mirages of steam shimmering off the asphalt. I shake my head to clear it. Maybe she'll give me a kitten.

As I come around the corner onto Rambling Rose Way, three houses nestled around a dead-end circle of black pavement, I inhale air, sharp with the taste of hot tar, and stop.

Three girls in bikinis—Kathy Zane, Sugar Evans and Jenny Hilliard, the cool Rolling Hills kids from my homeroom—lie on beach towels in the center of the lawn of the middle house, a transistor radio playing the tinny sounds of *Honky Tonk Woman*. Though he acts like he doesn't know it, they are obviously watching a shirtless boy—probably a high school boy, maybe even in college—washing his car, a red Mustang convertible. I stand perfectly still.

I can turn around and go back to wait for the bus to pick me up. If they see me like this, with my Bible in my hand, wearing panty hose and a church dress, they will know. The cool kids will know. Maybe I can hide the rest of my "One Way to Heaven" tracts somewhere and go back to wait for the bus and not tell anyone that I didn't give my personal testimony to every house in my territory. I bite my lip. God will know. Maybe I can just sneak by the cul-de-sac without anyone seeing me. That way I'll only miss these three houses. Jesus will probably understand that.

Muscles in the boy's back ripple as he bends to soap the hubcaps, and Kathy Zane says something behind her hand to Sugar Evans. They snicker. They're lying on their stomachs, propped up on elbows, toward me but with heads tilted to see the car washer, and the white lines of the straight parts down the middle of their sleek, wet, combed straight hair—blond, brown, black—seem like some definition of order, of perfection, that my world—with its broken pickup trucks and concrete block houses and horn-rimmed glasses taped together at the bridge and unshaven legs on order of God and Dad—can only tune into for a visit, like TV. Why would Jesus prefer my cluttered world to this tidy one? He belongs here, like in heaven. But these kids don't need Him because they already have perfection. Maybe He loves us because He's stuck with us. I remind myself that earthly riches aren't important. "In my Father's house there are many mansions," Jesus said. "I go to prepare a place for you," and I hope it's like this, like Rolling Hills. I drink in the scene of the cool kids on a hot afternoon one more time, making sure that none of those heads is turned toward me, then step very quietly off the curb to cross the street.

"Look!" I hear one of the girl's voices distinctly, even over the sound of the radio. I keep my eyes on my clogs stepping forward over the street tar. I pray, please don't let them see me. "Hey!" the voice calls. "Hey you! Kid! Um. . ." Murmuring. "Virgil! Virginia!"

I swallow. Now I have to look. They're all sitting up cross-legged, waving at me and grinning. I keep walking and half-wave in return. "No, wait!" Kathy calls. Why can't Jesus give me a break just this once?

"Hey Virgil! Come on over here!" When I look again, they all beckon.

I try to smile, but my jaw hurts. Heat pounds on top of my head, and my ears and the back of my neck flood with blood. Flame-face. My sweat-soaked slip grabs at my legs as I trudge to the edge of the lawn about fifteen feet downhill from them.

"Watcha doin'?" Kathy asks. Like smooth brown queens of the Nile, they pose on their towels, knees bent, glancing now and then at the car washer.

"Witnessing," I say. My voice is flat and dull.

Jenny smiles brightly. "Wow, cool man." She exchanges a glance with Kathy, whose hair is so white-blond that I have to squint. "Like on Perry Mason, huh?"

My brain winces inward. Is she making fun of me? I shake my head slowly. "No," I say. "I am going from house to house telling people my personal testimony about Jesus."

Jenny looks confused. "Huh?"

Sugar laughs. "You are sooo dumb," she says. "You know, like one of those Hari Krishna guys in the airport." Looking me up and down, she finishes, "'Cept they've got cooler duds."

The other two shout with laughter. Kathy chokes out, "But they both like the midi-length!" All three roll back on their towel-rectangles on the very even green grass.

I blink three times, hard, and suck in some hot air. What should I say? I step back. What would Jesus do? My upper lip feels very cool, and my breath pushes out of my chest. I can't pull it back in. My head is topless, whirling. I see pink. Then white. Colors slipping. Black.

Weightlessness. My legs dangling. Shoe falling off. I must be dead. Thank you Jesus for getting me out of that one. Praise Jesus, I'm dead. I'm going home to heaven. I see the white light behind my eyelids, and I want to see Him, standing there, holding out His open hands, making me safe again. Free. I blink into sun, then the car washer's face. "Stay still," he says. "Let me get you into the shade."

I stare up at him. Shaggy brown bangs in his eyes. Reddish side-burns. Little dots where his whiskers grow. Oh God. Oh no. I feel his hand under my thigh, supporting me, sticking to my nylon stocking. I force myself to tug the skirt of my dress. What if I'm getting my period? Sometimes I faint when I'm getting my period. What if Jenny and

Kathy and Sugar see? I glance back at them over the car-washer's shoulder. Jenny is carrying my clog with two fingers, away from her body, like it has cooties. "Ohh," I groan aloud and close my eyes again.

"We were just talking to her, Mike, really!" Sugar says. "And she just dropped down dead on the sidewalk. It's not our fault! Really!"

"Yeah right," Mike says. "I heard what you guys said. Uncool, man. Really uncool." The glare of the sun softens into shade and he sits me in a metal chair on the front patio. "Just go get her a cold drink, you little twerp." I lean over and put my head between my knees. No blood, thank goodness. I stare at the brick pavers between my feet, following the pattern until it repeats itself, then follow it back to my feet. Don't think, just breathe. The white spots fade. The others stand silently around me. Sugar doesn't go to get me a cool drink. I watch an ant wandering the maze of bricks. Left, right, back the way he came. Like me witnessing in Rolling Hills maybe.

"You okay?" Mike asks at last.

I sit up slowly and nod. "I think so." I swallow. Please God, don't let me cry.

Jenny holds out my shoe. "You dropped this." I take it and slide it onto my foot.

"What's your name?" Mike asks. "I'm Mike."

When I look up through the fence of my eyelashes, he's smiling. I bite my lip. "Virge."

"Like 'Virgil Cain is my name,'" sings Jenny. She laughs, then sobers at Mike's glare.

"Here," Kathy says, shoving my Bible at me. "I'll go get those. . . papers." My tracts are scattered all over the even green lawn and smooth black street like spots of shimmering white ice. She looks at one of the tracts and tosses it onto her towel. Maybe that's enough for Jesus. Maybe Jesus wanted me to faint so that Kathy Zane would take a "One Way to Heaven" tract. Maybe that's all God wants from me this time. It seems like a lot and not too much all at the same time.

Awhile later, when the black girl whose locker is over mine at school opens the door at 22 Rambling Rose Way, all I can say is "Uh." She is wearing cut-off, knee-length jeans shorts and a man's dress shirt with the sleeves rolled up and tail out. Her brown eyes study me, confused. "Uh, hi," I try again, and glance down to regain my balance. Her bare brown toes curl around spotless white strands of shag carpeting. Tendrils of air-conditioned cool lick at my upper lip. "Hi," I say. "I'm from Free Will Baptist Church and I'd like to share with you my personal testimony about Jesus." Past her, the house looks really modern. Wide stairs that seem to float in the air rise toward framed splats of paint on a landing. A lower-level room is furnished with leather-covered sofas and giant pillows—and even a fireplace! Does she live there? Is she a rich Rolling Hills kid too?

Dad worried a lot about blacks moving into Normandy Village; he said property values would go straight downhill and we'd have to move if some traitor sold out to a black person, but he used that other word that Mom says is mean and hateful. The day he heard that somebody had sold to a black family over in Marietta, he'd gotten so worked up that he forgot to yell for Lee to get out of the way when he dropped the four-by-four he'd been holding up for the addition he was making on the back of our carport, and it had hit Lee so hard on the head that he'd just sunk to the ground unconscious for a minute or two. "But you can't hurt a head that hard!" Dad had laughed, rubbing Lee's fuzzy crew cut. I'd gone to my room to read as soon as I'd heard Mom tell Dad the news and saw his face turn red and his eyes become that clear, colorless blue they get when he's mad. He'd looked like that when the government had said that our schools had to be integrated too. "Yankees got no business telling us how to run our schools, take care of our own," he'd said. But nothing much had happened, so far as I could tell, when school opened this year with the buses full of black kids from downtown unloading right beside mine. I guess I was a little scared of them at first, remembering how Mom always made us roll up the windows and lock the doors when we got off the highway to drive through that part of downtown where there had been riots in the spring after Martin Luther King got shot, but other than a few rumors of fights and some bad words inside the restrooms that I tried not to read because it wasn't Christian to call names, going to school with black kids seemed no more weird than anything else in junior high.

"Who is it, Melody?" a woman's voice calls from within the house.

The girl—Melody—keeps staring at me as she yells back, "Somebody from a church!"

I try to smile. "You go to Robert E. Lee, right?" I ask.

She blinks and shrugs. "Yeah, so?" She holds a paperback book in her left hand.

"Nothing. I—" I swallow. "I go there too. My locker's right under yours."

She looks at me harder, then begins to nod slowly, her head bobbing up and down as her brow unfurrows. "I thought you looked familiar," she says.

"I'm Virge. Virginia Young," I say.

"Melody St. James. Mel." She stands still and unmoving in the doorway, and the silence hums, damp with the weight of a humid Saturday afternoon. With a slight twitch at the corner of her mouth, she says, "Well, let's hear it."

I blink. "Huh?"

"Your personal testimony about Jesus."

"Oh." I swallow and hold out a tract. "I asked Jesus to come into my life and be my personal Lord and Savior, and He did. He saved me from all sin. He came to save us all from sin," I say. "Would you like to be saved too?" That isn't how Brother Frank made us practice, but my mouth seems to have a mind of its own. Mel stares and I shrug. "Jesus makes me feel safe," I say.

She smiles. "I know," she says. "Me too." Glancing behind her, she steps out onto the step and closes the door. "Come on," she says, and leads me toward a tall wooden gate.

Behind the house, the yard is lush with huge green elephant ears and hanging plants in baskets under tall live oaks. The air is cooler, and we sit on an iron bench that curves beside the brick walk. A tall metal object occupies a circular spot of lawn in the path. "What's that?" I ask.

"Art." Melody pulls her mouth down like she's tasted something bad. I snicker, and she laughs. "The people who live here like all this weird modern junk," she says. "Mama says they spend more on these hunks of junk than they pay her for a month of cookin' and cleanin'."

The gleaming thing is like the curved slide at the kiddie park, without the ladder. "Really?"

"Mama says some white folks ain't got no sense." Mel coughs. "Sorry. Some folks."

I shrug. "No sweat." I had forgotten to be scared of her because she's black when I thought I needed to be scared of her because she might be a Rolling Hills kid. "Do you live here?" I ask, thinking about that song *In the Ghetto* and the people who'd been in the riots downtown.

She shakes her head. "No, Sweetwater." That's out in the country past Normandy Village. "But Mama don't like me home by myself so she makes me come here every day."

"Lucky it's close to the school," I say.

She snorts. "Yeah, lucky." She looks down. "Feels dumb walking behind all these rich wh—uh, rich kids who're busy pretending I ain't back there walking behind them every day." Mel has to go the same way as Jenny and Kathy and Sugar, I realize, their perfect hair swinging back and forth down their backs as they walk. "That's why I'm glad I got Jesus walkin' with me," she says.

I smile at her, and she grins full into my face. "You go to church?" I ask.

"Yeah," she says. "Well, Sweetwater Baptist closed down last year, but when Daddy's around, we go downtown to church. Mama don't like to drive down there herself because our car is kind of rickety. And there's no other black churches close around here right now."

"I'm Baptist too," I say.

She nods. "I know. 'Member? You tol' me at the door."

My face warms with a blush. "Yeah, right."

"Mama don't let me go witnessing yet," she says. "And I am sure glad too. You must be awful scared sometimes—talking to people you never saw before—"

Something swells up in my chest. Maybe it isn't all that bad. "Yeah."

"'Course, it ain't safe for black folks," she says. "Not most places."

I hadn't thought of that. The steel sculpture reflects the dark greens of trees in blurry curves. No black people ever come to Normandy Village, except when the convicts in their orange suits clean out the ditches, and even though they're guarded by men with rifles, Mom makes us lock all the doors and close all the windows and stay inside no matter how hot it is. And sometimes guys fix the streets. And when Dad is working, we have Tillie who picks up the ironing once a week. I think of Melody's mom. Are we like Rolling Hills people? If Melody walked down our street, witnessing, some people might even be mean to her. Dad might be.

"It's not fair though," she says. "Mama acts like I'm some little baby. Won't let me stay home by myself. Won't let me out of her sight, 'cept when I'm in school. Won't let me wear pants to school. Won't let me shave my legs. Won't let me do anything."

Not fair. "My dad's the same way," I say. "Rules rules rules. 'Specially for girls."

Melody hunches, resting her elbows on her knees and chin in hands. "I wish my daddy was here," she says, her voice low. "He used to let me do whatever I want." My eyebrows arch up. "Army," she explains. "Vietnam. He's a Green Beret," she says. "A captain."

I flash back to Murray, his wheelchair rocking against the threshold as he cursed me.

"We're going to move back up North to New York City soon as his tour is up," she says. "Mama just came down here because her people are here."

"Maybe you can come visit our church sometime," I blurt out, then catch my breath. Part of my witnessing duty is to invite people to visit our church, but—

Mel looks at me sideways. "You think?" she asks. "I don't know—"

"Sure," I say slowly. "Why not? We're all God's children. And you're Baptist too—"

Mel looks skeptical, and I'm not too sure of what I'm offering. But God doesn't care about color, right? In the picture in the middle of my little kid Bible, Jesus holds out his hands to all the children—"red and yellow, black and white, they are precious in his sight" goes the song—and He says, "Suffer the little children to come unto me." Why shouldn't Melody come to my church?

Someone taps on the glass sliding doors behind us. Melody waves at the woman there and nods, and then she turns to me. "I got to go. Mama must be about done for today."

"See you at school then," I say at the gate. The sculpture catches the sun so that Mel is a silhouette. "Or church," I add. I can only see the pale palm of the hand she half raises in a wave.

When I finally turn the corner onto Rolling Hills Road, the last leg of my route, I'm so tired that I sit down to rest on the concrete bridge. Witnessing is hard work. The gully below is wide and deep because the trickle of creek can fill almost instantly in a downpour. A hurricane can overflow the banks. But in the lengthening afternoon shadows of live oaks, grapevines and palmettos, it seems like a ridiculous chasm for such a pathetic stream. It looks snakey down there. Dark. I hear the thread of water moving. Cars and a few tractor trailer trucks whoosh by, bouncing the bridge, the drivers staring out at me for an instant before they are gone. Rolling Hills Road is a bigger artery, a much older thoroughfare than the housing development, and traffic there moves quickly, destined for someplace, stores or jobs, unfettered by the meanderings of cul-de-sacs and pedestrians. My own school bus, as a matter of fact, comes this way every day to Robert E. Lee Junior High. There are few houses ahead, and I have tucked most of my tracts into the doorjambs and mailboxes of the neat suburban streets behind me, so my witnessing is almost done. Finally. The road seems awfully busy for me to cross—and surely those houses on the other side are in someone else's territory anyway. That leaves only the hippie house.

I look down into the dimness under the bridge and close my eyes. "Dear God," I pray. "Protect me and guide me that I may be your witness to the world." That guy in *The Cross and the Switchblade* went into New York City and saved the souls of junkies and helped heroin addicts kick their habits, holding them while they puked and had the shakes and hallucinated. It was a cool book. And God helped that guy—he even wrote a book—why shouldn't He help me?

You can see the hippie house from the bus window when we ride by on our way to school. Set back in the woods a little, it's just a regular old white Florida cracker house, wood-framed, a porch, ordinary. Parked in front, though, is a VW minibus with yellow flowers painted on it and fringe visible through the windshield, so it's called the hippie house. Once I heard one of the ninth-grade boys in the seat behind me on the bus say, "Bet you could get some weed from those dudes." "Weed" is marijuana—I know that from the Officer Friendly Day at elementary school, when all the sixth graders had a special assembly where the policeman showed a movie about how bad drugs were and handed out pamphlets that explained how to recognize them and named all their names. Marijuana is "weed," "pot," "Mary Jane," and it smells like burning rope—What does burning rope smell like? If you smoke marijuana, that is just the first step to getting hooked on heroin, which is just like Satan in your bloodstream according to the guy in *The Cross and the Switchblade*. It also makes you let down your guard, let Satan get to you in other ways too, like sex.

I suck in my breath and turn into the driveway of the hippie house. I raise my hand to knock on the front door as a man with a droopy mustache turns the side of the house pushing a lawn mower. He looks up at me on the porch and scowls. "Yeah?"

The door opens. A woman, hugely pregnant, in a flowered shift looks through the screen. "Hi."

I look back at the man. "What do you want?" he asks.

"Mow the lawn, Reggie," the woman says. "Being mad at some kid won't make it better." The guy yanks on the starter rope, frowning. "Wanna come in?" the woman asks. I open my mouth, but she's already fading back inside. I stand on the porch for a second, then open the screen door and follow her.

The house is warm—no air conditioner—but fans move the air and flutter the leaves of the potted plants cluttering every shelf and surface and hanging from macrame hangers before every window. It reminds me of Grandma's house in St. Mary's. Homey. Two little kids, a boy and girl about ten or eleven, lie on the floor in front of a television watching an old Godzilla movie. They roll their heads to look at me. "Who's she?" asks the boy.

The woman sprawls into a chair leaking stuffing and rests her hands on her belly. "I don't know," she says, reaching for a pack of Marlboros. She lights one and exhales. "Let's find out."

The kids sit up and cross their legs Indian-style, facing me. "Who are you?" says the girl.

My mouth is empty. They watch me like students watch a teacher. Both have silky black hair to their shoulders, and both are shirtless and barefoot. I haven't gone without a shirt in my whole life. I'm not even allowed to wear a two-piece bathing suit. But the girl doesn't seem uncomfortable. She stares directly at me, her face open and interested. She's probably not more than a year younger than me. The boy scratches his ear. "Maybe she can't talk," he says.

I find my tongue. "I, I'm Virginia Young." They don't seem much like hippies, except that they aren't wearing enough clothes and all have long hair. "I'd like to share with you—"

"Virginia, like the state?" asks the boy.

I nod. "Virge for short," I say.

"That's good," the woman says. "Virge. I like that."

"Yeah, me too." Who said that? "Crazy, man." From under the Indian print cloth thrown over the dining table, a mop of curly red hair pokes out. "I'm Wayne," the guy—about sixteen, I guess—says. "But you can call me Way."

"Faith," the woman says, then points at her belly. "And this is my hope."

"And I'm Love," the boy shouts and leaps to his feet holding his arms in a muscle man pose. "And the GREATEST of these is LOVE!"

he yells.

"Shut up, stupid," the girl says and punches his leg.

"Love is not stupid," Faith says to her. "And don't hit your brother either, Marilyn."

Marilyn? Faith, hope, Love and Marilyn? And Way? I look back at the table.

"He lives there," Love says, as if that explains everything. "Come out, come out, wherever you are!" he calls.

"Zora Neale Hurston said 'Love makes your soul crawl out from its hiding place,'" comes the voice from under the table, "but the rest of me stays here."

Both of them laugh, like this is an old game. Marilyn jumps up and stands in front of me. "You want to see my chicken?" she asks, then heads down the hallway toward the rear of the house without waiting for an answer.

I look back at Faith, who drags on her cigarette, grinning at me. "I'd like to share with you my personal testimony about Jesus," I say.

Faith smiles. "Sure," she says. "Go ahead." Then she laughs, loud hyucka-yucka-yucks.

"Do you go to Robert E. Lee Junior High?" the girl asks, coming back in. She carries a huge red chicken. "It's named for a bastard racist killer, you know," she says. She shoves the chicken into my arms, taking my Bible as she does so. "I go to Millside Co-op now," she continues, thumbing the gold-edged pages of my Bible so they flutter. "But I'll go to Robert E. Lee next year so I can get into medical school after college." She stares into my eyes. "I'm going to be a doctor," she says.

The boy snorts. "Booozuie!" His tone is taunting.

"It is not bourgeois," Marilyn says. "I want to help people. And besides, who else is going to take care of you guys when you're old?"

Faith laughs, snorting smoke out of her nose. The chicken looks at me with one red eye.

"Jesus died on the cross so that all mankind could be saved," I say.

"Kind?" says Way, hidden again by the tablecloth, his voice rising up like at a seance in the movies. "Man is not kind, man."

"That's a cool choker." Love scrambles up to stand beside me and touch the velvet ribbon with the embroidered rose around my neck. He smells of peanut butter, and his hands are streaked with dirt. My feet seem stuck to the floor, my hands mired in the bird's feathers. Love strokes the ribbon, then my neck under the ribbon. I shudder. "Can I have it?" he says, very seriously.

"Sure," I say. "Sure. Take it." He circles around and fumbles under my hair to unsnap it.

"Did you sin, Virge?" Faith asks suddenly.

I turn to her and blink. "Uh, yeah, of course," I say. "We're all sinners."

Faith grinds out her cigarette. She gathers her hair and twists it up to cool her neck. Under her arms are thick bushes of black hair. "What is your sin, Virge?" she asks. "What did you do?"

My tongue swells up again. The chicken's feathers stick to my palms, her tiny heart fluttering under my index finger. "Uh." My ears are hot. My mind flashes to Ricki Ann, to the way my go-to-sleep stories get mixed-up. But I am saved now. I shift my weight to the other foot. "Well, we are all sinners in the eyes of God," I say. "The Bible says, 'For all have sinned and come short of the glory of God.'" There, that's right, the right answer. I straighten a little.

"But what did you do?" Faith's eyes are soft, her tone insistent. "How did you come short of the glory of God?"

I blink. "We are all sinners," I repeat, but my throat closes. "Since Adam and Eve ate the forbidden fruit." I wish I were still sitting on the concrete of the bridge on Rolling Hills Road. I wish I were in the red and white church bus going home. "I was born a sinner, just like all people," I say. "Just like you."

Faith smiles. "Just like me."

"But Christ died for us," I say. "Don't you see?" My words tumble out. "He laid down His life on the cross—the Son of God died for us—and He rose up from the grave and lived again to save all of us from being punished for our sins. To save us from hell." I close my mouth. I want to run out the door. I want to sit down, watch the Godzilla movie with Love and Marilyn, and hold the chicken until it lays an egg in the lap of my Sunday dress. I want to disappear.

Faith smiles. She pats the arm of the chair. "Come here, Virge."

I stare. She doesn't move, doesn't stop smiling, doesn't stop watching me. My feet move forward. She reaches up for the chicken and stands it on the floor, then takes my hand and spreads my fingers out over her belly, which is warm and tight under the fabric of her shift. Faith's hand smoothes mine. The baby bumps, as if trying to reach out for me, and tears spring, cold and fat, out of my eyes. "This is no sinner," Faith says, her voice like the sound of deep water, husky and dark. "And Virge . . ."

Her hand tightens on my wrist. "You are no sinner either."

The door slams open and Reggie appears, sweating. "Damn, I hate mowing the lawn!" He sees me and his eyes dart past me, then back to me and Faith. "Aw shit, Faith."

"Stay cool, Reggie," Faith says. "She's just a kid."

"What Dad?" the boy asks.

"Nothing," Reggie says. "I just don't want strangers inside the house right now."

I follow his glance to the left of Faith's chair. Magazines. A weird plastic vase. Some tall rangy tropical plants. I look back at Faith, who is still holding my wrist, but now more loosely.

"Don't worry," she says. "Virge has already testified."

I wait, finally, back at the corner of Rolling Hills Road and Meadowlark Lane for Brother Carl in the red and white church bus to pick me up. I don't ever want to share my personal testimony again. I just can't. My tongue feels dead, empty, in my mouth. My body feels wilted and slack. The Steps to Salvation that were so simple and clear that morning are all mixed-up with other stuff in my head. I think about Murray, Mrs. Rosenbaum, Melody, the Rolling Hills kids, Faith and her baby who is hope bumping under my palm, Love, the guy named Way under the table, Marilyn, the chicken . . . And then I think about Ricki Ann and the way my go-to-sleep stories get mixed-up, the stuff I haven't told God about so I can be forgiven even though I am saved. I am backsliding; I know it.

I feel muddled, like I have looked too long at one of those black light posters Ricki Ann has in her room. But what did I see today? Just ordinary stuff. Everyday stuff. But what was true that morning doesn't seem so easy anymore. Jesus said "I am the truth," and that means the only truth. But that seems . . . I don't know. Too simple. I don't have the words for it. God, help me, I pray. Give me words. I lick my lips, rough and cracked against my tongue. I am so thirsty. I swallow and wait.

Backslide

I slip a little forward, a little sideways, a little backward, easing the truck around a sharp bend in the road. Where I am I? Bare trees crowd the dirt path, then open out into snow-covered meadows. I blink at the whiteness, the bright sun twinkling off the powder like stars. The snow is fresh and thick. Where am I? Going home. To the top of that hill. I brake, the tires sliding a little. The engine idles a quiet hum in the silence.

I see our home, white and square, the windows flashing sun, against the green hemlocks and blue sky like a picture in a story book in the distance. I wonder what Ruth is doing. Or will I arrive home and find St. Mary's or Renoir Drive, as I do in dreams, or somewhere else in some other time? Perhaps my father's new Green Acres. Will I get lost in the maze of some other self? The glass reflects sunlight, blinding me. I blink into the darkness, then the light. I hear my brother laugh. I hear my mother crying.

The airliner slides through air, the wings slicing clouds into thin strips outside the window against which I lean my forehead. My eyes leak and leak. My cheeks are wet. I am going home. Leaving home. I am flying, north maybe, or am I flying south? The bright clouds reveal no landmarks below. My brother's funeral. Lee. I cannot believe he is gone. My big little brother. The man I wanted to know. I will always love you, *Lee said. My witness. Witness to my life. Now he is gone.*

"Gone home to Jesus," *someone says to my mother. She tries to nod. Tears slide down her face again.*

Lee's three little children—Eddie, Mitch and Leigh Ann—wander from adult to adult. They do not understand. They will not know him. They will not know his great love, his huge heart. His silent fear of our father.

I slide forward. These boys will become young men who hate me, because I am not him. I am the sinner who lived. Lee will become a saint, no one they know. He will not be their witness, will never tell them of his life, our life. My father will tell his version, will bear a different witness. My father, too, will hate me, will erase me. I hear the silences deepen, everything, everywhere buried.

At the funeral I am given an envelope, a letter from Lee's old friend, Buddy. A man who has become a preacher. I remember that Buddy has a tattoo of a snake on his arm from an army stint. I remember that he lives now in Rolling Hills. Buddy is not here, but he has sent me a letter.

I have just seen my little brother in his huge coffin, his nose still sunburned from work, his skin puffy and cold, his wide shoulders too snug against the blue satin. I am drowning in jet lag, in humidity, everything blurry, as if swimming in a baptismal pool. I have flown home to Florida from my new home in the North. I am drowning in home.

*I am drowning in home, where my father stares into space, or at me, tears dampening his cheeks; where my mother prays, weeping through closed eyes, and tells me it's better that her son died than me, her daughter—*At least I know he's gone home to Jesus, *she says; where my sister-in-law wails, seeing his green eyes in mine; and where my little nephews and niece wander, looking for their father, trying to understand. What do they see? What do they really know? What will they know of him?*

I should scream out loud. He was my brother! He loved me! He didn't care that I was a lesbian! He loved me! Why can't you?

Instead, I sit quietly on a hard pew, wearing a dress and panty hose for the last time in my life, and unfold a letter handwritten on lined paper. My big little brother—witness to my life—lies across the room, not breathing, in a box. I sit in a place consecrated to love, and read the letter from a preacher with a snake on his arm: This is your fault. He's warning you.

Jesus sayeth, I am the Way, the Truth, and the Life, and no man comes to the Father except by me. Get straight with God, queer. This is your fault.

I stand behind my mother and father at the cemetery, a little apart already. Again. It's easy to be a good little girl again, that old good little girl, silent and a little apart. Across the old wall that divides the white section from the black in the old days, another clump of people stand around another grave. I wonder who has died over there. Whose witness and to what? Was her version dark like her skin? Was her vision blinded by light? By love? Or was she a survivor, her witness seasoned, like the old Jewish lady I met in that other time? Or is that now? Who has killed? Who has not? I think of the book I am writing at home up North. Home. How shall I testify?

The pastor is silent after his prayer. My mother leans on my father, who has sagged into old age. His hands are on the shoulders of Lee's older sons, the little boys looking around blankly. His widow sobs into the baby, Leigh Ann, in her arms.

I watch the children. I wonder if any of them will see this world through other eyes, and if he does, what will happen to him? Will she feel the weight of silence descend? Will he be sent to one of the new camps these Christians have established to fix—to silence—that kind of otherness, or some new kind of otherness? What will she testify? Will brothers and sister still love, still listen for their witness's voice, still let him speak? Will they witness the truth that is love?

I blink into the whiteness of clouds, of snow. I move my foot from the brake and let the truck roll ahead before sliding into first gear. I am going home through a maze of the back roads. My shoulder aches, and I think I must be sliding into Lee in that moment before his heart stopped. After I came home to the blinking phone message light, then my father's voice, "Call home, Virge; your brother has died; you need to come home." I realized that at the moment of my brother's death I had been at softball practice, learning to slide into a base in the mud and rain. My coach had laughed at our fears—a team of middle-aged women. If you don't learn to slide right—to get down at the right moment, at the right distance, to let the momentum carry you, guiding with weight and your hand in the clay, you can be injured. But if you know how, it's easy. You can sneak in under the tag. You can steal something fair and square, right under the catcher's nose.

I slide again, backward, and Lee laughs. This is our last conversation.

I've told him about playing a sport for the first time at mid-life. I don't know it's the last time I will hear his voice. I tell him how I love the game, the team, the way I live in my body when I play. He knows. He had always been the athlete in our family, always a part of another team. I hear my brother in the sound of the engine, in my head, as I drive, as I fly, heading home. "Tell it sister," he says.

The Eve Story,
or What Made Me Cut My
Crowning Glory

The library was like the calm clear pool where the spring bubbled up from the aquifer at the farm, a junior high school refuge. It was always quiet. The books made me feel safe. No one else came to the library, unless a teacher made them, which I couldn't understand. Compared to Normandy Village Elementary School, Robert E. Lee Junior High's library was an expanse of escapes, lives, stories that would last me at least a year. I tried not to think ahead to when I would finish reading everything there.

On the first day of school back in September, Miss Williams, my English teacher—my first black teacher ever—had told us to make a list of all the books we'd ever read for homework. She stood in front of the class, slender and small, in a perfect navy blue dress, her hair straightened and smoothed into a Mary Tyler Moore flip, chalk held firmly between long, manicured fingers, and spoke with the clearest, most pure voice I'd ever heard. "You will have one week to make your list," she had clipped out precisely, with no hint of any accent, just like Mary herself. "It shall be comprehensive and correct. Titles and authors, last name first—"

So I had started going to the library the very next morning, as soon as I got off the bus, and, beginning with the A's in the fiction section, I had copied titles and authors from the spines of the books I'd read, trying to resist the urge to check out all the ones I hadn't. It'd taken me two weeks of twenty minutes before school and skipped lunches (which I didn't mind since Ricki Ann had been ignoring me in the lunch room), and a trip back to my elementary school library after school (where Mrs. Ackerman, my old librarian, had greeted me with a hug and demands for me to "Please please come back and read to the kindergartners sometime! You do read so beautifully!"). The ten pages of scribbled titles that I had finally turned in to Miss Williams had been rumpled and smeared from so many days of carrying it around.

"I'll rewrite it neatly in pen if you want," I had mumbled, scared I was in trouble when she asked me to stay after class the day she returned the papers to the class. "I just didn't have time," I said, watching the tile floor under her gleaming black patent low heels. I sucked on a strand of hair, and bit my lip, poking my tongue into a sharp metal edge in my braces. I should have redone it before I turned it in.

"No, Virginia," Miss Williams had said. "That isn't it at all."

Then what? Did I fail the spelling test on Friday?

She held my list under my eyes. "Did you really read all these books?" she asked.

She thought I had lied. My throat got thick, and something pushed out from behind my eyes. I jammed my tongue into the metal point, focusing on the pain to keep from crying, and nodded once. "Yes, Miss Williams," I whispered. Please God, don't let me cry, I prayed.

"This is very impressive for someone your age," she said.

I had risked a glance up between brown strands of my hair. Mrs. Williams's eyes met mine, and she smiled with her perfectly even white teeth. "Very impressive indeed." The heat of a blush rushed up my neck, and I looked down again, letting my braces remind me not to grin. "If I may," she said, "I'd like to keep your list of books to put into your permanent file."

My permanent file! That's what they threaten you with if you're bad: "You wouldn't want this to go into your permanent file. . ." It follows you all through your life, and one mistake in seventh grade can ruin all your chances for success in life. If you messed up, everyone would know because it would be in your permanent file.

Early in November, I looked around the library at all the stacks of books yet to read. I'd been working on it, but there were thousands left. The silence was perfect. And somewhere down the hall in the office, my list of books lay quietly in my permanent file. "Very impressive indeed," Miss Williams had said in October. I looked down at the table and, behind the curtain of my hair, let my lips draw back from the metal of my braces in a smile to myself. I still wished I had someone to tell.

"Hi."

I looked up. Melody St. James, the black girl whose locker was over mine, the girl I had met while I was witnessing in Rolling Hills on that October afternoon two weeks before, stood by my table, holding her books in front of her chest like a shield. "Hi," I said.

"How come you're at school so early?" she asked. She rocked a little, up on her toes and back, and the round puffball of her Afro bounced.

"Bus," I said. "And this is the best place."

She nodded, looking around at the shelves and tables. Only the librarian in her glass-enclosed office looked back. "Pretty empty."

I glanced out the window toward the lawn where kids milled about and clumped into groups, laughing and shoving and talking. "That's just fine with me."

Mel lowered her books and stepped a little closer. "Can I sit here?" she asked.

"Sure," I said. Something in my chest lifted a little. Nobody ever sat at my table.

Mel slid her books across. "Mama decided it's better to drop me off on her way over to work instead of me walking from there or catching the bus at home." She sighed. "I think the rich folks don't like me walking out of their house to go to school. Neighbors probably said something. And Mama doesn't trust me not to miss the bus without her there at home nagging at me."

I didn't know what to say. Her mama and my dad sounded a lot alike. Mel took a paperback book off the top of her stack and slid it across the table. "You ever read this?" she asked.

I took the paperback and looked at the cover. A muscular man in old-fashioned clothes stood in the shadows of some kind of ruin while a woman in a low-cut long dress with thick blond hair, swirling in the wind like something alive, stood in the foreground, her hand over her breast, watching him. My palm felt damp, as if the book were making it sweat. This book was different from the books I usually read, like my favorite, *The Wind in the Willows,* which still made me laugh out loud when the Toad takes his friends for the wild ride. This book was going to make me feel something different, I thought suddenly. "No," I said. "I haven't. Is it good?" My hand clinched on the book, afraid Mel would take it back.

Mel nodded, her face solemn. "It's great!"

"Where'd you get it?" It sure hadn't come from the library shelves. I looked down at the biography of Marie Curie I had just checked out.

"Those rich people's house," she said. "Where Mama cleans. I just took it off the shelf when Mama wasn't around. They've got lots of them. They won't notice. And I'll put it back when I'm done." She was whispering and she kept glancing over at the librarian, making me feel like I was about to get in trouble. But I held tight to the book. "If you want, you can borrow it," Mel said. "I just finished that one."

"Thanks!" I said, breath rushing into my chest. I could keep it.

I read *The Secret Woman* by Victoria Holt at home that night in three hours, and then I read it again with a flashlight under the covers after Mom turned off my light and said good night.

When I had snapped off my flashlight, I stayed awake even later, adding new details from the book to the stories I thought up to go to sleep, the stories I told in my head, lying on my stomach with my pillow under me, rocking against my fist until I felt so good that I could sleep without hearing the snakes writhing beneath my bed.

Mel and I started meeting up in the library every morning before school to trade books from the art lover's shelves. Even though Mel and I weren't exactly friends, meeting her in the library before school made me feel less alone in school. We usually walked to our lockers together before homeroom, since her locker and mine were in the same corner, but we didn't talk much except in the library. No other black kids and white kids hung around together, so we didn't either. At least not so anybody noticed. We didn't have any classes together, so we just said hi if we met at the lockers. Maybe we didn't want the other kids to notice us. I don't know. We didn't talk about that.

In the girls' restroom down the hall from my English class the next day I prayed, *God, why wasn't I born a boy?* Cramps twisted my guts below my stomach. I wanted to puke. My forehead wham-wham-whammed with pain, and my skin was clammy with sweat, like I had just woke up from one of those dreams of black snakes wriggling across my floor. Kotex had failed me again. There was a blob of blood on the back of my skirt. What was I going to do? I sat bent in the dank stall, remembering the cold of the water from the old pump in the clearing at the farm, wishing I could wake up to that clarity again. But it was as if my head was stuck in mud, the cramping in my belly fuzzing my brain. What should I do? Why couldn't I just die?

Voices. I held my breath. The outer door swished open and closed. Giggling. "You're right, he is sooo cute!" I was trapped.

"Yeah. I know. But he hardly even looks at me." It was Ricki Ann. My best friend. My used-to-be best friend. She hadn't said much more than hello in the three months since school started.

"Is he going steady with anyone?" That was Michelle, Ricki Ann's new best friend.

I heard the scrape of a match, smelled a cigarette. They were smoking! "No," Ricki Ann said. "I don't think so. But he's a ninth grader. He'd never talk to me."

"What's he into?" Michelle asked, sounding like one of those stupid girl magazines I sneaked a look at sometimes when Mom was busy in the grocery store. "What can you do to hang out with him?"

I tried not to make any sound. "Well, he's in chorus," Ricki Ann said. "And drama club. But that's just not my bag, you know?"

Michelle snorted. "Yeah, I get you. Not the performing bear type, huh?"

"Something like that." I knew that Ricki wouldn't do those things because she's afraid inside. It's the kind of thing a best friend knows.

Ricki Ann paused, and then I heard her voice directed my way. "Hey, somebody's in here." Rustling. "Who's in there?" A toilet up the line flushed.

I stood up and pushed the toilet lever, and readjusted my clothes. "Just me," I called out. My voice wavered. I hoped they didn't notice. I smoothed my skirt and grabbed my sweater off the hook on the back of the door. My sweater! I wrapped it around my waist and tied the arms together, hiding the bloodstain on the back of my skirt. I would go to the office and ask to go home even though Dad would get mad about having to leave work for stupid girl stuff. I would just say I had the flu.

"Me who?" said Ricki Ann.

I opened the stall door and stepped out. "Me."

Ricki Ann's face went soft—she was glad it was just me—but then it stiffened smoothly into her normal mask-face. "Oh. Hi Virge." She gave Michelle a look. "No sweat."

"Perfectly good butt, wasted," Michelle responded, glaring at me.

I looked down at the water running over my hands, hiding behind my hair, trying not to shiver under Ricki Ann's stare, trying not to let on that I wanted to be back in the tree house on the farm last summer—when I was still twelve—leaning against her warm skin, watching her freckled nose wrinkle when she laughed. "Say," she said, her voice suddenly friendly. "You know Ronnie Lane, right?"

Of course. That was who they were talking about. I nodded, risking a glance at her as I reached for a paper towel. "He goes to my church," I said. She knew that, of course. It was like she was acting in a play or something. Like we were acting in a play. I picked up my shoulder-bag from the shelf and tossed the paper towel into the trashcan.

Ricki Ann grinned at me, but her face was weird. Wrong. Not whole. "We need to talk," she said, gathering her things and walking out into the empty hall beside me. She looked back at Michelle with a grimace. She was so close that I could feel her hair brush my shoulder. Maybe she wanted to be friends again. My head felt light, as if I had stood up too fast. I wanted to believe her, but then she said, "How have you been? Why haven't you called?" and I knew from her tone that it was all a lie. Be careful, I made myself think. "You've got to tell me everything," she said.

On Saturday, Mom and I went over to Southside to take Grandmother Young on her errands: the beauty shop, the grocery store, the garden center, the mall, and the vet. Grandmother still had a car, a Volkswagen Bug that I'd really like to have when I get old enough to drive. Her cataracts have gotten bad, so when it rained or got too hot, Mom and I helped out. Because Dad and Lee were out late at the stock car races on most Saturday nights, the three of "us girls," as Mom said, would pick up some Kentucky Fried Chicken and watch TV together. Mom and I liked *The Mary Tyler Moore Show* (we couldn't watch it at home because

Dad hated it), and basketball season hadn't started yet (Grandmother loved basketball), so when Grandmother let us choose that evening, Mary was what we picked.

Mary spun and threw her hat in the air. I liked that her song was about making it in the world . . . "after all," like nobody thought she would.

Grandmother snorted, her face reflecting the blue light of the television. "From bra-burners to this," she said.

Mom shifted uncomfortably, probably because Grandmother said the word bra. Mom was never very relaxed around Grandmother Young, Dad's mother. Nobody was really. She was always *Grandmother,* formal and kind of stiff, even a little regal, not like my grandparents on Mom's side, who I called *Grandma and Papa.* But there was something about Grandmother that I did like, the way that she was her own person, and who cared about anybody else?

A commercial came on. "It certainly is a change from the days of *Father Knows Best,*" my mother said, "isn't it? Those good old classics—."

Grandmother snorted again. "Maybe on TV," she said.

Mom tried again. "Not like it used to be—"

"And a good thing," Grandmother said, shutting Mom up. I watched the two of them, Mom trying to please everybody and Grandmother pleasing herself. And me. Just us girls.

"Your grandmother was a career woman in her day, Virginia," Mom said. "Did you know that?"

"I had a job," Grandmother corrected, her voice flat. "In Chicago. Teaching school." She glanced at me, then stared at the TV as Mary came back on. We watched in silence as Mary and Rhoda argued with Phyllis. When the next commercial started, Mom went down the hall toward the bathroom, and after she was out of earshot, Grandmother said, "I should have been a doctor. I wanted to be a doctor. But I was the only girl in my chemistry class in college. Almost the only girl in most of my classes. My father only let me go because my brother was there." Her face hardened. "And then he graduated, so I had to leave too."

"Really?" I said. I wanted to go to college myself. But I didn't want to be a teacher like Grandmother or a social worker like Mom. I used to want to be a preacher, but women weren't allowed. That's what the Bible meant by "Let your women keep silence in the churches." Now I wanted to be a writer, but last year I thought I wanted to be a TV news producer like Mary.

Mom came back, and we watched as Mary confronted Mr. Grant. We laughed at Ted. During the next commercial, Mom asked, "What was it like, being a single woman in Chicago back then?" Mom was always trying to make conversation.

Grandmother sat back from her TV tray. Her eyes focused somewhere beyond the television. "I lived with my brother," she said. "We went to ball games. I rode the trolley to work." I wondered what it would be like to live with Lee, all grown up. Would he still tell me I smell funny? Would we go to ball games? Would he let me borrow his clothes like Skipper borrows Ken's?

"Was it cold?" I asked. I'd never even seen snow.

Grandmother snorted. "Yes, cold." She nodded toward the TV, where Mary was brushing snow off her shoulders. I couldn't imagine it. Grandmother pushed her tray away and stood up. She was very tall. "But the cold wasn't why I left."

She carried her plate into the kitchen, and I looked at Mom. "She got married," Mom whispered.

Right after that weekend at Grandmother Young's, Ronnie Lane found me.

"Virge!" The voice, deep and masculine, came from somewhere high above my head. The hallway was packed, kids moving shoulder to shoulder, shuffling one way toward third-period classes. For me, civics. I always kept my eyes on the shoulder of the person in front of me, my arms wrapped tight around my books so that no sharp shoves could scatter them under all of those feet, and I watched for openings, ways to cut ahead, around, trying to get to where I was going quickly. I didn't want to be late. I didn't want to be anything except invisible in the crowd, just another fish in the current. But the voice called again, "Virge!" I looked up.

"Over here!" Ronnie Lane stood on top of the two steps that went to the chorus room, three or four girls hanging around below him. The light from the stage inside the room shined around his head, kind of like a halo. Did he know that? He waved at me. Me. My feet moved me forward. I felt dumb. Not just stupid, but like I didn't have anything in my mouth to make words with. I hadn't thought he even knew my name. A ninth grader knew my name.

"Hi Virge," he said, and reached down from his step to pull me into a half-hug. His cheek scratched mine, and his cologne saturated the air around us. He held my hand, not palm to palm but on the top, like he was keeping me from getting away, and said, "Look, I'm starting a Bible Study Group. You should come!" I stared. His hand was warm and kind of soft, not calloused like my dad's or Lee's. My neck burned. Blood rushed in my ears. "Every Thursday morning before school in Room Ten," he said. "You'll come, right?"

I nodded. My mouth opened, but nothing came out. His shaggy hair was thick and wavy—nothing like the strings that fell straight and thin around my horn-rimmed glasses and too-long freckled nose—and it framed his green eyes, soft round cheeks and full lips that were almost too pink for a boy's. He already had sideburns, reddish-brown and shaped long and wide. He laughed loudly. "Great!"

Ricki Ann was right. Ronnie Lane was cute.

He turned to one of the girls on the step below him and released my hand to touch her shoulder. I let myself be sucked into the crowd hurrying off to class.

As we all herded through the overcrowded one-way hall, I studied the couple in front of me. His left arm and her right arm crossed over in the back, their hands gripping each other's waist. From her wrist dangled his chunky ID bracelet. Going steady. They seemed to be concentrating hard on walking in step—left, right, left, right—both staring straight ahead, their attitude a studied nonchalance. Her long straight hair swung back and forth in a thick veil. I remembered Ricki Ann in my bed on that Saturday night before Labor Day, back when we were just twelve, just kids. Practicing with her. This—not that—was what boys and girls were supposed to do in junior high.

Why did God put Ronnie Lane and Ricki Ann back into my life in junior high after nearly three months? Her, smoking in the bathroom and walking close enough that I could feel the warmth of her arm. Him, a ninth grader, haloed on the steps of the chorus room, inviting me to study the Bible before school.

I trundled along the hall with the crowd and thought about the magic-markered heart under my bed, the words, *I love R.* Sometimes I thought I could still smell that black squeaky smell when I was reading or telling stories in my head, in my bed. Sometimes I imagined snakes in the darkness, watching Ricki Ann writing on the cool tiles. I remembered Ricki Ann's lips just hanging out, minding their own business and the way they felt against my own lips, and my face flamed.

Them talking to me was like magic. Maybe like God. Like something moving in my hands.

"He's gonna look like a girl!" Dad yelled from the head of the table at home that night. "Do ya wanna look like a girl?" His face boiled red, the little veins along his nose scarlet threads, and I could see the pulse in his temple. I wanted to escape, to disappear, but I was trapped at my place at the table, a green bell pepper stuffed with hamburger alone in the middle of my plate.

Lee, across from me, hunched his shoulders. He was sitting on his hands. He'll pay for this, I thought. I stared at my plate, glancing out through the lines of my eyelashes and veil of long hair from one to the other without moving my head. Mom's mouth pressed into a line.

"No son of mine is going to grow his hair like a gol-darned hippie!" Dad bellowed. I watched my hand move the fork to my bell pepper, scoop out some meat, and raise it to my mouth. I'm not here, not here, not here. Just finish and leave the table, I thought. "Sissie!" he taunted.

Lee blinked. Don't cry, I thought. Whatever you do, don't cry.

"He just wants to let it grow a little, Ed," Mom said. Pink bloomed under the freckles on her cheekbones. She didn't meet Dad's eyes. "Not long, just not quite so short."

"Not a flattop," Lee mumbled to his plate.

Dad glared at him, then at Mom. His own flattop was like a mowed lawn, every hair even. Lee had worn his hair cut like Dad's for as long as I could remember. I was glad Lee wanted to grow his hair out, but I was scared of what kind of accident would happen to him later. That's what always happens—accidents. Like the four-by-four that fell on his head when him and Dad were closing in the carport last summer. By accident.

"Just to the tops of his ears," Mom said, watching Dad. She dabbed her lips with her paper napkin, then returned her hands to her lap.

His lip twitched a little, and he glanced over at Lee, then back at Mom. "Not touching his ears, not touching his eyebrows, not touching his collar," he growled, disgusted. He threw the wad of his paper napkin onto the table, scraped his chair back and stood up, grabbing his iced tea. "Bring me some ice cream in there."

As Dad's La-Z-Boy slammed back in front of the TV news—*whoosh-clunk*—I swallowed the lump of hamburger and let my eyes meet Lee's. His grin was a little wavery, but he shrugged, his shoulders suddenly seeming wider, more muscled. I smiled. You won, I thought. You're brave. I wished I could say it out loud.

"'I will, therefore, that men pray everywhere, lifting up holy hands, without wrath and doubting; in like manner, also, that women adorn themselves in modest apparel, with godly fear and sobriety, not with braided hair, or gold, or pearls, or costly array, but (which becometh women professing godliness) with good works.'" Ronnie looked out on his congregation in Room 10 at Robert E. Lee Junior High School for a long moment, his green eyes pausing at one after another of the longing gazes of the girls sitting in the circle. I had told Mel and Ricki Ann about the Bible Study Group, and Ricki Ann had brought Michelle, and two girls from chorus were there, as well as another six or seven I didn't know. Mel was the only black person, and Ronnie was the only boy. You could tell he was practicing his preacher training on us even though it was supposed to be a discussion. But the girls who weren't churchgoers, like me and Mel, didn't seem to know it. I watched as each one of them met his eyes and blushed and blinked and smiled. Ronnie was good at it.

"These verses are God's message, through Paul, to the Christians, to His people," Ronnie said. His voice was low and smooth, gentle even, like the cypress woods in summer, with the hum of tree frogs and the heaviness of damp air. "Paul is recommending modesty to women, for it is the woman's job to keep men from lust and sin. Woman is cursed, because she yielded to the temptation of Satan, the snake, and ate the forbidden fruit. And she then deceived Adam."

Ricki Ann raised her hand. She crossed her legs and her miniskirt snuck up another inch on her thigh. Her black go-go boot swung a little rhythm. "Ronnie," she asked, her voice molasses-smooth and her eyes a little wide, "do you think that Jesus would be cool if he was alive now? Don't you think He'd be for love?" She pronounced it like luv. "Isn't He really about luv?"

Mel, sitting next to me, grunted, "Uhmph." Ricki Ann's question was weird.

Ronnie's smile, though, was broad. He laughed. "Well, of course Jesus is love, Ricki Ann!" He spread his hands, palms up, to us, just like the pictures of Jesus in Sunday school. "But that love must also be modest and godly." His glance dropped for a second to Ricki Ann's thigh, then he looked to the ceiling and sat down on the top of the teacher's desk. "Paul, in these verses, is urging the women in his church to be restrained, to keep men from temptation. He's telling the women that it's their job to say 'no' to men." Ronnie looked again into Ricki Ann's gaze.

Ricki Ann blushed and lowered her eyes so that we could all see the blue half-moons of eye shadow on her lids. A small smile creased the sides of her lips. She should be in the drama club, I thought.

I felt Mel's arm rising, tense and thick next to me. "What about men?" she asked, her voice soft, but with a note of something solid underneath.

Ronnie cleared his throat and his head swiveled toward us. "What's that?"

Mel shifted forward on her chair. "Well, don't men have some kind of responsibility too?" she said. "Why do women get all the blame?"

Ronnie held up his Bible. "Eve—" he began.

"Oh, come on," Mel said. "That explains why snakes crawl on their bellies and women have pain in childbirth, but that doesn't cut it with the sex thing does it?"

I couldn't believe what Mel was saying. She was challenging Ronnie Lane. A guy. Almost a preacher. My own mouth felt like it was full of sand.

"Isn't it something about the tree of good and evil and the tree of knowledge?" a girl on the other side of the room asked.

Ronnie nodded. "Paul admonishes women specifically, because they've shown themselves to be susceptible to temptation—"

"But doesn't that mean that men should be the more responsible ones?" Mel interrupted.

And Ronnie was ready. "Yes!" he shouted. "Exactly. Paul writes, 'But I would have you know that the head of every man is Christ; and the head of the woman is the man; and the head of Christ is God.' Men are in charge, but it is—as we saw in the scripture—the woman's duty to resist temptation by being modest."

I imagined the heads on top of each other like a totem pole—woman, man, Jesus, God—but I didn't see how that made women the ones to be responsible but not in charge of anything. My head ached, as if I were being pushed down by all those other heads on top of mine, holding them all up at the same time. And the tree question—I wasn't going to say anything; I was only a seventh grader. And a girl. But if we got kicked out of the garden because God was afraid we'd eat of the tree of knowledge as well as the fruit of good and evil, did that mean that we were wandering around in the dark? That God didn't want any of us to be wise? We had sex, and pain in childbearing, because we broke the rule about one tree; what would we have had if we had broken the rule about the other tree? And wasn't knowing about sex a kind of knowledge too? Not that I knew anything about sex. The Victoria Holt novels always stopped right after the man picked up the beautiful woman to take her to his bed.

The warning bell rang, and Ronnie made us all hold hands and pray. "Oh heavenly Father, lead us through this day in modesty and in submission to your will for us as men and women in Christ. Amen."

He stood at the door of Room 10, hugging each of us as we exited, just like the preacher after church. When it was my turn, my skin prickled at the scratch of his starched shirt, and he whispered "Thank you for coming Virge" behind my head. I had dressed in my favorite church dress, hem one inch above the knee, nylon pantyhose, no perfume or makeup. I am modest, I wanted to scream to Ronnie. See? But he was already reaching for the next girl.

Ricki Ann hung back, waiting to be the last to hug Ronnie, and he smiled as she approached him, almost shyly, and held his arms wide. She had unbuttoned another button on her blouse.

Mel waited for me at the door to walk to our lockers. She shook her head at the floor as she walked, but I didn't know what to ask her. I glanced back. Ronnie's head tilted down to hear something Ricki Ann was saying, and he draped his arm casually across her shoulder, slipping his hand under her silky orange hair.

"Hey Virge." On the day after the first Bible Study Group at school, I looked up from *The Secret Woman,* which I was reading for the fifth time, hiding it under my papers on the library table. "How come you're not at lunch?" Ronnie slid into the chair across from me. I caught my breath. His bangs fell down into his eyes and he smiled.

"Uh." I couldn't think. He was all by himself. Why was he in the library? Why was he sitting with me?

"I know, I know," he said, "you're a reader, a thinker." He smiled. "Like me."

I felt my face flushing red, and I smiled back, forgetting for an instant to keep my lips tight over my braces, then remembering and ducking, letting my hair swish forward to hide my face. "Uh, yeah," I mumbled. I hadn't ever thought of Ronnie as a reader or thinker. A preacher, sure. Maybe a good actor.

Sitting back in the wooden chair, Ronnie seemed to expand. His eyes swept the library. No one. "I'm doing some research for my AVC term paper," he said. AVC? My face must have conveyed my confusion, because he explained. "Americanism versus Communism. It's required for ninth graders."

"Oh." My mouth felt gummy, my head empty.

"My paper is going to be on the tensions between Americanism and Communism in the equal rights movements." He stopped scanning the room and looked at me. "You know, like Martin Luther King and the women's lib stuff, and even those homosexuals." His eyes met mine then darted off again. They were so green, and his lashes were so long. "It's like everybody wants equal rights and to be free and everything, but that's how the Communists get started." He frowned and shook his head. "I haven't quite got my thesis figured out."

I nodded, dumb. What was he saying?

"I mean, the Bible makes it pretty clear who's in charge between men and women, but that's in the church." Ronnie's eyes moved from the stacks of books to the door to the librarian behind me, then to meet my own eyes again. "You know, I've never even seen my mother in pants?"

I blinked. I tried to think of Mrs. Lane, who I knew from church, of course. She was older, and she seemed really sad, more like my grandmother than my mom. Ronnie was the youngest kid in the family, his brother Donny in college and his brother Lonny in high school. Mrs. Lane never did wear pants, I realized. Even my mom wore pedal pushers and culottes sometimes, below the knee, of course, and one-piece swimsuits with a little skirt. Mr. Lane was a deacon, like my dad, but he was funny, always joking around, even with me. I didn't think my dad liked him much, because he wasn't serious enough. But nobody could say the Lanes weren't godly.

Ronnie looked sideways at me, then down at his pencil. "You know Ricki Ann Purvis, don't you?"

I blinked. Oh. My insides settled downward, heavy. I felt my breath warm and thick in my chest, expanding. "Yeah," I said, nodding. "Kind of." I watched him. Ronnie Lane just wanted something from me, wanted me to get something for him. Ricki Ann. He stared at his pencil, at his fingers sliding up and down on it.

"She likes you," I said. Why? Why did I say it? In my ears, I heard my voice, kind of smooth, a little lilt at the end. My tongue felt small and quick, like a snake's, and my hands relaxed, flat against the table. I sat up straighter, my back muscles stretching up and expanding against the wooden slats of the chair, something loosening around my spine. I felt taller.

Ronnie's mouth twitched. His eyes met mine, then darted off to the side again. "Yeah?" he said.

I smiled, my lips closed over my braces. "Yeah."

"Miss Williams is putting my list of books I've read into my permanent file," I had announced, finally, that night at the dinner table.

Mom looked up from her dinner plate and smiled so that we could see all of her teeth. "Oh Virginia, that's wonderful!" she said.

"Bookworm," Lee taunted, out of habit. He grinned.

"She says it'll look good on my record for when I start applying to college," I said.

"That's right," Mom said, and lifted her fork full of rice toward her mouth.

On my left, Dad tensed, so I shut my mouth and sat very still. My heart sped up, fluttering in my throat. Maybe I should have waited until Mom was alone. He scraped his chair back from the table and folded his hands over his plate, elbows on the table. I stared at my plate, but I could feel his gaze, like blue ice on my neck.

"College," he snorted, like it was a bad taste in his mouth. "Huh."

Mom's fork wavered. She swallowed. "She's smart enough, Ed; why not?" Mom went to college, the first person in her family, but Dad went to Korea and then to work. Mom always said he was smart in a different way.

Dad laughed again. "Education's just a waste on a girl," he said. "She'll just get married anyway." He stood up. He wasn't even mad. It was just over.

I opened my mouth, then shut it, then opened it again. "No," I said. It was quiet, but I did say it out loud behind the stringy curtain of my hair. "I won't." Lee and Mom kept chewing. Nobody except me seemed to hear.

• • •

The day after that, which was Friday, I found Ricki Ann in the restroom. She stood at the far end, beside Michelle and a line of other girls in front of the mirrors, each head with a straight center part, the hair evenly halved and combed flat down the back and over the ears. It was like looking down a line of soldiers in helmets. Except for Mel, who stood at the first mirror with her pick, shaping her kinks into a smooth round globe. She met my eyes when I came in, but she didn't break our silence.

I did. "Hi," I said to Mel, and all the other girls stopped talking at once, looking from me to her and back.

Mel blinked. She swallowed. "Hey," she said.

I walked past her and all the others, watching me in the mirrors, to Ricki Ann. I dropped the folded note I had in my hand onto the little shelf below Ricki Ann's mirror. I jutted my chin out at her reflection. "From Ronnie Lane," I said, then turned and went into a stall.

Behind me, I heard "Ooo" and "Open it, open it!" and I sat down and waited. Ricki Ann gasped. "He wants to meet me after school!" she cried, and the other girls laughed and made sounds of envy. Someone had magic-markered a scrawl inside the stall door: *I love R.*

That night, Lee and I stayed with Grandmother while Mom and Dad went to a funeral in Tallahassee. Lee sat at the kitchen table looking at Grandmother's scrapbook. "Who's this guy?" Lee asked, and Grandmother and I both got up and hunched over the kitchen table to see. The man in the old brown and white photo was dressed in a big floppy cowboy hat, and belts crisscrossed his chest ending in two pistols in holsters on his hips. The men all around him looked dirty and tough. He was holding a beer can and grinning.

"That's your Pops," Grandmother said, "Your grandfather. My husband." Pops died when I was little, so I don't really remember him. I looked closer at the picture. He did look kind of like Dad, but he was laughing, so loose and relaxed that it took me a minute to see the resemblance. Dad hates drinkers. They're sinners, of course.

"Wow," Lee said. "Was he a cowboy? An outlaw?"

Grandmother laughed. "Hardly." Her long finger tapped the picture. "This is when he was adventuring in South America, working for the telegraph company. Gone off from us, as usual."

The picture on the next page was of a beautiful young woman with short hair and a fringed dress, a flapper girl. "Who's that?" I asked, pointing.

Grandmother hesitated, her fingertip stroking the side of the photo. I glanced at her face and saw that the lines in her face were soft. "That's me," she said. "Just before I was married."

The girl in the photo was smiling, her hands on her hips, and I could see that she was shaped something like me, wide in the shoulders and tall, with a long neck and arching eyebrows. Her hair was cut like a boy's. Grandmother sighed, turned to open the refrigerator and began pulling out dinner fixings, her face hidden behind the door.

I glanced around her cozy little house, the place she had designed and had built when Pops died. It was just right for one person, like Mary's place.

The face that had emerged in the mirror on Saturday morning at Grandmother's hair salon was mine and not mine. I kept my eyes on hers, on my own eyes. I heard the swish-click of the shears, the voices of my grandmother and her hairdresser, Albert, but it was as if they were all far away, beyond some kind of humming sound in my head, like tree frogs in the swampy cypress grove below the spring. Brown veils fell away. There were my cheekbones, my long neck. My eyes. Watch those green eyes. I saw that my lashes were long, my eyebrows arched. My lips were stretched closed over my braces. The cold of the scissors chilled my neck, and I shivered, something loosening down my spine. I fingered the lock of long brown hair that Albert had tied with a pink ribbon and laid in my lap after the first swish of the scissors. I would be the only girl with short hair in church, in the whole school, maybe in the whole world. Except I knew that Twiggy had short hair, and Terry Timmons the Channel 5 weather girl, though not Mary. I felt exposed. Albert's hands appeared, fluffing, and a can of spray hissed beside my ear.

"Dad's not gonna like it," said Lee, at my elbow. I met his eyes in the mirror, green like mine, and serious. My hair and his were almost the same length. A slow grin spread across his face. "That stuff makes you smell good though," he said.

"Let the woman learn in silence with all subjection." On Sunday, as Brother Bob read the text for his sermon, I followed along in my Bible, my finger gliding across the thin, scratchy paper of First Timothy, trying not to look at Ricki Ann's hair, smooth and shiny as sun on the surface of water, falling over Ronnie Lane's arm hugging her shoulder along the back of the pew in front of me. "But I permit not a woman to teach, nor to usurp authority over the man, but to be in silence," Brother Bob read. "For Adam was first formed, then Eve. And Adam was not deceived, but the woman, being deceived, was in transgression. Notwithstanding, she shall be saved in childbearing, if they continue in faith and love and holiness with sobriety."

When I got my first period, when I was twelve, Mom said, "Now you are a woman."

My cousin Maggie said, "You can have babies now," and her eyes got really wide.

And then Lee said, "You smell funny," even though he didn't know about me becoming a woman and all that. He'd held his nose and made a yech-face.

My face flamed hot and red, remembering. I wondered if being a woman explained why my tongue wouldn't move right anymore, like it wasn't part of the rest of me. Why had I said what I said? Why had I done what I did to get Ricki Ann and Ronnie together? I wondered if Ricki Ann and Ronnie, who were going steady now, were holy.

My index finger thumped the page of my Bible hard, and I jumped a little, surprised. It was like it had done it by itself, like when I jumped away from the snake without thinking, like magic. I glanced down the pew at the next person, Mrs. Harlow, whose mouth twisted. But not at me. She didn't notice. She stared at her own Bible page like she was trying to see through the book to her hand cradling it underneath. I reached up to unhook the strands of my hair from my ear to let it fall as usual in a thin, stringy curtain around my face, but the new short edges just barely brushed my cheekbones. I had forgotten again.

"Every man praying or prophesying, having his head covered, dishonoreth his head," read Pastor Bob. Ricki Ann snuggled into Ronnie's armpit. "But every woman that prayeth or prophesieth with her head uncovered dishonoreth her head, for that is even all one as if she were shaved. For if the woman be not covered, let her also be shorn; but if it be a shame for a woman to be shorn or shaved, let her be covered."

I wished I were sitting somewhere else, not behind Ricki Ann and Ronnie, but Mrs. Harlow had scooted over and beckoned me in next to her when I came in a little late. "I love your haircut," she'd whispered.

"It's so nice to see one of you girls with a different style!" So I was stuck.

I looked down at the words in my Bible. Pastor Bob was preaching about hair, but it wasn't very clear which rules he wanted us to follow. Long but not too long for guys, and not shaved for women . . . or was that about leg hair? Some folks thought women should be wearing hats again, but that was so square that it didn't seem likely to happen, not even for old ladies like Mrs. Harlow. Then there was this show on Broadway called *Hair* that we had all heard about on the news. People danced buck-neck-ed on stage. Long hair; no clothes. I couldn't imagine being without clothes on purpose in front of other people; changing for gym was embarrassing enough. Almost every girl at school wore her hair the same, straight and long and parted in the middle. The boys in the church had started letting their hair grow shaggy; maybe that was why Pastor Bob was preaching about it. The Rolling Hills boys grew their hair to their shoulders and beyond. The black kids had thick round Afros that bobbed when they walked. Grandmother used to say "That girl's got a good head on her shoulders" about me, but nobody much said anything about my head anymore. I wasn't stupid, but nobody seemed to care about whether I was smart or not, except maybe Miss Williams. Maybe I was supposed to be ashamed of my new hair. Dad hated it and Pastor Bob seemed to be preaching against it.

Pastor Bob read, "For a man indeed ought not to cover his head, forasmuch as he is the image and glory of God; but the woman is the glory of the man. For the man is not of the woman, but the woman of the man." I remembered my prayer—Why wasn't I born a boy? Maybe I was. If the woman is of the man, maybe we all are born boys. Maybe it's having to change into the girl that's so awful.

"Neither was the man created for the woman, but the woman for the man," Pastor Bob continued, and I watched the words under my finger, Ricki Ann's orange hair swishing just on the edge of my vision. That was why girls couldn't call boys for dates, why Ricki Ann had to wait for Ronnie to send her the note. And that was why women had to be pretty and wear eye makeup and have their hair fixed and smell nice, except weren't women also supposed to be unadorned? In *The Secret Woman*, the guy was dark and handsome, but he was also sullen and no good. He had a secret, a past, and the woman had to be beautiful and good, and her goodness finally won him over. She was pure. And what about Ricki Ann? What about Ronnie?

I looked up and toward the window for a second where I saw nothing but shadows and light through the frosted panes. I knew I shouldn't think about that book, especially not in church. I swallowed. God knew all my thoughts. He knew about that book. He knew about the practice kiss. He knew about my mixed-up stories, and how I get mixed-up in them. He knew how bad I was even though I hadn't confessed my sin to Him. "For this cause ought the woman to have authority on her head. Nevertheless, neither is the man without the woman, neither the woman without the man, in the Lord," Pastor Bob said.

I thought about watching *Mary Tyler Moore* at Grandmother's house last night, after my haircut. "Oh Rhoda!" Mary had said, having broken it off with her old fiancé again, even though he wanted her back. Mary didn't have a man. She didn't really need one, though she was always looking. She had a job. She had a cool apartment, a place that was all hers and no one else's. Rhoda came downstairs and they had fun together, without guys. They watched out for each other.

But I didn't have anybody. I touched my hair again, and I felt afraid. I clenched my eyes shut and prayed. I'm sorry. I'm sorry, God. Help me, please. Help me to be good, a good woman. Help me find a husband.

Pastor Bob droned on. "For as the woman is of the man, even so is the man also by the woman; but all things of God. Judge in yourselves; is it seemly that a woman pray unto God uncovered? Doth not even nature itself teach you that, if a man have long hair, it is a shame unto him?"

I focused on the back of Ronnie's head. Dark, silky locks curled over his collar, but not down his back. His elbow cocked back and his fingers twined themselves in Ricki Ann's orange strands. Something rose up in my chest like a huge burp, so I swallowed, blinked, and took a deep breath. I felt my throat closing and shut my eyes.

A warm hand closed over mine. Mrs. Harlow. "Are you okay?" she whispered. I nodded and watched her hand pat mine again, then withdraw.

"But if a woman have long hair, it is a glory to her," Pastor Bob read. "For her hair is given her for a covering." I tasted blood in my mouth. I had bitten my tongue. I'm sorry, God, I prayed. I'm sorry.

But I wasn't sorry. November had tangled me as tangled up as the stories I told myself to go to sleep. I wanted to be sorry, but part of me was not. I was backsliding. I knew it. I was scared, but I couldn't seem to stop.

Reunion: Ron

Ron will close his left eye to look through his right eye, the half of his new bifocal contact lenses that focuses far away. "Oh!" He opens both eyes wide. Virginia Young—the girl he knew twenty-five years ago and the woman who has just walked into his salon—Virge, past and present, advances and recedes, merging as his vision readjusts. Virge, the storyteller, the liar, the truth teller. The sinner. Like me, he thinks.

Ron lets his hands fall to his client's shoulders. Mrs. Eidleman pauses in her description of the fabric choices for the draperies in her redecorated dining room. He glances at her reflection in the mirror. "Oh, Mrs. E., I'm so sorry," he stage-whispers. "You know I'm just dying to hear about those window treatments, but do you know who that is?!" He cuts his eyes toward the door then back to hers.

She raises her eyebrows. "No, dear. Who?"

Ron leans close. "Do you watch Kora?" Mrs. Eidleman nods. Of course she watches Kora. "Well," Ron says, "that's Virge Young."

Mrs. Eidleman peers at the newcomer. "The writer?" she says. "What's she doing here?"

"Oh Ron," calls Brandi. She strides down the aisle to the back of the shop, her face working, eyes wide and mouthing a silent WOW! In her professional voice she asks, "Do you think you could work someone in after Mrs. Eidleman?" Her back to the front of the shop she whispers, "Oh. My. God. It's Virge Young. You know, from Kora."

Ron nods. "Of course, Brandi. I'm nearly done here. It will just be a few minutes."

"Didn't you go to school with her or something?" Brandi whispers. "Great!" she says. "Ms. Young just has a short time before her reading over at Borders." Brandi's voice drops again. "Oh. My. God." She composes herself to return to the front of the shop.

"You went to school with her?" Mrs. Eidleman asks, impressed. "What was she like?" Then, almost in the same breath, "Are you in the book?"

Ron poofs up the back of Mrs. E.'s flat spot and sprays her cowlick into submission. "Well," he murmurs. "She was always different. Quiet. A reader. One of the brainy kids. I was a bit of a smart-ass in those days, theater and all that." He rolls his eyes at her in the mirror. He doesn't actually know if he's in the book. He doesn't read all that much. He only knows what he heard in the news after the shooting on Kora, but Mrs. Eidleman will tip better if he can send her off with a good story for the bridge club. "You'd never recognize me in the book, but I'm there," he says, twirling her around and handing her the mirror to see the back of her head. "Read it again and try to guess." As she starts to protest, he cuts her off. "No, no, you tell me who you think I am the next time you come in." He unsnaps the protective cloth around her neck. "Then I'll tell all," he whispers next to her ear. Maybe, he thinks, I'll even read the thing before then.

While Mrs. Eidleman gathers her things—with plenty of time to fish some bills from her purse to tuck under the vase on his workstation—Ron steps over to the next chair. Jon's customer is gone. "Jonathan, dear." Ron leans close, an arm on the younger man's solid shoulder. "Could you do me a little favor and run over to Borders for a copy of *Sinner,* by Virge Young, before your next client?"

Jon shrugs out from under Ron's arm. "You must be kidding," he says. "You don't read." He crosses his arms over his sculpted pecs. God, what a beauty. "What will you do for me?" he asks.

Ron sighs. Let you keep your job, you big closet case, he thinks. But he smiles instead. "Oh," he says, "name your price, dear boy. Perhaps a cappuccino? A grande . . . ?" He winks.

Jon blushes. "Okay, yeah," he says. "Sure boss." As he leaves, he stares openly at Virge.

Ron takes Mrs. Eidleman's arm to usher her to the front. "Introduce me," she hisses through her teeth, smiling, pretending small talk. Ron, who has the last station, the primo spot at the back of the row beside the window overlooking the lawn and river, naturally, glares at the other stylists in the mirrors—whispering to their customers, glancing at Virge—as they pass through the alley of chairs. He'd personally recruited two of them from beauty school, and he'd stolen the other two stylists fair and square from other salons, plus Brandi, now standing behind the front counter, whom he'd dragged along from his last job when he'd opened his own place. The salon hums like a swamp, word of the celebrity in their midst making them all a little giddy.

"Ron, this is Virge Young," says Brandi, gesturing at the tall bleached blond. "This is Ron," she says, nodding his way.

She sticks out her hand. "Nice to meet you," she says. "I'm glad you could squeeze me in."

"Well of course," Ron says. "I . . ."

"Rhoda Eidleman." Mrs. E. grabs the hand Virge had offered to Ron. "I'm a big fan of yours."

Virge's face lightens with a broad smile. "Thank you," she says to Mrs. E. "I'm always glad to meet a fan." She looked again at Ron. "I hope you'll come over to the bookstore later. I'll be reading at six and signing books afterward."

"Oh you bet," says Mrs. E. "I'm gonna go home and call the reading group. You bet we'll come." She wedges her short body between Ron and the writer and stands looking up at the taller woman. "You got it right, you know," she says. "Those right-wingers, all their holy crap about this and that, their God is the only God. They come banging on my door seems like every day, telling me I'm going to hell because I don't want their Messiah. Stay outa my business is what I say. Just like you." She is still holding Virge's hand in both of hers, and now she pats her arm. "What they did to you was a sin," she says. "You know what my papa used to say about the Nazis? They come for the Jews and I said nothing because I wasn't a Jew. They come for the blacks and I said nothing because I wasn't black. They come for the queers and I said nothing because I wasn't queer. When they come for me, there was nobody left to say anything." She squeezes Virge's hands again before releasing them. "You said it right. We've all got to speak up like you and stop these holy roller nut cases from taking over."

Virge smiles. Ron doesn't know what to say. "Thank you, Mrs. Eidleman," Virge says. "That is very kind. I appreciate it."

Mrs. E. shrugs into the all-weather coat Ron holds open for her. "You look for me later at the bookstore," she says, jabbing her finger in the air. "I'll be there with bells on."

The doorbell tinkles and they watch her walk down the sidewalk. "Bet you get that a lot," Ron says.

Virge laughs. "Well, on the good days I do," she says. "Better that than the preachers and protesters. They'll be there this evening too, I expect." She nods toward the Borders across the street. "Like everything I was scared of when I was a kid come back to haunt me."

At the back of the shop, Virge Young's hair wet and a towel around her neck, she examines Ron in the mirror. "You look familiar," she says, then before he can answer, "Of course everyone around here does." She shrugs. "Home."

Ron steps to the side of the chair and puts his hand on his hip, jutting it out. He raises his hand to his heart and gazes off into the distance. "Remind you of anything?" he asks.

She frowns.

He drops his hand. "Must be the shaved head," he says. "I was losing my hair anyway, so I figured, why not?"

Her brow creases into confusion.

"Okay, imagine black hair slicked back." He clears his throat and sings the first line of the title song from *Grease*.

"Excuse me?" She looks like she wants to laugh but isn't sure if it's okay.

"Oh hell." Ron gives up. He faces her reflection. "Ronnie Lane. Former preacher boy at your own Free Will Baptist Church, Danny in the Robert E. Lee High School nineteen seventy-four production of *Grease*. My shining moment. I know you came to that show, don't try to deny it."

Virge laughs now, a full delighted ha-ha-ha. "Oh my God, Ronnie Lane!" She looks him up and down, takes in his jeans and designer T-shirt, the goatee and manicured nails, his silver hoop earring and the Superman tattoo on his forearm, and she laughs again. "I had such a crush on you," she says, "or something like a crush anyway. You know, back when you were going with Ricki Ann Purvis." She rolls her eyes.

"What do you know?" She puts her hand over her mouth, her eyes shining with tears. "My God."

Ron raises his hand to his heart again. "If only I'd known . . ." he says.

She snorts, giving him the up-and-down again. "Looks like that wouldn't have changed much of anything," she says. "I guess I knew you were a safe choice somehow."

He takes up his scissors and resumes the haircut, shrugging. "Who knew gaydar was born so young?" he says. "Imagine. I swear I couldn't believe it when I saw you on Kora, heard you'd gone and gotten to be one of those famous Yankee lesbians, all cool and out there. Nothing like poor little old me. And then you walk in here out of the blue, right into my little old beauty salon."

"Of all the gin joints in the world—"

Ron smiles. "Yeah. What're the odds?"

"So tell me your story," she says. "You know mine. The whole world knows mine. What's happened with you? How'd you spend the last twenty-five years? Are your mom and dad still around? Still going to Free Will Baptist?"

Ron hesitates. He combs up a section of her hair and stares at it. How to play it? What would she think of the truth? He thinks of her on TV. The truth. Ron watches his hands, the scissors and her hair, continuing to cut, forcing his voice to remain light, cheerful, silly. "Oh you know, boy grows up, goes to college, loses his virginity to a whole fraternity at once, flunks out of college, moves back home and sneaks out to discos by night until the cocaine ends him up in prison . . ." He sees that she is watching his eyes, and looks down again. "You know, your typical boy-gets-scared-queer story . . ."

"When were you in prison?" she asks.

The other stylists are trying to listen. Only one other client still sits in a chair, up front with Marva, but Brandi has wandered down to stand in a little cluster with Calvin at Donette's station, pretending to chat. The doorbell tinkles. Jon is back from Borders. They hadn't known about jail. Why did he say that so loud? Damn. How the hell had Virge Young made him say that? "Oh that was way back," he says, loud enough that the others can hear, "Eighty. Eighty-one. I was just a kid. Stupid. Fucked up." Virge raises an eyebrow. "Okay, yeah. I was queer before prison. Everybody knew it but me. I got it on with guys when I was high, but only when I was high. Hell, I was queer even before I got raped by that frat. That's why I was there, rushing, trying to get into the brotherhood. And then I got busted, and in prison . . ." He meets her eyes again. "Well, let's just say I got real clear about it in prison."

"My god," she says. "Ronny." She swallows, frowning, and bites her upper lip. "Your mom and dad?" she asks. Ron knows about her dad. Everybody knows about her dad. That's why she's asked.

"Dad died while I was in jail. Heart. Went quick." Comb, section, clip. Comb, section, clip. Ron tries not to think about his father, the way he cried at Ron's trial, the way he came to see him every week on visiting day, the lines in his face deeper and his skin gray. "And I went to live with Mom in the old house after I got out. I went to beauty school, got a job, stopped drinking and drugging, met guys in the bushes in the parks every once in a while, you know, stayed away from clubs for a long time." He shrugs. "Probably just luck I didn't get AIDS. I got scared, stopped having sex, stayed home." Ron is talking almost to himself, even though this isn't the way it usually goes. Clients talk; stylists listen and ask questions. That's the rule of the trade.

He gives himself a little shake and glances at Virge. "I was sorry to hear about Lee," he says, trying to right the conversation. "I wanted to come to the funeral, but—" But what?

"I know," she says, staring at him. "Those people who hate us. It's hard to face them. Hard to imagine what they're thinking about us." She doesn't blink. "Is that what you were going to say?"

Ron swallows. What is it about her? She was different when she was a kid. She'd been like a shadow then, a shade, on the edge of everything, or something. Now she stares back at him, waiting. Waiting for the story. He can't look at her, so he watches her hair sliding between his fingers. It's as if he needs to connect this moment with something twenty-five, thirty years ago. Maybe himself, maybe her. Ron shakes his head. "Mom got Alzheimer's in eighty-eight, and I was taking care of her when I heard about Lee. When she started getting bad, I bought this place so we could live upstairs, close to work," he explains, nodding to the tall Victorian ceiling of the old building. "She died three years ago." He stops and looks into Virge's eyes. "I never came out to her," he says, "but maybe she knew. Maybe not. I never really brought boys around or anything. No girls either, of course. Just couldn't quite fess up, you know . . ."

The haircut is complete, but Ron keeps combing and checking for uneven spots. The truth. Why did he rattle on? He hasn't heard his own story like that in years. Maybe never. When he meets men, he keeps it light, quick, airy. They don't want to know. Most aren't looking for anything long-term anyway, not with some bald fairy on the wrong side of forty. He looks up. Virge is watching him with something like sorrow. "What?" he says in mock horror. "Do I have spinach in my teeth?"

"Confession," she says, half to herself. "Asking forgiveness . . ." She blinks and meets his eyes. "Are you out now?" she asks. "Do you consider yourself out? Do you have a boyfriend?"

Ron smiles. "Well, I'm a bald middle-aged hair dresser with a manicure who buys jeans that make his butt look good. There's not much hope of not being out, do ya think?" There are creases like parentheses radiating out from his eyes. Old old old. Too damned old. "Of course, this is still the South. I don't make a big deal about it, keep my head down."

She frowns. "So don't ask, don't tell?"

Ron shrugs. "Something like that. Come on, look at you. It's different for you. You can be out there and nobody cares. You've got a career, a life up North. You've made it."

She tilts her head down so that he can razor the little hairs on her neck. "Like Mary Richards," she mumbles. "You know I wanted to be her back then," she says. "Back when I was thirteen or so." She closes her eyes. "God, that was a long time ago."

Ron smiles. "Sure," he says. "I mean, everybody basically must know about me, right? But being loud and proud around here is just stupid." He stops himself. That guy with the gun on Kora. "Sorry," he says. Who knew better than Virge Young about the danger of speaking out? "Gel?" he asks.

Virge nods. "Do you have a lover?" she asks. "Anyone serious?"

Ron looks in the mirror to see who is listening. All the eyes at Donette's station cut away at the same moment, except Jon's. He sips his cappuccino, staring directly into Ron's gaze in the reflection. Virge watches. Ron opens his mouth, then closes it. He works the gel into her hair and switches on the blow-dryer.

Virge turns to look at Jon. She meets Ron's eyes in the mirror again. "You know what Zora Neale Hurston said?" she asks. "Something I remember from back then, from seventh grade. She wrote, 'Love makes your soul crawl out from its hiding place.'"

Backslide

Rays of light blind me in flashes between dark shadows of forest as the truck parallels the setting—or rising—sun. Dark, light, dark, light—Where am I? What time is this? My head aches with squinting. The time of this journey home seems almost like the solstice, that longest day and shortest night, except that that is the summer solstice and I am traveling through cold, through white, through snow. Perhaps this is the other, the longest night, the shortest day. I hold the steering wheel with both hands, shoulder seeming to throb with the flashes of light. I want to stop, but I know the storm has only abated for a moment, and I need to get home. I need to build some momentum for the up-hills ahead.

For a minute, I am not myself. For a minute, I hear someone else's voice in my own head. I try to focus on the mirror, then twist to look back. Pain wrenches into my shoulder again. I gasp. "God." The voice of someone else in my mind. "God?" I repeat, but I am alone in the cab of the truck, going home to the top of the hill by the back way. Am I lost? Am I hiding? Is this the one who will forgive me? Should I try another road? Will I get home in time? In what time? Now? Future? Past? The truck has no clock on the *dashboard and I don't wear a watch.*

"God?" says Kora. "God," says Ronnie Lane, but he is all grown up, middle-aged, different. I haven't seen him in twenty years. Now he is some-one I don't know yet. But he is there in my mind, bald, tattooed, sad. How is he part of my sin? How is he part of my redemption? The sunlight flashes again into my side vision: dark, light, dark, light.

"Love," says Ruth, from the shadows. "Theories of love." I have slipped back again. It is 1996. It is dark save the image projected onto the screen of the lecture hall, a man overpowering a woman, lines from Foucault about power woven into the pattern. I hide in the back row, waiting for Ruthie to finish her guest lecture at the college, feeling like a spy. The projector clicks and advances with a mechanical hum and thunk, the room dark then light with another image—a Pieta, but instead of Mary and Joseph, two women—one with short hair like mine—cradle the Christ child. "And this one is from my series called 'Immaculate Insemination,'" Ruthie says. I know this painting from my apartment wall. Our apartment wall. It is our future, we think. We want children. We want a family. But our attempts have not yet worked. It has been three years of trying to believe that our children shall be flesh and blood rather than inventions of letter and image. We would rather rage or fight, but no weapon but faith seems to work.

The students in the room are invisible in the dark, watching and listen-ing as Ruth talks about her work, the slides flashing past. They ask questions about her process, the research she does and the materials she uses. For me, the slide show is a review of our history together, her history before me. A painting of a tree house lights the screen. "The 'Rehab Series,'" Ruth says into the darkness. Our rehab. When Ruthie moved in with me, we expanded my little apartment—just right for one person—overlooking the trees of Boston Common into a second apartment, knocking down a wall, to make room for us both. In the painting, the tree house is supported by two trees, one leafed in letters and the other in easels, brushes and tubes of paint. Thunk, hum, darkness. Then a white card on the screen: "Re-Membering." The images that follow are of body parts embedded with faces—friends, pets, fathers, ancestors, strangers—from photographs like jewels or scabs. These are the first paintings Ruthie made when we fell in love, moved in together. "We are making something new from the bits of something old," she had said. "Always re-membering our families, our selves." Thunk, hum, dark-ness. Thunk.

And then I am squinting into the brightness of snow and road and sun between trees again, and there it is, above me on the hill. Home.

"Ruth," I murmur aloud. I have sinned, but I have come out into love. I am heading for reunion, for home. I am remembering, re-membering, and I am inventing the beyond. I may be lost, sliding back and sideways and ahead. But I am certain that some part of me knows—like the magic that made my family—that it is a part of everything else, transforming past and future, sin and redemption, truth and invention into truth. I grin or grimace as I squint, trusting the wheels to turn me again toward home, and I can almost feel your hand—but who are you?—holding mine.

Reunion: Leigh Ann

She will be a spy, an escapee, an outlaw. Leigh Ann watches the woman from her perch in the big oak tree over her daddy's gravestone. The woman is tall and familiar. She's the lady in the pictures at Grandma's house, Aunt Virginia, "The Big Lezbo" Eddie—Leigh Ann's oldest brother—calls her. Leigh Ann doesn't know what that means, but Eddie says it mean and nasty and Mama always shushes him. Eddie's been the man of the family since Daddy died, but he's only eighteen so he's still gotta answer to Mama. Whatever Aunt Virginia is—or whatever a big lezbo is—must be bad cuz Aunt Virginia isn't really part of the family anymore, least not to Poppa, even though she's famous for writing a book and getting shot on *The Kora Lincoln Show*. Grandma goes up North to visit her and her roommate Ruth and the little babies, and she talks about her like there's no big deal going on, but that's just some big fake-out. Something is definitely screwed up about the whole thing with Aunt Virginia. And Leigh Ann is going to figure it out.

It's like magic, the way Aunt Virginia has just appeared out of nowhere at the cemetery on the same day at the same time that Leigh Ann has come to see Daddy. Like God wants her to figure it out. Leigh Ann isn't s'posed to come here by herself, of course, but Mitch—who is supposed to be babysitting her—couldn't care less what she does so long as she doesn't mess up his computer game. Besides, she's almost twelve now, plenty old enough to come to the cemetery on her own. She rides her bike real careful through the woods at the end of Renoir Drive, walks it under the expressway overpass at Fouraker Road, and locks it up to the fence post. She's been doing it for nearly a year now. She squeezes through the fence wires and walks under the trees, picking whatever flowers are in bloom to take to Daddy's spot. Some days she tells him about school or church, or about what she's been thinking. Some days she just sits quiet and listens to the trees whispering and the cicadas buzzing. She doesn't cry, though sometimes she tries to. The hard part is that Leigh Ann just doesn't remember Daddy much. He's the big guy in the video Mama watches sometimes. Her favorite is the one where he's splashing with Leigh Ann, who's just four, at the lake. But Leigh Ann doesn't remember that. She remembers a big big hand, rough and creased with oil, holding hers. She remembers his scratchy face against hers, and giggling. She remembers his deep voice in the front seat of the car talking to Mama as she fell asleep to the drone of the engine. She thinks she remembers green eyes, and she wants to see if Aunt Virginia's are still that same color.

She couldn't tell from the picture in the newspaper cuz it was black and white. Aunt Virginia is a writer and she's going to sign her books over at the Borders Bookstore. Leigh Ann read about it in the newspaper, but nobody knows that she knows. There is going to be a family reunion tomorrow, with all the old folks and people from Daddy's family getting together for a big dinner, but Mama still isn't too sure about whether they should go. "Cuz The Big Lezbo is going to be there," Mitch had said. "I'm sure not going." Of course, he'd just said that because Eddie was there and that's what Eddie would've said. Mama would make the final decision. Leigh Ann wants to go, but she doesn't have a vote. So she's decided to ride her bike to Borders and see Aunt Virginia for herself today. But she's come here first to see if Daddy has any opinion on the subject. She didn't think he would.

But here is Aunt Virginia visiting Daddy too. Leigh Ann looks down on the messy short hair, half blond and half dark. She wishes she could see her face, but she doesn't want to give herself away. She likes spying.

"Hey Lee," Aunt Virginia says. She rests her hand on the curve of the stone marker and sighs. "I miss you little brother." Leigh Ann watches her aunt's hands, pale and strong. Her fingers are long. They flutter, not fidgeting but moving and alive, stroking the stone then caressing the air. Her palms seem very white. The fluttering pale hands make Leigh Ann think of the time she watched a green snake shed its skin, the long minutes drawing out into an hour, more than an hour, as the creature dragged its belly against the sand, waving brilliant green and fresh in the warm air as the dry husk of old stayed behind. Leigh Ann still has the skin in her room.

Finally, Aunt Virginia reaches into her back pocket for a little notebook and withdraws a green pen from the spiral binding. She opens to a clean page and rests the pad on the narrow edge of the gravestone. She stares off toward the old drive-in theater screen across the highway. Leigh Ann watches from above, watches the pen hovering over the white paper. It touches down, and words in green ink scratch across the page.

Leigh Ann hugs the thick arm of the oak and stretches to see what her aunt is writing, but the angle is wrong. The woman smiles, frowns, closes her eyes, and writes some more. She cocks her head to listen, holding the pen lightly between her fingers. Leigh Ann holds her breath, waiting for something to happen.

The Stranger Story, or Why I Buried a Machete for Christmas

When we were little kids, Lee and me and the gang used to play a game in the woods behind Winn-Dixie that we called *Getting Lost*. We'd jump the ditch at the end of Renoir Drive and bushwhack through the kudzu vine and blackberry thickets, as straight as we could, in one direction—toward the sun, away from the sun, sun on our right, sun on our left—for about an hour, just to see if we could figure out where we were and find our way back home. Once we popped out all the way over on Fourakre Road and stood in a little bunch stunned for a second at the cars whizzing by before we remembered that one of our parents might be in one of them and ducked back into the leafy shadows. Once we found surveyor's orange ribbons in a wide swath, marking where the new expressway was coming through next year. Once we discovered the drive-in movie fence where the big kids had left empty beer cans and Cheetos bags while watching the movie for free. Once we found a little house, the size of a troll's house, and I whispered that it was a still and that the hillbillies were probably going to come after us with shotguns, and everybody shrieked and took off, running back through the woods, careless of snakes and poison oak, finally tripping and tumbling into a giggling heap. I knew it was really just a pump house for somebody's well. I knew there wasn't all that much to explore that I didn't already know in these woods. I knew that I couldn't really get lost, but even so, I liked the game.

After I turned thirteen, Mom said I couldn't go to the woods anymore. "Strangers," she said, her tone low and dangerous. I don't know exactly who she meant—I never saw anybody I didn't know in the woods—but the way she said it made me watch out for them. For men. *Strangers* means *men*; that, I did know.

I still went to the woods, but not with Lee and the gang, because he'd tell. Mom didn't get home from work until five, so I didn't have to lie to her. But instead of playing *Getting Lost* with the boys, on account of I had to keep it a secret that I was there, I pretended that I was a spy or an escaping prisoner, like on *Hogan's Heroes*. When I was stuck in my room because Mom was home, I would pretend that I was hiding out, like Anne Frank in the attic, except that she was hiding out with her family, and I was alone. And she was hiding from Nazis, and I didn't know who I was hiding from, or why.

My father ran away to fight Nazis when he was fourteen, but he didn't ever talk about it. One day, Lee showed me a picture he found of Dad in a marine uniform, looking even younger than the later picture of him in the album from when he was in the air force in Korea. He looked like a toy soldier in the marine outfit. He looked like Lee.

"Mom says they didn't find out he was too young for almost a whole month," Lee said. "Cool, huh?"

I remembered the guy in the wheelchair in Rolling Hills, Murray. "What happened?" I asked.

"Sent him home," Lee said, touching the picture on the edges with the tip of his finger. "Then he must've gone again after he was older, later." Dad was a mechanic in the air force when he met Mom. "I wonder if he got to shoot a gun, you know, when he was only fourteen."

I looked up at Lee. By then, his hair was shaggy and he looked different. He had gotten tall all of a sudden, as tall as me, maybe even taller, and I was the tallest girl in the seventh grade. He was about to turn twelve, but he was bigger than the other little boys. His shoulders seemed wide and he wasn't so chubby—Mom now said husky—and more solid. His upper lip was dark, fuzzy, and a black hair curled up from under his T-shirt collar, odd against his pink neck. "He probably shot guns hunting anyway," I said. There was something on Lee's face, and the words slipped out before I thought. "Is that a zit?"

Lee turned red. "Shut up!" he yelled, and his fist shot out and punched my arm. Hard. "Leave me alone!" He shoved back, his hand going up to cover the spot on his chin, and his chair clattered to the tile of the dining room floor. The light from the window silhouetted him. He wasn't a little boy anymore. My arm throbbed where he had punched it. He had done that a million times, all my life, just like I used to punch him, but it had never hurt before. For a minute that December afternoon, until he sank back down and mumbled "Sorry," I didn't quite recognize my little brother.

Ricki Ann started coming to our church all the time once she and Ronnie Lane were going steady, even on Sunday morning when she had to sit by herself on account of the choir got so small that Mrs. Felton, the choir director, came and asked all of us in the youth choir to join up with the adult choir on Sunday mornings. Even me. Even though I got so scared that it felt like almost nothing was coming out when I sang. But it was neat to wear a white robe like one of the heavenly host, and to give my testimony by just singing along with the others, especially something proud and tough like "Onward Christian Soldiers." And after we sang our special in the Sunday morning service, I liked that I could sit up there in the choir loft behind the preacher preaching and stare out at everybody. I could see who was dozing off, and who was getting moved by the Spirit, and who was making eyes at somebody in the choir—usually Ricki Ann blinking up at Ronnie, who sat in the row behind me. She acted like she didn't see me or know me even though it had only been four months since that night she had slept with me in my single bed before junior high school started. The night I had kissed her in the dark. By December, Ricki Ann acted like I was a stranger.

With Ronnie, Ricki Ann was different, always experimenting with new ways to hold hands—fingers twined or palms together or just pinkies—or trying to get him to go around behind the Sunday school building with her after the youth group meeting on Saturday night. When I saw them disappear around the corner one December evening, I went inside to the bathroom and cracked the window, keeping the lights off. I could hear what they were doing back there in the dark.

"Ummm." Smack, slurp. "Oh, Ronnie."

"Uhnnn. Uhnnn." Wet kissing sounds. "Ricki Ann."

A gasp. Breathing. Fumbling.

"Oh." More kissing. "No, Ricki Ann. Stop." Ronnie sounded out of breath.

"But I love you, Ronnie." Ricki Ann sounded smooth and cool, but her voice was husky.

"Ohhh." He drew in a breath. "Noo." It sounded like it hurt. "Stop. We have to stop." Movement. "My dad will be here soon."

I thought Ricki Ann was doing more than letting her lips just hang around, waiting to be kissed. I was kind of grossed out, kind of sweaty and itchy, but I couldn't seem to stop spying on them. It was like I was undercover, gathering information. It made me feel like I was in on it with them. Or maybe like God, knowing secrets.

"No, Ricki Ann, no." Ronnie's voice was deep, but it sounded weak. He was putting up a good fight in the narrow alley behind the church, but I could tell that Ricki Ann was wearing down his defenses. Funny, she was supposed to be the defender; he'd said so in Bible Study. I pressed my ear to the screen and strained to see into the dark through the two-inch crack of the open frosted window. The screen scratched my cheek, then moved, tilting inward. Uh oh. My hand shot up to catch it. A small, loud clack.

"Someone's in there!" Ronnie whispered. "Shh." They were listening.

I thought fast, reached back and flushed the toilet, then turned the water faucet on in the sink, splashing my hands and turning the crank of the paper towel holder noisily. Maybe they wouldn't notice that the light was off. I escaped into the dim hallway, slamming the bathroom door behind me.

Even though I snuck out of the Sunday school building by a side door, Ricki Ann and Ronnie were waiting.

"I knew it was her," Ricki Ann said, her hand latched onto Ronnie's arm like a vise. "You weirdo."

I couldn't breathe, and I was glad for the darkness, feeling the red in my face. Deep down inside, I was glad that Ricki Ann still knew me. She knew it was me. "Bathroom," I said. The word sounded like a breath, like the way you scream in a dream and nothing really comes out because your tongue won't move.

"Huh," she said. The door clicked shut behind me.

"Don't tell," Ronnie pleaded. "Don't tell."

I pushed past them, almost running toward the car where Mom waited.

During the fall and winter, whenever I heard Lee and the other boys going off to the woods, I slipped out of the house and followed them. I planned elaborate routes and inched silently along the ditches. I listened and watched and sat perfectly still for hours while they burst into loud battles, brutish and short, throwing rotten pears at each other's forts and trenches, and shouting gunfire sounds. Then they would lie around reviewing the highlights. "You're dead!" "No, you never got me!" "Did you see the way I fell out of that tree? Cool huh? Let me do it again. See, shoot me! Like this!" I didn't get it.

I found a little platform somebody had built not too far up on the side of a pine tree, probably hunters so that they could shoot deer, but it hadn't been used in a long time. It reminded me of the old tree house at the farm, made me remember Skipper, folded up in the knothole there, and the long, hot days in July when Ricki Ann and me had played dolls together. But the tree stand was smaller, only big enough for one person, and December was chilly, even in Florida. When I got bored with the boys' war games, I climbed up there and wrote in my notebook, drawing maps and making up codes so I could leave messages to myself or to the other spies in hollowed logs or special coffee cans buried at fifty paces north of the X. Sometimes I made up stories about a tribe of very tiny girls who lived wild in the woods, secret spies for a good queen of the forest. I called them the Izan, the opposite of Nazi. The Izan were warriors, but they never let themselves be seen.

One day in December, a twig cracked below, to the west of my deer stand in the tree, and I froze, my pen hovering over my notebook. Maybe an animal. I scanned the thicket toward the sound. A shadow emerged, moving slowly, bent and old. A man. I held my breath. A stranger.

He hesitated, standing still and listening. I watched with my muscles set like cement. He was a little hunched, wearing jeans and a plaid jacket. His long white beard floated out and twitched in a breeze. The sun was low and the sky orange. He cocked his head. A chopping, thwopping sound. "Uhhn," he said, and turned and strode off in that direction through the trees.

When he was gone, I shinnied down and followed, lifting each sneaker and placing it down carefully between dried leaves and twigs. His red jacket made him easy to see without getting close. But he wasn't paying attention to me, not watching for spies; he marched as fast as he could toward the chopping sound. A wind whipped up, blowing the stranger's beard out behind him.

He stopped at the edge of a clearing. "Hey!" he shouted. He waved his arms and started forward again, tilting and angry.

When I reached the edge of the trees, I saw Lee staring back at the stranger, who was almost running, even though he was old, toward him. I could see only the man's back and his beard flying to the side, but his fists were in the air and Lee's eyes were wide, his mouth open. Lee dropped his machete and ran.

When I went to Rolling Hills on December 20, the last day of school before Christmas vacation, Mrs. Rosenbaum opened her door and threw her arms wide. "Virginia! My little Christian friend!" The air from her house whispered out smells of mothballs and kitty litter. "Happy Hanukkah! Merry Christmas! Season's greetings! Come in, come in!"

Walter Cronkite shone blue from the television set in the living room, where a small but very fat orange cat slept like a fur hat hovering over the newsman's bald head. Mrs. Rosenbaum bustled off to where a pot steamed and rattled on the stove in the kitchen. "Sit down, Virginia! I'll be right back," she called over her shoulder.

I wasn't exactly supposed to be there, but not exactly not supposed to be either. "Can I go home after school with this girl, Mel, in Rolling Hills?" I'd asked Mom.

Her face got all smiley. "You have a new friend? Mel? Is that short for Melanie or Melody? What's she like? Is she in your classes?" Mom had even forgotten to correct me with "May I" instead of "Can I" in her rush of happiness. I felt a little guilty.

"She's just a girl," I said. "We read books together in the library in the morning." I didn't say "She's black." I didn't say "Her mother is a maid in Rolling Hills." I said, "She's been coming to the Bible Study Group with me."

Mom's grin had gotten even wider. "That's wonderful, Virginia! I knew you'd make new friends in junior high!"

So I had walked out of school with Mel on the last school day before our Christmas holiday and we'd gone to the rich people's house and sat in the garden with the art thing and read our books for an hour until her mom got ready to leave. Then I had walked down to see Mrs. Rosenbaum. Mel had told me that she had a little sign in her yard: "Free Kittens." My mother was going pick me up there, but she thought it was Mel's house.

I had a plan to explain the yellow kitten who stuck his butt up in the air and twitched his tail, preparing to pounce on the blue yarn I dangled under the edge of the chair.

"I think I'll name him Samson," I said. "Because he's like a big tough guy who's kind of a marshmallow underneath." I cocked my head back to feel the brush of my own short hair on my neck. Was my hair my strength, or was it the other way for girls?

Mrs. Rosenbaum laughed. "All men are like that," she said. "Don't let 'em fool you."

Walter Cronkite reported, "Today in East Orange, New Jersey, police arrested a man they say was one of Germany's most notorious war criminals."

Mrs. Rosenbaum sat forward and tightened her lips into a line. I followed the twist of her head to look at the TV. A policeman led a handcuffed old man from a house with shutters down a snow-lined sidewalk and helped him into the police car. The old man didn't look at the camera but at the ground. He reminded me of the pictures of Pops, my dad's father, thick and balding, a heavy brow. The camera cut to a woman in a white apron, a neighbor, who kept glancing from the big microphone in front of her to the camera to her hands.

"Well, he seemed so nice," she said. "Just normal. Nice to the kids." She wrinkled her brow and twisted her hands in her apron. "He lived here twenty years. Just a nice old man." She glanced to the left, and looked confused, worried. "I don't know. I thought I knew him pretty well—"

"Nazis," Mrs. Rosenbaum muttered. I looked at her. Her face was angry and tight. "They're everywhere."

• • •

Lee's birthday is only five days before Christmas. It always seems like we're going to church or decorating the tree or going to Grandma's house or something at the same time as his special day. Mom makes a cake and we give him presents, but his birthday always gets mixed-up with Jesus'. Sometimes it seems less special. On December 20, 1969, it was worse than that.

"I told you not to take that machete out of the tool shed!" Dad's face boiled, the veins blue and bulging in his temples. Lee tried to keep his shoulders up and back and square, tried not to move. Mom and I had just come in from Rolling Hills, and we stood in the front doorway and looked from one to the other.

"Yes sir," Lee said. He kept his eyes on the floor. "I'm sorry."

"What's the matter, Ed?" Mom said. I sidled in behind and around her, trying to keep my box hidden as I assessed the obstacles between me and the hallway that led to my room: sofa, coffee table, Dad. I pushed back into the corner behind the front door, hunched my shoulders over the box, and thought myself small, in a cave, a spy.

"He's gone and lost my machete," Dad said.

Get smaller, Lee, I thought, watching him. But Lee didn't shrink down as usual. His shoulders even seemed to swell up until he was almost as tall as Dad. "I used it to get Mom a Christmas tree," he said, jutting his chin out. "I . . . I dropped it yesterday and couldn't find it when I went back. But I got the tree," he said, pointing to the bushy cedar lying on its side in the family room. I recognized the sweet smell of the forest, and the tree. It seemed bigger inside the house.

"A Christmas tree!" Dad spluttered. "A Christmas tree!" Every year, me and Lee and Dad used to get in the pickup truck and go down to the farm and cut a cedar tree. Dad usually woke us up before daylight, and we would stop at Krispy Kreme for donuts. The sun would come up while we twisted and rattled down the misty maze of dirt roads, smushed together, three across on the bench seat of the pickup, Dad's arm resting behind our heads. Later, after we brought the tree home, we would get dressed up and Dad would take us downtown to May Cohen's to pick out a nice present for Mom from the three of us. But the farm was up for sale, on account of Dad being out of work again, and nobody wanted to go out there. "I was going to get a tree tomorrow," Dad said. Under the red, his face looked funny. His voice had a note of something small.

"You been saying that for two weeks," Lee replied. He didn't even hesitate. It was like I could see a grown-up man inside his face and body, covered by a thin layer of boy. It was like something was glowing, warm and big, underneath his skin.

I looked at Dad's hands, clenching into fists. I held my breath. Dad had never hit Lee that I knew of, except for official spankings or those accidents like the four-by-four falling on his head.

"Wait, Ed," Mom said. Neither Dad nor Lee looked at her. "I asked him to do it. I thought you were too busy, that it would be easier—" Her voice died into the silence.

Everyone seemed frozen. Dad's hands were still clenched. Lee stood tall, wide, chin out. Behind the smell of cedar tree was that of the cake, warm and sweet from the oven. It would have red icing, Lee's favorite color, a Christmas color.

The weight of the box in my arms shifted. Sounding small, Samson asked, "Meow?"

"Is that a *cat*?" Dad turned on me, and I couldn't keep my lungs from inhaling in short little gasps. He looked at me like he had never seen me before, like I was no longer that girl who sat smushed up next to him on the bench seat of the truck, his arm warm and sheltering behind my head. He had been so mad after I cut my hair that he had stopped talking to me. Now he looked at me like he didn't know who I was.

"It's okay, Ed," Mom said. "I told her she could."

His head swiveled toward her. He stood in the middle of us, like the hurt animal in a circle of attackers on *Marlon Perkins' Wild Kingdom*, except Dad wasn't exactly hurt and we weren't exactly attacking. "You?" he said. "Told her?"

"He's—" My throat was dry, and when I tried to speak, a hoarse rasp came out. My heart whammed at my throat. I thought of the stranger in the woods, the scrawny old man with the long beard, Dr. Ragland. I had recognized him from the picture Mom had showed us when she read the story in the newspaper. Dad had said he was crazy—Dr. Ragland—because he was fighting the state, which wanted to build the expressway through his land, the woods beyond the ditch at the end of Renoir Drive, the home of the Izan. "He could get a lot of money for his land," Dad had said. "Crazy old fool."

Then I thought about the machete, the Izan, warriors and spies.

Maybe Dad didn't know me because I had cut my hair but also because I had become different. Maybe I had become somebody else.

I swallowed, biting the tip of my tongue to wake it up, and tried again. "It's a present," I said, and pushed myself out of the corner and across the room to Lee. I felt Dad's bulk behind my shoulder, his fists just below the small of my back. I didn't think he would hit me. He didn't usually attack that way, only by accident, or with his words. But I wasn't sure any more.

I held the box out to my big little brother, and to the man I didn't know—but maybe I wanted to know—under his skin. "His name is Samson," I said. "Happy birthday."

The day before Lee's birthday, I had watched the stranger—Dr. Ragland—touch the little tree, half fallen over, like he was petting an animal. His palm had brushed the soft greenery of the branches, and the smell of cedar had filled my mind.

As he knelt, I understood that Dr. Raglan loved the little tree, that he loved all the trees in his forest. The orange flags that marked the new expressway meant bulldozers and chain saws, a massacre of trees a lot bloodier than my little brother chopping down this cedar for Christmas. I thought I knew what he felt. He finally stood up, kicked the machete into the weeds, and trudged into the woods away from me.

When I was sure he was gone, I found a stick to poke the weeds for snakes and dragged the machete out. The blade was cold and bright, reflecting the pink and orange sunset. A curl of cedar bark was stuck in it. When I ran my index finger down the edge, a thin line of blood sprang up. It tasted sweet and metallic on my tongue. The little tree lay still and broken in the dirt. I held the machete by its handle, feeling the odd weight of it in my hand, and used it to hack a shallow pit in the earth. I didn't really think about what I was doing, like moving in a dream, like flying away from the snake over the water. I didn't know why I was doing it. I let my body move on its own. I dropped the machete into the trench and scuffed the earth back over it with my sneaker. I scattered brown pine needles to hide the grave. I used a fallen branch to brush the earth, to hide my tracks.

Backslide

Snow flies at the windshield and the road blurs into whiteness. Where am I? I apply the brakes, pumping a little, and the truck stops, sliding a bit.

I will wait out this squall, I think, before going on home. Are you still here in the cab or in the bed of the truck with me? Are we going forward or back again? We are not lost, of course, just bushwhacking a little. The map is inside, near that place in the shoulder and chest that throbs and thunks. Do you hear the others calling, playing or hiding or wandering in the woods? They are not lost either, though many are afraid. We will each find our own way home.

And you. Are you God? Are you demon? Are you the part of me I have imagined into reality? Are you the story that is true or the fiction? The windows are frosting with our breath, beading as the defroster hums. Like tears, this warmth from inside us streaks the glass, revealing only white beyond.

Ruthie's tears stream down her cheeks. "He's dead," she moans. "I can't believe he's really dead." I am holding her, of course. A phone call from a policeman in Florida has informed my lover of the death of her father, from whom she has hidden for five years. She was his only child. He had raped her when she was a girl. And now he has written her out of his will, left a small fortune to a stranger, a drinking buddy, a young man. How will we find our way through this terrain? It is like a story, a soap opera, a melodrama. Not real.

I cannot know you, but I can imagine you. If you are God, you know me, know each of us. Are you my ultimate stranger? My ultimate friend? Will I know you at the end of this path? Are you, finally, inside me all the time?

Our journey home to Florida will be like all the other journeys home. I know pain is coming, because it has already happened. We will fly to Florida, and Ruthie will hear the lawyer read the will and her father will hurt her again from beyond this living. And we will discover a new shard of glass embedded long after the father's brutality to his child each time we make love. The stranger will take his ashes to scatter in water. We will re-member our lives. We will become less strange because we will stretch to face this challenge. Born strangers to even ourselves, we become known to each other as the story continues, as I inhabit you, as you live in me. We become the one we have always been. We journey home.

The snow pours from the sky, muffling the idling truck and me. I could die if the exhaust pipe becomes clogged with snow, but the pain in my arm— a man with a gun on Kora, I remember—is so sharp that I can't imagine how I might get out of the truck and walk around to clear it. And so, with-out a clear path, I shift into gear and drive on.

Reunion: Father

The diviner will be a girl. When Ed gets clear enough in his head to get a good look, he sees it right away. Jayce the diviner is a girl. Skinny and short-haired and dressed in cut-off jeans and a T-shirt with clodhopper work boots, but definitely a girl. Those guys down at the coffee shop must be having themselves a good laugh at his expense, sending him a girl diviner.

"How are you feeling, Mr. Young?" she asks again.

"Fine," he grumbles. "Just like when you asked two seconds ago."

She laughs. "Good." She sits back on the dirt. "That's what they tell you to do in the CPR training," she says. "Keep checking in with the person who's down. Keep them talking."

Ed grunts. He supposes she's right. Good to keep checking. "Yeah, thanks," he says.

She nods, staring off across the muddy pond he'd dug out with his bulldozer. "Nice piece of property," she says. "Building a house?" she asks, looking back at the slab foundation.

"Shop," he says. "Just a hobby farm. The wife and me live in

Jacksonville. This is how she keeps me out of her hair now that I'm retired."

"Ah," Jayce says. "Or maybe this is how you keep yourself out of trouble." She gives him a sidelong glance.

Ed laughs. "Okay, yeah. I s'pose it's mutual," he says. "And the grand young'uns, they like it some too." He flashes for a moment to his boys, the girl, Leigh Ann. "I like to keep a pony around for 'em, maybe teach them something about keeping a garden, fish in the pond."

"You want me to call your wife?" Jayce asks, reaching into her pocket for the little telephone.

Ed shakes his head. "Naw, she's out of town." He closes his eyes, trying not to think about where Mary is—up North—what she's doing. Traitor. No good Christian woman should disrespect her husband that way. "Nobody you need to call."

Jayce looks down the road. "How many grandchildren do you have?"

"Three," Ed says, without hesitation. Mary would say five, of course, but those babies Virge calls hers aren't no relation to him. The bastard babies of an unwed mother, far as he's concerned. That woman she lives with. Probably going to call her wife, too. He cringes. Far as he's concerned, Virge isn't no relation to him anymore anyway. No. He shakes his head. Get out of my mind. She doesn't exist anymore. "Three fine kids," he says. His voice seems louder than necessary. "Three," he repeats.

Jayce looks him in the face again, but she says nothing for a long minute. She watches the circling black bird in the sky, then gives herself a little shake. She grins again. "How are you feeling?" she asks.

Ed brushes an ant from his neck. "Dandy," he replies. She looks something familiar, but he can't place her. "You from around here?" he asks.

"All my life," she replies. "Starke. Daddy was a diviner, taught me since I had the touch for it. I tried going north, but it wasn't for me. Too busy, too fast, too dang cold."

Ed nods. "Too many Yankees," he agrees. "Lib'rals."

Jayce shakes her head. "No," she says. "I liked the people well enough. People are just folks, pretty much everywhere. Met a lot of nice ones. Just couldn't take the winter."

Ed remembers a snowy trip to Boston, a side trip to see Virge, to tell her not to waste her time on any more schooling, to settle down and find a husband. She wore her hair like Jayce's then. Maybe that was why the diviner seems familiar. He remembers the snow pelting the windshield of the cab back to the airport. That was the last time he'd seen her before Lee's funeral. Maybe that's when he'd started to wonder about her, suspect what she really was. If only she'd kept it quiet . . .

"How you feeling?" Jayce asks. "Any pain?"

Ed shakes his head, thinking about Lee, his big son waiting for him in heaven. Something to look forward to. He misses him so much. "No," he says. "Just tired. Real tired." Ed notices that the diviner's legs are hairy, and then he forgets the hair because he sees that one of her legs is deformed. Where the calf muscle is supposed to swell out from the knee, her leg is concave, a stick with almost no calf muscle at all. She had limped. He remembers her getting out of the truck, remembers that she limped. He tries not to stare.

"It's okay," she says. "It's hard to miss." She nods toward her leg. "Everybody looks at it."

"What, I mean, uh . . ."

"You mean, how did it happen?" She smiles. "Snake. Rattler. Stepped over a downed log and he was waiting. I was out in the woods . . ." She tilts her head toward the pasture and trees beyond. "Land a lot like this. My daddy's land that he left to me, my land now. Looking for a lost goat. Struck me hard in the calf. Double barrel of poison, I guess. I got back in my truck and drove like hell to the road. Lucky it was the left leg. Lucky the truck was automatic. Weaving all over the place, finally passed out. Came to on a stretcher. Somebody saying they'd probably have to amputate." She pats the withered muscle. "So I'm glad I got this much. Lucky. All in how you see it, I reckon."

Ed keeps silent for a minute. "Saw a snake right before I went down," he says. "Moccasin. Big one. S'pose it made my heart jump a bit."

The diviner looks at him. "That so?" she says. "Whad'ya know? And me the one already on her way to save you, snake-bite survivor. Humm." Something odd in her eyes, a look he can't decipher.

"Funny, huh?" he says. "My daughter almost got bit by a snake once too." His head feels a little swimmy. He remembers that summer, the day she and her friend had come screaming across the pasture, white as ghosts. He remembers walking back into the swamp with Virge, even though she was so scared, the way she had clung to his hand, hers clammy and small. He remembers the hum of cicadas in the trees, the heavy weight of the humidity that day. A lot like today. He watches the buzzard, circling overhead again, lower now. Her whole hand had trembled as she pointed across the muddy creek. "Over there," she had whispered in the woods that day. "He's over there." He'd sent her back toward the house, and now he feels the trigger in the curl of his finger again, sees the monster through the narrow sight of the 30.30. The gun kicks hard into his shoulder in recoil. "Uhn."

"Mr. Young?" the diviner asks.

The Free Speech Story, or How the Age of Aquarius Dawned on Me

"There's a new single fella in our church," Mom said.

Aunt Lil, her baby sister, was home visiting and we had gone over to St. Mary's to Grandma and Papa's house for the afternoon. Uncle Lester and Dad were both already asleep in front of the TV, and through the kitchen window I could see Lee and our cousin Jeffy playing catch, one of those chilly but warm January afternoons. The women—Grandma and Mom and Aunt Lil and Carolyn, her roommate, and my cousin Magnolia (Maggie for short) and Aunt Naomi (Maggie and Jeff's mom) and my cousin Lisa—were cleaning up after noon dinner.

Aunt Lil laughed. "Is that so?" she said.

They're always trying to fix Aunt Lil up with somebody. She was over thirty and not married, so she was an old maid, though nobody ever said that out loud, and she didn't much seem to care anyway.

"The new youth minister," Mom said. "Mid-thirties, I guess, maybe forty. Never married." She hesitated.

Yuck. What was Mom thinking? Brother Eugene had to weigh about four hundred pounds. Sure, he laughed a lot, and I supposed he was godly, but Aunt Lil was a fox: lots of freckles, sparkling green eyes, a little white frosting on her short brown hair, and a laugh that was open and easy. Not a match for Eugene anyway.

"What's wrong with him?" Carolyn said.

I looked up at her, and she winked. She stood next to Aunt Lil at the sink, drying. I was putting the silverware away in the drawer next to her, on the other side. Carolyn was really tall and not bad looking herself. She'd been Aunt Lil's roommate since college, and now that she was an assistant principal at the elementary school her church runs, and Aunt Lil was done with law school, both in Atlanta, they were still roommates.

"He's fat," I said.

Aunt Lil and Carolyn laughed. Even Grandma, sitting over at the kitchen table while we did the work, chuckled.

"Virginia," Mom said, hesitating with the Saran Wrap for the bean casserole she was covering. "That's not kind."

"Well, he is," I said. Big forks, little forks, knives, spoons. My tongue touched a sharp place on my braces, way in the back, reminding me to respect my elders.

"He's just a big man," Mom said. "Maybe a little husky—"

"No thanks," Aunt Lil said. "I'll take Virge's word for it."

My chest swelled up like it was full of something, and I felt my tongue tingling on the edges. My teeth clicked together and my lips drew back from the metal braces before I could stop them. I smiled.

Later, I helped Aunt Lil work on her car.

"Hand me that wrench, will ya, Virge," she said.

I stood close to her in the shadow of the raised hood of her Corvair convertible, watching while she tightened the new battery cable down. Uncle Deke was leaning in alongside the car so that his cigar smoke clouded under the hood. "You ought'a just sell that car instead of fixin' it," he said.

Aunt Lil wrinkled her nose and glanced at him. "Deke, do you think you can smoke that stinking thing somewhere else?"

He grinned, the cigar clenched between his teeth. "Why this here's the finest smell on earth," he blustered. He took it out and waved it around. "A real man's cee-gar. A man's smell. Put hair on your chest." Aunt Lil straightened. Uncle Deke put the gross brown stub between his teeth. "Right, Ginny?" he said to me.

I hate *Ginny* even worse than *Virginia*, but I knew that Dad was listening from over on the back stoop where he was smoking a cigarette. "Yes sir," I said. That's what we always have to say when a grown-up asks us something. It's just the way it is—*yes sir, no sir, yes ma'am, no ma'am.* No matter what.

Aunt Lil handed me the tools and slammed the hood shut so fast and so hard that Uncle Deke stepped back in surprise. Then he grinned. "Unsafe at any speed, ain't that what they say about these Corvairs?" he asked.

"Yep," she said. "That's what they say." She folded her arms over her chest and looked at the little white convertible with a sad smile. "I've been thinking about sellin' it," she admitted. "But nobody's gonna want to buy it."

Uncle Deke snorted. "Just take it down there by the tracks and I bet-cha you could sell it to some young nigger feller don't know no better."

Aunt Lil inhaled. "Deke, you know I don't like that word."

Mom didn't like that word either, and she always told me and Lee later, after Dad or somebody used it, to never ever use it. *Hateful,* she called it. *Ugly.* I felt ashamed of Dad when he used it, like he was dirty or uneducated or something, but lots of grown-ups still say it, especially men. When I thought of Mel, I blushed. How could I think I was her friend when my father used that word for black people? Even when Mom said *colored* or *Negroes,* my skin crawled. It was like the words themselves in her mouth tasted funny, like she didn't know how to say them natural.

Of course Uncle Deke knew that Aunt Lil didn't like that word. That's why he used it. She knew it too, but she was still mad. He chuck-led and grinned. "What?" he teased. "You mean *nigger?*"

Aunt Lil's hands clenched. It was a good thing I was holding the wrenches. She made this sound like a little growl. "Deke—" she warned.

Uncle Deke is a KKK-er, or at least that's what Lee says. I don't know for sure, but I believe it in my gut. He's mean about black people, and my cousin Lisa—his little girl—seems downright scared of black people. She goes to a special private school that they started in their town when integration came. She says all the white kids go to it.

"You ain't turned into no nigger-lover up there in the big city, have ya?" Uncle Deke asked.

"You know what I think, Deke," Aunt Lil said. "And if you'd use your head to think instead of butting it up against a brick wall or sticking it in the sand like an ostrich."

The image of toad-shaped Uncle Deke bent over with his head stuck in the sand, his hand waving the smoking cigar around in the air, popped into my head, and a laugh snorted out of my nose. I choked it in and looked down. Maybe nobody heard.

Silence. I felt Uncle Deke's little reptile eyes on me. Through my lashes I saw him lift his cigar to his mouth and take a long pull, watching me. "Wa-all, Ed," he said, finally, drawing out his syllables. And my dad stared at me. "Didn't 'spect you of all fellas to be raisin' up little lib-rals over there."

I swallowed, standing very still. Look away, I willed. Nobody to see here. I didn't laugh. There was no sound. No daughter. No girl over here.

"Black people have got the same rights as anybody else," Aunt Lil said. "That's just plain common sense. They're equal to me and you, and you know it, Deke. You're just scared."

Uncle Deke puffed on his cigar, his lip curling.

Dad stood up on the concrete stoop, threw his cigarette butt down and ground it into the dirt, twisting the heel of his shoe hard. He spoke distinctly. "*Niggers* . . ." He drew out the ugly word, long and snarly. "Should know their place," he said. I remembered the snake, the way I couldn't move. I froze, waiting. He looked at me, his eyes chips of iron, and then he spat into the flower bed. "Like children."

At the end of the day, Aunt Lil and Carolyn backed away in the white Corvair convertible, the top closed tight, of course, since it was January. At the end of the driveway, the little car stopped and pulled forward again, up to where I stood with Grandma and Mom and Lee and all my cousins, waving good-bye.

"Hey Virge," Aunt Lil called, motioning me to the window. My lips pulled tight around my braces as the corners of my mouth drew back in a grin, and I jogged over.

Carolyn handed her something, which Aunt Lil passed through the window to me. It was a forty-five record in its paper envelope. "We bought the album," Aunt Lil said, "so we don't need this anymore." She smiled, and I realized that her smile was like Mom's, but without the little overlap, the snaggle. "It's a good song," she said.

I stepped back as she shifted into reverse and they backed down the drive again, pulled out into the street, and drove away.

Lee ran over. "Whad'ja get?" he asked.

"A record," I said. I slid the disk from the paper. (This is the dawning of) The Age of Aquarius.

At my January orthodontist appointment the next week, Dr. Rose grabbed my chin and wiggled. "Loose," he said. "Loose." When I re-laxed my jaw, he jammed it up and forward. "Okay, bite." I clamped my teeth together, lips drawn so that he could see inside. He poked his finger into my cheek and pulled it out to look toward the back of my mouth, left side, then right. "Good, good." His breath was sweet. I had a close-up view of his mutton chop sideburns and huge mustache; each black and red hair sprouted from an individual indentation in his skin. I could probably inventory them, I'd seen them so often—every other week for two years. On the other hand, if my mouth was covered I doubted that Dr. Rose could pick me out of a line of three other kids.

Dr. Rose and Mrs. Rosenbaum, his grandmother, weren't anything alike, except they both had a crinkly way of smiling, their eyes wrinkling at the corners. But where Mrs. Rosenbaum was old and faded and said whatever was on her mind, Dr. Rose was cool and closed in, at least with me. Of course, I was just a kid to him, a mouth. He was a grown-up, a doctor, the orthodontist. He was probably not much younger than my mom, but he seemed like a whole other kind of person, like he had walked out of the television set from *The Mod Squad* or *Laugh-In*.

Dr. Rose wore a brown and red paisley shirt that day, the buttons undone so that his chest hair fringed out in the vee between the collar points, with brown hip-hugger bell-bottomed pants. It was a cool outfit, kind of like my favorite pantsuit, but with a better shirt. The music in his office wasn't the usual stuff with no words, but the 5th Dimension on a new eight-track stereo sound system—he had pointed to it first thing when I sat down. "Far out, huh?" he'd said. And I'd nodded, dumb before his hipness.

I didn't tell Dr. Rose that I knew his grandmother. I couldn't quite figure out how to say it. I wanted to, because maybe he would look at me differently, really see me. But between having his hands in my mouth while he yanked and tightened and shaped new little metal torture devices and my own tied-up tongue, I couldn't.

Dr. Rose hummed along with the music: "This is the dawning of the age of Aquarius . . ." The same record Aunt Lil had given me. It was from that neck-ed show, *Hair*. The Supreme Court said that theatres couldn't make actors put their clothes on because that would be censorship and the Bill of Rights guaranteed freedom of speech. And taking your clothes off for a play—something somebody wrote, like a story—was the same as speech. Pastor Bob said the whole country was headed for a dark time, maybe the Rapture and The Last Days and Armageddon, all starting with rock 'n' roll music and drugs and sex, and now the Supreme Court going to the devil's side saying pornography was free speech. He seemed awfully happy about it to me. I didn't have much to speak up about anyway, and being neck-ed in front of people was a freedom I reckoned I could do without. But it kept sticking there in my head that you can write down anything you want—any truth, any lie—in a story and nobody can stop you because we're all free in America.

Dr. Rose put his silver wire-cutters—dainty and shining and clean, not at all like the greasy, red-handled ones in Dad's toolbox—into my mouth and snipped the main wire on my upper teeth. Ahh. It was like my teeth let loose a sigh, relaxing and stretching their shoulders wide. Free.

I hoped that whatever wires Dr. Rose was going to put in my mouth next weren't going to be so tight that my head would hurt all night, but I knew that was stupid. Of course he was going to tighten my braces up; he always did. He was probably going to give me those little packages of rubber bands to tie my jaws together too. After a trip to Dr. Rose's, my jaw always throbbed and it felt like the bands pulled my whole head into my own mouth, like I was squeezing my skull between my teeth.

"Hmmm," he said. "Bite," he ordered. This time he didn't wiggle my chin to loosen it. He let me clench my teeth by myself. He wasn't even that close to me. I bit. He stared at my profile from the left, then rolled on his little stool around in front of me, stared, and then rolled to the other side. Weird. It felt like my jaw was a statue in a museum, or maybe one of those bits the scientists use to figure out what the monkey-men looked like—they're wrong, of course; Pastor Bob says that evolution is the devil's work. Dr. Rose put his fingers to his own lips, tapping them in time with "This is the dawning of the Age of Aquarius."

"Come with me," he said, lowering my chair.

In one of the little side rooms in the back, Dr. Rose reseated me, this time on a stool, and took a photo of me while humming along with the stereo. The walls were lined with drawers. I remembered the little room from way back when I first started coming to Dr. Rose, from when I first got braces three years ago. Even before I got saved the second time.

He had his back to me, rummaging in one of the drawers, singing. I bet he knew all the words to all the songs on the whole album, not just the main songs that they play on the radio, the ones on my forty-five. When he turned around, he had a photograph in one hand and a set of teeth in the other, like a mouth without a face.

In the photograph Dr. Rose held out to me, my lips were drawn back like I was grinning even though I wasn't. I remembered when he took it three years ago, the first time I came to the orthodontist, before braces and before my haircut. Before I got saved. I had been scared, kind of curious about what was going to happen, but mostly scared, because I knew that dentists always hurt, even if you gave them a fancy name like "orthodontist" and mod sideburns and clothes. I could see the scared look in my eyes in the photo now.

But that wasn't what Dr. Rose wanted me to look at. He traced the profile of my jaw on the picture. "Look at the way the teeth protrude here, the receding of the lower jaw." He raised up the plaster teeth in his other hand. "See how the lower jaw is set back, accentuating the protruding front teeth?" It looked like my mom's smile in his hands, except that her buck teeth were a little more snaggled, overlapping each other in front. "This is the cast we took of your teeth on your first visit here," Dr. Rose said. My teeth. The taste of the gunk filling my mouth rushed back to me. I'd nearly barfed. My finger went up to touch the teeth in his hand.

"Ah—" The beautiful blond lady who was Dr. Rose's assistant came in, holding another picture, the one Dr. Rose had just taken. "Thank you, April," Dr. Rose said.

She rested her hand on his shoulder and held the new photo next to the old one in front of me. "Nice," she said. I wondered if they were boyfriend and girlfriend, or whatever you call grown-ups who were going steady.

He didn't seem to notice her at all. Dr. Rose touched my jawline in the new photo. He didn't have to say anything. We could all see that it was different, moved forward. The teeth in front, my lips drawn back to show the braces, lined up just barely in front of the lower teeth. My face was leaner and longer. I was different.

While April set the new plaster mold in my mouth, I concentrated on breathing through my nose, my eyes closed. I wouldn't gag. Dr. Rose's Aquarius song moved into the part about letting the sun shine in. "Okay, open," April finally said, and she pried the gunk out of my mouth. She rinsed my teeth with the little water sprayer. Even with just that gentle warm pressure, they felt like they were about to fall out of my head, loose now that they were free of the bands and wires that had held them tight for three years. They felt naked.

"I'm tellin' ya, folks, it's comin'—" Pastor Bob leaned out over the pulpit toward us and lowered his voice. "It's comin'," he warned again. "The Bible says that the graves shall break open and the souls of the saved will fly up—*flyyyy UP!*—to be with Je-e-sus." He said it with three parts, the middle 'e' louder than the others, his voice settled into the rhythm that makes a sermon a song. It made me think about those black-and-white movies on *Creature Feature* on Saturday night where some old evil pasty-faced guy with snaky eyes hypnotizes people by chanting at them. Of course, what Pastor Bob did was holy. And I was under the spell too. I couldn't see how anybody in the church could help but be.

Someone yelled, "Praise the Lord!" and someone else followed with "Amen! Praise the Lord!" I felt the Spirit starting to move among the congregation. The dark windows seemed to pull us all in closer and quieter than in the morning church service. It felt like Satan was lurking just outside with the sinners and rock 'n' rollers and drug addicts and sex perverts. Pastor Bob's Sunday night series on The Last Days had been packed, helped by the big witnessing campaign in the weeks after Christmas. It was almost like a revival service, except there was no visiting evangelist, just Pastor Bob. That night late in January though, I thought maybe he had got the Spirit almost as good.

"Imagine that," he whispered. "Imagine those Last Days." He stared out, his brows drawn down and forehead creased. He seemed about to cry, his voice almost trembling. "Imagine. The Antichrist movin' among us—maybe even right now—and wars and rumors of wars, and disease and pestilence. People feeling pretty scared—" He had already told us that The Last Days were upon us. The European Common Market was the ten toes of the lion that the Bible warned was a sign of The Last Days. I shivered. The Antichrist might be alive, walking around right then on earth. Pastor Bob had said the week before that he'd heard that the credit card companies wanted to tattoo people with invisible numbers, right on their foreheads or the backs of their hands—just like The Mark of The Beast in the Bible. He had explained how those numbers translated into 666, but I'm not so good at math. I had decided I wouldn't ever get anything tattooed on my head or hand, invisible or not, because you never knew whether it might be the sign of the Antichrist.

"And then, BOOM!" He slammed his Bible down on the pulpit near the microphone so that everyone in the sanctuary jumped. "The sky splits open and those angels trumpet, and the graves in the cemeteries bust open and all the Christians that ever were alive on this earth, and all the Christians that are alive now, are called up, RAISED up, to Je-e-sus!"

He paused. "Amen!" and "Praise God!" jumbled together around the room. People were getting excited about going home to Jesus, I guessed. When Pastor Bob talked about how the prophecies in Revelation were getting fulfilled, he got kind of giddy, like he couldn't wait for the Rapture and the Last Times and Armageddon, and all the Christians in the church got happy with him. I thought there must be something wrong with me, because it just made me feel scared and sad. I didn't really want the world to end. Sure, I wanted to see Jesus, but not till I was done with living here. Part of me—the backslider part—wanted to see more of the world, even if it was filled with sinners, before God destroyed it.

I heard the door at the back of the church open. "The souls of the saved," Pastor Bob said in a hush, his mouth close to the microphone, "go home to heaven, free of this earth—freeee—" He stopped in mid-sentence, his face changed. He blinked, looking over our heads toward the back of the room. I turned with everybody else and looked over the blur of pale faces to the main door. Mel and her mother and a tall man in a uniform, holding his green beret in his hands—three black people—stood in the doorway of my church. Time stopped.

• • •

Pastor Bob smiled, but his brow wrinkled like it hurt. He was full of joy at being one of the saved, but real concerned about those poor folks out in the congregation who were lost and going to hell. His voice was low and somber, like it always got when he was gearing up for the invitation to come up front and get saved, but it seemed like Mel and her mom and dad had broken his spell a little when they came in. It didn't seem like The Rapture was about to happen any minute anymore. I could feel them sitting somewhere in the back behind my left shoulder, and I was pretty sure everybody else could too. It was too bad they hadn't arrived earlier, when we all stood up and welcomed the visitors before the sermon. Pastor Bob had gotten back into his rhythm after they came in at the start of the preaching, but he was ending right on time instead of going on forever like he usually did in those Sunday night services. Of course, the invitation could have still kept us there late if he was feeling like there was an unsaved soul that the Lord was working on.

I worried that it might be me. Even though he had lost his rhythm a little, Pastor Bob's sermon had gotten my heart racing and my palms sweaty. What if I wasn't really saved? What if I still wasn't forgiven for my sins? What if that was why I kept on sinning, breaking rules, dishonoring my mother and father, cutting my hair, stealing the machete, lying, reading those books that made me feel funny, telling those stories to myself at night, practicing kissing with Ricki Ann in the dark? I knew I must be backsliding, because everything that was happening kept getting all mixed-up in time. I felt like I was whirling through space on one of those Apollo missions. And what about those times when I wasn't even sure I was still me?

"Let us pray," Pastor Bob said.

I wanted to be born again, again, for the third time. I sang "Blessed assurance, Jesus is mine" along with everybody else, but I couldn't be sure I was really saved. What if I wasn't? What if it didn't take the second time like it didn't take the first time? What if I still wasn't forgiven?

I was scared. I didn't really want to be left on earth with the sinners when The Rapture came. I already felt alone. Before The Rapture. What would happen if all the Christians—Mom, Dad, Lee, my family, Pastor Bob, Ronnie and Ricki Ann, Mel, all those people in my church who had always known me—what would happen if they were all gone in the twinkling of an eye like the Bible said? What would it be like to be really alone?

I'daccepttheLordJesusChristintomyheartasmypersonalLordandSavior and got born again the first time when I was six. "Mommy, I want to get saved," I'd said. She'd grinned that wide, snaggle-toothed smile that was so open I'd do anything to make it happen, so wide I wanted to fall into it. Right before that, she'd been sad about something. Me getting saved was going to make everything right. I'd been scared then too, after they said in children's church that heaven was only for people who had been saved. Besides, all the bigger kids, like Ronnie Lane, were getting baptized.

"Oh Virginia, that's wonderful!" Mom had said, grinning her wide grin. Baptists don't believe in baptizing babies like Catholics do. They'd told us that in children's church. We believe a person's got to accept-theLordJesusChristintotheirheartastheirpersonalLordandSavior of their own free will. That was my church's name: Free Will Baptist Church. Maybe Mom had been sad about me getting old enough to have a free will and not choosing Jesus with it. Maybe it was because Dad had bought another pickup truck with his paycheck and we had to eat Cheerios for supper all week.

Mom had taken me to see Pastor Bob. I remember sitting in his office. I remember a picture of Jesus standing on the edge of a cloud that Pastor Bob said was painted from a real photograph a Christian lady had taken out of the window of an airplane—"I reckon He's making some test-runs for The Rapture," Pastor Bob had laughed. I remember that he asked me some questions. I remember praying, and that he told me what to say. I remember my mouth moving, but I don't remember the words.

I got baptized too when I was six, right after I prayed with Brother Bob and marched down to the front of the church on that Sunday morning to make my publicprofessionoffaith—which just meant that I stood there and faced the congregation, didn't even have to open my mouth, because I'd already prayed with Pastor Bob in his office—and joined the church officially—even though I'd been going to Free Will Baptist Church since before I was born. Born from my mother, that is.

At the beginning of the evening service that night, the lights dimmed, and the deacon helped me down the stairs into the turquoise water of the glass baptismal pool. I held my arms to my sides until my robe was good and wet so it wouldn't float up, gave Pastor Bob the clean handkerchief from my dad's drawer, then grabbed onto his hairy arm like I was supposed to. He held the hanky in front of my mouth and pinched my nose shut and raised his other hand.

"Virginia Young has professed her faith in the Lord Jesus Christ. Buried in the likeness of his death—" He pushed me backward into the water. My feet slipped out and I gasped. Chlorine filled my mouth. I saw my hair swirling around my face like snakes. I was going to drown. And then, by the lever of his arm that I was hanging onto, Pastor Bob pulled me back up into the air. "—His resurrection!" I choked and coughed.

"Praise the Lord," said someone in the crowd. And the deacon on the other side helped me back up the stairs. Was that it? Could anybody see through my wet robe? Did I feel different? I remember licking the taste of chlorine from my lips. I remember feeling a little sick. I remember feeling mixed-up.

That crazy night in January, even though I was scared and thought maybe I needed to get saved again, I kept myself still, mouthing the words all the way through three verses of the invitation hymn. I was frozen, along with everybody else in the congregation. I didn't want to get born again again anymore. I didn't want to go anywhere near the front of the church.

Mel and her mother and father stood up there in a little bunch. They had slipped out of their pew on the first verse, the man in his green uniform, his black Bible under his arm, leading the woman by the hand and her leading Mel in a little chain up the aisle to the front. The singing had faltered as they passed each row, growing weaker and thinner until, by the time they reached the front, it sounded like when the children's choir was forced to perform up in front of God and everybody on Sunday morning.

Pastor Bob wore this funny look on his face when the little group finally made it to the front. He shook the man's hand and they bowed their heads together, talking low. Mel's mother tilted her head in too, listening, but Mel—my friend—just stood there, holding her mother's hand, staring at the floor. I was sure glad that it wasn't me up there.

Pastor Bob sang along with the congregation, staring up and toward the back of the church with his eyes wide and blinking. Dad and one of the other deacons had hustled up front during the second verse, had a quick little whispering conversation with him, and stepped off a little to the side, like guards or something. Mel and her mother and father kept in a little row in front of the pulpit, facing us. Mel hadn't stopped looking at the carpet. Captain St. James was almost at attention, huge and still and black, holding his wife's hand, his jaw squared and eyes moving to meet stares from the congregation.

Pastor Bob blinked and took a deep breath. He gave Mrs. Felton a nod, and she ended the verse with a flourish of her hands over the keyboard of the organ. The church almost quivered, everybody straining to hear.

Pastor Bob cleared his throat and twisted his neck against his collar and tie. "Praise the Lord," he squawked, his voice breaking. He didn't sound joyful at all.

This was when he usually announced all the people who had come up front to get saved or to join the church. Baptists are not only believers in free will, but they're also democratic, so if somebody wants to join up in the church, either after a publicprofessionoffaithintheLordJesusChrist or by moving their membership from some other church, the members will vote out loud right then. Nobody ever objects or votes No. I had never really thought about it much before that night, because it was a part of the little ritual of what happened after the invitation song. I thought I knew what was about to happen. My mouth was suddenly full of something thick, and my tongue felt like lead.

"This is Captain Abraham St. James, his wife, Margaret, and their daughter, Melody," said Pastor Bob. "They come to us this evening, on promise of letter, wishing to move their membership from Sweetwater Baptist Church." Pastor Bob's mouth moved with the words just like always, but, like me, everybody seemed to be really hearing them for the first time. Mrs. Harlow, next to me, had pulled herself so tall and straight that she was like a flagpole. Her fingers, curled over the back of the pew in front of her, were white at the knuckles.

Up front, Captain St. James thrust his shoulders back even farther and smiled, his teeth gleaming. Mrs. St. James also smiled, but nervously. Mel kept her eyes on the floor.

Over in the opposite corner, my dad glared out at the church congregation. His face was red. His ears were red. His neck looked like it might explode out of his white shirt collar and tie. I could see the vein on the side of it pulsing. His eyes scanned, stopped, scanned, stopped. Steel gray. Very small. I looked down before they got to me.

"Do I have a motion to accept?" Pastor Bob mumbled. He sounded like he had a mouth full of marbles.

Mrs. Harlow surprised me, tipping up on her toes and practically shouting. "Motion to accept!" She looked like the picture of the angel

Gabriel in my Bible, announcing the birth of Jesus to the shepherds. Her face glowed.

I couldn't help it. My eyes darted to Dad. His lips were white, drawn back from his teeth, like the awful grin of a monster on *Creature Feature*. His eyes drilled into mine.

"Second?" the preacher squawked.

Silence. My hand-sweat was sticky on the leather cover of my Bible, which I clutched hard. Mrs. Harlow twisted and swept the congregation with a look, her face almost white with light. I shut my eyes, as if praying, to block out Dad's stare. Then I did pray. *God, help.* My tongue sought out where the rough place on my braces should have been, but it was smooth. My braces had come off on Friday. I opened my eyes to the front. Mel bit her lip, still staring at the floor. Her mother's eyes were glassy. I felt Dad daring anyone to speak. My tongue glided along the slick enamel of my teeth.

Maybe my words slipped out into the church that Sunday night because there was so much room in my mouth, maybe because my teeth were smooth without the braces there anymore. Maybe the words appeared in the air in the same way I had floated over the creek the day of the snake. Maybe I saw something in Mel's eyes when they rose, her face tilting up from the carpet at the front of the church, to meet mine. Maybe I just said it because we're all free in America. Maybe because nobody could tell me not to.

"I second," I said.

Backslide

The truck fishtails on ice, then swirls back and around in a slow donut. I blink, dizzy, turning into the spin. Which way was I going? Is this backward or am I sliding ahead into the future again?

The forest flashes past in slow motion, four green quadrants, the intersection of the two frozen dirt roads an X with me at the center.

The green blurs in the spin, into Ruth. My Ruth. I feel her hands holding mine, even as the momentum of the spin pulls us apart. I blink, focus on her face, her smile, her eyes, the ice rink blurring into a white circle spinning behind her. I need to say something. I need to speak, but I am caught up in the drama of holding on, of not letting go. And I am afraid.

We are skating in Boston, my first time on ice. It is our third date. I am in love with her already. Her grip is tight on my hands as we twirl. She laughs, like the music of a perfect choir, and I join in, even though I know I am about to lose my footing, the skates sliding out from under me, and fall hard. I know it because this moment has already happened, years before the man with the gun, before Kora. But I am back here with her in that first moment now. The pain is coming, but I have to speak.

"I think I love you," I say. And her hand flies to her mouth, as I knew it would, her eyes wide. When her hand releases mine, I slip backward. My feet slide from under me. The sound of my butt on the ice is like the sound of the snake falling into the sand. Thunk.

And then she kneels between my knees, her hands astride me. "I love you too," she says. "It's as if I have always known you."

I close my eyes as Ruth kisses me and in the dark of my mind see the words in Miss Williams's neat script on a sign over the blackboard in my seventh grade English class: "Love takes off masks that we fear we cannot live without and know we cannot live within." James Baldwin. *I hear the magic marker squeak and smell it again*: I love R. Yes. I want to hold on. I want to be free. I want to shout this love to the world.

I will call my brother down in Florida in the evening of this day, to tell him about ice skating for the first time. "I'm in love, Lee," I will say. "With a woman." I will hear him breathe through the miles and years again. "I'm a lesbian," I will say, at last.

I cannot stop the words from leaving my mouth, any more than I can stop the skates from flying up, the ache of the thunk *to the ice. Or has that yet to come? I can't stop the speeding boat or the pain coming at me in the V of white water either. Will that be soon? Hasn't that already happened? And what about the pain in my chest? Where does that pain come? Is it in me? Which part of me?*

"Don't tell Dad," Lee says. "I will always love you. You will always be my big sister," he says. "But don't tell Dad. You don't know what he will do."

I feel Ruth's arms around me, smell her breath. I feel her hands holding mine, squeezing tight. I try to squeeze them back. I want to say the words again. I want to speak, but I can't seem to make my tongue move. Neither can I stop the pain coming, so I give in, lean back into the warmth of her and try to trust the momentum that is God, or magic, or love.

The Story Story, or How I Couldn't See the Signs

Screams woke me up in the night, a strange yowling, full of pain and desire at the same time. I sat up, afraid. Who was it? What was it? Dad? Was he in my room? Was he screaming at me again, the way he had after church?

"What were you thinking?" he'd yelled. "You eat my food, live in my house, you do as I do!"

I'd been sure he was going to hit me. He was going to hit me. His fists were clenched. His face was purple. His eyes were slits.

I sat with my knees together on the sofa, my hands clenching my Bible in my lap, trying not to shake. Trying not to breathe. I looked down at the carpet.

"Ed," Mom said. "Ed—"

There was a gun in the closet behind him. A shotgun. We weren't allowed to touch it. I hoped he wouldn't think of it. He was mad enough to kill me.

"What?" he screamed. "What do you have to say, Mary?" He turned on her, and I looked up, worried that he would hit her instead of me. "They're all laughing at me. Man who can't even control his own family." He went still.

Mom reached out as if to touch his arm. "Ed," she soothed. "They're not. They're not. She's just a girl," she said. "They know about having children," she said.

He sagged. His fists loosened a little. "She's no child of mine," he said. "A devil." He blew air out of his nose like a bull, his mouth working. "Satan, right here under my roof."

I sat still, trying to be invisible while he went to the refrigerator and got out ice cream, slamming the freezer door, then flipped on the TV and collapsed into his La-Z-Boy, *whoosh-thunk*. Mom nodded toward my room, and I silently went, undressed and got into bed and waited to die, waited for everything to go silent.

The yowls changed tone, then another voice joined in, higher pitched. Outside. It was outside. The sound was sad, yearning, afraid and angry, all in the same moment. I wanted to put my head under the covers. I felt the tears I had sucked in last night filling my head again.

Now it seems like something I should have understood.

Dad thumped through the living room, then the kitchen. The screen door slammed. The faucet outside under my window squeaked, then water rushed. "Scat!" he yelled. I knelt on my bed and looked out. He was holding the hose, directing a spray of water toward the back fence where a cat's green eyes reflected the kitchen light before it turned and ran away.

The next morning, I waited for the bus, like always. Spring buds swelled on the azaleas, little dots of hot pink and purple revealing the gaudy colors to come, but our breath still puffed out in clouds as we stood in loose clumps at the bus stop, the kids who smoke cigarettes—or pot—just inside the edge of trees, the rest of us burrowed down into our coats beside the road. Some mornings in February the ground is frosted white, but by the afternoon, we will all have shed down to our sleeves, coats bunched in sweaty clumps with our books under our arms. I hoped it would be one of the last cold mornings. I felt numb, mummied in my coat. Maybe everything would change again in spring. Maybe things would go back to the way they were.

I never talked to anybody at the bus stop. The only kids in my grade were the Gonzales twins, two rangy dark-skinned boys who passed a basketball back and forth, mocking each other in Spanish. A monkey lived on their carport and all the moms told their kids to stay away from it on account of it bit and might have diseases. Their mom didn't speak any English, so whenever the teachers wanted to have a conference with her, the kids did the translating. Lee said that the mom never knew how much trouble they got into. "Lucky ducks," he said. My next-door neighbor, Shirley, was in the ninth grade and sang in the chorus with Ronnie Lane. She hadn't really talked to me since she went off to junior high two years before. I guessed she figured she'd be in high school next year, so what was the point of talking to a stupid seventh grader now? Shirley brushed her hair at least one hundred strokes three times a day, so that took up a lot of her time too. That morning she was putting on her makeup—mascara and eyeliner and cherry pink lipstick—while puckering and squinting into a compact mirror. She was an only child and her mom and dad were older; Shirley got away with a lot of stuff even though she had maybe more rules from her parents than even me. The only other kids at my stop were Stanley Pitts, Roger somebody, and Mean Dean, a bunch of eighth- and ninth-grade boys who smoked pot and had straggly long hair and drew things—boys' things, spouting like geysers—and dirty words on the backs of the bus seats. I kept my back to all of them, looking toward the traffic light for the orange bus, praying that there would be a whole empty seat so I wouldn't have to stand or ask to sit beside anyone else. I especially hoped I could sit by myself that day so I could read over the story I had written for English class.

Hot air rushed out when the bus driver opened the doors in front of me. Good, I was the first one on at my stop. I hauled my armful of books and notebooks up the steep steps and turned to look down the long aisle. Kids jammed nearly every seat. The radio was blasting Bob Dylan singing "The times they are a'changin'," and kids were shouting conversations over the volume. The air was smoky with tobacco and pot. Mrs. Cox, the driver, didn't care. She was a tough, stringy-looking woman with an on-the-edge wildness—or maybe it was fear—in her eyes. Every couple of weeks, usually on the ride home, she would get mad and pull over to the side of the road and stand screaming down the aisle: "Shut up! I'll take the goddamn radio out of the bus forever and then you'll be sorry! Shut up! Shut up! Shut up!" The kids in the back row would laugh, and every now and then one would get up the nerve to yell something back, but most of us were scared enough of Mrs. Cox that the bus would be silent for the rest of the ride home.

That morning, like most days, kids with window seats slept with their faces against the glass; the boys in the back cupped cigarettes in their hands, bending below the seat backs to take drags; popular or slutty girls put on makeup; couples held hands or made out, kissing in disgusting slobbery mouth exercises; and some kids scrawled out math solutions or finished reading homework assignments. I kept moving toward the back. It looked like there was a whole row empty about four seats from the rear. When I got there, though, I discovered a boy lying with his face on his history book, snoring. Dang. Should I poke him awake or find another seat? I looked around.

Mean Dean bumped me from behind. "Are you going or not?" he snarled. I scootched to the side, letting him wiggle past and into the last row with his friends. No other seats were empty. "Hey Sheryl," Mean Dean said. "Wanna ciggy?"

The girl in the next-to-last row on the left, sitting in front of Dean, turned and gave him a grin. "Sure," she said, reaching over the seat back.

"Naw," Dean grinned. "You gotta come back here and sit on my lap if you want it."

Sheryl hesitated, but just for a second, then shrugged and slipped around to the backseat. Good. A seat for me. I slid quickly into it as Mrs. Cox jerked the bus into gear and Sheryl lurched into Dean's arms. What was she thinking?

I opened my notebook and took out my story, "What Made Her Change."

Sheryl and Mean Dean wasted no time in finishing their cigarettes and getting down to the business of necking. I heard the smacking and slurping behind me. It was nothing like *The Secret Woman* by Victoria Holt or *Thunder Heights* by Phyllis A. Whitney. Dean might have had a deep seam of honor under his dark exterior, but I doubted it. Besides, he had pimples. And Sheryl didn't seem like the brave good-hearted virgin who could save him. Did she think she was?

I smoothed my short story for English. I hoped Miss Williams liked it.

Virginia Young
English B
February 24, 1970

What Made Her Change
by Virge Young

She was often looked on as odd and she knew it. No one paid any attention to her and she had often wondered if anyone noticed her. She often felt lonely and depressed. But after many years of this she just withdrew and lived in a world of her own. Of course she still went to school with the same people she always had, but to her they really didn't count.

Her parents were always very active and so were her brother and sister. They all had their friends and parties, but somehow she didn't fit. People didn't pay much attention to her, but she watched them carefully and she knew a lot more than people realized. Animals in any shape, form or size were a different matter. She was always bringing in orphaned animals. All animals seemed to understand her as much as she understood them, especially her cat, Vic.

The girl often left early in the morning to take long walks, often staying away all day. Vic would always go too, following the girl like a dog. One day she went on one of these walks and didn't return. She wasn't missed until the next morning. Her family all had dates or parties that night and everyone thought she was asleep in her room as always. The next morning as soon as they realized she was missing, her family called the police and organized a search party.

Meanwhile the girl and Vic saw two people in the woods separated by a small stream. They didn't know each other, and they were sad and lonely apart. Vic told the girl a spell and gave her a special stick. When the girl wrote the words down in the sand with the stick, the two people suddenly flew over the stream toward each other. They hugged and kissed, and they were no longer sad. Later they got hungry. Vic told the girl some more words to write in the sand. The candy bar in her pocket *suddenly became ten candy bars. She gave some to the two people. The girl gathered twigs and Vic told her the words to write in the sand to make a fire. All the scary things in the woods like snakes and wolves ran away and hid in the darkness.*

Late that night the news came, the girl was found and safe. When she returned, the girl was a changed person. She was happy and no longer secluded. Of course it took a while for her to overcome her shyness but she was a really changed person. She was still a wonder with animals and as she grew older, she went to college and majored in veterinary medicine. She lived alone with animals ever after. Sometimes she left special words written in the sand, but no one ever found out what changed her that night in the woods.

Ricki Ann came late to first period English again, just as we were passing our short stories to the front. She looked pale and a little shaky when she came in and whispered something to Miss Williams. I passed her desk on the way to the pencil sharpener and smelled something sour, like puke. Was Ricki Ann sick? I watched her face, hoping she'd meet my eyes. Looking for something.

Mel got weird after I seconded the motion for her and her mom and dad to join up with our church. When I came into the school library in the mornings and sat down at her table, she wouldn't even look up from her book. Some days she didn't even come to the library. The whole family came to Sunday morning services, but they didn't come to Sunday school, and Mel just said "Hi" when I chased them down as they were hurrying out to their car afterward. I thought she wanted to be part of the church. I thought she'd be happy, be my friend in church too. I thought she'd be grateful.

A week later, the cafeteria din of kids' voices and clattering trays suddenly hushed beside my usual table—a Nobody table where none of us knew each other and most of us did homework or read in our own little individual bubbles. I looked up from Victoria Holt. Ricki Ann walked past, on her way to the back left corner where her friends sat, and in her wake, the volume rose again. One of the girls across from me turned to the girl next to her and whispered something. The second girl's mouth circled into an *O*, and she looked again at Ricki Ann.

My used-to-be-best-friend's face was blank. She didn't see me, as usual, but she didn't seem to be seeing anyone or anything else either. She was wearing the pink flowered mini-dress with the empire waist. She had worn it on Monday too. Twice in one week. Weird.

"I think she's pregnant," Mom said a couple of weeks later, holding Sammy up to rub her face in her fur. Samson had turned out not to be a boy kitty but a girl kitty. Mom closed her eyes and put her ear to the cat's side. "Umm, what a beautiful sound," she said. "She's got her motor running." She stroked Samson's head with long white fingers. "Poor little baby. You're too young to be a mother, aren't you?"

Wow. Kittens! "How long will it take?" I asked.

"I'm not sure," Mom said. "Two months maybe? Why don't we look it up in the encyclopedia?"

It took me a few tries to find it in the *Britannica,* under R for *Reproduction, Animal.* "Nine weeks," I told her. "That's just over two months."

"Right," Mom said, Samson now sleeping in a relaxed *O* in her lap. "And she's probably a couple of weeks along, too. So that makes the kittens due around the middle of April."

"How do you know how far she's along?" I asked. I wanted to know. Samson didn't look much different to me, maybe a little rounder, but not much.

Mom's face flushed pink and she looked away from me, down at the cat. "Umm." She swallowed. "Well, do you remember how the cats were yowling out back a couple of weeks ago—?"

The night Dad nearly killed me.

Then I blushed, understanding. "Oh," I said. I got it. Cat sex. I remembered the sadness and fear and desire in those voices beyond my window. Was that love? Was that sex?

"Hi," I whispered to Mel, sliding into a chair and glancing at the librarian's desk to make sure she was busy. The library was empty, as usual, except for me and Mel.

"Hi," she said, keeping her eyes on her paperback, a new Victoria Holt novel. It looked like Mel was over halfway finished with it. I bent my head close to the table and sideways to try to read the back cover. Mel flattened the book on the table, and I looked up to meet her eyes. She blinked.

"Is it good?" I asked, even though I knew that it was. They were all good.

Mel just shrugged. "I guess." She looked back down at the page.

I couldn't figure out what was wrong with her, but I was too excited to ask just then. "Mom says I can walk to your mom's work after school with you today," I said. "She's going to pick me up at Mrs. Rosenbaum's on her way home at four. I want to tell Mrs. R. about Samson. I don't think Mom told Dad, but Mom says it's fine for you and me to hang out after school, so long as it's okay with your mom." Dad would have exploded, but I didn't say that. "I told her it would be," I said.

Mel hadn't looked up from her book again. She was completely still.

I wanted to reach over and touch her hand, but I knew that would be wrong. Girls don't touch in junior high, except to help each other with makeup or hair or something like that. I didn't know what to do. "It is, isn't it?" My voice cracked in the middle of the question.

Mel shrugged again. "I s'pose," she said.

I didn't know what to say. Didn't she want to hang out with me anymore? What had I done? I fluttered the pages of the novel on top of my notebook with my thumb. Something inside my chest felt like it was caving in; I felt my ribs bending inward, their pointy ends jabbing soft stuff—my lungs, my heart.

"Maybe I should just go to Mrs. Rosenbaum's," I said. "If you're busy or something—"

Mel's jaw tightened, but she didn't look up. "Maybe you should," she said.

But we walked together through Rolling Hills that afternoon, a block behind the cool kids. I had decided to just ignore what she said in the library, so I waited at the lockers and fell into step with her on her way out. We had walked about four blocks in silence.

Kathy Zane looked back over her shoulder at us, then turned and said something to the others. They glanced back, then started laughing to each other, their backs twisting into mean shapes. "See how it feels?" Mel said. She watched the sidewalk and our feet.

"They're just snobs," I said.

Mel snorted. "They're whities," she spat.

My breath sucked in and I looked hard at her.

"What?" she said. "You think you're different than them?"

I stopped walking, stunned. What was she saying? I felt my mouth hanging open. I felt like I was going to cry. "But—"

"Don't bother," Mel said. "I know, I know. I'm supposed to be glad you voted for us to join your church." She crossed her arms over her books in front of her chest, as if they were armor. "My father says you're all alike. He says you don't even know what you're doing. You think you're helping us, but it's just because you don't want us to be too strong, too powerful." Mel's voice was cracking. I thought she might cry too. "Don't bother to be nice to me," she said. "I know it's just because you feel guilty. You just want to be some kind of hero."

Hero? Me? I was just lonely. "I wanted to be friends," I said. "I thought you—"

Mel bit her lip, staring at the ground again. "Don't matter anyway," she said. "We're moving up North."

It felt like someone had punched me in the ribs, like I was about to fall over backward. I stood in the middle of the sidewalk with my mouth open. Moving away? I wanted to touch Mel's arm, but I couldn't move. I saw tears in her eyes. I saw that she was not really mad at me. She was just trying to make me not matter so that it didn't hurt so much. She was trying to make me disappear.

I handed over the Victoria Holt novel, and Mel reached up to put it back on the shelf at the rich people's house. My toes curled around the strands of soft-scratchy shag carpet. I watched my friend's back, stretching up. She had gotten taller in the months I'd known her. She slid in the book she had been reading, then shrank back down to normal size and faced me.

"I'm sorry, Virge," she said. "I didn't mean it. I'm just—"

"Yeah," I said. "It's okay." The St. Jameses would be moving before Easter. To New York City. My shoulders felt tight with trying not to feel sad, closing over the emptiness. It was too soon.

She turned to her books and pulled out a slip of paper. "My address," she said. "Will you write?"

I took it from her, and studied the thin white roughness and the blue ink marks. "Yeah," I said. "I'll write."

"*Pregnant?*" Mrs. Rosenbaum threw back her head and laughed. "Oh my Got!" she crowed. "Vell, vell, vell. Big bad Samson is a girl." She shrugged. "It's hard to tell with the little ones, you know," she said, picking up a kitten from the tangle on the sofa and holding it to her cheek.

I was still dazed from the sun and the walk home with Mel. I was still dazed from what Mel had said. I blinked and swallowed and tried to smile at Mrs. Rosenbaum. "Yes ma'am," I said. "I thought she was getting killed in a fight out back when I still thought she was a boy. It sounded like a baby screaming."

"Oh please don't call me 'yes ma'am,' Virge," Mrs. Rosenbaum said. "It makes me feel so old." She smiled, but her face slackened and her eyes glazed over. She rubbed the kitten's fur. "Poor little girl," she said. "So young for that." She sighed and sat back into the pink flowered cushions. "Babies having babies. Rape babies."

My mouth fell open. I had heard that word on the television, but nobody had ever said it out loud around me. Rape. Was that what had happened to Samson?

Mrs. Rosenbaum seemed to have gone somewhere else. She was still sitting there, but her eyes were closed and she seemed to have shrunken smaller, sinking into the sofa with the flowers bigger than her head. Old people do that sometimes, I knew from Grandma's house—go somewhere else in their memories. I started to ask if she was okay, but Mrs. Rosenbaum murmured, "Poor little girl."

"Yes, ma—Yes, Mrs. Rosenbaum," I said.

Her eyes flew open and she grinned. "Call me Miriam," she said.

I smiled. "Okay, Miriam." It was harder to say than I expected, probably because *yes ma'am* had been drilled into me since I was a baby. Mrs. Rosenbaum—Miriam—was the first old person I had ever called by their first name without "Pastor" or "Brother" or "Aunt" or "Miss" before it. I sat up straighter and stroked Falstaff, who had curled into a ball on my lap. "D-don't you think Samson wanted to have s-s-sex?" I asked. I had said it. I swallowed. "Isn't it natural instinct?" That's what it had said in the *Britannica*; I'd read the whole article under *Reproduction, Animal,* as well as *Reproduction, Human,* after Mom left my room that day. I'd written down some of the big words and practiced saying them out loud high in my pine tree and then in the deer stand in the woods later: *spermatozoa, Fallopian, follicle, estrus, ovum.* It was like some secret language. I traced the diagram of the female reproductive system from the book into my notebook, but I couldn't figure out how that looked inside of me. Mom had given me a box of tampons back in sixth grade when I got my first period, but I couldn't find a hole down there to put one in.

Mrs. Rosenbaum's face was serious. "I don't know," she said. "Maybe. They always wail like that, even when they're older, but I think the little ones, like little Samson, must be terrible afraid, especially the first time. Don't you?"

I nodded. "It sure sounded like that," I said, remembering the screams in the night.

"And sometimes it's hard for the little ones to have babies," she said. "Sometimes the babies die."

I swallowed. Not Sammy's though. Please God, not Sammy's.

"Sometimes the mother dies because she is too small," Miriam said.

I blinked hard, my heart beating fast. "But what can I do?" I asked. "Can I do something to make Samson okay?"

Miriam shook her head. "No, Virge. Nature vill take its course, I think." She reached across and patted the back of my hand, which was gripping the arm of my chair. "It will probably be fine," she said. "Don't worry. Nothing you can do." She sat back again, settling the kitten into the clump of its brothers and sisters. Her voice was very soft when she murmured, "Zer was nothing to do for my little girl."

I blinked at Mrs. Rosenbaum—Miriam. What did she mean, *my little girl?*

She looked up from her hands and directly into my eyes. "My little daughter, my Hannah, was raped," she said. "The guards at the camp," she said. "My grandson was born when Hannah was only thirteen years old. And she was fine," she said, "at first. It was later that she died." Her face was plain and soft and smooth, but her eyes were glassy with tears. "Little girls like your Samson can be fine," she said. "They can. But there is not'ing much you can do. Sometimes nature must take its course. Sometimes you just got to put faith in Got."

I was on my knees beside the sofa before I knew what I was doing.

I picked up Miriam's hand from her lap and held it, holding my breath at the same time. I didn't know what to say. Miriam wiped away the tears from her cheeks with her other hand. I traced the veins and sinews through the skin on the back of her hand with my thumb. I didn't know what to say, but touching her hand seemed to be enough.

Holding Mrs. Rosenbaum's thin hand on that February afternoon, I thought again about Mel, about losing Mel. First Ricki Ann, then Dad, now Mel. What was I going to do without even Mel?

"I'm sorry you lost your daughter," I finally said to Mrs. Rosenbaum. "Miriam."

Her hand squeezed mine tight and released it. She patted my head twice. "Life is about losing, Virge," she sighed. "A little here, a little there. It is what we keep—like my grandson the dentist—it is what grows from what is gone that matters."

My period was late in February. A whole two weeks late according to the calendar Mom had given me when I first started my periods in sixth grade. I stepped inside my closet—I keep the calendar on the inside of my closet door because it would be too embarrassing if Lee or somebody else saw it—and counted again and again. Forty days. It was always twenty-six or twenty-seven days, for over a year now, except that time when it came early at twenty-four days and I bled all over myself at school. I never wanted that to happen again. I hate it that it's not exactly exact every month—it's better if everything stays exactly the same, dependable—and I had gotten pretty good at noticing the signs that it was about to start—little cramps, feeling all swole up—but it was never that late before. I wasn't sure what to do about it.

Ricki Ann was absent from school for a whole week. I wanted to call her and ask, "Are you okay?" But she wouldn't want to talk to me. And I wouldn't have been able to see her or touch her hand through the phone lines. And those wouldn't have been the right words.

Mom stopped at the STOP—the only stop sign in St. Mary's—at the end of Main Street, and stared out at the shrimp boats and brown river beyond. "Well, we aren't going to make it home in time for church," she said. We had been at Grandma and Papa's the whole afternoon, just me and Mom, eating a big dinner and sitting around listening to the old people talk. That's what they do on Sunday afternoon—visit. Great-Aunt Belle came over and Miz Ledbetter and then Uncle Sonny and old Grandma Rose, who's not really anybody's Grandma on account of she's the third wife of my grandma's daddy who died before even my mom was born. I like the stories they tell, even though I'm not so sure they're much true. They sound true.

"I've kind of been wanting to go over to that little church up past Woodbine where they've been seein' the signs," Mom said. "What do you think?"

She stared straight ahead, not looking at me, so I knew she was feeling a little funny about it. She still wore her green polyester Sunday dress and pearls, but the curls of her perm seemed limp and her face tired. She didn't want to go home, I thought. Or maybe she really did want to look for the signs.

Since Dad had stopped talking to me over that thing with Mel and her folks, I didn't like being at home either. Maybe it was hard on Mom too. And I did want to see the signs, because it seemed like I couldn't see much of anything clear anymore. If I could see the signs, maybe it would be like Jesus or God was showing me something, a message out of the muddle the year had made of me. I shrugged like I didn't care and reached out to twiddle the radio knob. "Sure," I said. "Why not?"

Mom smiled. "Why not?" she repeated, and shifted the Buick into drive.

I thought about school as Mom turned the car to follow the river west. On the inside of the door in the girl's restroom stall that I always used, someone had drawn the profile of a pregnant woman just below the "I love R." The belly of the woman was round and protruding. An arrow pointed to the belly and the artist had scrawled "SLUT" underneath.

Ahead of the car, the orange light faded into the marsh ahead.

"In Youth Group, Ronnie Lane said that he heard that the Lord's been making some test runs for The Second Coming," I told Mom, making conversation. The road grew black as night came, except for the oval of our headlights and the center lines flashing by. We were deep into the backwoods of south Georgia on a two-lane blacktop, the stars brightening between gaps in the trees. It was spooky, but also cozy and warm inside the old car with Mom. I figured she grew up riding around on these roads before they were paved; she must have had a feel for where we were going.

"How so?" Mom asked.

"Well, he says there's been three different people—a young guy, an old couple and a traveling salesman—who've been driving down the road in the country, and they see a hitchhiker—a guy with long blond hair, kind'a scruffy—and even though they don't usually pick up hitchhikers, something just makes them stop. And the guy gets in and he's real quiet and polite, even though he kind'a looks like a hippie." I glanced over at Mom, who had a weird twist to her mouth. "And the hitchhiker starts quoting scripture, and they get into a conversation about religion and The Second Coming and all that. And then it gets kind'a quiet in the backseat." Mom bit her lip. "And when the driver turns around, thinkin maybe the hitchhiker's gone asleep, he's just vanished!" Mom smiled. "Do you think it's true?" I asked. I knew Mom was a True Believer and she liked stories as much as I did, but I didn't know if she really thought magical stuff like that happened.

"We-ell," she drew out the syllables. "Anything is possible for God, of course. And those stories must come from somewhere," she said. I thought maybe Mom wanted to believe it. Maybe I did too. Telling the story out loud made it seem true. "But I don't know," Mom said. "I think miracles happen, even if you don't see them with your own eyes."

"How come we don't get big miracles like in the Bible these days?" I asked. It was one of the things I liked best about the Bible, those stories about Jesus turning the loaves and fishes into enough food to feed the multitude, or the one about Saul getting struck blind on the road to Damascus, or the one about Lazarus getting raised back up from the dead. Even the Old Testament stuff—all those plagues and stuff with Moses, the burning bush and the parting of the Red Sea, him smiting the stone so water gushes out into the wilderness—I wondered what it was like for just a regular person to see all that.

Mom paused. "Well, Jesus isn't here for one thing," she said. "Since He died and rose again, and then went up to heaven to be with His Father, we don't need big miracles—or we're not supposed to. His resurrection was the big one. That's supposed to be enough for us to believe—'Faith is the evidence of things not seen,'" she quoted.

"Sort of the grand finale," I said.

Mom laughed. "Well, sort of—at least until The Second Coming, I guess."

"So what about the story about the hitchhiker? Do you think that's a miracle? Or a sign of The Last Days?"

Mom squinted into the lights of an oncoming car. "Maybe," she said. "But it's kind of like a story I heard when I was a girl, way back when. A story about a stranger who quotes scripture then disappears. Maybe it's the same story, only updated."

"Or maybe Jesus has been making test runs for a long time," I said.

The car was silent for awhile, except for the scratchy voice of the DJ on the radio and the whine of the tires on the black road. Maybe it was the same story, the same way Aunt Belle and the other old folks tell about the great-great-great uncle who was a Civil War cook and got his arm shot off into the soup and they ate it anyway on account of they were so poor and hungry there toward the end. The strains of music became clearer as we rounded a curve. "Oh, I love this song!" I turned up the volume on the radio and sang along with the words I'd managed to figure out to "Lola." Something about being a man, Lola being a man.

Mom drew her breath in fast, then reached out and turned the dial. "Aw Mom."

She found an easy listening station. "That's better," she said. "No words."

"Why do you think Dad hates black people?" I said, finally. In the dark and the whine of the highway, I had been thinking about how strange it was at home with Dad pretending like I wasn't there. I had been watching him, waiting for him to be in a good mood, waiting for him to get over being mad at me. I brought him iced tea without him asking. I shined his Sunday shoes. I changed the channel from the Tarzan movie to the stock car races when he came in the room. I spent four hours practicing the piano on Friday night, playing his favorite songs—"Dixie" and "Rock of Ages"—over and over again, hoping he'd hear that I was sorry I'd made him mad. I had been praying for him to like me again. But nothing. He didn't look at me, didn't hear me. I thought I had seen the corner of his mouth twitch when I called Lee a bozo, and he drank the iced tea I left on the table by his La-Z-Boy, but his eyes didn't even shift in my direction when I put my elbows on the table at dinner. How could he just erase me like that?

Mom finally said, "I don't think he hates black people, exactly. It's just the way he was raised." She kept her eyes on the road and her hands at exactly two o'clock and ten o'clock, just like it said in the driver's handbook.

"Then why's he so mad about Mel and her family?"

Mom shook her head. "I don't know for sure." Her fingers stretched then relaxed on the wheel. "Your dad doesn't like things to change," she said. "He wants everything to be the same, to be the way they always have been. And the way he was raised—the way we were all raised back in those days—black people and white people didn't much mix."

It was more than that, though, I knew it. I thought of the things Dad said about black people, and it wasn't so different from the things he said about Lee, or Mom, or me. The way he made fun of people, laughing at them and mimicking them. It was funny for a little bit, but he kept on going, and then, all of a sudden, it wasn't funny at all and you just felt awful.

"I remember when I was a girl," Mom said, "just learning to drive. Mama asked me to go over and pick up Rita, the black lady who did our ironing. So I got in the car and drove over to where she lived on the other side of town by the mill, and she came out and started to get in the backseat. And I said, 'Oh, why don't you sit up front here with me, Rita?' I wanted the company and it just seemed silly for her to sit in the back. So she got in and we drove on over to home. But when we drove up and Mama saw us, I could tell she was mad. And she took me aside and she said, 'Mary, you just can't do that. Let a black person ride up front with you. That's just not done.'" Mom paused and blinked a few times. "And that was just wrong. I know that now. But you know, that was just the way things were back then."

"So you think it was the same for Dad?" I asked.

"Oh sure, maybe more so," she said. "We all went to different schools back then. He might've played football against the black high school, but he wouldn't have socialized with any black people." She smiled and glanced over. "Not like you and Mel."

And all over again, I felt that throb of pain in my chest of her leaving soon.

"It's been forty days since my last period," I said, changing the subject.

Mom's face jerked toward me and we both tilted in the little swerve of the car, her pearls swinging as her knuckles whitened on the wheel and she steered back over to our side of the white line. Her black patent leather pocketbook tipped, and lipstick and compact rolled around my feet. Even in the dim light, I could see the shadows of freckles under the powder on her cheeks. Her nylons whispered when she braked, and I wondered if she ever wished she could wear jeans, as I did, between Sunday morning and evening services. She might kick her heels off and nap on Sunday afternoon, but we'd never see her in anything but her Sunday dress. Mom blinked fast six, seven times and swallowed, then swallowed again, her Adam's apple bobbing up and down. "Are you sure?" she finally asked, her eyes focused straight ahead.

"I counted the days on my calendar about a million times." I felt scared, because she was scared. What if I was dying of cancer? Maybe a late period was a sign of some terrible disease.

We passed another abandoned gas station, a faded sign for an alligator farm, a house set back from the road, its lighted windows draped with a vine so that the leaves and the silhouettes inside seemed the same. From the corner of my eye, I saw that Mom was biting the side of her lip. She took a deep breath. "You haven't been down in the woods, have you? You haven't seen anybody, any men, someplace like that, have you?" Her hands looked stuck on the steering wheel. "Nobody's tried to talk to you. Nobody's done anything to you?"

My eyes lost their focus on the darkness and the road. I thought about Dr. Ragland, the boys playing war, my tree and the Izan. I remembered witnessing to Murray in the wheelchair and Faith, Love, and Marilyn, and Way under the table. I thought about couples: Ricki Ann and Ronnie Lane, Dr. Rose and his nurse, April; Sheryl and Mean Dean. I imagined climbing down from the deer stand in my tree to find someone waiting for me, someone who took my hand and said something to me, someone who wanted to read my journal, who liked what I'd been writing. I thought about my story for English class, "What Made Her Change?" All those words from the *Britannica* seemed etched in the air: *spermatozoa, Fallopian, estrus, ovum.* I heard Mrs. Rosenbaum say that other word—*rape.* I blinked. The road and the Buick became loud again. Mom thought I'd been raped.

"No," I said. "Nobody talks to me," I said. "That's not it." It made me sad to say it. Like I had erased something.

I heard Mom's breath rush out, like she had been holding it, and in that sound, I heard some magic dissipate, like the spell was brushed away with the sand.

The sign for the little church in the backwoods was a small white square, lit from inside: THE CHURCH OF THE HOLY WORD. The building was a white concrete block rectangle with a wooden steeple perched over the front door and tall frosted windows along each side. The dirt yard in front was jammed with cars, and people stood in clumps outside the windows on each side, mumbling quietly and cocking their heads from side to side. Mom and I got out of the car and walked over.

The lights were on inside, and everybody looked up at the frosted glass. Mom put her finger to her lips and tipped her head. She had reapplied her lipstick and smoothed her skirt, reaching up under her hem to pull down her slip in the safety of the car's open driver's door before we had walked over. She looked thin and small and ordinary, a woman with a short permanent wave hairdo and knee-length polyester dress, a tan London Fog raincoat covering it, against the chill in the air. She looked like a proper church lady. But she wasn't that old, I realized. No older than the woman named Faith on my witnessing route, pregnant with Hope. My mother wasn't like that Faith. I looked back at the windows of the church. All I saw were streaks from the lights inside coming through the panes.

"Do you see it?" a short lady in front of me asked.

Her husband shrugged. "Don't know what I'm s'posed to see," he said.

"There." She pointed to a window. "The three crosses, just like on Calvary."

The man tilted his head one way, then the other. "Hmmph." He didn't sound convinced.

I was disappointed. The man's "Hmmph" echoed in my own chest. I closed my eyes and prayed. What is it that you want me to know, God? What is it you want me to see?

Mom reached over and pulled me to her side in a warm hug in front of the little church in the woods. "You'll be fine, Virge," she whispered. "It's normal for a young girl. You're fine."

I let myself relax a little into her side. Her touch felt good. She touched without thinking, without warning or caring what anybody thought. That was how she was like Faith. The lights in the windows shifted a little as I leaned toward her. I kept my shoulders tight. I wished I didn't have to hold anything safe with Mom, but I couldn't help it anymore. It was like I had been on guard for so long that I couldn't let go of that part of me that was on alert, even with her. "Do you see it, Mom?" I asked, nodding at the windows. "Is there a sign?"

She sighed and squeezed my shoulder. "Maybe," she said. "Maybe."

The note in English class in February originated with Michelle, Ricki Ann's new best friend. The minute she came into class I could tell that she was excited about something. Her eyes were round and shining and her chest was puffed out. She was grinning with her mouth closed, like if she opened it something would fly out. She made eye contact with Kathy Zane, who mouthed 'What?' with her eyebrows raised. Michelle grinned and slipped into her desk, and while Miss Williams took attendance, she wrote a note and folded it into a tight, tiny triangle.

"Pass your homework to the front," Miss Williams said. "Be sure your heading is correct in the upper right-hand corner. Does anyone need the stapler?" A couple of kids raised their hands, and Miss Williams walked around the room, stapling papers.

Michelle dropped the note over her left shoulder onto the desk behind her, which was the seat next to mine. I could see that she had written, TO KATHY ZANE ONLY! PRIVATE!! DO NOT OPEN!!! on the outside of the triangle. Kathy was in the desk behind me, so the boy in the desk behind Michelle closed his palm over the note and held it across the aisle toward me. I reached out and he dropped it into my palm. I held it for a second, passing it in my lap to my left hand, trying to feel the words inside through the folds and paper. Then Kathy poked me hard in my back and hissed, so I bent my arm over my shoulder, ready to drop it onto her desk.

"Virginia Young!" Miss Williams said. "Are you passing notes in my class?" I swallowed, the triangle in my palm suddenly sweaty, the points poking into my skin. She was back up front at her desk, staring at me. I nodded. "Bring it up here," she said. "Now."

"Writing is a powerful thing, Virginia," said Miss Williams. I stood alone in front of her desk after school. The note from Michelle to Kathy was unfolded in front of her. "When you write something down, whether it's true or not," she said, "you make it seem true. Sometimes you make something real."

I swallowed and took a breath. "It's not my note," I said. "I don't even know what it says."

Miss Williams folded her hands together on top of it and sighed. "Well," she said. "I hope that's true. I know you and Ricki Ann Purvis are friends. I hope you wouldn't do that to her."

When Miss Williams passed back the short stories the next day, I found the note from Michelle to Kathy stapled underneath my paper. Miss Williams didn't say anything. She just looked at me. Maybe she thought a friend should know. The words inside the triangle folds said, "R. A. P. is P-G!!!" That was all. I didn't have to guess at what the letters meant. And I didn't feel surprised either.

On my short story, Miss Williams had written, *Very good, Virginia! I love the magical cat! What a mystery! But what did make her change?*

The thing was, I didn't know myself. Something in the woods. Something about the magic cat. The spells and the stick she wrote them out with. But she changed. Something happened and she was okay. She was fine. At least, I think she was. I think she will be.

Reunion: Mary

"Mom, you're not going to believe who I ran into!"

Mary Young will look up from her menu at the tall woman coming toward her from the inside of the restaurant and smile, then frown. Some days she just can't believe she has a forty-three-year-old daughter. Virge keeps her shoulders back and chin high, and she walks with confidence. Her freckled face and green eyes—from my side of the family, Mary thinks—seem to be lit with attention, always listening. She seems so strong. How did I raise such a woman? Mary thinks. And what did I do to turn her into this, a lesbian, a sinner? What did I do wrong? What made her change?

"I chose an outside table," Mary says. "I hope that's okay. I thought it would be better with the children." Her eyes look past Virge to the door again, but no one is behind her daughter. "Aren't they coming?" she asks.

Virge smiles. "Yes, Mom," she says. "As soon as they wake up from their nap. Ruth's bringing them over from the hotel in the stroller."

"Are you sure it's safe?" Mary asks. She knows she's said it before, a half-dozen times, but she can't help it. After that terrible man on Kora . . . "They're not coming to the bookstore, are they?"

Virge shakes her head. "No Mom, of course not." She pulls out a chair and sits down. "Ruth's going to take them to the park to play after we eat, while you and I go to the reading . . ." Mary watches as Virge stares at her menu, not looking at her. "Or you can go with them to the park if you'd rather."

They both look up at the clatter of the double stroller wiggling through the doorway. "Hi!" says Ruth. The kids break into grins when they see Virge, who stands up to help. Georgia, the little girl, whacks her feet against the footrest, and Jesse, the boy, wriggles, straining against the safety straps.

"You're so big!" Mary exclaims. "Oh, they change so fast!" she says. They change so fast, she thinks, watching her daughter with her children.

It's been three months since she went to Vermont to help out during Virge's recovery from the gunshot. Three months since Virge woke up, looked into her eyes and accused her. "Mom," Mary remembers Virge saying, "I could have died."

Mary bends to the children's level. "Hello Jesse! Hello Georgia!" The waitress carries a high chair over to their table and goes back to the corner for another one.

The kids examine Mary for a minute, then Jesse crows. "Gama!"

"It's Grandma!" Virge laughs. "Can you say 'Hi Grandma'?"

I failed her, Mary thinks. I should have known. That's what Virge had meant three months ago, lying in her bed in that big farmhouse they'd bought in Vermont. "Mom," she had said. "When I was a girl, I thought God hated me because I could never be good enough." Mary remembers the tears streaming down both their cheeks. Her girl was still alive. "Your God hates me, Mom. He made that man hate me. He hated me when I was a girl, made me feel like a failure, and he makes people want to kill me now." And Mary had prayed then, prayed to that same God. But she knows Virge was accusing her, accusing Ed as much as God. I should have been a better mother, should have protected her better.

"You are perfect," she had said then, three months ago, sitting on the bed to hug Virge's uninjured side. "You are made in God's image. You are good. You are my daughter, and I will always love you."

She looks at the little family of women and children. Perfect, she thinks.

"Hi Mary," says Ruth, smiling. The little ones garble. Ruth holds out an arm and they hug, less stiffly than before the shooting, the days spent together taking care of the woman and children having drawn them closer. Mary reminds herself to relax into the hug. She really does like Ruth, if only . . . No. Mary blinks. She won't let herself think about it. She pats Ruth's back. "It's so good to see you," she says, meaning it.

Mary watches the girls wrestle the children into the chairs, move salt-and-pepper shakers and the little vase of flowers to the far side of the table, find toys and bibs in the diaper bag, and push the stroller out of the way. They are good mommies, she thinks; they're genuinely enjoying their children. When Virge had turned forty, Mary assumed her daughter would never have this experience, and it had made her just a little sad, but relieved. She'd set that fear—and that hope—aside.

She'd thought she would just have to worry about the books. What would her daughter write next? How much would it hurt? How would Ed take it? Of course, now it was as if he had erased Virge. He didn't ever talk about her, didn't want to hear about the babies, didn't want to hear about any of it. He probably wouldn't even have known his daughter was on Kora if it hadn't been for that crazy man, all the publicity that had stirred up, and Mary going up North to help out afterward. And her daughter is a new woman with these babies in her life. Maybe more of the Virge she has been becoming all along, Mary suddenly thinks.

Jesse, seated next to her, grabs for her arm and Mary takes his little hand in hers. "Are you glad to see your Grandma?" she asks. "You cutie-pie." He grins, seeming at a loss for words, then screeches and gargles something in his own language. She laughs. "They're adorable," she says. Little Georgia stuffs a fistful of oyster crackers into her mouth. Mary looks at her daughter, who is looking from Jesse to Ruth to Georgia across the table and smiling with pride, glowing with happiness, Mary thinks. She reaches over and touches Virge's hand. "I am so happy for you," she says.

Virge squeezes her hand back. "Yes," she says. "Me too."

After they order and the food arrives, Virge returns to her original subject. "You won't believe who cut my hair at the salon down the block," she says.

Georgia grabs a handful of peas, which squirt between her fingers.

She licks them from the back of her fist. Jesse tips his head back, sucking hard on a sippy cup full of juice, mesmerized by the light dancing through the leaves overhead in the courtyard.

Mary looks at Virge again. "You got your hair cut?" she asks. Even after all these years, she can't get used to the blond. Everyone in the family is brunette. And so short, so messy. She would never have guessed Virge had just come from a beauty salon. "I mean, who?" she corrects herself.

Virge laughs. "It's okay Mom," she says. "I know you don't like it." She glances at Ruth, a private look, the kind you exchange with a husband or . . . Mary looks down at her salad.

"Ronnie Lane," says Virge. "Can you believe it?"

Ronnie Lane. Mary blinks. She remembers the boy from the church all those years ago, of course, especially since Virge wrote that book. One of the sinners in it. Like her, she thought, though that woman is not her. She swallows and stuffs another bite of salad into her mouth.

"Really?" asks Ruth. "What a coincidence."

"He's gay," says Virge. Mary glances around. Good. No one is sitting near enough to hear. "A big gay hairdresser!" Virge marvels. "I couldn't believe it."

"No kidding," says Ruth. "Wow!"

"Oh his poor mother," Mary says, regretting it immediately. "Oh, I mean, she had such a hard life." No, that isn't right either. "Her other boy disappearing like that, and then I heard Ronnie was in jail of all things." She looks down at her plate. "I went to her funeral," she says. "That's what we old folks do, go to funerals." She thinks back. "He didn't look gay," she says. "He was as bald as a cue ball," she remembers.

Virge laughs. "Oh Mom," she says, then nods. "Yeah, he said that about prison." She shakes her head. "He's sure changed." She pauses, gazing off into the trees overhead. "But maybe not," she continues slowly. "He's maybe the same, only more so. Maybe just . . ." Mary watches her face, the furrow of her brow as she searches for the word. "It's like he was wearing a mask back then, a costume, but now it's like the costume is him, or it was him all along." She chews slowly. "Like he's grown into it, or . . . revealed," she says. "Maybe just owning all the parts of himself instead of silencing something." Virge picks up her knife and holds it like a pen, doodling indentations into the white tablecloth, still staring up into sky. "Were we all were like that?" she murmurs. She gives her head a shake and refocuses, grinning. "It was sure weird to see him again anyway."

"What did he say about himself in the novel?" Ruth asks.

"I don't think he'd read it," Virge answers. "And it's fiction, remember? He's not in it."

Mary shakes her head. "Fiction," she mumbles. "That mother sure looks a lot like me."

Virge pauses. "Maybe a little, Mom, okay?" She sighs. "But it's fiction. It's not you. It's you changed into someone else, a character." She takes a bite of her salad. "You'd never do what that character does," she mutters.

Changed. Mary considers her daughter's words. "You mean divorce?" she says, feeling suddenly angry. "You know I don't believe in divorce, Virge." She swallows. "It's just not done. 'What God hath joined, let no man rip asunder.'"

"Huuhn!" Virge snorts. "That's a good one, Mom. Ever tell it to Dad?"

Mary thinks of Ed, then. He doesn't change. No layers there to strip away, nothing revealed over time, except maybe to her. "He's a difficult man," she admits.

"You know, Mom," Virge says, her voice softer, "we wished you would divorce him, me and Lee, all those years ago. We talked about it. He was so mean to you."

Mary's heart aches at the mention of Lee, her boy, gone so long, so young. He hadn't had time . . . not nearly enough time. "Poor Lee," she says.

"Poor Mom," Virge says, touching her arm.

Mary draws back. "You think you know me, Virginia," she says, "but you don't. I am not 'poor Mom.' I am saved. People only change in Christ. Change is not a revelation. Change is a redemption from sin. Revelation is the end of time. The Second Coming of the blessed Savior. The Rapture. God's plan will make sense then, only then, and I pray for you, for your soul." She sits up straighter then, and speaks more gently. "I love you, my daughter. You are a good person, but if you're not saved . . ." Mary bites her tongue, remembering how she almost lost this one too. "I pray for you every day," she says.

Virge and Ruth exchange a look. "Mom," Virge begins. "I am not going to—" She stops. "I love you too, Mom," she finally says. "I am as saved as you are, but in a different way. I know you believe in only one way, Mom, but I can't follow that path."

The girl baby lurches suddenly, and a glass of water spills on the table. Ruth lunges for it before the glass rolls off the table. The moment is broken. Mary is troubled. She doesn't like to hear Virge say that she will not join her in heaven for all eternity. There is only one way, one truth, one life, and that is Christ. But she can't let herself believe that her daughter is truly lost.

They talk about the plans for the afternoon and evening, for the next day. The reading at Borders will be the last of the book tour—interrupted in March by that awful man on the television show—and then the girls will go to Virge's class reunion—"What a hoot that'll be," Virge says—while Mary stays with the children in the hotel room. Tomorrow will be the family reunion.

"We'll put them down before we leave," Ruth says. "They should sleep the whole time we're gone. And we have two rooms, so you can watch TV."

"We won't stay late," Virge continues. "We have to be in St. Mary's to catch the nine o'clock boat to the island tomorrow morning."

Ruth pulls out the wet wipes from the diaper bag and begins to clean Georgia's hands and face. The little girl grimaces and leans away, whimpering. "Oh, come on," says Ruth. "You know I'll win."

Mary thinks of her brothers and sisters and their wives and husbands, and all the children too—all grown, with children of their own—together again, waiting out there on Cumberland Island, staying at that fancy hotel. Mama and Papa and the other old folks were all gone home to Jesus now, the old house sold, but the young ones were drawing the family all back together again, organizing this reunion. "Oh, I'll be on that boat too," she says. "Wouldn't miss it for the world." If only Ed would come. She will at least call Janice later, ask her again to bring Lee's children. They needed to know their daddy's family. Mary offers up a silent prayer for God to grant her this little miracle of everyone together again for the reunion on the island.

Virge looks at her watch. "Guess it's time to head over to the bookstore," she says. She scrubs at the apple juice stuck to Jesse's cheek. "Are you sure you want to come, Mom?" she asks, keeping her eyes focused on her son. "There will be protesters, you know." She frowns, still not looking up. "Christians. Probably from your church even."

Mary watches her daughter. She loves her. She admires her. She is afraid for her daughter's soul, but she has to trust what she feels, the still small voice of God inside that tells her to love her child, no matter what, above all else. She still prays for a miracle, but she has to trust that ache inside her chest that loves this child, this woman. I should have known something was wrong when she wrote that story in seventh grade, Mary thinks for the thousandth time. I should have known. Virge laughs at Jesse, who is reaching up to grab her hair. But here she is, Mary thinks, all grown up, happy, strong, successful. Maybe I couldn't have changed anything anyway. Maybe I couldn't have known any better back then. Maybe she didn't change so much after all. Maybe this Virge had been that Virge all along.

"I know," Mary says. "But I want to be there."

Backslide

The snow falls so thick now that I see nothing but white, nothing but white. Like inside a church, perhaps. My thick sweater and winter coat make it hard to move my arms on the steering wheel or to shift, and I feel the cold even with the heat on full blast. The wipers slap back and forth, but I only glimpse bits of trees and what might be rocks or animals—white wisps or wraiths—through the storm. I don't want to miss my next turn, these roads familiar but tangled. I want to get home, and I know it will take longer going this back way. The others, my family, will worry.

The truck rumbles low in first gear, creeping along, slipping a little. My mouth falls open as I suck in a breath and heave it out in a sigh over a thick tongue. I want to say something, but I am alone with my self. My selves. I still seem to hear voices, shouting even. The snow flies toward me through the beams, and I feel the vertigo of seeming to fall backward again.

I sit between my mother and father in their church, my brother, Lee, and his family behind us. Janice is pregnant again. I am home on a visit from the job I have taken farther south in Florida, living at a beach. I do not belong here, but the old women remember me anyway. They act as if I have never left, though I am now in my thirties. I slip back and forth in time as I look around the church, noticing black faces among the white. How long ago seems that day that Mel and her family stood at the front and became members here. I wear pantyhose, a dress. A disguise, perhaps.

The pastor—a man I do not know—is preaching. He points to a cluster of four young men in the front right pew. "They have repented," he shouts. "They have been saved. Born again." They look small to me, afraid. Though the rest of the church is filled, the ushers even lining the aisles with extra folding chairs, the pews around the group of four are empty. They are gay.

"This AIDS," the pastor shouts, "this AIDS! Why that's just God's curse against this sin, this evil. But these men are saved now! They have repented! They have turned away from that lifestyle, that abomination against God!"

I feel sick. I cannot let it slide over me. I have done so for too long, let my parents believe that I am the same as always, divorced now and alone. Living a happy single life at the beach, in a little house that reminds me of my Grandmother Young's, just right for one person, like a nun's cell. But I am no nun. I am sure that my parents worry that I don't go to church. I know that they pray I will find a good Christian man, a miracle. That will never happen. Next year I will go to graduate school to buy myself the time to write a book that will tell the truth. I will become a different kind of preacher. Mine will be a different gospel. I will move north, finally, and embrace my sin.

I watch the ex-gay men in the front pews. We all do. As they hunch, studying Bibles in their laps, carefully apart from each other, the preacher moves on in his sermon to a joyful interpretation of the most recent signs of the Last Days. "AIDS is God's warning to all of us!" he shouts. "He's coming, brothers! If this"—he points to the ex-gay men—"ain't a pestilence, I don't know what is!" The old quiver in my gut makes me sad now. The "Amen!"s and "Praise the Lord!"s around me nauseate me. These people hope for the end of times. They rejoice in war and disease and natural disaster, for these things mean that Jesus is coming back for them, His special people. Why would they want peace in the Middle East? Why would they worry about global environmental destruction? Their religion tells them that these things surely mean they will be proven right all along very soon. The worse the world gets, the happier they are. I wonder that America cannot see that Christians of this ilk are dangerous. I wonder how I—one of the backsliders, the dangerous ones—can tell that story.

I cross my legs, encased in nylon, and close my eyes.

I have begun dating women in the year since my divorce. I go to nightclubs where men like those in that little pen of pews up there used to dance and laugh and love, the same way I know that I will love. I think of my friend, John, who is like another brother. A poet. He is HIV-positive. He is dying. He is in love. He is not cursed, except perhaps by a country that forced him into dark alleys searching for love.

I believe I will find someone who is like my dreams, my old mixed-up, going-to-sleep stories. She will be like me, but not me. We will not be evil. I am not evil. I am not a sinner, not a backslider. I am just me, Virge Young. I have a voice—voices—and I must not be silent.

And like the magic that carried me away from the snake, like the magic that lifts me into my own body, the magic that opens my mind into other minds and selves and times when I write, I rise from the pew and past my father's legs into the aisle. "No," I murmur. "No." Mrs. Harlow meets my eyes and nods. My brother closes his eyes, seems to sleep, his nose sunburned, his shoulders snug in his Sunday suit. I hold my chin up and turn to face the preacher. "No," I say aloud. "You're wrong."

But this is not what happened. This is what I should have done, not what I did. I sat there. I sucked it in. I hid my self. I sinned.

I stand and leave the church, heading home. Toward Renoir Drive? Green Acres? My little house like Grandmother's at the beach? St. Mary's? The snowfall clears suddenly to a few huge drifting flakes, and I see it up ahead: the white place at the top of the hill.

The Egg Story, or What Clouded the Biggest Natural Event of My Time

Sometime last year I started telling myself stories to go to sleep. After I finished whatever chapter I was on in whatever book I was reading and turned off the light, I would tuck one of my pillows between my legs and start imagining a story where I was somebody else and somewhere else. I mixed pieces of movies and books in with pieces of real life, but my stories always ended pretty much the same, and then I would go to sleep. In March I realized that the endings had changed, and when I would remember them the next day, my face would flame up and I'd get sweaty. My stories were wrong. I worried that maybe something in me was wrong.

I was always on an island in my going-to-sleep stories, like Cumberland Island, which is a real place that Papa used to take us to on his shrimp boat before he retired. It always pops up in the old folks' stories, because they used to go out there all the time, but I only barely remember it. Rich people owned the island, so there's these mansions that are abandoned and falling down, but there's no bridge to the island, so it's mostly wild and empty now. My uncles talk about fishing and hunting and adventuring over there. And families who have boats can go over for picnics and beach days. What I remember from when Papa took us are these big live oak trees bending over palmetto bushes, like the ceiling of some green mansion that sways. And soft sand dunes reaching down to a beach where there's almost nobody for as far as you can see, not like the beaches we usually go to where you have to stake out a spot with your towels and blankets and umbrella and picnic lunch and beach toys between loads of other folks with all their stuff. On the island, there was nobody but us, all the way until the white and the blue disappeared into each other. It was the emptiest and freest feeling ever. And horses. I remember the wild horses that live there, left all those years ago by the rich people when they moved away.

So in one of my favorite going-to-sleep stories, I was on an island, standing or lying on a beach that was long and white and empty. Sometimes I had been shipwrecked, like Robinson Crusoe. Sometimes it didn't matter how I had gotten there, just that I was alone with that free feeling on that long white beach. Sometimes the story got really complicated about how I built a house under the live oak trees, or set up a tent and found water, or moved into one of the abandoned mansions and fixed it up so it was better than new. That used to happen more back when I was fixing up the tree house out at the farm. Usually I would get so caught up in the details that I'd just fall asleep before the ending. Last year though, I realized I had been skipping over those parts to get to the good parts—that's how I thought of them, *the good parts*—quicker.

Somehow in the story, I always got a horse. Sometimes it was a white stallion that I slowly befriended, sometimes a painted foal that I raised up because its mother had abandoned it. It was always a beautiful horse that loved me, and it was always named Pegasus, for the magical flying horse. I held my pillow tight between my legs and it became Pegasus as I imagined galloping down the beach in the surf, the wind in our hair. I rocked myself against my pillow, like I was riding Pegasus, and this wonderful feeling built up and rushed through my head so I felt my heart pounding with the surf. Those were *the good parts*. And then I fell asleep.

In March, the endings of my going-to-sleep stories got weird. I would be riding along and I would see another person lying in a little niche in a big rock, which was kind of strange since there are no rocks on the beaches around here. But I did see a beach like that once when we went on The Big Trip to Disneyland in California. Anyway, it was usually a girl. Sometimes it was a real cute guy who had long hair, but usually it was a girl. And I would ride up and say "Hi!" and ask her if she was lost or something. Usually it got dark all of a sudden, except maybe for a big full moon. I would offer the girl a ride on my horse, and I'd bend over and hoist her up in front of me and hold the reins with my arms around her.

And then—this is the really weird part—I would become the girl I had just hoisted up, and I'd feel the arms around me, and I'd think maybe it was a boy behind me. He always had shaggy hair, and the arms around me felt safe and the body behind me soft and warm. The full moon would change to a fingernail moon. And then we would ride. Sometimes we would be suddenly naked, but I wouldn't feel wrong like I do when I'm naked in real life. And sometimes the hands would let go of the reins—Pegasus was such a good horse that he didn't need us to guide him—and would start touching my thighs or my titties—and I'd find myself doing that in my bed. But I tried not to think about that because it ruined the story to think about real. Or we would kiss, and I'd kiss my arm inside the elbow like Ricki Ann showed me last year, or my other pillow. And the rocking of the horse and those hands made me feel that warm hot good feeling just before I went to sleep. The moon would be round in my mind again.

What was weird was that I couldn't keep it straight in my head whether I was the boy or the girl in those stories. It was kind of like I was both of them. And I knew that wasn't normal. You can't be both. It isn't natural.

Dear Virge,

How are you? I am fine. Our new house is nice, but it's very, very crowded here. The houses are all real close together without hardly any backyards at all. I painted my new room pink. It's still real cold here and we even got out of school for a snow day today, so I thought I would write you a letter. My new school is okay. I have already read all the books for my English class, and the spelling words are easy. The library is really big. We have joined the Baptist church in our neighborhood, and it has white and black and Spanish folks in it. We're not the only ones, so Daddy likes it better. He says that this is how the whole world should be. Equal. Now to the *BIG NEWS*. I have a boyfriend! His name is Paco Martinez and he is Spanish from Porto Rico. He's got ~~these GORGEOUS brown eyes and black hair with bangs that kind of~~ fall into his eyes. He likes to play chess, which is how we got together, because the chess kids play in the library. He wrote me a note and asked me to go steady with him and I wrote back yes. He wrote back to me to meet him in the refernce section and I did and he gave me his ID braclet to wear and then he kissed me! He wants to go out west and live on a ranch someday, even though his father wants him to be a doctor. He is Catholic, but not very much. He doesn't go to church except at Easter and Christmas and he says he is not sure he even believes in God, which is our only problem. (Other than me not being allowed to date until I'm in high school.) But I'm sure I can help to lead him to the Lord. Please pray for me and Paco. I miss you very much! How is Samson and Mrs. Rosenbaum? How is school? Please write!

Your friend 4-ever!
Melody St. James

In March, old Mrs. Toad, my natural science teacher, lifted her chin from the folds of her neck and blinked. Would she haul herself up out of her chair to talk to us or just sit there? "Class! Class!" she croaked. The talking ebbed a little and a couple of final crumpled-up pieces of note-book paper thunked into the trashcan hoop. "Class!" Mrs. Toad—Mrs. Tomblin is her real name—shouted this time and pushed herself up behind the desk. She really did look like a toad, and the fact that she had spent all of October on *Amphibians and Reptiles,* making us memorize lists of names and showing movies and slides every day and sending us into the marsh and swamp and woods looking for new "specimens," stuck her with the name forever. We had just finished our unit on *Plants,* which for Mrs. Toad seemed to be mostly about mushrooms, specifically the activity of making spore prints on pieces of white cardboard that came out of Dad's shirts from the dry cleaners. To tell the truth, I liked the spore prints—searching under the azaleas around Grandma's house for different kinds of mushrooms, the musty stink that arose when I lifted their caps carefully off and set them on the white cardboard, the stickiness on my fingers, the round spirals and swirls in pinks and yellows and oranges left by the spores that fell from the caps. I knew I was supposed to be learning something about mushroom sex, but mostly I liked the designs, the way that nature was making this beautiful picture we couldn't usually see. I suspected Mrs. Toad thought that too, even though she taught science, not art. She gave me an A for *Plants.* And now we were on to *Space.*

"Today we will be preparing for the biggest natural event of your time!" Mrs. Toad shouted. The hubbub settled a little lower. Even Tommy Craddock, who was in the band and couldn't sit still for more than five minutes, tapped a little stutter on his desk with his drumstick pencils, then stopped. That made the rest of the kids look up, startled by the silencing of our backbeat.

"On March seventh, next Saturday, the southeastern United States will be blacked out in a total eclipse of the sun," Mrs. Toad said.

"Cool," said the kid with the Coke-bottle-thick-lens glasses in the front row seat. The boys in the back snickered.

"This week's vocabulary will be related to this event," Mrs. Toad said, "and you will each construct a sun shade to view the eclipse safely. Your homework on the weekend will be to observe the eclipse and write a report of your observations." She tapped her yardstick sharply on the blackboard behind her. "Today, you will look up these words and read Chapter Twelve to find the definitions." I had already been writing them down, because that was what we did every Monday in natural science. The hum of kids talking started to rise again and Tommy thumped his bookcase bass drum twice. Mrs. Toad shouted, "Silence!" Her tiny black eyes squinted at us through silver cats-eye glasses. She slammed her fist into the desk so that the little glasses chain around her neck shivered and the folds in her neck quaked. "The vocabulary list is due tomorrow, and the answers to the questions at the end of Chapter Twelve are due on Wednesday. We will have a movie tomorrow—" A little cheer erupted from the back of the room. Mrs. Toad raised her voice higher, "And on Thursday we will make our sunshades in class. On Friday will be the vocabulary test—"

Nobody was listening anymore, partly because this is what we did almost every week in natural science. The next week we'd have more vocabulary on Monday, another movie on Tuesday, a review on Wednesday, some activity—probably drawing and labeling something—or another movie on Thursday, and a test on Friday. Maybe we'd study the eclipse some more, or maybe we'd move on to something else—I was guessing it would be *The Planets,* since that was the next chapter in the book. Kids would talk through most of every class, and Mrs. Toad would yell or slap her yardstick on her desk when we got too loud. And the next week would be about the same. She had already slumped back down into the dark corner behind the desk, marking the attendance book and ignoring us.

I opened my science book to Chapter 12, *The Solar System,* and began to read. I could have just skimmed through to find the twenty-five words on Mrs. Toad's list, but I was a little excited about the biggest natural event of my time.

This is what I was thinking in March: Sex was sin, and that was bad. Sin was Satan. But we're humans, and if we don't have sex, we can't have babies. So sex was good, but only if you were married and doing it to have babies. The Bible and Mom made sex sound kind of awful, but songs and movies and even the Bible also made it sound kind of good. With or without baby-making. And the *Encyclopedia Yearbook 1970,* which was about 1969 and came in the mail in March, had this whole article called *Biology of the Future* about how scientists can make babies in a petrie dish, like we made bacteria in natural science with pond scum and mold on an orange peel, I guessed. It said that a woman would be able to go into a store and pick out her baby by a label and have her doctor implant it in her without any sex at all. But nobody seemed to be talking about giving up sex completely, so I had started to think—except it was a sin—it wasn't all that bad. With or without baby-making.

People are born sinners, because of Adam and Eve and the snake and the apple, which seemed to have something to do with sex too. And then "For God so loved the world that he sent his only begotten Son" to save us from our sins. People had to accept Jesus and then their sins got forgiven. If they didn't accept him into their hearts, they were still sinners and when they died, they would go to hell with Satan for all eternity. Christians would still get tempted by Satan all the time, and they had to resist Satan, but even if they slipped up a little or backslid a lot, they were still forgiven and would go to heaven for all eternity when they died. But sometimes people didn't really really really mean it when they accepted Jesus into their hearts; maybe with one tiny little corner of their minds they still didn't believe that he was really the Son of God. And then they were still sinners.

I kept worrying that a tiny little corner of my mind was keeping me a sinner damned to hell, a backslider from Jesus. When I thought about those mixed-up parts of my go-to-sleep stories, I worried that I felt bad because I must really still be a sinner and damned to hell, even though they made me feel good. Except they were just stories. It was the part where I was mixed-up about being the boy or the girl that I worried about the most. Was Satan putting those stories in my head? If God made me, didn't he put the stories in my head? What was wrong with me?

The movie in natural science was called "Eclipses: Celestial Shadows." Most everyone in class was talking or throwing spitwads, stopping now and then to write in the answers to the diagram and list of *Key Terms* Mrs. Toad had handed out before she turned on the projector. Mrs. Toad seemed to be asleep, tilted way back into the shadow behind her desk and her chin resting in the folds of skin around her short neck. The definitions appeared in white words at the bottom of the movie screen after the spooky deep-voiced man explained something, and we're supposed to fill in the blanks. The scent of that purple mimeograph stuff on the paper filled my head every time I bent low to write in an answer in the dark. I added in little extra explanations of my own to help me remember later, even though I'm pretty good at just plain memorizing.

Umbra—*the shadow region over an area of the Earth where a solar eclipse is total. The very darkest part.*

Penumbra—*a partial shadow between completely shadow and the completely light. The last little bit of light on Earth before the whole sun is dark when the moon comes between (SOLAR ECLIPSE).*

Photosphere—*the surface of a star. The sun is a STAR.*

Chromosphere—*an incandescent, transparent layer of hydrogen gas, thousands of miles deep, above the photosphere of the sun but separate from the corona. Chromo means red, so it looks kind of red or pink. But see-through.* 1,000₄ OF MILES DEEP!

Corona—~~the luminous ring of gas outside the chromosphere of the sun.~~ *This is the ring around the SUN that you can see when the moon comes between the Earth and the sun (SOLAR ECLIPSE).*

Bailey's Beads—*the bright spots of sunlight around the edge of the moon's disk right before and after the central phase in a solar eclipse. Exploding gas that jumps up from the sun.* LOOKS PRETTY COOL!

For the unit test, we would have to be able to tell which thing—sun, moon, or Earth—was in the shadow and which made the shadow to explain the difference between a lunar eclipse and a solar eclipse, and we had to be able to label the different parts of a solar eclipse on the diagram. The spooky-voiced man kept saying "Don't look at a solar eclipse!" in a lot of different ways. "You can go blind!" when the sun comes out of the shadow and burns up your eyeballs. the man said you could look at lunar eclipses, because what you look at is just the moon and it is just a big rock, not a star, and the shadow was just the Earth coming between the sun and the full moon.

Lots of kids didn't even bother to fill in their papers, because Mrs. Toad would put all the answers up on the overhead projector the next day and you could just copy them down and memorize them for the test. Sometimes I read during the Tuesday movie, but this was going to be the biggest natural event of my time.

Dear Virge,

How are you? I am fine. Thank you for writing me back. We are studying about the eclipse in school too, but it's not going to be so much up here in the north as it is down in Jacksonville. You are so lucky!

Paco and me are still going steady, but I can't wear his ID bracelet except at school and we can't let grownups see us holding hands or even just together who know my parents because my father got real mad when he heard that I had a boyfriend who was Porto Rican. He says that its not natural. That people of diffrent colors shouldn't get married and have babies cuz then the children will be mixed-up. And besides, I'm not allowed to have a boyfriend until I'm sixteen. That's forever! Paco says his mother and father are even more mad, both cuz I'm Afro-American and cuz I'm not Catholic. But I love Paco so much! He is so nice to me and kisses so good. But we can only be together at school. He says that he will love me forever, no matter whether our parents like it or not.

Please write and tell me what the eclipse is like. My teacher says that roosters crow sometimes! And animals go to sleep because it's dark!

Your friend,

Melody St. James MS+PS4ever

"It's not natural!" my brother, Lee, yelled. I sat still in the dark closet on Tuesday after school, trying to breathe my cramps away. You can't hear much from my bedroom, even with the door cracked, because of the bend in the hallway to the living room, so whenever I wanted to hear something, I sat in my closet with my ear pressed against the wall. Most of the time their conversations were stupid, but now and then I'd find out something they'd done that I could get Lee in trouble for or could use to get him to do my chores for me. Sometimes I just sat in the closet even when I wasn't listening in on anyone, letting my eyes adjust to the dim light, enjoying the feel of my dresses brushing the back of my neck and hair. The smell of shoes was like earth and animal skins. It was like I was in a soft cave where I knew all the shadows because they were all my own stuff.

"Is too!" yelled Buddy Gaines, his best friend. Boys yell a lot, and that makes it easy to hear them through the wall. Lee walked home with his pals after elementary school got out at three, and my bus dropped me off around the same time. Lee was always hungry, so the guys would eat and watch *Dark Shadows* on TV until Mom came in at five. Sometimes I watched too, but mostly I just went to my room and did homework or read. If I had cramps, like today, I would lie down on my bed or sit in the dark of my closet, trying not to cry. Sometimes I did cry anyway because it hurt so much. God, why didn't you make me a boy?

"My big brother, Steve, says if you do it too much, hair will grow on your hands!" said Buddy. They were talking about masturbation. I didn't know what that meant exactly, except that boys could have sex by themselves. In the Old Testament, men were always getting in trouble because they "spilled their seed on the ground" instead of making their wives pregnant, which was masturbation. Those pictures scrawled on the backs of the bus seats of boys' things gushing like fountains were what it looked like, I guessed. I knew it was bad because it was sex without being married and making babies. And it was a big sin. Lee would have to do dishes for me forever if I could find out he had been doing that. I fiddled with the laces on a shoe next to my knee. Could girls do masturbation?

"My dad told me I'd go blind," said Lee. I couldn't imagine Dad talking about sex to Lee or anybody else. Mom had just given me this little book called *The Natural Rhythms of the Female Body* and a couple of days later asked if I had any questions. I didn't ask any because it just seemed too embarrassing, but that book didn't make any sense at all to me. The cramps sure didn't feel natural.

I heard Mom's car pull into the driveway.

"But when it happens without you doing anything," Buddy said, "without your hands, like sometimes at night when you're asleep, it's okay. It's just natural."

"No way, man," said Lee.

Dang. I heard Mom open the front door. The pain in my gut flared again and I was already in the dark, so I prayed with my eyes open. Why God? Why didn't you make me a boy?

On Wednesday, as usual, Mrs. Tomblin reviewed the movie and the chapter with the answers to her worksheet and definitions list on the overhead projector. Then she said, "And now I need two volunteers." She rolled the overhead projector cart up the aisle to the front, whamming it against desks as she went. She whacked into John Stone's feet, which he always sprawls out because his legs have gotten so long all of a sudden, and he said, "Whoa!" in surprise. The class went quiet, everybody stunned by the change in our routine.

Mrs. Toad scanned the room over the top of her little glasses and bulged her cheeks out. "Well?" she said. "Volunteers?" Nobody moved. Tommy Craddock's drumstick let out a little tap on his desk, and Mrs. Toad's little black eyes zoomed over to him. "Mr. Craddock then," she said. "Front and center. And get that globe off its stand."

He heaved a huge sigh, hauled himself up from his desk, pulled the blue and green globe off the stand on the bookshelf, and slouched to the front of the room where he tossed it from hand to hand like a basketball.

Mrs. Toad looked down at the grade book on her desk. "Miss Young," she said. My heart stopped. "You seem to have a good grasp of this subject." I couldn't breathe. My face flushed hot in the darkness. "Come to the front please."

I unstuck my thighs from the wooden seat of my desk and slid out, holding my skirt down. I watched my feet on the tile floor, hoping I wouldn't trip over anything.

"You shall be our moon," Mrs. Toad said. She pointed to a spot between her and Tommy in the front of the room, and I stood there. "As we have learned," she said to the class, "in the solar eclipse, the Moon"—she pointed her yardstick at me—"passes between the sun"— she waved her doughy hand in front of the lightbulb of the overhead projector—"and the Earth." She pointed at Tommy, who tossed the globe up in the air, caught it on the tip of his index finger and tried to twirl it like the Harlem Globetrotters. "Stop that this instant, Mr. Craddock," she shouted. "Treat the Earth with some respect, please!"

Everyone laughed. I stood as still as I could in the darkness, trying to be small, my shoulders hunched down and my head bent. Tommy held the Earth up so that the projector light shined on the United States.

"Face the Earth, Miss Moon," Mrs. Toad said. I heard snickers from the darkness. "During a solar eclipse," she said, "our Miss Moon will cast her shadow on the Earth." I stood there. "Miss Moon?" she said. I looked back over my shoulder toward her, but the overhead projector light blinded me. "Move between the sun and the Earth, Miss Moon," I heard her say.

Watching the globe in Tommy's hands, I shuffled left. The shadow of my head crept over the blue-green surface until it was dark. I imagined what I looked like from my seat, my face dark, the back of my head shining. I could feel the heat of the light on my hair, but I was looking into the dark. I could see my own shadow over the place I live.

Mrs. Toad walked past me and tapped the globe with her yardstick pointer. "And so," she said, "this darkest part of the shadow is Miss Moon's umbra."

Dear Virge,

How are you? I am fine. NO. I am NOT fine. My father took me out of regular school and is making me go to a school with NUNS that is ALL GIRLS! I might never get to see Paco again! My father and mother are watching me like a hawk. It's so unfair! It's like I'm a prisoner. I hate them. I hate the nuns. I hate it here. I hate everything. I wish I was dead. Please write!

Your friend,
Melody St. James

The sun scopes we made in natural science on Thursday were just cardboard boxes stuck together into an angle with masking tape and a little mirror fixed at the top that was supposed to shine the sun and shadow down onto white paper. You could only look at the paper so that you wouldn't go blind looking right at the sun. I could tell that it wasn't going to look anything like what the eclipse looked like in the movie. Tommy Craddock used his cardboard scope for a new drum sound, and somebody used the masking tape to stick a "Kick Me" sign onto the back of the kid up front with the glasses.

I put my sun scope to my face, holding it up toward the light. It was stupid. I wanted to see the moon shadow over the sun. I wanted to see Bailey's beads. Even if it fried my eyeballs.

I wasn't supposed to listen, but when I heard Mom say "Virge's friend," my ears pricked up. Dad had come home from his March deacons meeting, which was once a month on Saturday morning, and slammed the front door and yelled "Mary!" Lee was off with his friends somewhere, and I was reading in my room. Right away I knew Dad was agitated about something, which is not unusual after a deacons meeting, and I didn't pay attention to their voices until I heard my name.

I crawled into my closet and pressed my ear against the wall.

"You don't mean Ricki Ann Purvis!" Mom said. The wall was dry against my cheek and ear.

Mumbling. "—that Lane boy," said Dad. Ronnie, I thought.

"Oh no!" said Mom. It was about Ricki Ann being P-G. I felt my face getting hot in the dark. "Well, I don't think she and Virge are so close anymore . . . not around . . . last summer."

I strained to hear Dad's voice, my ear aching. Something, something—"He says it's not his—"

I blinked and saw spots of light. Not Ronnie's? Then whose?

By the time Mom knocked on my door after her talk with Dad after the deacons meeting, I was out of my closet and sitting on my bed pretending to read. She opened the door a little and peeked in. "Can I talk to you, honey?" she asked.

I knew what about, because I had heard Dad say "See what you can find out." But I just blinked like I had been deep inside my book and said, "Uh, sure, Mom."

She twisted her hands together and sat first on the edge of my bed, then moved over to the chair at the desk. One of Dad's old white dress shirts, blotted with dried paint, hung loosely over her slacks, and the lemony smell of furniture polish wafted from the cloth in her pocket. A scarf covered her hair. She stared at my bulletin board, at the postcard about my homeroom from way back in August, the lock of my long hair tied with a pink ribbon, the silver wire from my braces, the wrinkled "One Way to Jesus" tract, and my story with Miss Williams's round red writing: *Very good, Virginia! I love the magical cat! What a mystery! But what did make her change?* The note from Michelle to Kathy Zane was still stapled to the back, but Mom didn't look underneath the story. She touched the diviner's stick with her index finger, and her wedding ring and diamond engagement ring reflected gold light on the wall. She looked out the window. Her mouth seemed thin and weak without lipstick. I noticed a smudge on her forehead. Finally she asked, "How's school?"

I shrugged. "Okay." My heart beat a little faster, getting nervous, and I was curious about how she was going to get to the subject. I yawned and tried to sit up straighter, tucking both hands under my stretched-out legs. I felt sorry for Mom so I said, "We're having an eclipse today. I have to watch it for natural science."

She smiled and sat down in the chair again, tired from house-cleaning. "Yes, I heard about that on the news. That's interesting." She crossed her ankles and studied her dirty white sneakers, not listening as I explained about the shadow of the moon—the penumbra, then the umbra—crossing over the United States and especially Florida.

"It's the biggest natural event of our time."

Mom swallowed. She hadn't heard a word. "Listen, Virge," she said. I cocked my head and waited. She watched her hands in her lap, twisting her rings around her finger. "Virge, have you talked to Ricki Ann lately?" she asked. Her fingernails were short and ragged.

I told the truth. "No ma'am." It was mostly that Ricki Ann hadn't talked to me, but it was still the truth. "She's been absent a lot lately." And she wouldn't talk to me anyway, I thought. "And she stopped coming to church too, I guess." I thought I knew why.

Mom swallowed. "Hmm." One of her fingers tapped the back of her other hand. Her knuckles were stretched pale. She glanced at me quickly, then away. "Have you, um, heard anything about her? I mean, about why she's been out of school?"

It was my turn to look at my lap. If I said no, I'd be lying, and that was a sin, especially to my mother. But I didn't really want to say what the note said. "I, um, heard something," I said. "But I don't know if it's true." I swallowed. "It's kind of bad."

Mom took a breath. "What did you hear, Virge?"

I looked up and met her eyes. "It might not be true."

She nodded, not smiling. "What might not be true?"

"That Ricki Ann is pregnant." The words seemed like marbles in my mouth—slick and hard—and when I said them out loud, they hung in the air of my room like stones.

Me and Mom stood on the front porch of Ricki Ann's house, waiting for somebody to come to the door. The yard full of rusty cars and truck parts and chickens and a tire swing and broken bicycles was empty of people. "Maybe they're not home," I said, hoping that the words would make it so. I wanted to run back down the dirt drive and get into our car and roll up the windows and get away fast. "I don't want to miss the eclipse," I said. "It's for homework."

Mom's mouth drew into a little line. She had put on a clean striped blouse and had brushed her hair and put on makeup, but she still looked tired. She knocked on the doorjamb again. She didn't want to be there any more than me, but Dad had sent us. We heard noises inside. Dang.

Mom took a deep breath and let it out.

When Ricki Ann opened the door, I was almost as surprised to see her as she was to see me. Of course I had known she might be there, but I had just figured that with seven kids in the house, the odds were that somebody else would answer. Her eyebrows jumped, but the rest of her face remained that mask she had perfected. "Yeah?" she asked.

"Hello Ricki Ann!" Mom said. "My goodness, I haven't seen you in so long!" Her voice sounded fake.

Ricki Ann didn't move. Her expression was like a flat rock.

"Who is it, baby?" her mother yelled from the shadows inside.

Mom grinned. "Oh, I just stopped by to buy some eggs," she said brightly. One finger reached up and touched the small gold cross on the chain at her neck.

It was a lie. The Purvises did have a sign on the road that said FRESH EGGS, and that was what Dad had told her to say, but the real reason we were there was to see if Ricki Ann was really P-G and try to find out if Ronnie Lane was the daddy. I wanted to shrink down to the size of a sheet of paper and slip between the cracks in the floorboards of the porch. I wished I was dead.

Mrs. Purvis came to the door, still in a nightgown and slippers though it was afternoon, tying her pink bathrobe cord tighter. A cigarette dangled from her lip. "I think we got some," she said. "Joe-Ray," she yelled back into the house, "go on out back and see can you get us a dozen eggs for Miz Young." She pushed the screen door open and stepped out onto the porch. "I'd ask you in," she said, "but the house is a mess."

Ricki Ann stood still, staring at me. I stared back at her. She looked the same, but pale against the shadows of the room behind her.

"Joe-Ray!" Mrs. Purvis yelled again. No answer. I remembered Joe-Ray, Ricki Ann's second oldest brother, kind of short and greasy, always grabbing at her and hugging her in close and rough or tickling her until she almost cried. Mrs. Purvis shrugged at Mom and said back over her shoulder. "Ricki Ann," she said, "I reckon you'll have to go on out there and fetch the eggs." She grabbed Mom's arm and walked her down to the porch swing on the end. "Come on and sit down with me, Miz Young. I ain't seen you in a coon's age."

Ricki Ann sighed and turned back into the dark toward the back of the house.

"Virge, you go on with Ricki Ann," said Mrs. Purvis. "I reckon you know the way good enough." She laughed.

I opened the screen door and followed Ricki Ann down the hall toward the kitchen door in back. She didn't speak and she didn't turn around.

I watched as Ricki Ann reached under a hen and pulled out two eggs. The hen pecked at her hand, but she ignored it and red dots welled up on her pale skin. She turned around and held the eggs toward me. "Pull your shirt out like a basket," she ordered, and when I did, she placed them next to my belly. She looked at me, meeting my eyes. "I guess you heard," she said.

I swallowed and nodded. "Yeah."

She shrugged. "It don't matter anymore," she said. "It's gone."

I wasn't sure what that meant. "What's gone?" I asked, then bit my tongue.

She grimaced. "The baby, stupid." She swiped at another hen, and it flew off its nest, squawking and flapping, red feathers floating upward in the draft it made. Two eggs. Ricki Ann picked them up and placed them in my shirt. "It miscarried."

I held my breath, then swallowed. The eggs stretched my shirt. They were still warm from the hens. "Oh," I said. Stupid.

"Don't matter," she said. "Probably better anyway." She moved toward the shadows in the back of the barn where more chickens sat on hay nests in boxes. The air was sweet and heavy and dusty with motes shining in the dim light from one small window in the loft overhead. Something rustled, and some hay floated down. "Who's there?" Ricki Ann said, and I heard a note of fear in her voice. "That you, Joe-Ray? Daddy?"

Silence. We stood quiet for a minute, listening, then Ricki Ann shrugged and reached under another chicken. This one, a fat red one, didn't even open her eyes. I wondered if she was asleep or if she just didn't care.

I knew what I was supposed to ask, what Mom—Dad—wanted me to ask, but I was scared. Ricki Ann wasn't my best friend anymore. I wasn't hers. Nobody was my friend. And my tongue felt like a lump of clay inside my mouth. Lifting it to speak, to ask that question, seemed like hoisting a boulder. "Uh—" I drew in a deep breath. The words came out low, barely above a mumble. "Who—" I couldn't finish it, but

I had to. "Uh, is—was—"

Ricki Ann had stopped and was staring at the hay- and chicken-poop-covered floor. I wanted to cry. Why did anybody care? I hated myself. I hated Dad for making Mom make me do this. Why couldn't everybody leave everybody alone? I took another deep breath and blew it out. "Ronnie Lane says it's not his," I said.

Ricki Ann's face was in shadow, the back of her head lit with the beam through the loft window, her orange hair glowing. The scuffle from above came again, and she cocked her head to listen. Her eyes watched mine. She slowly looked up, then back to my eyes, serious, like she was a dog trying to tell me something. "It was his," she said, and looked up again. She spoke deliberately, each word slow and even. She looked up again.

"But—it—don't—matter—any—more—cuz—it's—gone." She looked at me. Her eyes seemed to have lost all their color, and I felt like I was staring into the snake's eyes again, that hot afternoon last summer with the cicadas buzzing a never-ending song. She held my gaze with hers, then drew it upward to look at the loft floor again. "I'll never tell," she said a little louder, as if talking to someone up there. Her face shone with the sunlight for a second, and then the light dimmed with clouds.

Saturday night, I was exhausted, but I couldn't sleep, not after seeing Ricki Ann in the barn, not after the eclipse. I wanted to tell myself a story, get to the good part, the weird part, and go to sleep, but my stories were sinful. They were something to do with sex, like masturbation, because they made me feel so good, and so bad afterward. And the part where I was mixed-up between a boy and a girl must surely be a sin, because that wasn't natural. I wanted to be good, normal, ordinary, so I prayed for help. God, I'm sorry. God, I'm sorry. Tell me what to do. Tell me how to be good.

Pastor Bob always said that all the answers we needed were in the Bible, God's own holy word, so that night, after the eclipse, I held my Bible closed and thumbed the soft pages with my eyes closed. God, show me how to be good. I got a little chill through my thumb, which seemed like it might be a sign or an answer back from God, so, with my eyes still closed, I opened my Bible and let my finger point down onto the page. This is what God had to say about how to cure my mixed-up, am-I-a-girl-or-a-boy go-to-sleep stories:

"And it was about the sixth hour, and there was a darkness over all the earth until the ninth hour. And the sun was darkened, and the veil of the temple was torn in the midst. And when Jesus had cried with a loud voice, he said, 'Father, into thy hands I commend my spirit,' and, having said this, he gave up the ghost."

My heart jumped in my chest, burning. My head ached. I couldn't breathe. I had turned to the part where Jesus dies up on the cross and there's an eclipse. Did God want me to give up the ghost? To die? Was that the only way for me to be good?

If I didn't believe God was answering my prayer with those words about giving up the ghost in my Bible, then maybe He wasn't answering me at all. Maybe He wasn't even there. That made me feel so alone. No. That couldn't be it.

I just wouldn't tell myself any going-to-sleep-stories. I turned out the light and lay there. The snakes rustled under the bed. I thought about Jesus making the eclipse happen when He gave up the ghost. I imagined being buried behind a stone.

Dear Mel,

How are you? I am fine. I am sorry that your mother and father are being so unfair and keeping you and Paco apart. It's so romantic! Just like Romeo and Juliet, which is a story by Shakespeare that Miss Williams gave me to read the condensed version of for extra credit. It was good! Not as good as Thunder Heights by Phyllis A. Whitney, but still good. I hope you don't mean it really that you wish you were dead, but I know how you feel sometimes. Even though it was romantic for Romeo and Juliet, killing yourself is a sin. And it's pretty bad for everybody else too. Like Bobby Miller, Lee's friend, whose Dad blew his brains out all over the garage. Bobby couldn't even go to school for that whole year. And then they moved away. God gave us life, right? So killing yourself would be a sin, right? How could you face Jesus in heaven if you had killed yourself? I have thought about that a lot.

Other news. Ronnie Lane didn't get to preach for the first time with the other guys at the church who have got the call to go to seminary. It's a big MYSTERY about why, but I think I know. It has to do with RA and the letters P-G. But it might not be true, so I don't want to say for sure.

The eclipse turned out to be not so great because the weather got cloudy that day. It got kind of dark and spooky, but I didn't see the penumbra or the umbra or Baily's beads or anything. It was just kind of like a really cloudy afternoon. Oh well. So much for the biggest natural event of my time.

Write back!
Your friend,
Virge

Backslide

Something thup-thup-thups a rhythm, like the surf on a beach. I blink into sun, a bright halo behind the white of a thick wet snow falling. The weather has changed again. The windshield wipers slap back and forth and I struggle against the steering wheel, trying to keep the truck to the middle of the road. It is hard to see the edges, the turns. I'm still driving home. This route is not the Steep Way, but bad weather makes it treacherous anyway. I wonder if I'm going to careen off into a ditch or tree, get stuck, have to hunker down and wait for rescue. I almost hear the sirens and smell the antiseptic, but then I fall back into the driving, trying to stay focused on the road. Not on my throbbing shoulder, not on the destination, but on the road.

And then I am flying into space with my arms spread wide. Like a swan dive. A swallow dive. The Fool. I have stepped off into the air. Who am I? Is this really me? I hear voices in my head, me and not me. Where am I? Has this moment happened yet? Who do I think I am? This is not natural. Something is wrong.

I fall into a blue sky and the yaw of a wide canyon, the silver sliver of a river rushing up at me. Rocks. Rocks! Will I die? Surely I will die. I'm about to die. My body is my own in that instant, flying toward rocks and water, and I understand the magic in every cell of it, every atom. Even the air through which I fly is a part of me. We are joined. And I know I want to live, even if I am afraid. As the water changes from silver to the blue of sky, I feel a gentle tug on my body harness, and return, slowing, the weight of my body still stretching the cords that hold me, then I bounce back up again toward the bridge, flying, like I used to imagine the Rapture. Like I flew away from the snake when I was twelve. Like magic.

At the apex, stillness. Life. Heaven. Then I plummet again toward the rocks and silver water. The cords bounce me back up again, two, three, four times, and finally I dangle at the end of my ropes. As I wait for the guys above to start the winch, pulling me back up to the bridge, I think of where I have been, why I am here. Where I am going.

It is 1990. I am going home once again. South, close enough to my mother but far enough from my father to be safe. I have had a new job for a year, teaching high school in Florida, and a little house near the beach, just right for one person. I write every day. My first story has been published. In therapy, I have begun to talk about my dreams, all of them, even those where I kiss a woman. I want to kiss a woman. I have said it to my therapist— to myself—aloud: "I think I am a lesbian." This summer I have been to Denver to reclaim my stuff, to sign divorce papers, to begin again. Born again again.

"Isn't it a lot of work to keep these parts of yourself separate?" my therapist repeats in my head. I shake it, ignoring her again. No, I think. Not hard. Necessary. Separate selves, separate lives, separate truths. This is the road I'm on right now.

The guys on top of the bridge help me over the railing.

"Ready for more suicide practice?" asks one. "How was it?"

I have paid them $100 for three jumps. I am gasping, the adrenaline pumping my heart fast. Right now. This moment. Stay in this one moment. My face is stretched with a grin. I nod. "That was great! I was really just there! Right there!" They change the harness, double- and triple-check everything. This time I will fall backward.

They help me up and over the railing again. I hold on, perched with my toes on the bridge, back to the deep canyon. They count down: "Five, four, three, two, one!" and I fling myself back into space.

I want to let go of something. I want to step out into space, to take a risk, to let go. At a Renaissance fair during my past year alone, I had paid a woman to tell my future with Tarot cards. "The past and passing," she said, tapping the Death card, "is about letting go, about shedding a skin like a snake, transformation." I thought of my marriage, the divorce creaking toward finality, and the baby that had never been. I remembered the snake in the swamp, so many years before. The reader slid a card on top of Death. "The Fool," she said, "is your future." She had smiled at me. "Time to take the leap into the unknown, to let go. Risk it all."

I bunch my thighs and fall backward into space, arching my back, like I imagined when I was a girl, but no tree limbs whack into my body, breaking off. There is only space. Only letting go. Only flying, falling, the Rapture reversed. My heart thumps fast as I lie back, the blue sky and canyon walls turning upside down until I see the bridge above me again, the bands attached to my ankles and body harness stretching out. I feel at one with everything. I feel the gentle tug as my head points down toward the river and rocks below, and I am sprung up again, into the air for the short flight before another free-fall back toward the river. Suicide practice.

But this is the opposite of that, I think, bouncing at the end of the cords like a bat, waiting to be pulled back up. I have come here to fall backward toward death and to be lifted up again into a new life. I am born again again, into someone new. No rules to guide me, except those inside me, like the urge that made me reach into my wallet and count out cash to leap into space. I am free. "Isn't it hard to compartmentalize?" asks my therapist. No. No. No. I won't answer that. It's fine. I'm fine.

I close my eyes into darkness and see the halo of sun around shadows, beads of light that seem to spring out into space. Like me. A smile stretches my face. I am Bailey's Beads. My heart pounds, thub-thub-thub. I no longer fear the next step into air. I am eager for it.

Reunion: Ricki Ann

"Wow," Ricki Ann hears a woman behind her say. "I can't believe she came to the reunion. Did you see her on Kora?" Ricki Ann can't move, watching the dance floor.

"Were they in our class?" a man's voice asks. "I don't remember any dykes in our class." He snickers. "There was that faggot who was ahead of us a couple of years . . ." Ricki Ann listens, watching the women moving together—forward, backward—in the rhythm.

"Yeah, sure," the woman replies. "But she wasn't . . . um . . . like that back then." She pauses. "I don't think." She laughs. "She was one of those kids who read books in the library all the time."

"Who is it?" the man asks.

The answer comes from several voices at once. "Virge . . . Virge Young." Ricki Ann wonders if anyone in the class knew the name before the television show, the shooting. She wonders how many have read the book. She wants to die from shame.

The people who aren't dancing have gradually turned to watch the dance floor, the famous lesbian who had once been invisible among them now dancing with another woman. "Right here in front of God and everybody," someone whispers. Ricki Ann holds her drink tightly, trying not to move, trying to keep her face blank, listening to the voices.

"I knew her brother," says a man. Tommy somebody, Ricki Ann thinks. "Lee. On the football team . . . a year behind us. Real nice guy. Died a couple years ago, you know."

The first woman scoffs. Had she been a cheerleader? She is tanned in that leathery way you rarely see anymore, a sun goddess. "Duh," she says. "It's in the book."

Laughter. Ricki Ann doesn't know what she feels. Everything. Nothing. Maybe nobody has connected her to Virge, to that chapter in the book. She wants to step back into the crowd, stand closer to the wall, the shadows, but there are too many people crowding her.

"Pretty hot, huh," slurs a man. "What I wouldn't give to be a slice in that sandwich." Other men snort appreciatively.

"Disgusting," a woman's voice says. "Pig." Laughter.

"I think she was in my English class back in junior high or something." Another male voice. "One of the smart kids. Kept to herself."

The song transitions into a disco beat, something they'd played at the prom. The kid disc jockey is sliding back and forth through the thirty years in disconcerting leaps. This music makes Ricki Ann remember pastel tuxedos, sprayed hair. Virge had been practically invisible by senior year of high school, certainly not at the prom. Ricki Ann tries to remember her back then . . . Virge had had a job at the supermarket and Ricki Ann had seen her there, smiling, talking to an old lady as she rang up her groceries, like a grown-up, like a friend. And one day, stuck in the traffic jam from the student parking lot, she had looked over to see Virge behind the wheel of a little brown car, alone, nodding her head to the music on the radio, her eyes focused far away, like she was somewhere else, maybe someone else.

Ricki Ann remembers Virge from the library too, maybe senior year, standing over a big book, an atlas, her eyes moving with her finger across the page. Planning her escape, Ricki Ann suddenly realizes. Her palm itches, and she curls her long, manicured nails inward to scratch the scar where the barbed wire fence snagged her, an old habit. Virge, dancing with her partner now, laughing, relaxed, having fun, seems to have become someone else, someone whole and unafraid. Ricki Ann thinks again of the senior prom, her perfect date with the captain of the basketball team. The perfect dress. She remembers the limo, the hotel room out at the beach, all those jocks and their girls, the booze and pot and some kind of pills. He'd only asked her because she was a sure thing. She watches Virge pull the redhead close as the music slows. Everything went downhill after that, Ricki Ann thinks. Maybe since even before then.

"Can you believe her?" Michelle says loudly. "Flaunting that lifestyle like that. I mean . . . Well!" A few murmurs of approval, agreement, but just a few.

"Oh, give me a break," comes a woman's voice from behind. Ricki Ann glances to her right. A thin woman with dark hair and small, fashionable glasses, a trim pantsuit. Another one of those smart kids, but one of the popular ones, the Honor Society bunch. Michelle has turned to face her. "What do you care?" the woman asks.

Michelle splutters. "Why it's a sin!" she says. "They're just trying to make it seem normal, pull this country down. It's not normal. It's not natural. It's . . ."

The shorter woman takes a step toward Michelle, like a terrier challenging a bulldog, Ricki Ann thinks. She feels her lip twitch. "I know I think all the time about what you do in your bedroom," the woman says.

"Ewww." Another woman in the little group makes a face.

The woman with the glasses turns to her. "Exactly," she says. "What business is it of ours what anybody else does in private?" She waves her drink glass at Michelle, who has taken a step back. "You people are a bunch of perverts."

Michelle gasps and opens her mouth.

"You're obsessed with other people's sexual behavior," the woman says. "What else would you call it?" A few people laugh.

"Aren't you that lawyer?" someone asks. "Weren't you on TV?"

The woman laughs. "Stacy Lake," she says, tapping her name tag. "And yes, I am a lawyer."

"Oh I remember you," another woman says. "You represented the abortion clinics back in the Eighties. That whole bombing conspiracy thing. Something about how close protesters could get."

Ricki Ann looks more closely at the woman, at the same time trying to step back from the edge of the dance floor again. The two beefy men behind her smell of whiskey, ex-football players, no doubt, and they form a solid block between her and escape. She doesn't want to be here at all anymore, for Boomer's business or anything else.

"A baby killer!" Michelle says. She looks truly horrified, alarmed to be in such close proximity to the woman.

"Here we go," sighs Stacy Lake. She squares her shoulders at Michelle. "I represented a woman's right to control her own body. In this country, for the moment anyway, my body is my business." She nods at the dance floor. "Just like theirs, and—" she sweeps the little group with a look— "just like all of yours."

Ricki Ann snorts. Other people laugh.

Michelle glares. "This country was founded on Christian princi . . ."

"Oh stop it," says Tommy-something. "She's right. I'm a Christian too, but it's God's job to judge, not mine." He lifts his drink in a toast toward the dance floor. "They're happy, pay their taxes, don't bother me. More power to 'em." He sticks his hand out toward Stacy. "Tom Craddock," he says. "I think we were in Latin together junior year."

Michelle turns back to Ricki Ann. "What're you laughing at?" she hisses. She isn't done with being the center of attention. Ricki Ann feels the others looking at her. "You're one of them, aren't you? We all know who you were in the book. We all read about you." Ricki Ann's face grows hot, but she doesn't move. "Did you really miscarry that baby?" Michelle snarls. "How many have you miscarried since then?"

"Who's that?" Ricki Ann hears someone whisper. The music has stopped, and the DJ is talking. Where is Boomer? How can she get out of here?

Michelle looks satisfied, one hand on a hip, chin tilted up. "Humph," she snorts. "Always thought you were better than us," she says. "Didn't you?" She shakes her head. "Dropped me just like you dropped her." She pauses. "Well thank the good Lord you did," she says. "Because you were leading me down the path straight to hell. I see it now. I found the Lord because of you," she says. "And just in time. You would've turned me into one of them—" she nods toward the dance floor—"too, wouldn't you have? Lezzie," she hisses.

The group behind Michelle is silent, maybe embarrassed, Ricki Ann hopes. She crosses her arms slowly. She feels sick, but she keeps stiff while her mind skitters for a response.

"You have got to be kidding," somebody says behind her. A warm hand flattens onto Ricki Ann's shoulder, and the scar in her palm tingles. Ricki Ann knows who it is. Virge.

The Sickness Story, or How I Rolled Away a Stone

I didn't tell anybody about my mixed-up sickness. I didn't tell myself those stories to go to sleep. I didn't sleep much. I hoped that was good enough for God.

Some nights I read until the sky turned pink and I could see the words without my flashlight. Some nights I fiddled with my transistor radio, trying to pick up stations in other languages, usually Spanish, sometimes from Cuba where nobody was free anymore because of the communists. I wondered if the voices were talking about freedom. Once I picked up a revival broadcast from the North Georgia mountains, and I tried to imagine what mountains felt like. Except for the big trip to Disneyland when I was six, and which I don't much remember, I hadn't ever seen a mountain. How would it be to climb up and up, to pull yourself toward a pinnacle where you could look down on the earth, like up in my pine tree, except that the earth below would bend into folds and crevices instead of being flat and even, with nothing hidden and everything in plain sight?

I didn't climb my pine tree anymore. The morning after God turned my Bible to the page where Jesus gives up the ghost on the cross and the whole world goes dark in the middle of the day—the eclipse—I had climbed my tree one last time. Up there, above the house and Normandy Village and all of Jacksonville, watching the sun come up, wishing I could see the ocean and Cumberland Island, I had closed my eyes and imagined how it would be to just let go. To fall backward. I could feel how it would be, like flying at first. Flying. Branches would shout out with a snap as I hit them. They would slap against my back. I breathed in sap, my face sticky against the rough bark of the tree. I was crying, hugging the trunk with both arms. I didn't want to let go. I didn't want to let go. I hugged it tighter, crying like a girl. It took me a long time before I could climb down, trembling so much I could hardly breathe. At every branch, I expected God to push me or break it off. I expected God to kill me. When I got to the bottom, I collapsed flat onto the ground and stared back up into the limbs and blue sky. It all whirled and whirled into a blur of colors. I was a backslider, if not something worse. Damned to hell. But I didn't want to die.

Sometimes I just sat in the dark in my room, moving my hands in front of the flashlight, making shadows of elephants and witches on the wall. Sometimes I looked out the window, watching the dark street for raccoons and possums, burglars and stray cats. It was like there was nobody in the world but me.

When Samson started poking out on both sides like she'd swallowed a cantaloupe, and we could see the babies inside her belly move when she was lying down, which is what she did most of the time, Mom took all the stuff out of the bottom drawer of the chest of drawers in the utility room and made a bed of an old towel inside and left it open enough that Samson could crawl in. Of course, Samson went behind the washing machine to have her kittens instead.

"That's what cats do," Mom said.

Mom squeezed herself in behind the washer and pulled the kittens out, one by one, and stuck them in the drawer. And then Samson. Samson hung limply, draped across Mom's long white fingers, and her fur was wet and bloody. Without lifting her head, she let out a weak yowl.

"You stay out of here," Mom said, her forehead wrinkled up and the edges of her mouth pulled down. "Samson doesn't seem right. She needs some time to feel better." After she tucked Sammy into the drawer, she shut the door to the utility room and went right to the bathroom to wash her hands.

The night after Samson had her kittens, I read my Bible, because that was what I did when I couldn't sleep. I liked Psalms and Proverbs and the Song of Solomon. The words were pretty. I found the part they read at Bobby Miller's father's funeral:

"Yea, though I walk through the valley of the shadow of death, I will fear no evil."

I was afraid of evil, but I thought maybe what was inside me was more evil than what was in the night. I wasn't really afraid in the dark anymore. When I thought I heard snakes on the floor, I would just make myself turn on the light and put my bare feet down onto the tiles, as cold as the water gushing up from the aquifer through the old pump in the clearing at the farm. I wished I could put my head under that water again. What magic kept me from being kilt by that snake back then? Maybe God. Maybe something inside me. Was it the evil or the good or something else?

I watched the dark outside that night, thinking of Sammy in the utility room with her kittens. Through my window, I could see my pine tree moving slowly in a breeze, the moon peeking in and out through clouds. Something in me wanted to go out there. Even alone.

One by one the five little kittens died. Mom wouldn't let me and Lee hold them or even get close, except for the funerals in the backyard. She brought Samson food and water every few hours. She sat in the dark utility room alone, holding Sammy in her arms, coaxing her to eat from her fingertip the special chicken liver that she had cooked for her. "Come on, baby," she said. "You've got to eat." Part of me wished I were Samson, so sick that Mom would call me *baby* again, hold me in her lap, rock me.

But Sammy wouldn't eat. She got skinnier, her fur duller, and in a few more days, she was dead too.

We buried her in a shoebox beside the kittens. Lee made his dog, Hulk, wear a tie, and I made a cross to put at the head of her grave by hammering two two-by-fours together. I wrote on it, "In loving memory of Samson The Strong. R.I.P."

That night I started writing stories down on paper in the long sleepless nights. Not my mixed-up-going-to-sleep stories, or stories about a girl who mysteriously changes, but stories that I had heard the old folks at Grandma's house tell or stories about people I didn't know at all. And it was like I became them for a little while. I could see in my mind what the old black man's face looked like when he offered my great-great grandfather the pail of mare's milk for his sick daughter. I could hear his voice. I could think my great-great grandfather's thoughts. I could feel the cry of his little daughter in my own chest, weak and small. I could hear the voices of my mother and her mother and the ironing lady, Rita, as they talked. I could feel the steering wheel under my mother's hands and see the way the black woman next to her in the front seat clutched her handbag. I could feel what it was like to be as small as one of the Izan warriors in the forest, and I could feel the power of the Izan queen's hands when she laid them on my head before I set out on my mission. I could feel what it was like to be inside my little brother's body as it swelled up to man-size, and the ache in his head after Dad dropped the four-by-four on it.

I wrote out what Bobby Martin saw when he walked into the garage after school that day. I tasted the gun metal in his father's mouth. I felt on my own hands the rubber gloves that the church ladies wore later, and I felt my own stomach rising up as they mopped up the bits of Mr. Martin's brain from the concrete floor.

It was like the real world already lived in little pieces of other people inside my head, even though I knew I was sort of making it up. The details seemed so real that sometimes I thought they were more true than true stories. Sometimes I believed them more, because those other people were all parts of me, the good parts and the evil parts.

What I couldn't imagine was how Jesus looked to Mr. Martin in that instant, the boom of the gun still thundering in his head. All I could see was light sliding away backward into dark.

I looked out my window into the dark. I had almost filled up a whole notebook. The burglars and rapists and witches and snakes under my bed were just shadows I had made into real. What about the boy-me and the girl-me in the going-to-sleep stories? Which one of them was shadow? Which was real? Did it matter?

Miss Williams, my English teacher, had written out all these quotes on white paper in her neat red cursive and posted them on the walls of Room 10. One of them said, *"Love is the difficult realization that something other than oneself is real."—Iris Murdoch.* I thumbed the pages of my notebook. It all seemed so real, so me and so not me. Was what I wrote some kind of love?

The pen in my hand moved across the page again, and I watched it, almost like my hand was separate from me. I saw the diviner in my mind, striding out over the Bahia grass without looking, the willow twig balanced in his hands, trusting it to lead him to water. The pen between my fingers felt like his willow branch. I wasn't afraid of the dark anymore, no matter how alone I was. Writing down that story, I knew something other than me was out there. And it was inside me too.

Ronnie Lane glared when I came into Room 10 for Bible Study before school on the Wednesday morning before Easter. They had already started, so I just slipped into the first empty desk by the door. I would rather have been in the library, but it wasn't the same without Mel. Only five other girls were in the room, mostly seventh graders like me. No Ricki Ann. Ronnie was talking about the events leading up to Jesus' crucifixion, the week before it, which was exactly what the preacher always does the week before Easter in church. His bell-bottoms were creased and hung low on his hips, held up by a bright orange belt, but he also wore a wide tie with a mod print under his denim vest. Nobody wore a necktie in school except teachers. He had let his sideburns grow long and bushy. He was trying to be a hip preacher, I thought, or something.

"So Jesus enters the city with a parade," he said. "People throw down palm branches in the streets and hail him as Savior. What happens in one short week that causes him to be hung up on a cross as a criminal?"

A girl started to raise her hand, but Ronnie kept going. He didn't want an answer. He was preaching now.

"After the Last Supper with his disciples, Jesus goes up to a garden on the Mount of Olives, Gethsemane." Ronnie paused for effect. "And there he tells his disciples to wait for him while he prays." He lowered his voice. "But it's very late, and they fall asleep." He made his voice sound sad. He shook his head, frowning, his mouth turned down, and sighed. "And while his friends sleep, he prays to his Father, 'Take this cup from me,' which means that He knows what is going to happen— that His Father, God, is going to turn away from Him and let Him be killed—and that if there's any other way to save men from their sins, please, Dad, do that instead."

I thought about my own dad. He wasn't exactly talking to me yet. But on the afternoon I told my mom what Ricki Ann said—her exact words, "It's his," and that I wasn't sure if that meant Ronnie or something else—Dad had said, "Virge, get me a glass of iced tea." First words he had said direct to me since Mel. So maybe he wasn't so mad anymore about my haircut and about me standing up for Mel and her family in the church that night or whatever it was that had made him disappear me. He still looked at me like I had turned into some alien from outer space, when he noticed me at all. I was glad I still had Mom, but I thought I understood how Jesus was more afraid of his father turning away than of dying on the cross.

A skinny girl who still didn't have any boobs raised her hand just a little, then lowered it, then raised it again. Ronnie smiled at her, baring his teeth, which were clenched. Her voice was very small. "Why did He have a cup?" she asked.

Ronnie grimaced. "No, no, it was a met-a-phor," he pronounced slowly. I could almost hear him thinking: *stupid.* "The cup rep-re-sents the work He knows is ahead of Him, dying for all our sins." The girl shrunk down into her chair. "Got it?" he asked. She nodded, biting her lip. Ronnie sighed. "Okay." He glanced at the clock, then back at the lectern where he had his notes.

I was betting that this was the sermon he wanted to preach at church but they didn't let him. Nobody would have asked questions then. "Jesus' prayer," Ronnie continued, "is 'Father, all things are possible unto thee. Take away this cup from me; nevertheless, not what I will, but what thou wilt.'" Ronnie looked right at me and pressed his hand against his chest. "Jesus surrenders himself to his Father's will. Whatever God demands or asks, Jesus accepts his fate. It's His Father's will that Jesus should die for our sins." Ronnie was trying to tell me that he had surrendered to God's will, to his own fate, but I didn't believe it. He was just plain mad.

Ronnie read, "And he cometh, and findeth them sleeping, and saith unto Peter, 'Simon, sleepest thou? Couldest not thou watch one hour?'"

Ronnie looked back up at me. "Even his best friends—" he said. He blinked and glanced around at his little congregation. "Three times He goes and prays, asking His friends to watch, but they just fall asleep. What kind of friends are those?"

Was he saying I was a bad friend? But I hadn't been his friend, had I? No more than Ricki Ann's anyway. The back of my shoulders dragged downward, and I couldn't breathe. But somewhere inside my head something throbbed, No, you're wrong. I didn't like that feeling. It was like something was boiling up, without me making it happen, without me in control. Like when I lifted over the creek away from the snake last summer, like when the baby in Faith's belly moved under my hand and she said I was no sinner, like when I raised my hand to second Mel's church membership. But this feeling was also hard, and maybe not so magical. It was like I was mad too.

Ronnie kept on talking, preaching, and I tuned back in to what he was saying, lifting my chin and staring at him. "—And after that little betrayal, a bigger betrayal. His own disciple, Judas, one of his twelve best friends, kisses Jesus to show the guards who to arrest." This time, when Ronnie Lane stared at me, I glared right back.

The door opened. His voice went weak right in the middle of his next sentence. He stopped. We all turned around to look. Ricki Ann.

She walked to a desk, keeping her back straight, staring at him, and slid in.

Ronnie swallowed. He looked down at his notes. "Um," he said. He closed his eyes, then opened them. "The Bible tells us," he said, then stopped. "The Bible tells us that after Jesus gives up the ghost, he is taken down from the cross and placed in the tomb. His, uh, His mother, Mary, and some women prepare him for burial, and . . ." Ronnie's voice quavered. He loosened the knot in his tie a little. He took a breath. He had skipped way ahead in the story, left his lesson about the Garden of Gethsemane and how Jesus' friends betrayed him, and jumped right over into the resurrection. That story always made me wonder how Mary felt, burying her son who was also the son of God, then finding Him alive again. Ronnie looked down at his Bible. "Uh," he said.

Ricki Ann folded her hands on the desktop and her sharp little chin tilted up and forward. All of the Bible Study group seemed to be holding its breath.

Ronnie looked gray, but he kept stumbling along in his sermon. Or some sermon. His eyes darted to the clock, back to his notes, over our heads, and, every few minutes, directly at Ricki Ann. Bright red blotches bloomed on his cheeks. I thought he might be sweating. He fumbled in his Bible, turning to a page he had marked with a piece of paper.

"And the women came to the tomb and found the stone rolled away," Ronnie said. He stopped, and blinked. "Uh, His mother, Mary, and Mary Magdalene, and, uh, some other women who ministered to Jesus on his journeys . . ." He glanced at the clock. "They go in and see a young man, an angel, shining with light, sitting there. And he says, 'He is not here, but is risen!'" Ronnie looked at Ricki Ann, then away. "Uh, so then Jesus appears again and again, proving that he is not dead, but resurrected."

Ricki Ann's hand rose into the air. It was as if the rest of us were watching a play. Ronnie's face paled. His mouth hung open. He blinked. Ricki Ann's hand was unwavering. Her face was blank. "Wasn't she the one who was caught in the act of adultery?" she said.

Ronnie Lane's thumb stroked the brown leather cover of his Bible. He stared at Ricki Ann, his eyes wide, like an animal caught in head-lights. "Uh," he said, then looked down and started turning pages. I heard one of the thin sheets tear. "Mary Magdalene—" he repeated. "Uh—"

"You know the one I mean," Ricki Ann said. "The Pharisees bring her to Jesus and say, 'Look, we caught her *doing it*'"—Ricki Ann said the words harshly—"'and the law says we should stone her.'" Ricki Ann sounded tough, I thought. Mad.

Ronnie's upper lip shone with sweat, and he licked it, still turning pages in his Bible, the paper rustling and ripping. "I, uh, think that was some other woman," he said. "Not Mary Magdalene." He kept fum-bling, not looking up.

"But what did Jesus say to that woman, Ronald?" Ricki Ann taunted. "What did your Savior say?"

I imagined stoning, how those little rocks would feel, pelting into your body like hail, the voices of the men yelling, the way you would notice the insects on the ground as you fell and covered your head, try-ing to live, trying to escape the pain. I remembered that last time in my pine tree. I stared at one of the quotes on the wall: *"Love makes your soul crawl out from its hiding place."—Zora Neale Hurston.* The words in my mouth, then in the air of Miss Williams's classroom, Room 10, seemed to spring up from somewhere deep inside me. "That's it," I said. The other seventh-grade girls, Ronnie Lane and Ricki Ann all turned to look at me.

"Let he who is without sin cast the first stone," I said. My tongue felt alive and light, as if something had been lifted off it. My mouth opened again, and I said, "And then, to live again, He rolls away the stone." I knew it made no sense, except maybe to me.

Ricki Ann squinted, brow wrinkling. Ronnie Lane just stood there, glad he wasn't in charge anymore, and the other girls blurred away. My mouth felt empty, as if it had been stuffed with something and I hadn't even known it, and now it was clean. I stood up and moved toward the door, my back to all of them, before the bell rang and before the closing prayer.

When I got home from school that afternoon, a week after we buried Samson, Mom opened the door of her room, which was dark behind her, and whispered to me. "Virginia, can you come in here?" She had stayed home from work that day, sick, sleeping I guessed, observing the half-moons under her eyes. School, Ricki Ann in Bible Study that morning: all my thoughts stopped when I saw my mother. She looked really sick.

I stepped into Mom's room, shut the door behind me, and a dark warm sweet smell enveloped me.

Mom collapsed back onto the edge of her bed. "Virge, will you look at this for me?" She was asking me for help as if I were a grown-up, her voice somehow sounding like mine when I had been younger. It seemed so long ago that I had been too afraid to call to her in the night when I heard snakes on the floor under my bed. She unbuttoned her nightgown at the waist. Her hands parted the thin fabric. "Do I look yellow to you?" she asked. Her voice trembled.

She was. Her belly, her whole body, was yellow. Her skin was hot. "Mom," I said. "I think you're really sick."

She stared down at her stomach and nodded. "I—I—" She looked up at me. Her eyes were yellow too. She was afraid. "Can you call your dad for me?" she asked.

I found the number, written in her neat cursive, on the emergency numbers list taped to the wall in the kitchen. I wondered if anyone had ever dared to dial it before, to interrupt him at work. Two numbers had been marked through, from previous jobs he'd lost. "May I please speak to Ed Young?" I said, when the shop answered. "It's an emergency."

I could hear men's voices, machinery and tools clanking in the background. I imagined the smell of oil and exhaust fumes, the phone dangling from its cord while the answerer went to find Dad. I imagined him scowling, shaking a cigarette from the pack he dug out of his pocket as he walked over. I heard someone laugh.

"Yell-ow," he said.

My breath caught in my chest. I coughed. "Dad," I said. "It's me. Virge."

Silence. He exhaled. "Yeah?" he said, his tone flat. Mean.

Didn't he care? I swallowed. I thought of Mom in the bedroom, yellow, scared, waiting. I felt the mad surging up into my temples again. "Dad," I said, and I heard myself and I sounded tough. "Mom's sick. You've got to come home. She needs to get to a doctor. She's real sick. She can't get out of bed."

Silence. I heard something metal fall to a concrete floor, clanging. I heard him exhale, maybe cigarette smoke, maybe anger, maybe something else. "Lemme talk to her," he said.

"She can't get out of bed," I said. "Dad—" I made myself sound like a grown-up. "You've got to come home now." My back felt stiff and straight and tall. My chin lifted. The plastic receiver felt slick with sweat. "If you can't," I said, "I'll call an ambulance."

He sniffed. I heard his hesitation. Maybe he was afraid of losing his job. Maybe he just didn't care. "Huh," he coughed. "Yeah," he said. "Okay. I'll get there soon's I can." He hung up.

I stared at the emergency number list for a minute, listening to the dial tone. He would come, but when? The ambulance would cost money. I wondered if I could figure out how to drive Mom's car. Hers had a stick shift. Sometimes we had to push it to get it going. I decided I'd give him an hour.

I went to the refrigerator, got out the orange juice and took a glass to Mom. I helped her sit up to drink it. I could feel the heat of her fever through her nightgown as I touched her back. "It'll be okay, Mom," I said. "I talked to Dad. I'll get you to a doctor."

Dad's truck pulled into the driveway fifty-three minutes later. When he came into the bedroom, he glared at me, but then he saw Mom, whose hand I was holding. His eyes went wide.

"I'm sorry, Ed," Mom said.

But he didn't say a word. Together we helped her out of bed. "Get a robe," he ordered me, and I did. We put her slippers on her feet and, leaning on us on either side, she shuffled out and slid into the truck. I shoved the passenger door shut while Dad got behind the wheel. Mom had already closed her eyes. Her skin looked even more yellow in the afternoon light. "You wait for Lee," Dad said. "Both of you, stay home."

After the truck roared around the corner, I sat on the front step hugging the dog and scratching his belly until Lee rode up on his bike, about an hour later. He swerved into the driveway and stood on the brake, looking back to see his skid mark after he stopped. He straddled the banana seat and leaned over the handlebars. "Hey," he said. The dog danced toward him, barking. Lee looked up fast when I explained what had happened. His eyes were round. He wiped his brow on his sleeve. "You called Dad at work?" he asked. "He came home from work?" he said. He looked at me with new respect.

Even as it got dark, they didn't come back.

I did my homework at the dining room table. Lee read comic books, sitting across from me. The phone didn't ring. I put a frozen pizza into the oven. We didn't say much to each other, but got plates and ate, then watched TV. We didn't argue about what to watch. Nobody told us to go to bed, so we just stayed up. We didn't turn on the lights, just sat in the blue glow of the TV. We didn't talk. We had some ice cream. Lee dripped on the carpet, but he got a dishrag and cleaned it up without me saying anything. I locked the doors. Lee fell asleep on the sofa, and I draped a quilt over him. He seemed like a little boy again. I sat in Dad's La-Z-Boy, and kicked it back, *whoosh-clunk,* so that my feet were up. I watched the late news, breathing in the leather, safe and strong in that familiar smell.

The next week, Easter Sunday, Lee and I were at Grandma's house. Papa—Mom's father—always planted his garden on the first full moon after Easter. On Easter afternoon, I kicked the plow, which was lying beside the shed, and it clunked over into the dirt. I had changed out of my stupid dress and nylon pantyhose. The dishes were done and the leftover ham wrapped up in the refrigerator. My cousins kept hiding their eggs and hunting them down, over and over again, but I was too old for that. Their shrieks in the front yard made me feel sad. Papa and Uncle Deke and Uncle Junior, and even Little Sister Willis—all the men except Dad, who hadn't gone to St. Mary's at Grandma's for Easter as he usually did—were snoring in front of the TV. The women, except Mom, were rocking on the front porch. Mom was in the hospital this Easter.

Lee sat between the furrows of last year's garden with his dog, Hulk, between his legs, his Sunday pants covered in dirt. Hulk had been digging around the roots of the little blueberry bushes in Papa's garden. Papa hated dogs, but he had let Lee bring Hulk over to St. Mary's when they took Mom to the hospital on account of everybody felt sorry for us, I guess. And Dad would've forgotten to feed him.

"Papa's gonna be mad," I said.

Lee shrugged. "I don't care," he said. The dog slobbered mud on Lee's neck and Lee laughed. "No!" he shouted. He hugged the stocky little mutt and buried his face in fur. "Nobody's gonna mess with my dog," he said, sounding like a little boy. "My cat already died, and he's my dog."

"Better not let Papa find out about his berry bushes," I said, and started kicking the dirt back into the holes.

Lee grabbed my pant leg. His eyes were glassy, and his voice small. "You think Mom's dying?" he asked.

I looked away. A pale full moon shone in the dimming blue sky overhead. I wondered if the flag still marked the spot the astronauts walked last summer. I didn't know how to answer. Was Mom going to die? How would we survive without her?

Even though he was tall and thick in the shoulders, Lee looked like a little kid sitting in the dirt with his dog lolling over him. I felt scared too. I wanted to cry. But Lee needed me to be his big sister, grown up, strong. I wanted to hug him like a little kid, but I wasn't sure he would let me.

I squatted down to be closer to Lee between the furrows in the garden earth. I held my hands with the fingertips touching, my arms resting on my thighs. I tried to keep my face smooth. "I looked it up in the encyclopedia," I said. "What Mom's got. Hepatitis."

Lee patted Hulk on his head, scratched under the dog's chin and down to his belly. Finally, he looked at me. "Is it bad?" he asked, his eyes big. "Why won't they let us see her?"

Inside, my heart thumped harder and harder, and my palms dampened, but I kept my voice even, and I looked right into Lee's eyes, like a grown-up would. "The encyclopedia says it can be fatal," I said. "And very contagious. That's why they won't let us see her. And why we had to go get those shots. But I don't think Mom's going to die." I hoped it was true.

Lee didn't look at me but at an ant struggling up the hill of earth we had made trying to hide Hulk's digging. The ant slid, waggled its little feelers in the air, then strained back up and over another little clod of dirt, a twig, a grass leaf. At the top of the ridge, the ant hesitated in the sunlight. Lee reached down, picked the ant up between two gentle fingers, and put him back down into the valley of the furrow, as if he were an ant-god. The sun had nearly set; the ant was in the shadows again. It started struggling up the hill.

"You better get cleaned up before Grandma sees you like that," I said.

Lee nodded and looked at my face. "Sure wish we could see Mom," he said.

I put my hand on his shoulder. "Yeah," I said. "But it'll be okay." I felt muscle under his shirt. He was sweaty. Would he take care of me someday? "We'll have each other," I said. "We'll be okay."

Easter night seemed almost like day under the full moon. When I went outside, careful not to slam the screen door, I wondered why Hulk wasn't on the porch where Grandma made him sleep. I hoped he didn't get into the garbage. I suspected Lee might have snuck him into his bed.

I sat on the stoop, breathing in the smell of something sweet, listening to leaves swish, watching the shadows. Dad had called. Mom was better. She would be home from the hospital soon. Me and Lee would go home on Tuesday, and Grandmother would come over from Southside to stay with us. Best not to miss too much school. And when Mom came home, I would help take care of her. I wished I'd heard Dad say it himself, so I could have listened for the truth in his voice. But he had just talked to Grandma. Her face had relaxed as she listened to the phone, and the lines around her mouth had softened. Mom was her daughter, and I didn't think her face could lie about her own child, so it must be true. Mom wasn't going to die.

In the moonlight I saw moss swaying in the treetops. Part of me wanted to climb up, but I was still afraid. I thought about those mountains up North.

After a bit, I stood up and walked out to the garden. White light reflected off the plow blade. It was the first full moon after Easter. I picked up the handles and settled my fingers into the smooth places worn into the wood like fingerprints. My hands must have grown during the year. The plow hoisted easily, lighter than I expected. The moonlight on the blade shifted then half-darkened as I pushed it deeper into the earth. The dirt welled up on either side of the plow, and I stopped to pick up a small stone that glowed white in the moonlight. I rolled it back and forth in my palm. I breathed in the earth and the night. I turned back to the house. I needed to sleep.

Backslide

In sunny spots my truck tires mire in glop and ruts so I push down on the accelerator to power ahead in a kind of strange slow motion. The twists of the maze of roads—or something—has me a little dizzy. My body is loose and relaxed though. When the truck slides on a sheen of water over frozen mud in the thick shade of a hemlock forest and seems to float over the road— sliding, flying—I even laugh aloud. The giggle flutters in my chest. I cough. The rumbling of the engine in four-wheel drive is like a low, serious voice. My father's or Lee's, maybe God's. Maybe my ex-husband's voice. Maybe the low voices of everyone together again, at home, waiting for me.

Spring. I think it's spring. Snow remains only in dirty patches on the north sides of boulders. The tip of every maple branch is thick with a deep pink bulb ready to explode into new leaves. Funny. No one has tapped these trees. No spigots or buckets sprout from the trunks. But I know the sap is rising, pounding like blood. I feel stickiness on my fingertips. Sweetness on my tongue. I navigate the truck with fluid, easy turns of the wheel, one-handed because my right shoulder aches, upward through the maze. I'm going home the long way, the back way. Yes, that's it. A patch of fog envelops me.

I look through the haze, a cloud of smoke, at my husband. It must be about 1985. I haven't left him yet. I am still in Colorado. His eyes closed, he lies back in the sun against a rock. He puffs at the joint held between his delicate fingers to get it going, then inhales a long draw. In the pause before he exhales, I slip back another four years to his proposal, back to 1979. We had been living together in an old Airstream trailer, silver and rounded at the edges outside, paneled with real wood and ingenious cubbies inside, in Florida again. Living in sin.

My father came to see me. He stood in the driveway. "Whore." He spat the word.

I remember the tears, wet on my face, and the words in my head: Better whore than the other thing, the truth. At least I stood there, facing him. At least I stood up to him. "It's my life," I said.

"Go to hell," said he.

Why didn't I confront him? What did I have to lose?

I slide a little forward in time. After my father left, this man who had been kind to me, gentle, who rolled joints of the sweetest sensimillia for me—the man I had chosen to make love to me because I knew he would be kind, because I had to make love to some man, because I had to dispel those dreams—dreams of women's lips on mine—said, "Would it be better if we were married?"

And I guessed maybe it would be. Oh, I was an idiot. I was a child. The wetness drying on my cheeks itched as I nodded. It would be easier for my mom if we were married. Even though he is much older than me. Even though he has children and an ex-wife. Even though he is a Jew. My dad hates him, and maybe that is why I love him. I think I can imagine his thoughts, his life, even though it has been so different from my own. I was a child, escaping. Maybe it's because his is a different way, a different path. A different truth. A different, smokier light. Maybe I am just sliding along the easiest path, sideways, against and with at the same time.

He passes the joint to me as I slip again into the mid-1980s and inhale, sinking into that soft-muscled place where I can float without worrying about the things I dream, the things I think, even during sex. Especially during sex. Because it's fine to just float. Let the weights lift away from my heart, from my mind, from even this body. I can slide into anything, anyone, any time, and it's okay. It's all one. I don't have to worry about God or hell or Dad or who I am—what I am—because it's all good. Dad should be relieved that I married a man at all—older, divorced, Jewish, but a man. I do love him, I think.

Someone, hiding in the smoke, peeks out from behind a stone, inside. She giggles. "You silly girl," she whispers. "You're disappearing yourself now." Her fingers on the rounded edges of the rock are claw-like. "You're still trying to be a good girl."

It is 1985. I am taking courses at the University of Colorado, riding the bus up the highway a couple of days a week between shifts at the supermarket. I am going to be a teacher, and maybe a writer too. That old dream. I can't write stoned, because the people in the stories get mixed-up. It still scares me. I know it's the old brainwashing; my Psych class helped me figure that out. But I can't stop that feeling, because it's not just the Baptists that think those mixed-up people—queers—are bad. How can they live that way? And now that gay disease is killing them. Instead, I write stories before anyone else is awake about a small town in Georgia, living inside the minds of people I once knew or people I imagine. If I am going to teach kids, I am going to have to stop smoking weed completely. I can barely look my stepkids in the face. It's dishonest to hide in this smoke. I know I'm sliding, but maybe I'm also going somewhere.

I pass the joint to my left, and the woman who takes it from me lets her fingers rest against mine for a moment longer than she should. Who is she? I feel that old compass needle swing. Toward love maybe.

When I am clear of the fog, I see that this road is a dead-end, a forest cul-de-sac. Through the rumble of reverse, like that of a stone moving, I hear a woman say, "Breathe baby. Breathe."

The Protest Story, or How Demons Get Ahold of a Soul

On account of I've been getting up at five a.m. since I was little, I was the first one to see the newspaper in the morning on May 5, 1970. I usually read the whole paper, but that day I couldn't get past the picture on the front page.

The girl's arms were wide, her hands open. One knee touched the sidewalk, and I could feel the grit digging into her knee through her paisley slacks, but I knew she hadn't felt anything. Her face was twisted in pain, agony and grief, her brow wrinkled in confusion, her mouth open with a cry that was silent in the photo. I could feel that cry in my chest. She looked about eighteen, only five years older than me.

The long line of the boy's body stretched across the page in front of the girl. I could tell that he was dead without reading the words below the picture, even though his face was turned away and his arms were tucked under his chest like he was sleeping. I could tell by the way the moccasins on his feet turned sideways. And by the scream on the girl's face.

A couple of kids on the bus had black bands around their arms that morning. When we passed the hippie house, a bedsheet with a peace sign spray-painted on it hung from the front porch. The Volkswagen van was crammed with signs. The one I could see said U.S. OUT OF CAMBODIA. Faith and Way were standing beside the van, and as we lumbered past they turned and held their fingers up in the peace sign, V.

In the cafeteria at lunchtime, Ricki Ann and her new best friend, Michelle, put on armbands made out of notebook paper colored with a black magic marker. Black magic markers squeaked at nearly every table in the lunchroom. It was supposed to be for the kids who had been killed at Kent State. I watched Ricki Ann, two tables away from mine, talking with Michelle. Since she had been back to school, her face seemed to stay blank all the time. I had seen her pass Ronnie Lane in the hall one day, and she hadn't even blinked. Her mouth moved when she talked to her friends, and she smiled, but the rest of her expression stayed completely smooth all the time.

The smell of magic marker reminded me of the words under my bed: *I love R*. It reminded me of that last time she spent the night. It reminded me of kissing her, and then of the way my going-to-sleep stories got mixed-up into something sinful. I hunched down behind my book, listening to the squeak of markers at tables around me.

A magic marker dropped between me and the page. I picked it up before it fell to the floor and looked up. Ricki Ann and Michelle Mitchell stood over me.

Should I make an armband? Would they like me if I did it? Would Ricki Ann be my friend again? I thought of the words under my bed, the last night we'd spent together, the day of the eclipse. No. If Dad found out . . . I put the marker down on their side of the table, and it rolled back and forth.

Ricki Ann's lip lifted in a little curl, her face blank.

"Figures," said Michelle. Then she hissed. "Virgggg—" She made my name into a curse.

Ricki Ann set the magic marker on its end before me, a little tower, and turned and walked away.

• • •

The story about the National Guard shooting students at Kent State University came on the evening news, and Dad's La-Z-Boy slammed to the floor so he could sit forward. Me and Lee looked at each other. Keep quiet, I said with my eyes. Don't move.

Soldiers stood on a little hill partly under a picnic shelter, crouching and pointing rifles and pistols. Their faces were hidden behind gas masks. They looked like the plastic army men that we used to play with in the dirt hole out back. Then the picture of the girl on the sidewalk again.

"Idiots," Dad said. "Serves 'em right."

Dear Virge,

Paco and me met at the library downtown, and you'll never guess what! We saw a PROTEST march! It was cool. Kids had signs and chanted stuff like "H-double hockey sticks NO, WE WON'T GO!" Paco says it's just like when the Pilgrims started the war of independence against the British. I was a little scared, cuz of those kids who got killed at Kent State. But there weren't any soldiers like there at the library. The kids just walked by on the street yelling and some people in cars honked their horns and some construction guys cussed them.

I hope you are doing fine. I'm glad that school is almost out. I think I am getting through to Paco a little about getting saved, except that he says that Catholics believe in Jesus already. The only difference is that the Pope is in charge of their church instead of regular people. Did you know that Protestant means somebody who protested against being told what to do by the Pope? I learned that at my new school. So it's like the kids at the library some I guess. Except they're against Mr. Nixon.

I miss you alot! Write me again soon!
Your friend,
Melody St. James
MS+PS4ever

• • •

"The word demonstration," said Pastor Bob, a week later, leaning out over the pulpit, confiding in us, the whole congregation, "contains the word demon." He made a worried face. He shook his head sadly. "These children," he said, "are being led by—" He paused for drama. "Satan!" he hissed. "These demonstrations—" The word tasted bad in his mouth. "Are the work of the devil."

A chorus of "Amen!" in deep voices scattered through the church. I glanced at the pew across the aisle from me where the other teenagers sat. Ronnie Lane's face was hard. The boy next to him, his brother, Donny, shook his head back and forth in an emphatic "no," his long blond hair brushing the lapels of his blue suit. He was wearing a peace button. A girl in the row behind them passed a note forward. She was scowling.

"These children," said Brother Bob, "have forgotten the word of God!" He held his Bible up in the air. "The fifth commandment, one of God's very first laws for his people, reads, "Honor thy mother and thy father, that thy days may be long upon the earth!'" He shook his Bible in the direction of the youth pew. "God not only gave the law, but he promised a reward for following it! The government is like a parent, children! Our leaders are like our fathers! We must honor them! We must not show disrespect to them! And if we do not honor them," he gasped. "Why, if we do not—! We will not live long upon this earth!"

Male voices, even men who didn't usually speak up in church, said "Amen," "Praise the Lord!" and "You tell it, preacher!"

The kids across the aisle shifted and muttered. Donny scowled and leaned forward. Ronnie grabbed his arm and whispered something.

"Demons!" shouted Pastor Bob. "Demons are moving among our children, brothers and sisters!" He closed his eyes. "Let us pray for our children."

During the prayer, I heard the rustling, so I twisted my head to look back through my eyelashes. Donny Lane stood in front of his pew. Ronnie tried to pull him back down. A girl in the row behind them opened her eyes and stood up too, then the girl to her left and the boy to her right did the same. The girl thrust her chin forward. The boy next to her grabbed her hand. Donny scowled down at his little brother, who was still pulling on his arm. "Buzz off, kid," he said out loud. People opened their eyes and looked, even though Pastor Bob hadn't said "In-Jesus'-name-we-pray-Amen" yet. I saw Mr. Lane, who was an usher standing at the back of the aisle, take a step forward, then hesitate. Donny wrenched his arm free and pushed past Ronnie into the aisle. The three kids behind him followed as he marched past his father, who had closed his eyes in prayer again, face stiff and tilted down, and out the door.

Dear Virge,

I've made a big decision. If Paco won't be a Baptist, I will become a Catholic. I talked to Sister Anne Margaret, who is my Religion teacher at St. Michaels School for Girls. And she talked to my mom and dad. They flipped out. My dad wants to take me out of St. Michaels, but mom says no not so close to the end of the school year. I told my dad that he can't tell me what to believe. He wanted to spank me but mom told him that I was too big for that now. This way if I can't be with Paco I can be a nun. That will show my dad. He's so unfair! The big Catholic church is really neat too. Lots bigger than the Baptist church, which is just a store with the windows painted over with white paint. But they have guitars for music sometimes at St. Mike's and the priest is a real young guy with long hair. I still have to go with my mom and dad to church at their church, but I'm praying to God to help me be a good Catholic anyway. I go to confession before school, which is weird but kind of good cuz you know right away what you have to do to get God to forgive you, like repeat chants and prayers and stuff. It's pretty easy, really. I have to study a lot of stuff, but Sister Anne Margaret is helping me.

I hope you will understand and still be my friend.

Melody St. James

Everyone in our house on Renoir Drive seemed suddenly tense, as if something were moving under the surface, some current pushing the four of us along like debris, swirling us into unexpected snags and riptides. The rules that we had been following without thinking suddenly seemed to be changing, but none of us was sure whether we should act the same or, if different, how.

On one ordinary Saturday afternoon in May, Mom, home from the hospital, lying on the sofa, said, "Lee, please go shut the car windows."

Lee didn't look up from the Tarzan movie he was watching on TV. "Aww, Mommm," he said.

"NOW!" Dad shouted.

That ordinary May Saturday was hot, and the air conditioner hummed, shutting out the rest of the world except me, reading a novel, and Lee, watching *Tarzan*, and Mom reading a magazine and dozing, and Dad eating a sandwich at the table. Some time passed. I don't know how much; I was lost in my story.

"Did you shut the windows in the car like I asked?" Mom said. Her recovery had been slow. My job was to bring her magazines and cool water and her medicine when it was time. She opened her eyes and stared at the ceiling.

Lee sighed. "Yeah," he said.

Dad's face reddened. "What's that?" he yelled.

Lee rolled his eyes. "I mean, yes ma'am."

A little while later, when Mom shuffled back into the family room from the bathroom, she glanced out the front window and put her hands on her hips. "Lee," she said tiredly, "I thought I asked you to close the car windows."

Lee looked up from the TV. "Uh, I forgot," he said.

Dad slammed his La-Z-Boy to the floor. "You said you did it, boy," he growled.

Lee groaned. "Okay, okay, I'll do it," he said.

Dad put his hands on the arms of his chair as if to stand up. "You'll do it now, boy," he said.

Lee dragged himself to his feet. "Okay, okay," he said, then muttered, "—sheesh."

Dad half-rose from his chair. "What?" he yelled.

Lee was halfway out the door. "Uh, yeah—yessir," he said.

Around five on that ordinary May afternoon, big rainclouds bloomed up and darkened the skies and thunder rumbled. Mom sat up from her nap and looked out. "Oh Lee," she said, sounding exhausted even after her nap, "you forgot to close the car windows."

The first raindrops began to splat onto the driveway.

Lee stretched out long on the carpet in front of the TV and yawned.

"Aw, Mom, it's raining," he said. "Do I have to do it now?"

Dad opened his eyes. He'd been napping in front of the TV, but I could tell he'd been awake and listening. "What did you say?" he growled.

"Why can't Virge do it?" Lee asked. "She's not doing anything but reading a stupid book."

Dad was out of his lounge chair then, standing over Lee. "Your mother told YOU to do it!" he screamed, his fists clenched and his face red.

Lee scootched away from him and got up slowly, back to the wall. "But why?" he whined.

"Because I said so, that's why!"

I slipped down the hallway with my book to my room, but in a few minutes, I heard Dad's belt through the wall: *SMACK SMACK SMACK.* In Lee's yelps, I heard rage. The currents under the ordinary May afternoon had hidden something, had churned something to the surface. But what? I didn't understand it.

Later, after the rain had stopped and a heavy wet mist hung just above the grass and street, I smelled something funny from the back porch.

Dad had left in his truck. Mom had fallen asleep again. Lee knelt on the concrete of the porch melting army men with a cigarette lighter into green puddles. He glanced up at me.

"How come you never get in trouble?" he asked.

I thought about it. Dad had acted like I hardly existed since I turned thirteen. He had just disappeared me after I stood up for Mel in church. He hardly seemed to see me. It was like I was a ghost.

I hadn't told anybody about my mixed-up stories that were a sin. I remembered the last time Ricki Ann had stayed over, the magic marker words under my bed. Only God knew about that.

Lee clicked the lighter flame and watched me think.

Donny Lane had disappeared in the night with his clothes and a toothbrush. He didn't even leave a note. We had prayed for him at prayer meeting. His mother's eyes were dark-circled and her whole body sagged. Ronnie had stopped the morning Bible Study group.

Lee waved the flame of the lighter over the barrel of the green man's rifle, and it drooped. "It's like if you do something," he said, "you're invisible. Nobody pays attention. You go read a book or something, and everybody forgets." We both knew that he meant Dad. The little green gun started to drip. "How do you do that?"

He was right. I wasn't sure why or how I got away with breaking the rules. I wasn't sure why he didn't. Maybe nobody much cared about the rules I broke, except me. Maybe it just wasn't important.

I watched the army guy's helmet slipping down toward his shoulders in the lighter's flame. "Gotta keep your head down," I said.

Lee looked up at me. After a second, he laughed. I liked that about my little brother; even when he was his saddest, he liked to laugh.

I blinked. "For now," I said, thinking aloud.

Back in my room, I picked up the May 5 newspaper from my desk. I cut out the pictures of the girl and boy from the newspaper, and the one of the soldiers, and pinned them to my bulletin board next to the old postcard about my homeroom assignment, the lock of my long hair tied in the pink ribbon, the cedar Christmas tree bark shaving, the metal wire from my braces, my letters from Mel, and the PG note stapled to the story I wrote with Miss Williams's comments in red on the bottom: *Very good, Virginia! I love the magical cat! What a mystery! But what did make her change?* I took down the diviner's stick and hung it up again so that its V was down. I got the same marker Ricki Ann had used from my desk drawer and drew a magic marker circle around the diviner's stick on the cork of the bulletin board so that it looked like a peace sign.

I put one knee down on the floor beside my bed. I held my mouth opened and my arms wide, posing like the girl in the picture. It felt like I was waiting for something to fall into my grasp, or like something had been lifted out of my hands. It was the same way I'd seen people at church hold their arms up to heaven when they got the spirit. It was the way I imagined Jesus must have looked in the garden, asking His Father to take His cup of fate from Him. I twisted my face in agony and confusion, in anger swallowed by loss, to try to match her expression. I thought maybe I felt the same way Jesus must have felt. I wondered how He had faced his future.

Reunion: Father

Ed feels a breeze on his face, which is damp with sweat. He thinks he hears something rustle, like feathers, wings. And another sound, a wailing, far away. He is afraid to open his eyes. Has Gabriel arrived for his soul? Have the buzzards found him? Have the winged devils come up from hell?

"Mr. Young?" The voice is soft, familiar.

Ed blinks. The diviner waves a clipboard back and forth over his face. "Huh?" Ed says.

"You went away there for a minute," Jayce says. "You back now?" She stops fanning him and picks up his wrist between her thumb and fingers, checking his heart rate. Ed blinks again. She looks worried. "How are you feeling Mr. Young?" she asks. "Can you answer me?" She watches him. "What do you feel?"

Ed blinks again, trying to clear the dark edges from the blue sky overhead. "Okay," he says. "Heavy. Tired."

She holds a water bottle to his lips. "Have a sip," she says. She cocks her head toward the road. "I think I hear the rescue coming."

The water is cold, good. Ed licks his lips and closes his hand around the wet plastic. He remembers Lee. He remembers looking down at Lee, lying on the ground, just as he himself is now. He remembers his son blinking, just like this, and it is strange, as if he is where Jayce is now, looking down on himself, looking up at himself. Strange. The diviner stands and limps toward a backpack she has left on the ground.

"My son died like this," Ed says aloud. "Heart. Aneurysm. Blood clot. Broke his leg and tried to work in a cast. He worked for me." He watches as she leans on her cane to pick up the pack, her withered leg unable to support weight. "Clot from the leg to the heart they said. He just dropped down on the job. Fell to the ground. Lay there just like this."

"Tell me about your daughter," Jayce says, her back to him as she lifts the bag.

"Died." Ed continues his thought about Lee. The diviner turns and walks back. "Just like this."

She is a shadow against the sky. "She died too?" she asks. Her tone is flat, not shocked. The backpack hangs from her hand.

Ed swallows. "No." He coughs. "No." He is so thirsty all of a sudden. He lifts the bottle to his mouth and tries to suck, but something in his chest is heavy and won't let him breathe in.

The diviner kneels and places one hand over his heart. "My father died of a heart attack," she says. "In his sleep. Quiet. At peace. Just slipped away." Her hand on his chest is warm and light. She takes the water bottle and squeezes it so that a little water pools on his tongue. "I caused him some trouble, like kids do, but he always loved me." She puts the bottle in the dirt and grasps his hand. "I miss him," she says. "I miss my father."

Ed swallows and closes his eyes. "Yeah," he says. Something seems to tickle or move under his shirt, under the warmth of the diviner's touch, the weight of something heavy, the prick of something sharp.

"He taught me to witch the water," she says. "Everything I know."

Ed's skin prickles, not quite itching, but something there, maybe just below the surface.

"He used to say to me," she continues, "J.C . . ."

Ed frowns.

"J.C., he'd say, trust what you feel, mark the spot where you feel it. That's all there is to it. Just an ordinary magic."

Ed looks up at the diviner, her face dark before the sky. "Yeah," he says. "I seen a diviner work before. The way you bring the water up outa dirt is somethin . . ."

She shakes her head. "No," she will say. "I just mark the spot where I feel it. You're the one that's gotta drill down and tap it, get it out of the earth."

Ed watches a thread of dust spin up into the sky beyond the fence, toward the road. The rescue? He listens but hears nothing but the hum of cicadas.

"Like . . . what you do about love," she says. "Love makes your soul crawl out from its hiding place."

"Had a diviner mark a spot once before," Ed says, talking almost to himself. "Another farm. Way back when." He and Virge passed the orange flag in the middle of the pasture that day she almost got snake-bit, on their way to the swamp to kill the snake. He held Virge's hand. "I always regretted not getting around to digging that well, see if something was down there." Her fingers twitched, he remembers, like something was trying to get through her skin.

Backslide

I hear sobs, someone crying, out of the darkness of the forest closing in on each side of the path. Where am I? Not lost, just winding around the back way through a maze of roads toward home. I must be close now.

My hands close around the steering wheel, but it isn't the wheel of my truck; no curve. My arms are apart and I am standing in the cold, breathing hard. The crying is not a child's, the way the twins wake me in the night sometimes; this sounds like a woman, afraid. My shoulder throbs. I must have pulled a muscle. That's it. I've pulled a muscle, skiing. I am on Telemark skis, sliding through the trees, panting. A wind whistles and the trees click-clack; warm air blows into my open mouth. Maybe that is what I heard. I kick out into a clearing below a tall mountain, bare and jagged white against the blue Colorado sky.

It is 1978. I have escaped west, dropped out of college. Why was I there anyway? College education's wasted on a girl. And I'm a woman, not a girl. I sent in ten dollars to get a metal bracelet that says ERA. "Women need to have a constitutional amendment to be equal," I said to my mom. Dad snorted.

I saw a flyer for a meeting about women's rights on campus. I went and watched the door from across the street. The women who entered seemed to know each other; they were friends; they looked cool, too cool for me to be one of them. Some of them looked like men, tough and short-haired. I didn't go in.

Teacher, librarian—those are women's work. I want to be something else; I want to say something, not like a preacher does, but more beautiful. I want to write again. The woman T.A. who taught my composition class chose one sentence from each student's first essay to explain some kind of grammar problem. The sentence from my description of Cumberland Island was last on the sheet she handed out. "What's wrong with this one?" she asked. I wanted to die, to disappear into the floor. Silence. "Nothing," she finally said. "It's perfect. Beautiful." And later, when she made me come to a private conference, she said, "You are a writer, Virge. You have something."

But how could I be a writer when I hadn't ever really lived? How could college teach me to write? And how could I write with Mom and Dad and everyone else right there, an hour away? How could I write with that feeling like God was looking over my shoulder?

I had silence and solitude alone in my little apartment off campus, and I wrote every day, story after story, on my electric typewriter. I fell into other lives, other voices, all in my head, but sometimes I got scared all over again. The people in my stories got mixed-up sometimes.

A man who worked at the Winn-Dixie where I was working to pay my tuition and rent asked me to go out with him to hear a band in a bar. He seemed safe, gentle and kind. He had a lot of stories from the Sixties, when he was a hippie and went to protests. But I was scared of him too. But at least he was a man, someone who wanted to go out with me. I had my first beer. I had my first dance. The one seemed to make my body move into the other, but his arms around me made me feel safe and trapped at the same time.

After he kissed me good-night at my door, I dreamed about my professor, the woman who said I had something. I dreamed we were in her little office, our knees nearly touching. I dreamed she said, "You are something, *aren't you?" I dreamed I leaned in and kissed her.*

Then a big hand on my head pushed me down under water. I couldn't breathe. The water became stone that I couldn't heave away. I woke up gasping in the humidity of a Florida summer night, my heart pounding. I was about to die. About to go to hell. Maybe I should. Maybe I should. I was sick, maybe possessed by a demon, but when I thought of Bobby Martin's dad and felt the cold of his gun in my mouth before he blew his brains onto the garage wall, I knew I was too much of a chicken.

Instead of starting my sophomore year in the fall, I threw away all the stories I had written, packed up my stuff in Gus, my car, turned my savings account into traveler's checks, quit my job at the Winn-Dixie, and headed west toward something completely different. A different way. Toward some new truth. Following the light of the setting sun. Away.

Mom made me promise to visit relatives along the way. I mapped out a route that went to each of the places they lived, but at the top of the Continental Divide—in the big gap between family—Gus started to cough, and I coasted down to a gas station in the resort town below. A golf cart like my Aunt Belle's sat in the parking lot. "Just needs some adjustment for the altitude," the attendant said when he looked under the hood of Gus. "But I can't get to it till tomorrow."

So I found a motel and checked in, bought a paper and read it all the way through. The gossip column reminded me of St. Mary's, small-town chitchat, and the classifieds listed dozens of jobs for the upcoming ski season. I had never even seen snow. I wanted to see snow. I went to the resort employment office and they hired me on the spot as a housekeeper, a maid. "You'll be off by noon most days," the woman said. "So you can ski all afternoon." A room and a season pass came with the job. Skiing? I had never even seen snow.

I moved into a dorm room with another woman, Annie, who was from Minneapolis, like Mary Tyler Moore, for the six months after that day in October. It snowed and snowed and snowed, piling up nearly two hundred inches at the top of the mountain. I did women's work in the morning— making beds, vaccuuming, scrubbing toilets—and I skied every afternoon. Annie took me to bars with other ski bums in the evenings. I didn't write because I was too busy living, making stories out of life, really living. I didn't write because I was never alone. I found my tongue. I drank. I smoked pot. I laughed and talked. I dated boys. But sometimes I felt Annie's accent on my tongue instead of my old Southern twang. Sometimes I dreamed about her tongue touching mine.

I slide a ski out ahead of me, looking up at the mountain ridge. Annie again. I dreamed I kissed her. I still taste her tongue on mine. I am damned to hell. I am terrified.

The wind sweeps up from the valley, warm with the thaw, and I hear the crying again. The ridge above me seems to shift, to ripple, the whiteness sagging inward. I hear rumbling. A clump of snow tumbles downward, *gathering momentum, the hill sliding with it. An avalanche. I hope no one is in the canyon or on the traverse.*

I watch, imagining being buried where everything is white. Sliding in white. Turning over and over, not sure which way is up or down, heaven or hell, backward or forward. No one. Everyone. Someone.

Someone cries as I slide into white. The cold becomes warm, a warm wind in my mouth, in my heart. I am numb. Numb is good. I am not afraid. I will die in pure white. I give in to the slide.

The Funny Story, or Why My Great-Aunt Belle Drives a Golf Cart

"Virrggge . . ." Everywhere I went in the last weeks of junior high, someone hissed my name behind me. "Virrggge . . ." I knew it was Ricki Ann or Michelle or one of that crowd, but when I turned to look, they'd all look past me, pretending nothing had been said. I heard their snickers.

What had I done? Rummaging in my locker, my back stiff, head hunched into the sweaty metallic scent of the dark box, I prayed quickly: *Help God.* Seemed like I was always doing that, though some part of me no longer expected Him to hear. *Help me God. Help me get through seventh grade. Help me get through junior high. Just a few more days. Help.*

It was funny. Until the last quarter of the school year—everyone suddenly taller, the boys meatier and sweatier, and nearly every girl's polyester blouse swelling out with breasts—Ricki Ann had hardly seemed to see me. Mom called her new junior high friends "a fast crowd" in her tssking tone. Ricki Ann hadn't come to church at all since she broke up with Ronnie Lane. I didn't expect her to say "hi" when she saw me in the halls, and I'd thought there was nothing worse than not being best friends anymore, nothing worse than not being friends at all, but then she made me disappear. For a while, I had wanted to be like them, to be one of them. Then it had gotten even worse than being invisible. "Virrrggge . . ." behind my back, over my shoulder, in my ear. My name, my own nickname, short for Virginia, which I hated, and the only alternative to Ginny, which I hated more, had become a curse. But why? Keeping my head down, I shut the locker door as gently as I could and took a deep breath. *Just a few more days, God.* Maybe I was just praying to myself.

"Virrrggge . . ." Michelle held her pre-algebra book in front of her face. I knew it was her. She bent over, giggling, and then a crowd of football players, ninth graders, jostled me aside. Between their jerseys I saw Ricki Ann's eyes, the blue eye shadow and pink powder like a hard mask. She didn't blink, and the smile on her face was nowhere else inside her. I could see that. Tears welled up in my throat, but I swallowed hard and faded back into the other hall, even though it was one way the other way, so she wouldn't see.

Because I knew she could see inside me. I knew she could.

On final exam day in English, Miss Williams leaned back against her desk, arms crossed, and watched us scribble. I knew all the answers and finished the test early. I put my head down on my desk, still holding my pencil. Since I still wasn't sleeping very well at night, I tried to catch up in school when I could.

And then my palm was suddenly wet. The pencil softened. Then it was cold. It wriggled. A snake! I screamed and dropped it.

The clatter on the floor woke me up, and kids all around me were laughing. I focused on the completed English test turned upside-down on my desk. My heart pounded, and my face burned. I couldn't believe I had screamed out loud.

"Viiirrrgggee—" hissed Michelle. Then she snickered. I wished I was still invisible.

"That's enough, class," said Miss Williams.

The boy across from me picked up my pencil and handed it to me. I put it down on my desk and watched it, still feeling it wriggle in my palm.

The English class kept tittering. Most of the kids weren't finished with their exam. Miss Williams put her hands on her hips and glared. I slumped lower in my desk.

Ricki Ann glanced back at me, then looked stolidly ahead. I tried to inhale the tears that were gathering in my nose. *Jesus, please make me disappear.*

Miss Williams scowled as if the chaos was all my fault. My throat constricted. I put my face back down onto the cool pages of my test and let my vision blur into the white.

The class quieted, and I heard the squeak-tap of Miss Williams's heels advancing down my row. I shut my eyes and prayed harder. *I'm sorry, I'm sorry, I'm sorry. Please God. Please make me invisible.* She stopped next to me and I could smell her perfume. Her cool finger touched my arm.

"If you're not feeling well, you can go to the nurse," Miss Williams said softly.

I sat up, but kept my eyes down and shook my head no.

"Maybe you should go wash your face, then," she said.

I could see her smooth brown nylon-cased legs, slim and perfect. I felt all the other kids looking at me. My face was probably blotched from being asleep, my hair tangled. I nodded and slid out of my desk. I followed Miss Williams to the front of the room.

She sat at her desk and began to write out a hall pass, then hesitated and looked around the room. "Who else is finished with the test?" Hands shot up. "Ricki Ann Purvis, why don't you go with Virginia?" she said.

I drew in my breath and felt my face flare again. I kept looking at the gray tile floor, but I heard Ricki Ann's shrug and the jingle of the hippie bells on her leather-fringed purse as she stood up. Miss Williams ripped the note off her pad and gave it to my former best friend, and I followed her plastic go-go boots out of the room and down the empty, echoing hallway.

I walked to the sink, Ricki Ann behind me. The fringed bag jingled, and I heard her rummaging in it. The water rushed, icy and soothing, over my hands. I watched my palms fill and thought of the spring below the tree house at the farm, the day last summer when I laid with my face to the wooden floor, the warmth of Ricki Ann next to me, her smell, the curve of her breast under her shirt. Before junior high. Back when she was my best friend. Before I had become invisible.

I glanced up and met her eyes in the mirror, watching me, the heavy blue eye shadow like bruises, her expression hard. Mocking.

I bent and splashed water on my hot, blotchy face in quick bursts. Ricki Ann hurumphed.

Why did she hate me so much? I forced my eyes up to the glass again. Lines of stringy red-blond hair shielded her face as she looked through her bag. Did she know I had told my mother what she said? But she had hated me before that. She had erased me because of something else. Behind her, graffiti on the sterile, institutional green tile of the girls' restroom: *Fuck!; Marybeth loves Robert; Mr. Collins is a fag.*

My ears burned, and I opened my own purse, took out my comb, and tried to focus on my reflection, on smoothing my short brown hair, on making the part straight. It was all wrong. My eyes, rimmed in red, made me glad for the thick lenses and heavy horn rims of my glasses, even though I had begged and begged just last week for gold metal granny glasses like John Lennon wears. "Too flimsy," Dad had said. "You'll just break 'em."

"But everybody else—" I had started.

"If everybody else jumped off a bridge . . ." Mom chimed in from across the table.

I studied my face in the mirror, rubbing the red spot on the bridge of my nose where headaches always start. Yes, I thought, I would jump.

A match scratched. Ricki Ann lit the cigarette between her lips, staring at me. I sucked in a breath. We could be suspended. I felt like a possum in the headlights, a pink-eyed pathetic prehistoric remnant, mesmerized by the flame, helpless and naked. She waved the match out and let her blue lids slide lazily closed, then open again to meet my eyes.

"Gonna tell?" she dared, her lip curling into a half-smile, "Virrggge?"

That hiss. I fumbled my comb back into my purse.

Ricki Ann laughed once in a loud, "Ha!" and the harsh exhale of sound echoed off the tile in the restroom. "Want one?" she sneered.

Air caught in my chest. I swallowed. I thought of all the times I had seen Ricki Ann and her friends slouched just like this against the sinks, that same slit-eyed expression as they watched me, snickering at me, through the smoky haze, while I sidled along the walls around them. I had mostly stopped going to the restrooms at school because I was afraid

I would be accused with them when Miss Cutler, the stern-jawed Dean of Girls, made one of her sweeps. Ricki Ann's smoke drifted up toward the window, ribboning in the beams.

"Come on, Virge," she whispered. "You know you want to."

I bit my lip. She smiled a little. I did. I did want to. I still wanted to be like them. I wanted to be with them. With her.

I gnawed the inside of my cheek. I had seen a wooden paddle with holes in it hung behind the door in Miss Cutler's office when I'd had to wait there for my father that time I got my period early and bled on the back of my skirt. I thought of my father's eyes, the same hard empty blue as Ricki Ann's. I thought of his belt. "My dad'll kill me," I'd heard Michelle say once, laughing. They all said it like that, the exaggeration manipulating their mouths, their eyebrows, into cartoons. My dad really could kill me.

I could almost feel Ricki Ann's breath as she blew out the smoke, hissing a little. I slipped back, remembering the way that breath had smoothed the skin of my neck when we used to sleep together. When we were still best friends.

I turned. She smiled with the corner of her lip, not a real smile, but a hard, twisted thing.

I looked at the floor. My mouth opened and my words caught in my chest, but I stuttered them out. "It's against the rules."

Her laugh barked. Her arm snaked, waving the cigarette back and forth under my eyes. "Be bad then," she whispered, "Virrggge."

I closed my eyes, but I could see Ricki Ann there anyway, slouching casually against the bathroom wall, her miniskirt tight and her shirt stretched over the silhouette of her bra, a subterranean map. Behind my closed lids, the black plastic skin of her go-go boots glinted, clinging to the curve of her calf. Her long straight orange hair, divided by the pale line of her center part, was like a helmet, her blue eyes were thin slits under the heavy powder of her lids, and her tongue slipped out to moisten her lips.

Please God, I prayed. *Help me.*

"Be in the world, not of the world," Ricki Ann scoffed. "Funny, huh?"

My eyes opened with my mouth, but something closed in my chest.

"Yeah, I heard some of that crap," she said, taking another long drag. "Boooorrrinnng."

I didn't know what to say. Back when we were twelve, when we were friends, I would have. I would have opened my mouth and words would have come out, something flip, something half-smart, and we would have laughed. Maybe we would have made up some game, pretended ourselves into some other place, some other, magic world. But now it was different. Serious. Like the way God had suddenly become serious.

Ricki Ann watched me, silent, and I knew what she was seeing: too tall, too fat, too ugly. Thick horn-rimmed glasses. My skirt brushed my knees—"modesty before the Lord God," Mom said—the run in my suntan nylons patched with clear nail polish, the hair I wasn't allowed to shave rumpled and visible through them. I wasn't one of them. In the world, not of the world. I would never be one of them. I felt my shoulders sagging inward, like wings folding over.

Ricki Ann cocked a sandy eyebrow and offered her cigarette pack to me.

I shook my head. "No, I can't," I said.

Ricki Ann snorted, dropped the cigarette pack back into her bag, and turned to the mirror to examine her makeup, the butt hanging from her lip making her look like someone much older. "Cain't," she mimicked, drawing out the long A and singing my twang. "You cain't have no fun, cain't do nuthin' little Virrggge, kin ya?" She smirked, holding my gaze in the reflection, and took the cigarette from her mouth. "Little cracker," she said. "Little goody two-shoes." She let her eyelids drop into a squint. "Little Virrggge-in," she hissed.

I blinked. *Virgin.*

My Great-Aunt Belle weighed about three hundred pounds, all soft and spreading-out powdery flesh, but she was tough as old collard greens inside. Ricki Ann would have called her "a real character." You could see it in the flint of her keen little eyes. She looked you up and down—seemed like right into you sometimes—and said in her nasally drawl, "Looky here . . ." and then you were in for it. Us kids knew to get out of the way of her cane and her comments, but grown-ups, especially strangers, had this way of being obliterated by Aunt Belle that was something to see.

I got to spend a whole month in St. Mary's at Grandma's house when school was finally out in June. The end of seventh grade at last. Lee had to go to summer school on account of he failed math, and Mom didn't want me at home alone all day while she was at work. I think they wanted to get rid of me. Great-Aunt Belle dropped by Grandma's house every couple of days. She reminded me of Mrs. Rosenbaum, the way she saw everything and wasn't afraid to speak her mind.

Aunt Belle's car backfired and shuddered to silence and I heard the squawk of the door hinges out back. She drove the four blocks to Grandma's house in her battered old Chevy on account of it was too far and too hot to walk with her weight and all. Grandma looked out the screen door and said, "Belle's here," and Papa thought of something that needed doing down in the garden and slipped out through the kitchen door. I was pretty sure that I had mostly mastered invisibility again, so I just burrowed deeper into "I Am Jane's Ovaries" in the *Reader's Digest*—it had a lot of good stuff about anatomy and sex and other grown-up stuff—and pricked up my ears for whatever gossip might spill from Aunt Belle's mouth.

Grandma held the screen door open and Aunt Belle struggled up the steps on her thick legs. "Howdy," she panted, plopping herself, as usual, into the smallest chair in the room, spreading her legs wide, and flapping the skirt of her dress so I got an unsettling view of Aunt Belle's rolled-down nylons, pasty thighs and white panties.

"Lord 'a mercy, it's a hot one, ain't it?"

I looked quickly back at Jane's Ovaries as a blush and a chill collided at the nape of my neck. I felt Aunt Belle's eyes on me.

"Now whose young'un are you?"

I swallowed and looked up, blinking like I was so deep in my reading that I hadn't quite heard.

"Why you know Belle," Grandma said, "that's Mary's girl, Virginia."

"Virge," I mumbled.

"Mary's girl? Well, I'll be! I'd a'thought you was a boy with that short hair."

I flinched inside but kept my face blank. Aunt Belle's eyes had gone narrow, the slits emitting thin beams directed at me. I didn't squirm, but I wanted to. I hoped I wasn't yet grown-up enough to be a target.

"Come over here and give old Belle some sugar," she said. I immediately wished I were more grown up.

I put down my *Reader's Digest* and got up to hug Aunt Belle's neck, a slightly more grown-up version of "giving some sugar." Her skin was damp and she wasn't wearing a brassiere. When she grabbed my waist from her sitting position, my head got smushed down below her chin. I closed my eyes to keep from looking into the soft quaking crevasse of Aunt Belle's cleavage. She yanked me in hard, then let me go, patting my rear end. She grabbed my thigh just above my knee and squeezed.

"Ain't lost none 'a yer baby fat yet," she said, "have ya?" My breath caught in my chest like I had been punched.

I also felt grown-up again all of a sudden, and my shoulders stiffened straight after their initial sag. That was the kind of thing Aunt Belle said mostly to grown-ups.

She looked me up and down, and I knew that moment of sheer nakedness I'd seen terrify my Uncle Junior's new wife, Lucille, when she'd met Aunt Belle the first time. The bride had withstood all the family introductions, from Reverend Sam, Mama's second cousin who handled rattlesnakes when he got the spirit, to Great-Grandmother Willis, who can't move and had been lying like a limp doily in the front room at Aunt Darlene's since I can remember, to Little Sister Willis, the retarded boy who was really most near sixty now and wouldn't let go of your hand if you let him hold it, not to mention the near thirty or so mostly regular kin. And then Aunt Belle stomped up and stood looking at the pretty, plump young woman in the mod, orange-flowered sundress, looking up and down with those sharp eyes, leaning heavily on her cane. "So you the one gone and married our Junior," she'd said.

Lucille had held up pretty good, I had to give her that, even though Little Sister Willis was still clinging to her left hand, which I knew from experience was probably sticky with sweat and popsicle and Lord knows what. Lucille had stared right back at Aunt Belle and said, "Pleased to meetcha, Miz Ledbetter. Donald's told me so much about you."

I heard a couple of snorts from the folks who were close enough to hear that. I was being invisible, sitting on the back stairs watching and listening, and I reckoned maybe Uncle Junior—I'd never heard anybody call him Donald before—hadn't told his fiancée enough about Aunt Belle. Because she looked right back into Aunt Belle's eyes as they swept up and down her, from the orange headband to the orange toenails between the white straps of her new sandals. I figured what Dad says about dogs you don't know was true about Aunt Belle too: You don't ever look 'em in the eye unless you want to get ripped to shreds.

The room had gotten pretty quiet, because we kinfolks who were old enough to know, knew what was coming. As awful as it was when it happened to you, you didn't want to miss it when Aunt Belle leveled someone else.

The bride had swallowed, but she kept looking at Aunt Belle. Uncle Junior cleared his throat. "Uh, Aunt Bu—" It was a feeble effort. His Adam's apple bobbed and he opened his mouth to try again.

Aunt Belle's eyes swept from their inspection of Lucille to Junior. "Whall, Junior," she drawled. No one moved. "You shore do like 'em big, don'tcha?"

That was when Lucille got the same naked look I was pretty sure was on my face that afternoon. Lucille had kind of lurched, but Little Sister's hand was still glued to hers and caught her from stumbling. Her face paled, her jaw slackened, and her eyes darted to Junior. His face was red, but when he opened his mouth, nothing came out. Lucille made her back stiff. Meanwhile, everybody waited, holding their breath. I had figured out then that it was sort of a grown-up test—how you acted toward Aunt Belle.

So when Aunt Belle pinched my baby fat, I just swallowed and said, "Yes ma'am." She chortled like her old Chevy after you turned off the key and let me go.

"Violet," Aunt Belle shouted to Grandma, who was just coming in with a glass of iced tea. "I reckon I got to go to the DMV and get myself a new driver's license."

Grandma's brow creased, then smoothed out. She took a long sip of her tea and held it to her forehead. Aunt Belle guzzled hers down in one long draught, then dug out an ice cube and held it to her throat. Grandma was Aunt Belle's baby sister, and Aunt Belle had pretty much raised Grandma, but Grandma knew how to handle Aunt Belle like nobody else.

"Now Belle," Grandma said. "Didn't you decide maybe it was time to stop drivin' and give that old car to Joey?" She sipped from her tea glass.

Aunt Belle snorted. "Land sakes, Violet. That boy don't 'preciate nothing." She rattled her ice cubes. "He says it ain't cute enough fer him. Says he'd just sell it when he goes back to New Orleans anyway." Grandma shifted uncomfortably in her chair and glanced at me. Aunt Belle didn't bother to drop her voice like most folks did. "You know, Lord forgive me for sayin' it 'bout my own child, but I declare, I b'lieve that boy is funny."

Grandma sat up. "Virginia, why don't you go out to the kitchen and get your Aunt Belle another glass of iced tea."

I looked up, blinking like I hadn't really been listening. "Uh, oh, yes ma'am." I put my magazine down and reached for Aunt Belle's iced tea. She fished the ice cube from between her breasts and popped it back into the glass.

"Yes sir," Aunt Belle continued, oblivious to Grandma's grimace. "Livin' over there in that French Quarter with that other fella, wearin' all them flowerdy shirts and lettin' his hair grow so long . . ."

I tried to walk slow. Folks said it that way sometimes, "funny," and I knew it had something to do with men like Cousin Joey. It wasn't just his clothes and his hair, because there were plenty of other guys who looked like that these days, like Tom Jones and Dr. Rose and the hippies. It was one of those grown-up codes I hadn't been able to break yet: *funny.*

Grandma shushed Aunt Belle, and I went on out to the kitchen. It wasn't funny-haha, so it had to be funny-odd. When Dad said it, he made his voice go high and fluttered his fingers. It must be something bad because his face looked like he tasted something gross. Mom would just give him that weird embarrassed look she got sometimes and say, "Oh Ed." Of course, Mom got that look at a lot of stuff, like when she heard that Tonya Freedland was going to join the air force and told me, "Well, you know some people say that women who go into the service are all *lesbians,* but I don't think that's true. Tonya's a fine Christian girl and I think it's a good choice for her." Her eyes had kind of glazed over when she said the word "lesbian," and I didn't want her to be embarrassed more, so I'd just nodded, "Uh huh." But I had looked it up in the dictionary later. I couldn't figure out how joining the air force would make Tonya Freedland have something to do with a Greek island. Her uniform was pretty sharp though. That was right before I cut my hair short and Dad said I looked like a boy, and Mom got that funny look on her face again, like when I got the C-minus in Home Ec: "Well at least you passed," she'd sighed.

I came back into the living room with Aunt Belle's iced tea just as Grandma said, "Well, I reckon I'd better go to the DMV with you then." Aunt Belle took the glass and drained it. I watched the thick layer of sugar in the bottom ooze toward her mouth.

"Tomorra', first thing," Aunt Belle said. "We'll go shoppin' over to Cloth World and out to Morrison's Cafeteria afterward."

Grandma sighed and nodded.

Aunt Belle heaved herself up out of her chair. "Well, it's been mighty nice vistin' with ya'll this afternoon. Violet, you tell that husband of yours I was sorry to miss him."

She gave me this speculative look up and down. I braced myself. "Don'tcha worry none 'bout that little bit a baby fat, girl, now ya hear?" I grinned weakly, and she handed me her empty tea glass. "Boys like somethin' they kin grab onto."

Aunt Belle drove fiercely, her head flung back and her elbow out the window, gas pedal mashed to the floor. Her rearview mirror dangled, held to its stem with Scotch tape. I sat with my feet crossed under me on the backseat, trying not to look down where I could see the gray tar of the highway rushing by through the holes in the floorboard. Grandma was stiff and straight in the shotgun seat, clutching the door handle with one hand and her handbag with the other.

"Get outa the way ya goll-darn log truck!" Aunt Belle yelled.

I had decided to come along so I could get a driver's manual to study for my learner's permit even though I wouldn't be old enough for another year and a half. I figured you could never study enough.

Aunt Belle jerked the steering wheel to the left to pass, then stomped the brake and jerked back to the right to avoid the oncoming car. She shook her fist out the window as the other car wailed its horn in passing. Maybe I shouldn't have come along.

The logs on the truck seemed about four feet from our windshield, held on only by a couple of chains. They bounced when the truck bounced. Aunt Belle craned her neck to see around the truck, then swerved into the other lane and mashed the gas pedal again. Another car was coming, but this time she just grinned wickedly and hunched farther over the wheel like she was urging a horse to go faster. The Chevy roared because it had no muffler, but it didn't pick up speed. I closed my eyes.

When we cut back to the right, I could feel the heat of the truck's engine through my window. I looked up and saw the driver's eyes popped really wide and the vein on his neck bulging. I was supposed to be scared, but the rearview mirror swung wide and I saw Aunt Belle grin. Her hard, glittering eyes met mine. My breath caught in my chest. Suddenly, the exhilaration of passing that truck was more than just reck-lessness, it was a calculated thrill, like smoking in the restroom with Ricki Ann—something I suddenly wished I had done. The other car jerked off onto the shoulder and the road opened straight and flat and dull before us, the mirages melting as we barreled on. I grinned.

Aunt Belle winked.

"Belle!" Grandma sounded like a teacher, her voice a warning that Aunt Belle and I both recognized. Aunt Belle let off the gas a little, and I studied the back of her head. Had she really winked at me?

At the DMV, Aunt Belle took a number and we sat as close to the electric fan as we could. After awhile, a man and a young woman—not much more than a college girl—sat down across from us, and the baby the girl was holding started to fuss in the heat.

"Poor little thing," Grandma said.

"Yes, ma'am," the woman said. "And he's got a heat rash too." Her voice was clipped and precise. They were Yankees.

Grandma tskked sadly.

Aunt Belle's eyes narrowed and she studied the couple carefully. I held my breath. The man kept reading his magazine. His hair was graying, but shaggy over his collar and ears, and he wore wire-rimmed glasses and a bright, splashy tie with blue jeans. Grandma and the woman talked about remedies for the heat rash.

"I just never imagined it would be so hot down here," the woman said.

"So you're from up North," Aunt Belle said. It sounded like an accusation. The man glanced up, then back to his reading. I swallowed and felt Grandma tense up beside me.

The girl smiled. "Why yes," she said. "We've just moved from New York." I liked the way the words clipped from her tongue. She sounded smart. I wondered if Mel was going to start talking like that. I wondered if I could.

"My husband is a professor at the college," she said proudly. Aunt Belle's eyes were like iron. I felt sorry for the girl. She didn't suspect a thing.

Aunt Belle sat back in her chair and crossed her arms. "Is that so?" she drawled. "Your husband's a professor, is he?" She gave the man another long look. I cringed . . . trick question.

"Yes, ma'am," the woman said, rocking her baby again.

"And where's your husband today?" Aunt Belle asked, her voice as thick as the sugar syrup in the bottom of an iced tea glass.

The girl blinked and the man looked up. Even the baby stopped fussing, confused maybe by the sudden silence. She looked at the man, then back to Aunt Belle. "Why, this is my husband," she said.

"Ummmhmm," Aunt Belle replied. She folded her hands primly together over the pocketbook on her lap and pressed her lips together. Sweat trickled down my spine.

"Number thirty-two!" the clerk shouted.

"Belle," Grandma said, her tone warning.

The girl stared at Aunt Belle's eyes, trapped. Aunt Belle nodded slowly, glancing for a second at the man, then back at the girl.

Grandma stood up. "That's your number, Belle," she said.

Aunt Belle planted her cane and pushed herself to her feet. "Waall," she said, standing close to the couple and looking down at the girl. She drew out her words in long syllables: "An ole man gener'ly *does* make a better husband."

Aunt Belle passed the written test and the eye test with no errors. "And I don't even wear specs!" she crowed.

The man behind the counter seemed tired and unimpressed by a seventy-year-old woman with twenty-twenty vision. "Officer Shakespeare will be along directly for your road test," the man said. "Wait here."

I slumped down below the counter, trying hard to reestablish the invisibility Aunt Belle had pretty much blown. I thumbed through the little paperback handbook of Georgia driving laws, hoping the couple from New York wouldn't have their number called before Aunt Belle went for her driving test. Since I actually lived over the state line in Jacksonville, I would have to study all over again for the Florida learner's permit when I turned fifteen, but it was a book and it made me look busy and I figured driver's tests were probably about the same wherever you went.

Grandma spoke low to Aunt Belle. "Belle, you got to try to be nice now. Calm down and shush and try not to make anybody else mad."

Aunt Belle snorted. "Officer Shakespeare, what kind of name is that?"

Grandma poked her hard. "Belle, that Officer Shakespeare can make sure you never drive a car again," she warned. "You be nice."

"Shakespeare was the guy that wrote *Romeo and Juliet*," I said. "I read it for English class."

Aunt Belle scowled at me. "Is that so, now?"

I felt like I was about two. "I made an A on my report," I mumbled.

"What's some English playwritin' feller got to do with the rules of the road is what I want to know?"

I wasn't doing too well with my invisibility, so I slid down to sit on the cool tile floor.

"Mrs. Belle Ledbetter," the clerk called out.

"You be nice, Belle," Grandma reminded as Aunt Belle raised her hand and waved.

"Over here!" she yelled. The sack of flesh under her arm flapped. "I'm Belle Ledbetter."

Two very shiny black shoes tapped over to us. I could see my reflection in them. I followed the crisp green crease of the pants to a fine pale hand holding a clipboard, a thick black belt, and finally to a brown shirt with silver badge that swelled out over breasts. I scrambled to my feet.

"Hello, Mrs. Ledbetter," she said in a low voice. "I'm Officer Shakespeare, and I'll conduct your road test today."

Grandma poked Aunt Belle and gave her a look, but Aunt Belle was staring at Officer Shakespeare. Her hair was short, like mine, and brown, like mine. Her nose was freckled, like mine, and she was only about an inch taller than me, on account of I had got a growing spurt this year. I wished she were wearing a gun. I had shot Ricki Ann's dad's Colt .45 when I was twelve, and I liked the way it made you feel big and strong as any guy. Not that this woman needed anything besides that uniform and that badge to look big and strong. Officer Shakespeare smiled at me. Even though her uniform was like a man's, she didn't look mixed-up at all.

"You all will have to wait here for Mrs. Ledbetter," she said. She was saying it to both me and Grandma, but the way she looked right into my eyes made me feel like one of the grown-ups.

Grandma went stiff beside me and I glanced over. Aunt Belle was dead calm, her eyes glassy, like the ocean before a squall. Officer Shakespeare must have felt it too, because she didn't say anything for a minute. Aunt Belle looked her up and down. I watched her chins unfold and settle back on top of each other like an accordion as she tilted her head up and down, up and down.

"Mrs. Ledbetter?" Officer Shakespeare seemed puzzled, but she stared right back at Aunt Belle.

Aunt Belle fished in her pocketbook and pulled out the jelly jar she always kept in there. Deliberately, she unscrewed the cap and spat a wad of tobacco juice inside, all the time trying to stare down Officer Shakespeare. She screwed the lid back on, tight. Extra tight.

"Officer Shakespeare," Aunt Belle said.

"Yes ma'am?" Officer Shakespeare wasn't even sweating, but my fingers were stuck together and I heard my teeth grind.

"You looky here," Aunt Belle said. She gestured at the uniform with her jelly jar, raising it up and down like some religious thing.

"Belle," warned Grandma.

"That getup," Aunt Belle said. She unscrewed the lid again, spat brown, retightened the lid. "Waaallll." Her syllables were getting longer. "You shore do look like a feller in that getup."

I felt like a balloon so full I was about to hiss air. Grandma trembled like a tightwire beside me.

Aunt Belle waited for her target to collapse. Like Lucille had done when she'd run from the house bawling, dragging along Little Sister Willis who wouldn't let go her hand. Like the old husband just a half hour ago who'd turned so bright red I'd thought his neck was going to bust his tie, and his young wife who'd joined her baby in his yowls. Like I'd wanted to when she'd squeezed my baby fat the day before.

But Officer Shakespeare just smiled. I felt lightheaded, studying that smile. She kept her eyes locked with Aunt Belle's, waiting. It was like I was about to learn some new language or a complicated formula, the answers to the test. I felt naked. I felt almost like I used to at the end of my stories, before I went to sleep. Aunt Belle stopped chewing. The fans whirred. The bell on the door jingled as someone left. Officer Shakespeare just smiled.

Finally, she lifted her clipboard. Aunt Belle snorted out a short breath, and then she blinked several times. She blinked! I caught my breath as she fumbled with her jelly jar, nearly dropping her pocketbook. Aunt Belle had blinked. Officer Shakespeare nodded, just slightly, and glanced at me, still smiling. For a second, I thought she had winked. "Shall we take that test now, Mrs. Ledbetter?" she said.

I don't know for sure what happened on Aunt Belle's driving test while Grandma and I waited at the DMV, but afterward, when Grandma was driving the Chevy home, Aunt Belle turned around and looked me up and down for a long time. I tried to look her in the eye.

"You're a funny one," she said, "ain'tcha, girl?"

So Great-Aunt Belle drove a golf cart now. Cousin Joey came to St. Mary's to sell the Chevy because she lost her license, and he was lots of laughs, always teasing me. He had his mama's little black eyes, but his eyes twinkled, even when he squinted. He looked at me, up and down, ruffled my short hair and said, "Oh, girl. Just you wait. You are gonna be something." I didn't know what that meant, but I laughed anyway. Joey was funny—funny ha-ha. Maybe he was funny-odd too, but whatever that was couldn't be so awful.

Joey bought Aunt Belle a golf cart so she could still get around St. Mary's since she couldn't walk on account of the heat and her weight and all. Lying in the hammock under the wisteria vine, reading the *Reader's Digest* while the cicadas droned on, I eyed it, just sitting there in the driveway while Great-Aunt Belle visited with Grandma. Ricki Ann would have said maybe we should steal it for a joyride. But Ricki Ann wasn't here. And even though I heard her voice in my head suggesting it, like God maybe, I wasn't Ricki Ann. I wasn't sure who I was or what I was, or which parts of me were sin and which were right, but I wasn't mixed-up about that.

Failing the driving test didn't slow Aunt Belle down much anyway. On our way out of town at the end of June in St. Mary's, heading home for a couple of weeks before my big trip up North, me and Mom passed her in her golf cart on the highway, electrically silent, the pedal mashed to the floor. The tasseled fringe of the little cart whipped back in the wind, and my Great-Aunt Belle drove, license or no, with her bare arm slung along the back of the seat, grinning her fierce grin, a long trail of log-truck drivers cussing behind her.

Reunion: The Dead

Bunch of Bible thumpers and idiot screamers. Belle—the shadow that is Belle on this other side called dead—mashes the pedal to the floor and bounces her golf cart—an *intention* of a golf cart now—up onto the curb. Not a one of the protestors moves an inch; they just keep yelling and waving their signs. Fools, alive and wasting that one good life, this one glorious day. Belle hoists herself off the seat and passes right through the window glass and bookshelves. She wants to see this writer. Mary's child. All growed up.

The bookstore is full of both living people and the ghosts who are shades of their old selves. Belle recognizes most of them.

Her boy Joey over there in a flowered shirt. Bein' funny'd done him in. Pitiful. Should've lived a good long life, but he let that gay disease catch 'im. He waves and she drifts over. She'd nursed 'im along those last months, after that feller he lived with went first. Buried 'em both in her own family plot. Cuz they was family.

"Hey Mama," he says. "Quite a crowd for our girl, huh?"

"Yes, indeedy," she replies, looking around. Near a hundred foldin' chairs, mostly filled with people, and a fair number of shades too, though they is harder to count. Now that one . . . "Ain't you her grandma on t'other side?" she asks.

The shadow that was Iris Young when she lived wafts to the back of the bookstore, ignoring the fat ghost who has spoken to her, and watches as Virge arrives. Iris doesn't speak anymore, not on this side. She has lost the habit. Or maybe something in her has just grown to fruition.

That woman, Mary, who married her son, Ed, is with Virginia. She's held up well, Iris thinks, older now but still vigorous, a young old woman. The bookstore manager escorts them to the front of the room. Where is Ed? He should be here. He's still among the living. He ought to be proud. Iris would like to tell him that.

Virge looks like me, Iris thinks. Tall, long nose, serious green eyes . . . definitely a resemblance. And a writer and a college professor, too. A career woman, just as she would have been had she gone to medical school instead of marrying. She cringes, remembering that last outburst at the nursing home, not in her right mind: "You can't tell me what to do! I have a college education!" Oh, no regrets now, she thinks. That's for the living.

She watches her daughter-in-law, Mary, take a place in the front row, sitting up straight and tall. The woman has some backbone after all. I could have been nicer to her, Iris thinks. I wish I'd taught my son better about love, that love doesn't flinch from the truth. Then she shakes herself. No use regretting anything now.

When the writer sits down on top of the table at the front of the room to read, the ghost who was her brother, Lee, is reminded of his big sister high in a pine tree with a book. All alone up there. She smiles and looks around. "Thank you for coming." She nods toward the front of the store where the protesters still chant outside. "Thank you for being brave."

Brave, Lee thinks. He'd told her not to tell Dad, not to come out to the world. She'd done it anyway. Good for her. More like him than either of them had known. Or maybe he was more like her. Lee wonders if the silence feels like a four-by-four falling on your head. Like being dead.

• • •

Virge takes a book from the stacks on the table, white titles screaming from red covers: *Sinner*. "This chapter is titled 'Funny,'" she says, and begins to read.

Why that's me, Belle thinks. She chuckles. If that young'un only knew. She pokes her elbow into Joey's side, or tries to. He doesn't feel it, of course, but he feels the intention, glances at her and smiles. "You always did tell it like it was, Mama," he says. "Nothin' got by those keen little eyes."

Lee grins at the description of Aunt Belle. He'd "borrowed" that golf cart once and got the tar whipped out of him. But man, it was fun. He'd had a glorious ride. A short and glorious ride. Just one day alive.

His kids, growing up without him, have fun at Green Acres with his dad now. The old man buys the boys minibikes and sticks cash in their pockets. The big man. The rich man. Grandpop. They don't know that dark side of Dad. His dad's eyes had been dark with something in that last human connection Lee made on his last day alive. Love? Sorrow? Fear? Maybe something the old man wanted Lee to take away with him into the shady place on the other side.

Virge reads, "I think my dad really could kill me." She glances up, directly at Lee. Does she see him, see his ghost? She blinks. She shakes her head and looks back at the page, swallows and reads on.

Virge is evidence, Lee thinks. Dad can't just wish away his hard, mean part. Why won't he choose the work of love? I wish folks had bigger hearts, Lee thinks. His dad, his sons, himself. He lets his attention drift to his girl, to Leigh Ann. Her heart is big. She's brave too, he thinks. No. No regrets.

Iris thinks about love as Virge clears her throat. It leads you to lose yourself—a little like dying—but then, if you're brave or lucky, you open your eyes and see that you're not alone, and you live again. She observes the little girl on the sideline, her great-granddaughter. You're not alone, Iris thinks. Live this glorious day.

Virge pauses to sip from a plastic water bottle, those ugly, ubiquitous substitutes for beautiful clean glasses . . . And when Virge glances up, she looks right at Iris, as if seeing her.

Sometimes they do—people see shades, see ghosts. But like Virge now, they usually just blink, shake their heads, look down at the page again and go on.

Something in Belle—like the heart she had when she was still alive—swells as Virge finishes the story, and Joey laughs aloud. Virge glances their way. Naw, she can't see 'em. Belle grins. Virge smiles and sips from her water bottle.

"The last time I saw my Great-Aunt Belle was at my grandmother's funeral," Virge says to the audience in the bookstore. "I hadn't come out yet, not to the world, to my dad, but I was divorced, dating women, had my hair cut all spiky short. I felt like I'd finally figured something out." She smiles, remembering. "We all went to the cemetery. A glorious late spring day. And Great-Aunt Belle drove up in her golf cart." The audience laughs. "And she came up to me and said, 'Now whose girl are you?' And I told her, 'Mary's daughter.'" Virge pauses and looks out into gaps in the audience where, it seems, she sees something. "Aunt Belle," she says, "looked me up and down and up and down. I just stood there, waiting to take the hit."

The audience laughs on cue. Belle chuckles. "I waited." Virge pauses. "Aunt Belle looked me up and down, and then she said, 'W'alll'—just like she always did—'w'alllll' . . . and then, 'you shore did grow up to be a beauty.'"

Virge ducks her head. "No one ever said anything like that to me before. Thirty-something years old. And I will always believe that it was not physical beauty that Great-Aunt Belle saw, but the truth of who I was, who I had finally come to be."

Joey's ghost puts his arm around Belle and hugs her close, or at least that is the intention Belle feels. Sentimental fool. She nods at the young'un across the room. "You see that one?" she asks Joey.

"Aunt Belle always said it like it was, no mincing words. No silences." Virge stops.

The girl, Leigh Ann, stands a little apart, on the fringe of the group, watching and listening. The crowd outside was smaller than she had expected, only a dozen protesters from First Baptist, holding signs. She didn't know any of them, but she had still waited until the preacher started leading them in a prayer to slip out of the alley where her bike is stashed and into the bookstore. The room inside is crowded too, stuffy with bodies and shadows. Now, watching this woman—a real writer, her Aunt Virge—talk, the big stack of red and white books behind her, she feels less afraid.

The writer looks around the room. "Anybody want to ask questions?"

Leigh Ann squeezes her copy of the book in her hand. She will have to take off the cover before she gets home, or maybe she can hide it somewhere outside the house. This is her own copy, not the one she read in the library. She paid for it with her own money and nobody can take it away. Maybe she will get Aunt Virge to sign it somehow, but how, without Grandma Mary seeing her? People in the room rustle, resettling, now that the reading part is over. "Questions?" Aunt Virge asks again.

The girl's arm rises of its own accord, lifting up into the air without her meaning it to, like magic. Like that chapter about the girl in the book. Her heart beats faster. The writer looks around the room at the waving hands. She points at Leigh Ann. "Yes?"

Her throat feels open, her teeth slick, and her tongue alive. "Where do your ideas come from?" she asks. "I mean . . ." She hesitates. "How do you know what all those other people in the book think? How do you make the characters so real? Are they real?" She feels naked, like everyone is looking at her. She suddenly thinks of Daddy and wishes he was here. Aunt Virge smiles, and the girl feels something else, something surging through her, but not her. Something stirring in the air around her.

"Good question," says the writer. "I know these people in the book because they are all in me. They are all parts of me. Sure, parts of them are real, but most of them—the characters I write about—are just that . . . what I've made up from bits and pieces of myself and my experiences." She pauses and looks around, hunching forward on the tabletop. "It seems like they're real because they almost are—at least to me. Because they are parts of me. Like ghosts. Like shades of me, shades of the true me, the real world."

Leigh Ann tilts her chin up. She wants to tell her aunt, the writer, that she, Leigh Ann, is real.

The writer smiles, continuing. "An odd old friend of mine once said to me, 'You've got to love your words, love your characters.' I think that maybe love is part of why these characters seem real. I love them, every one of them unlovable, every one of them a sinner, because they are all in me. The novelist Iris Murdoch once said, 'Love is the difficult realization that something other than oneself is real.'"

Leigh Ann cocks her head, memorizing the line. The writer squints at Leigh Ann, her brow furrowing as if she is trying to see something or remember something. Someone coughs. Leigh Ann sees Grandma Mary lift up in her chair, straining to see into this part of the room. Daddy would have brought me here, she thinks. Leigh Ann feels a rustle in the darkness around her, almost a little shove. She inhales, then raises her hand again. The writer blinks, then nods. "Aunt Virge," Leigh Ann says, "I am real."

Backslide

The truck slides on the gravel, the frozen mud of spring perhaps, nearing
the top of the hill, the long way around. I've been traveling this way so long,
lost in the maze, that all these roads seem the same. When I get there—
home—everyone will be waiting, like at the reunion—though that has not
yet happened—or at a Sunday dinner in St. Mary's, a holiday. Maybe the
civil union we have planned for August, the joining of our family. Ruthie
and the twins and me. Maybe my brother and his children, my grandparents, Mom and Ricki Ann, Ronnie Lane, Mrs. Rosenbaum, old Aunt Belle.
Maybe even Dad. But some of them are gone on. How can they all be here
in the cab of the truck with me? In me? Is this road almost ended, or am I at
another fork, another cul-de-sac?

I feel the tires slip, but this time on wet asphalt, not snow on gravel. It
is 1975. The rain pounds down hard on the roof of Gus, my first car, and
the wipers slap back and forth, back and forth. I'm driving south instead
of north, but direction doesn't matter, so long as I'm driving away forever,
alone, away from Dad.

I can't believe I have escaped. Graduated from high school. Saved up *enough to pay for my first semester at the University of Florida. Convinced Mom to let me go, to help me find a little apartment off campus, two rooms upstairs in an old house with a private entrance, bathroom and kitchen. I was too afraid to live in a dorm, to share a room with another girl. What if I dreamed about her? What if I had those feelings? The old lady's apartment is just as cheap, and I know I'll be safer alone. The windows in my new place look out into a yard filled with ferns and palmettos, dark under the spreading limbs of live oak trees. It reminds me of the view from my old tree house at Green Acres, or of being in St. Mary's at Grandma's house, or in the campground on Cumberland Island, where I spent the summer. The park service is making the island a national seashore. Protected forever. My cousin, Maggie, and I worked there for two weeks, and it was just as I imagined it would be, just like a going-to-sleep story, but real. Without the tamed horse. With mosquitoes and snakes. Without any kisses. But safe. Surrounded by water. Away.*

Stories are why I am going to the university, I think. Dad says I should do something to get a good job, study business maybe, but I want to keep writing stories. He doesn't have any say anyway. He thinks education's a waste for a girl. At least I can be an English teacher like Miss Williams. Maybe a librarian. I'm not sure. Mostly, I just want to be away.

Florida 301, the four-lane highway that spans most of the 80 miles from Jacksonville to Gainesville, curves through the hilly heart of Florida, through Starke's strawberry farms and pecan groves, giving way to orange trees and cold spring-fed rivers like the Itchetucknee, where the aquifer burbles to the surface further south. I drive slow, feeling the tires slip in the rain puddling and channeling on the pavement, scared of losing control. I think I'm scared of who I might be when I get to my new life at college, especially when I remember what happened to me that summer when I was thirteen. I'm still scared of hell too, because it still seems so real sometimes. And I've been scared of Dad all along. I see that now. At least whoever I'm going to be will be the me that's been hiding safe inside, or maybe all the mes that seem to live in my head.

I wish my drive to college were north, but I can't afford it, even with a scholarship, and Dad won't help because education's a waste on a girl. He's wrong. I won't waste it. And even if I don't get a great job, at least I'll be on my own. Free. And someday I'll go north again, like that summer I was thirteen. Part of me is already there, left there. I wish I could have said that to Dad, wish I'd been brave enough to tell him. It feels wrong to keep it inside, to only be able to say it to him in my head.

Gus hydroplanes a little and my hands grip the wheel tighter. I'm passing the state penitentiary, the turn-off toward Green Cove Springs where somewhere in the maze of dirt roads is the old farm, Green Acres. I drove out there once after I bought Gus, but I couldn't find the way. I remember bouncing into Ricki Ann in the back of the pickup, looking backward into the dust. I wonder if Skipper is still in the knot hole. I still think about the snake, about flying away from the snake, like magic. I wonder if I've left that part of me behind forever. I wonder if I'll always be this alone. I wonder if this feeling of Gus flying over water, a little out of control, on my way to a new life, is the same kind of magic.

The Horses Story, or How I Came to See Into the Aquifer

At the end of my stay in St. Mary's, I accidentally-on-purpose broke my old horn-rimmed glasses so that I would need a new pair. First I tried dropping them onto the concrete porch, and when that didn't break them, I just stepped on them. The crunch under my shoe gave me a thrill like when Aunt Belle passed the log truck, even though it was a sin to waste hard-earned money. I thought I could talk Mom into those John Lennon granny glasses. Even better than that, though, Dr. Allen said I should try contact lenses. "It might keep her from needing a new prescription so often," he said to Mom.

It was almost like my sin paid off. I hardly felt guilty at all, because with the contact lenses in, I felt like blind Saul after he got saved and got his sight back and took a new name, Paul, to show how he'd changed.

I blinked and blinked again. The words in the diplomas on the wall seemed to jump out at me, black and sharp. The instruments on the countertop gleamed, each an individual and purposeful shape. I opened and shut my eyes, and I didn't care that the contact lenses rubbed against the insides of my eyelids. I could see more clearly than ever in my thirteen-going-on-fourteen years. I didn't know the world had such fine lines.

"How does that feel?" Dr. Allen asked.

Like I've got something in my eyes, I thought. But I said, "Okay." I blinked again. Wow. "It's fine," I said. I looked at Mom. I could see every single hair on her head instead of the general outline of a hairstyle. I had never noticed the little lines next to her eyes and mouth. She smiled, and I grinned back. "Wow," I said. It was like I had never seen anything before. Everything had edges, definition.

"You'll get used to the discomfort," Dr. Allen said. He twirled away on his little stool. Behind me. I could see him even as he went around me! With my glasses, he would have blurred away as soon as he moved to the side. "You won't even notice it after a while," he said.

At the end of July, more than a year after the astronauts first walked on the moon and a few days before I would leave for my big adventure up North, I put my face mask into water—my new contact lenses making everything clear—and looked down into a turquoise blue cavern called Blue Hole far, far below. I looked into the aquifer.

I fought with my arms and legs to keep my inner tube stationary against the river current. Mom had told me that hundreds of gallons well up from Blue Hole every second, from limestone caves under the land. The aquifer bubbled up to make the Itchetucknee River, where the church youth group had come to float away a summer day. The water was very clear. My legs kicked silently below, stirring up millions of white bubbles.

The trip took all day: two hours riding in the beds of pickup trucks to get there, five hours of floating down the river, lunch, and the two-hour truck ride home. We met at six in the morning, the tar parking lot of the church already warm under our feet. As we started to pile into trucks, Dad grabbed my arm. "Nope. You're riding with me." He gave me a shove toward his truck. "Right there." He pointed to the part of the bed closest to the cab, in the middle of an inflated truck tire tube. I boosted myself up the side and settled in, trying to hold my thighs up off the sides of the tube so they don't look so fat.

"Cool." Ronnie Lane dropped into the tube next to me and grinned.

My contact lenses rubbed the insides of my eyelids a little when I blinked. Why was he sitting next to me?

Ronnie had unbuttoned the top buttons on his shirt so the shiny black hairs growing down the middle of his chest showed. "You sure look different without glasses," he said.

I flushed. "Uh, thanks." I noticed that his belly pooched out over the waistband of his cut-off jeans shorts. His skin was pasty under the black hairs.

The backs of my legs grew sweaty, but I didn't dare move them on account of the black inner tubes had soaked up the sun while we roared down the highway, blistering hot where they hadn't been shaded. Me and Ronnie sat with our backs to the cab of the truck, and five other kids lounged on tubes along the sides of the bed and toward the tailgate. I felt Dad behind me, driving, his glance now and then in the rearview mirror. Going backward and forward at the same time reminded me of going to Green Acres down the maze of dirt roads, but everything was different now, all mixed-up. Ronnie sat next to me instead of Ricki Ann. I could see the road receding clearly, and my mouth was empty of metal. I was thirteen.

I was glad the wind and the tires on the road were so loud. Ronnie tried to yell something to me a couple of times, but I couldn't hear what he said. His mouth formed words that rushed away into the wind. I kept my eyes squinted so that my contact lenses wouldn't blow out in a stray gust, watching him, and shrugged to show that I didn't understand. He had pimples on his neck, and his mouth seemed fleshy, his lips too red.

When the trucks finally got to the river, to the clear, cool pool of little springs that began the Itchetucknee River, I stood up and stretched, then sat on the side of the truck to slide off. Ronnie Lane, who had jumped down first, reached up, grabbed my waist, and lifted me off and onto the ground, pulling me toward him so that I stumbled into his chest.

"Hey, sorry," I said. Why had he done that? I didn't need help. I pushed back quickly, mostly because his skin was all clammy with sweat, and hairy. His hands pressing into my sides made me feel squeezed, but not in a good way or a brotherly hug way. Just funny.

Ronnie grinned. "No problem, Virge," he said. He tried to lay an arm across my shoulders, but I slipped out from under it. What was wrong with him?

I ran with the other girls to the water, slipped out of my shorts at the edge, and dove in, coming up gasping with the shock of the freezing spring water. My head hurt like I had swallowed ice cream too fast. I blinked the water out of my eyes. My contacts. I had forgotten about my contacts. What if they washed out? I kept my head up, shivering, and kicked back to the edge.

Ronnie still stood beside the truck, but my dad was talking to him. Ronnie Lane is cute, I kept telling myself. That was what girls said. He's cute. That was what I was supposed to think. But it seemed wrong, weird—not exactly like a sin, just mixed-up. I didn't trust him. If he thought I told on him and Ricki Ann, why was he being nice to me? He would be going off to high school the next year. Why would he talk to any seventh grader, even one going into eighth?

I treaded water, watching my dad's face, serious and stiff, like a mask. I couldn't hear what he was saying, but Ronnie's eyes widened and when Dad walked away, Ronnie shook his head. I guessed he was cute, but the thought of his arm on my skin made me shiver and my stomach clench. Maybe it was me. Maybe something was really wrong with me.

At Blue Hole, divers in black rubber suits with tanks and flippers swam down, dwindling smaller and smaller in the turquoise water below me, then vanished into the cavern, the aquifer. I had never seen under water before, because of wearing glasses, but my contact lenses were secure within my swim mask. It was so clear. Even down below the water the world was sharp, everything defined and distinct. Grasses waved greenly at the edges of the river. Fishes swerved in and out. More little men in black rubber swam into the spring's current, then disappeared into the turquoise opening. I tried to imagine what it was like in there, getting darker and darker, a labyrinth of tunnels branching off. All of the earth pressing down and the water pushing past to escape. Dependent on that tank on your back for breath. The silence.

I gave my tube a push back upstream, took a deep breath and tried to dive down, swimming against the water gushing from Blue Hole. The current was too strong. I needed flippers. I popped back up and grabbed my inner tube before it got too far toward the bank. Ronnie Lane and some high school girls were floating past in the river.

"He said he'd kill me!" Ronnie's voice floated across the surface of the cold water. I held my tube with one hand, keeping my head on the side opposite the group, listening. "Can you believe it?" He laughed harshly. "Like something out of the Old West or something." The girls laughed too. "What an old fogey," Ronnie said.

"Poor kid," said one of the girls. "He'll probably never let her go out with guys."

"Yeah," said another one. "Wow."

Ronnie's voice deepened, mimicking my father. "Stay away from my daughter, boy."

I twirled my tube so that they floated on past without seeing me, down the river ahead of me. I swallowed in a deep breath and put my face mask into the water again, but I didn't see anything but turquoise. The clear plastic of the mask was blurry inside, with tears.

I liked to died when I saw the snake. I was alone on the river, float-ing behind the rest of the group, looking down through my mask, lying on my stomach across the top of my inner tube. The grasses twenty or so feet below bent and fluttered with the current, like long green fin-gers waving me ahead, downstream, toward something. I saw fishes and sunken logs, another world down there. Clean and clear. I wondered if it was really silent or if it burbled in a language for different ears. The sun blazed into the skin of my back even though I was wearing a T-shirt over my swimsuit—Dad's orders—but my legs and face, and my belly through the inner tube hole, were numbed in the spring water.

At first the snake looked like a weed, one of the grasses far below, black against the green. My heart started, then thrummed hard and fast against the rubber tube. Black, a water moccasin. Too skinny to be a cottonmouth, but just as deadly. The mask pinched as my eyes went wide. I wanted to jerk up, but I controlled my body instead, held it still, watching. Don't breathe, I thought, don't move. It was far away. At least twenty feet down. I let the current carry me. The snake wound between the weeds, crossing to the other side. I could see every detail: black eyes, tiny nostrils, slick black body. It was beautiful.

That weekend, me and Lee went to the auction with Dad to sell off the livestock from Green Acres. Dad didn't pay any attention to us, as usual, but at least he had let us come along. Or maybe Mom made him take us. Dad kept scribbling numbers on a scrap of paper, figuring out how much he was going to get after the auctioneer took his cut on each of our cows. The man in the dirt ring below sang and shouted and pointed, and I didn't understand a word until he yelled, "Sold!" and the cow or horse or goat was led back out of the ring. I wondered what it was like to be able to speak that language. I wondered if anyone really understood it, or if he was just making it up as he went along. It was like Brother Floyd when he got the Spirit and spoke in tongues at church, except his eyes rolled back and he spat a lot.

Lee jabbed me in the ribs and pointed. "Look," he said. "Isn't that Ricki Ann?"

It was. She wore a white cowboy hat and pointy-toed boots. She was with her dad, sitting across the ring from us, a little lower down. I wondered why they were there.

Mom's hospital time had been expensive, and Dad was still laid off from the State Road Department. He had been a day worker down at the docks for most of the last year. A man from Sears had knocked on the door in June and asked Mom to give him her charge card. He took these little scissors from inside his jacket and cut it up right there on the front porch. Mom cried for a long time after he left, and when Dad came home, she told him we were going to have to sell the farm for an even lower price, and the livestock soon. He hadn't even yelled. I couldn't hear exactly what they said through the wall after that, just his low voice and Mom crying.

Ricki Ann laughed at something her father said just as our mule, Gus, was led into the ring. I remembered how it felt to ride Gus last summer with Ricki Ann's arms wrapped around my waist, both of us cradled in the mule's swayback, rocking together across the Bahia grass meadows at the farm. I remembered when I could talk to my father like she was doing. It all seemed so long ago.

Ricki Ann and her dad looked like they were having fun. I wondered if she remembered Gus, down in the auction ring. Her dad had his arm stretched out along the back of her seat, and he kept hugging her in close. Something about the way they leaned into each other bothered me, but I didn't know what it was.

"Dad, can I go get a Coke?" Lee said. "I've got my lawn mowing money."

Dad shrugged without looking away from the auctioneer. "Yeah, sure. Stay out of trouble." When Lee stood up, Dad said, "Virge, go with him."

The auctioneer said, "Nnnn, nnn, nnn, THIS fine mule—nuun, nnnn, nnnn, nnn, WHAT am I bid?"

Lee bought me a Coke, then we hung over the railing at ringside. I watched the auctioneer's mouth, trying to slow down what he was saying, trying to translate the language he was speaking. "Hummm, nnn, nnn, hummina, SOLD!" he yelled.

Gus seemed to look at us, his eyes rolling in fear, as he was led out of the ring. I hoped whoever had bought him would be nice to him. Lee and I followed around to where they tied him up to give him some good-bye pats. Gus flopped his ears and nuzzled at my pockets, looking for carrots, but I didn't have any. "Be good, Gus," I whispered in his huge soft ear. "I'll miss you."

Lee put his arms around Gus's broad gray neck and hid his face. He was crying, I thought. I reached out and patted Lee's broad shoulders. The muscles under his blue Hang Ten T-shirt felt hard. "Don't worry, Lee. He's a good mule. He's tough. He'll be okay."

A tall woman in jeans and a white T-shirt stepped up, stuffing a man's wallet into her back pocket. "Hey there," she said, grinning. "What's that you're telling my mule?"

"His name is Gus," Lee said defiantly, stepping back and wiping his wrist across his nose. "He's a real good mule." Gus bobbed his head and poked his nose into Lee's ribs.

"That so?" she said. "Guess you must know him pretty good then."

"He was ours," I said. The woman reminded me of Officer Shakespeare from the DMV. She looked at me, and I flushed. "We just rode him around sometimes. He don't know how to plow or anything. Just a pet mostly."

"But he's a real good mule!" Lee said.

The woman laughed. "Okay, I get it." She reached into her back pocket and pulled out a carrot. Gus waggled his ears and snorted, reaching for it with his teeth bared. "Hey Gus."

"It's short for Pegasus," I said. "I named him."

The woman laughed again, a nice musical sound, low, like the wind chimes over Grandmother's stoop. "Excellent," she said. "Isn't he something then! A flying mule!"

I liked the way she said that word without a drawl, clipping the syllables, *ex-cel-lent.*

The auctioneer stopped at the end of a sale and the arena hummed with voices, thumps of animal feet, laughter. The woman who had bought Gus led him away to a trailer. He was going to be what she called a "companion" for her quarter horse. "So he won't be so lonely," she said.

Lee liked that. "He won't have to work," he said. "He can just hang out with a friend."

We climbed up the board fence around the arena to watch. The teenager who worked for the auctioneer led in a young paint horse. He picked up his feet, stepping high, and his haunches rippled as the kid urged him into a trot around the ring. His black-and-white mane and tail fluttered out behind him. He stopped short, raised his head, neck curving, and flared his huge nostrils into a snort. "Just like a cowboy and Indian horse," Lee commented. "Sure is pretty."

"Yeah," I said. Just like one of the wild horses I used to imagine riding on the island in my mixed-up go-to-sleep dreams.

Then the auctioneer started his song, mumbling into his microphone, spinning to look and point up into the seats above him, first here, then there. He pointed at Ricki Ann and her dad, then back to the other side of the arena. Mr. Purvis nodded when the auctioneer looked at him again. I heard a rise in the song, then a dip. The auctioneer pointed again. Back and forth. Then, "SOLD!"

When they appeared at ringside, Ricki Ann's dad didn't recognize me, but she saw me right away for a change. She smirked. "My father just bought me that paint gelding," she said without even a hello.

"Cool," said Lee. "He's a beauty."

We watched the horse stamp the ground of his stall and nuzzle the rails.

Ricki Ann cocked her head and smiled at her father with her mask-face. "I told him he had to," she sang in a high-pitched, fake voice, "because I'm such a good girl. Didn't I, Daddy?" She blinked at him with her eyes half-closed.

Mr. Purvis smiled at her, then looked me up and down. "Why Virge Young, I didn't even know who you were! You're different! What've you done to yourself? Gone and growed up while my back was turned!"

I flushed and grinned. Mr. Purvis always made me feel exposed, like I couldn't hide. He always seemed to see you, even when you didn't want him to. Ricki Ann acted different with him than me with my dad. Sometimes I felt scared around him, but not because he was big like my dad—he wasn't—and not because he was mean—he was actually extra friendly—but because he made me feel funny.

He put his arm around my shoulders and hugged me in close. That too, all that hugging and touching, was different about Mr. Purvis; we didn't do that so much in my house. Especially not my dad, at least not since I'd got my growing spurt and my first period and turned thirteen and all.

Mr. Purvis turned me to face him, hands on my arms, holding me still. "Let me look at you," he said. "No more metal on that beautiful smile, no more glasses! A grown-up gal's hairstyle. That's must be it! Why you've gone and grown into a real beauty, haven't you!" I shifted a little, hoping he would let me go, but his hands were strong. "You are something, aren't you?" he said.

I felt antsy, wrong somehow.

His breath smelled of peppermints. He was not much taller than me, so his eyes were nearly level with mine. They were Ricki Ann's color, pale blue, and his lashes were nearly invisible. His mouth smiled, but those eyes seemed magical, pulling you down to a bottom that was too far away.

"How about a kiss for your old pal?" he said. His grip on my arms hurt as he pulled me toward him, puckering his lips. The heat from his body made me lean away. I tried not to squirm, but the hairs on the back of my neck stood up.

Ricki Ann grabbed his bicep and twisted him toward her. "Come on, Daddy," she said. "Let's think of names, why don't we?"

Mr. Purvis turned, releasing my arms, and I stumbled backward.

Lee caught me. "I gotcha," he said, his voice low. He held his hand against my back.

I couldn't breathe. What was that? I felt shaky, sweaty. Scared. Why?

Mr. Purvis glanced over at me as Ricki Ann led him toward the stall. "Why don't you come over sometime, Virge?" he asked. "We miss you, don't we honey?" His smile and his eyes didn't match. His soothing tone seemed to mask something. His eyelids half-closed.

Ricki Ann's eyes met mine. She held her father's arm close to her body, hanging on to him like she used to hold on to Ronnie Lane. She took his hand and twined her fingers into his. I remembered the lock on her bedroom door.

When he had let me shoot his Colt .45, Mr. Purvis had put his hands over mine, and the memory of his body close behind mine made me feel sick. His hands had forced mine to hold steady, his peppermint breath in my ear—*See it, Virge. See the target. Now squeeze. Real gentle. Squeeze the trigger . . .*—and the huge boom had jerked me back into him hard. He had laughed, his hands brushing my breasts as he set me upright. My stomach churned.

At the auction that day, Ricki Ann said simply, "Yeah, sure." But her eyes bored into mine, hard and clear, seeing me and making sure that I saw her when she shook her head very slightly, once, *no.*

Dad was quiet on the ride home, so me and Lee were quiet too. Rain drummed on the roof of the pickup, and the wipers *slap slap slapped* back and forth. The radio had been broken for years. We were all three wedged along the bench seat—Dad, me and Lee—on account of the rain. I wanted to say something. I wanted to ask Dad why he'd told Ronnie Lane to stay away from me. Was there something wrong with me? Why didn't he talk to me anymore? Why didn't he know me? I wished I could make him see me again, but I didn't want to do anything to ruin that peaceful feeling of being next to him either. I thought about Mr. Purvis and Ricki Ann. I felt safe with my father's arm across the back of the seat behind my head, Lee on the other side. I felt safe as long as I didn't move, as long as I kept my mouth shut.

I wondered if Ricki Ann would let Michelle ride bareback with her on her new horse, his muscles moving under their legs, one hanging onto the other's waist, chest to back. I wondered if her father would buy her a saddle for the new paint horse. I wondered if he would let Michelle shoot his gun. If Ricki Ann would ask her to sleep over, behind the locked bedroom door.

Dad sighed, a deep sad sound of breath going away. "Sure would've liked to keep that mule for you kids," he said. What he meant was that he'd sure like to have kept the farm, his Green Acres. Something simple and wild, land to be tamed and plowed, bulldozed, something like his grandfather might have had. But it was never really tamed. Even Itchetucknee, all those hundreds of people in inner tubes floating down the river, docks and scuba divers, a road, picnic tables—it was wild under the surface. Springs welled up. Snakes.

"It's okay, Dad," said Lee. "We'll get another farm."

The rain fell harder, pounding on the roof. Dad even let off the gas pedal a little. He reached out along the back of the seat to tousle Lee's hair, bumping the back of my head. "Yep," he said. "I reckon." His arm was warm behind my head, and I felt safe, almost like when I was still twelve, still a little girl.

The movie was after the auction, after the Itchetucknee River trip, after getting contact lenses, after St. Mary's and after that long year of seventh grade. Maybe July was the beginning of the whole story of me backsliding. Maybe the story began *last* summer—a year ago July—with the astronauts walking on the moon, the snake nearly killing me, *I love R.* under my bed. The movie changed things though. Everything changed.

The movie was *Butch Cassidy and the Sundance Kid.* My favorite part was when Butch and Sundance wrapped their hands together in the belt and leapt off the cliff into the river far below.

Lee said what I was thinking—"Cool!"—out loud.

Buddy shushed him. "Hey man," he whispered, "don't get us caught."

I looked away from the screen and up and down the rows of cars just on the other side of the tall chain-link fence. It was the end of July. Nobody was patrolling, nobody was even looking our way. We were hidden in the trees outside the drive-in theater at the back of the woods at the end of Renoir Drive. I stretched out on the low thick limb of the live oak and looked up at the full moon. Cicadas chirred around us. Except that I wasn't holding on to someone else, I felt like Butch or Sundance, flying through the blue sky off the cliff, sliding down the canyon, riding the river. I couldn't believe I was out in the middle of the night, watching a movie that Mom said was too adult for me, without paying for it, breaking all the rules.

I'd overheard Lee and Buddy planning the adventure through the wall of my closet, and I'd decided I wanted to go too. I kept thinking about the snake under the water at Itchetucknee, about the way I'd felt when Aunt Belle passed the log truck. And I really wanted to see the movie too. It wasn't hard to convince Lee. He'd even grinned. "Really?"

he'd said. "Goody-two-shoes?" he'd laughed. And here I was, breaking the rules. Maybe that was my favorite part.

We couldn't hear the words from the speakers hanging on the sides of the cars except when somebody shouted or they shot guns, which was a lot in *Butch Cassidy and the Sundance Kid,* so it was almost like an old-timey silent movie, especially at the beginning when the words were on the screen and the picture was tinted brown. But the huge picture screen edged by the leaves and moss of the oak, the hard limb under my butt, and, mostly, the fact that I had snuck out after dark into the woods to watch a movie that Mom and Dad thought I was too young to see made it the best picture I'd ever seen. I tried to read the lips of the actors; I made up the words I couldn't quite hear.

When the woman undressed while the Kid held a gun on her, pretending to be a stranger, all three of us went still. When he put his hands inside her nightgown, I felt my heart beating fast. Were we going to get to see what happened where the romance novels left off? I could feel what it was like to be inside the woman, the Kid's hands on my skin, and I could feel what it was like to be inside of his body too, the way her skin felt under his touch. It was funny, like in my old go-to-sleep stories, as if I were both of them.

On our last family trip to the drive-in, Mom and Dad had taken us to see *True Grit* with John Wayne, Glen Campbell and Kim Darby. Dad liked John Wayne, maybe because they were built the same, big and blocky. Kim Darby was my favorite. She was this girl, Mattie, in the movie, who was just about my age, and she hired Rooster Cogburn—John Wayne—to take her to track down her father's murderer. Her short brown hair was cut just like mine, and she pushed both of the men around. When they tried to push her around—or sweet-talk her, which is what Glen Campbell did—and treated her like a baby or said that women couldn't do something, she just pushed back. She got her way, mostly. She wasn't afraid. She just broke the rules they laid down, or talked back to them, kind of twangy, but also proper, like a Yankee, sounding smart.

Sometimes I practiced talking like Kim Darby or Mary Tyler Moore or the woman who bought Gus or the Yankees at the DMV the day Great-Aunt Belle lost her license. I tried to tighten my jaw and stand up straight like Kim Darby as I spoke.

Katharine Ross in *Butch Cassidy and the Sundance Kid* was not much like Kim Darby in *True Grit,* except that she was a woman on her own in the Wild West. She was more focused on those two guys with the blue eyes than on making her own way. I wondered what it was like for her when they were gone. They didn't seem to notice when she left them alone together in Bolivia—on account of she didn't want to watch them die—near the end.

When Butch and Sundance tried to lose the posse that was tracking them by both riding one horse, I got worried. It reminded me of my going-to-sleep dreams, the way the Kid wrapped his arms around Butch's waist and they rode hard, like a creature with two human heads, a horse head, and four feet, but it also reminded me of *True Grit*. I had liked that movie until the end. Kim Darby had shot the bad guy with her father's enormous pistol, but he pushed her into a pit with a rattlesnake. She couldn't move. The snake had stared at her, its tongue fluttering and rattles shivering, face level. She hit at it with a little branch, screaming for help.

On account of all my experience with snakes, I had known that wasn't such a good idea. *Stay still*, I had wanted to say. *Don't move at all.* But she hit at it until it struck, biting her on the arm, and then John Wayne shot it and rescued Kim Darby from the hole. I had snake dreams again that night.

But as bad as that part was, the worst part in *True Grit* was where John Wayne hauled Mattie up onto the front of her little horse, Blackie, and rode as fast as he could make the horse go to get her to a doctor. Mattie had yelled for him to stop. "Blackie's all played out!" she yelled. "You'll kill him!" But John Wayne had just slashed the little horse to go faster and faster until he had fallen down, gasping, and died.

I held my breath until Butch and Sundance let their horse go. No dead horse in that movie.

I also didn't like that Mattie gave her father's big pistol away to John Wayne at the end of *True Grit*. She should have kept it. I thought she would have grown into it.

At the end of *Butch Cassidy and the Sundance Kid*, the sounds of guns echoed loud out of the speakers hanging from the cars, and all over the movie lot, car engines started up, breaking the spell. Lee said, "Guess we better get home."

I stretched, lifting my butt up from the hard limb of the tree. Before I scrambled down behind the boys, I looked back at the screen. Butch and Sundance were frozen in a brown photograph, rushing ahead with guns drawn, not dead, even though there was no way they could have made it out of there alive, surrounded by the whole Bolivian army and all. Together, friends forever. Never dying, eternally between two worlds.

Dad was waiting when Lee and I tried to sneak in through the back door at nearly midnight, Butch and Sundance still frozen in brown and white on that screen in my head.

And then Dad's quiet, hard voice came from the darkness. "Go to your rooms."

He came into my bedroom unthreading his belt from his pants. He wound it into a black loop, holding the buckle in his hand. I had never been so scared. My chest felt like it was going to explode. He could kill me, I thought.

His eyes gleamed. His face was stiff. "Lie down," he said. I had never seen him so mad.

I bit my pillow, trying to breathe and not to breathe, tears that I wouldn't let loose pounding in my head. He hadn't spanked me since I was a little kid, twelve. I couldn't believe he was going to spank me. I wouldn't scream. I wouldn't cry.

THWAP! The belt flattened across my butt. I bit down harder, swallowed the sound into my burning chest. THWAP! He hit harder. I could feel his rage. He was on an edge. He was trying to hurt me. THWAP! I wouldn't yell. I wouldn't. THWAP! Faster. THWAP! THWAP! Harder. I saw red through my closed eyes. THWAP! He couldn't do this to me. THWAP! I was thirteen. THWAP! I was too old to be spanked. THWAP! The pain radiated down my legs. THWAP! He hit my bare thighs. THWAP! I was scared, but I wouldn't yell. THWAP! He wanted me to yell. THWAP! He wanted me to let go, to cry. THWAP! But I wouldn't. THWAP! I wouldn't let that empty feeling come. THWAP! I held something in, feeling full. THWAP! I gasped. To cry would be to lose something important.

Then he laughed. One short harsh, *ha*. He'd laughed like that when Glen Campbell spanked Mattie in *True Grit* too. I had hated it. I hated him.

"You think you're something, don't you?" he said, pausing in his rhythm. He breathed hard. "Not as long as you live in my house," he said. "Never," he growled. THWAP! "Ever." THWAP! "Do anything." THWAP! "Without." THWAP! "My." THWAP! "Permission." THWAP! "Again." He stopped.

My back throbbed. My butt was numb. The backs of my thighs stung. I could hear him over me, breathing hard. He could kill me.

I held everything in. My whole self, all the parts. But I was not crying. I won. Escape, I thought. I can escape in four years. He won't ever touch me again.

My Schwinn five-speed bicycle with the brakes on the handlebars—my birthday present last year, before we were broke—skimmed the road so fast it was like I was flying. I had been afraid of the bike for a while after I forgot about the handbrakes and smashed into the back of the car in the driveway while my feet were back-pedaling like mad, trying to stop, but after I came home from St. Mary's, while Mom was at work, me and Lee and his friend, Buddy, had taken some bike trips. As long as we were home at lunchtime when she called, she didn't find out.

The day after *Butch Cassidy and the Sundance Kid,* I didn't care if she found out. After what Dad did, I didn't care about anything except escape.

I was going to see Mrs. Rosenbaum because she got away from the Nazis. If she could get away from Nazis, I could get away from Dad. I had decided to start by riding my bike to Rolling Hills.

I had named my bike Peg, short for Pegasus, the winged horse. I urged Peg on down Fourakre Road, across Normandy Boulevard, and past the entrance to the drive-in theater, following the school bus route toward Rolling Hills, imagining we were galloping down one of the white sand roads on Cumberland Island. I could almost feel some other part of me, the part of me that used to make up those going-to-sleep stories maybe like a ghost or a dream come into my real life. I kept my legs pumping hard on the pedals, trying to shake off that feeling by breathing hard, watching the white line on the black tar, the mirages of steam disappearing ahead.

I stopped at the hippie house because I thought maybe Faith would give me a drink of water. Riding all the way to Rolling Hills in the middle of July was hot work. The hippie house seemed empty though, nobody home. The lawn mower sat in the yard, rusting, and the screen hung sideways on its hinges. She must have had her baby by then. I wouldn't have minded holding it even though I was kind of scared of babies because they were so small and floppy. I thought I might have liked to know the hippies better. I knocked again. The house echoed.

I looked in the window. The weird potted plants that Reggie hadn't wanted me to see were cut off, stems sticking from the pots they had occupied. The table that the boy named Way had been living under was covered with newspapers and dirty dishes, but no one was underneath. No red chicken stalked the room. The long-haired half-naked children, Marilyn or Love, were gone.

Back on my bike, I took the long way, around Rambling Rose Way and into the cul-de-sac. It was like I was going back over my witnessing route, but all mixed-up. The guy in the wheelchair, Murray, was popping wheelies in his driveway. His hair was longer, and his arm muscles bulged, exposed by his sleeveless T-shirt. He twirled and balanced on two wheels, completely in control of the chair. He reminded me of the dancers in the ballet Mom made me watch on TV—hoping to convince me to take ballet lessons . . . no way!—as he stopped in an impossible pose, sweat shimmering and biceps quivering. He concentrated, his face blank, focusing inward or on his body and balance. From the open door of the van parked in the drive I could hear *Raindrops Keep Fallin on My Head* playing on the radio. He didn't even look as I passed, my bike tick-tick-ticking as I coasted.

The Rolling Hills clique of Kathy Zane, Sugar Evans and Jenny Hilliard lay on their stomachs on beach towels on the same green front lawn, but they didn't see me. Their bikinis revealed dark brown skin, gleaming with oil. All three heads were turned to the left, blond, brown, black hair cut in straight lines and swept back off their shoulders. Their eyes were closed, faces empty. I wondered what they were thinking or dreaming. I wondered if they thought about God, or if they got mixed-up in their dreams. I wondered if they planned for escape, if anybody did but me.

Pegasus tick-tick-ticked, coasting by, and not one of them moved or opened her eyes.

A big truck was parked in front of Mrs. Rosenbaum's house. I braked, remembering to squeeze my hands, and stood astride Peg on the steaming asphalt street. Was she moving? Where? I gasped with the heat and the ride, and my heart pounded in my temples. I felt a little funny. Two men hauled the sofa with the flowers bigger than my head out through the front door.

I got off and wheeled Peg up the walk and leaned her against the garage. The front door stood open. I heard voices inside. "Hello?" I called, then knocked on the doorjamb. "Mrs. R.? Miriam?" The television was gone and the paintings were stacked against the wall. It was hot in the house, no air-conditioning blowing out the door. "Hello?"

As if from faraway, I heard an answering "Meow?"

"Not another one," said a familiar voice, and Dr. Rose walked into the living room, looking around, cocking his head to one side to listen. "Oh!" He saw me. A funny look crossed his face. He blinked. "Can I help you?"

He didn't recognize me. My tongue slid over my smooth teeth. I felt my lips slip back in a smile. "I'm looking for Mrs. Rosenbaum," I said. "Is she here?" I didn't recognize my own voice. Maybe he didn't recognize me without my glasses. I felt dizzy and discombobulated.

Dr. Rose swallowed, staring at me. "I'm sorry," he said. "Who are you? How did you know my grandmother?"

I looked around at the nearly empty room. "I'm Virge Young," I said. "I, uh. She gave me a kitten. I came around after school sometimes and we talked."

His forehead furrowed. He still didn't know me. "I remember her saying something about a girl," he said. "From a church—something—"

"That's me," I said. "But that was just once. Then we were, uh—" I hesitated. "We were like friends."

Dr. Rose swallowed. "Shit," he said. He rolled his eyes up to the ceiling. "Uh, okay." He rubbed his hand over his mouth. "Listen." He stopped. "I'm sorry." He swallowed again. "My grandmother died last week," he said.

I made myself think only about my bike, about Pegasus, the flying mule, the flying bike, escape. Mrs. Rosenbaum. My bike. In the movie, Butch Cassidy rode his bike with Katharine Ross on the handlebars, her hair flying in his face, laughing. The pitchman in the Old West town had said the bicycle was the new invention, the coming of the modern age. "The horse is dead!" he'd yelled. Then Butch had pitched the bike down the hill before they ran away to Bolivia on account of the special posse that was after them, on account of the new banks that sacrificed beauty for not getting robbed.

I tried to think only about the bike in the ditch, its wheel spinning. My own bike ticked under me. I tried not to think about Mrs. Rosenbaum gone. Dead.

I wasn't worried about her soul, even though she wasn't a Christian.

I'll see her in heaven if there is one, I thought. Will she still have that mark on her hand?

Something drained away inside of me as I rode, emptying into the air current rushing past my ears. The sound of escape. A piece of me felt dead.

I had refused to look up when Dad stood at my doorway, threading his belt back through the loops of his pants. If he wouldn't see me, then I wouldn't see him. When he shut the door, I wished for a lock. I wished for a map to some other place.

I rolled over, and the tears that I had held inside pounded as if all the water in a baptismal pool or all the water of the aquifer was dammed behind my eyes, inside me. I put one cool hand on my brow. I slipped back to the day I had painted myself with the blue eye shadow in the tree house: my feet, my heart, my hands. The plywood under my back, green leaves overhead. The moon on the horizon. I reached up to touch the diviner's stick, hanging from the bulletin board over my bed. The wood was rough and dry under my fingers. They tingled. I touched my own warm skin. I thought of the island. I'm alone riding a wild horse on the beach, I began in my head, and I told myself a story. When I got to the good parts, I didn't care that I was mixed-up.

Backslide

Is this my turn? Is this home? I squint into the light, into the water blurring the glass. It feels like home.

"Virge." I hear Ruthie's voice, urgent and soft. "We're here. I'm here. I love you."

Where? Who? Is this home? I turn into the drive. The pain that radiates up my arm is so intense I want to scream, but I can't. I feel the tail of the vehicle shoot out. The tires lose grip. We spin. We slide.

And then I am walking up the long white sand road on Cumberland Island. Palmetto bushes crowd the edges, the width of one car, forming green walls, and the arms of live oaks arch overhead, a ceiling that drips Spanish moss. All is silent but for the buzz of cicadas, the muffled hush of the surf on the beach. The road is completely straight, disappearing into a dot at the farthest reach of my vision. It is the summer after my high school graduation, 1975. I have been on the island for a month, working for the park service as a laborer, building the campground at High Point. I have been here so many times in my stories, it feels like home.

Today is my day off, and tomorrow I will leave on the morning boat, go home to Renoir Drive, pack up all my things and escape to college. For now, though, I am walking this long, straight road. I am on my way to Plum Orchard, one of the old mansions, to explore and to have lunch on the porch, and then return the five miles back to the dormitory, arriving too exhausted to join in with the other kids at the last bonfire, where they will pair off and disappear into the dunes. I don't belong to them. I belong to the sea turtles who haul themselves onto the shore in the moonlight, scoop out hollows in sand and deposit eggs, which they leave to fend for themselves, to ripen and hatch into little turtles who scurry on another moonlit night back to the sea.

A dark line stretches across the road ahead. As I walk toward it, I remember my grandmother's story of a drive on this same road in her uncle's old truck, of a snake so thick that the truck bumped like going over a log, and of how they never saw the head or the tail in the brush on either side. I think that the line ahead of me must be another very big snake. I am loathe to go on, to get closer. I have almost been kilt by a snake. But there is no other road on this island. There is no other way now. I will not be afraid.

But this will not be a snake. I stand still and look down at the shadow. This will not be the last time I see it or hear it or feel it.

Thirty years later, I will settle in a place that has only garter snakes— shiver-inducing, but not lethal. I will build a house on a hill where I can stand and observe the way a snake moves, slow or fast, unblinking, silently shedding skin again and again. I will learn not to run away or to bring the blade of a shovel down cleanly across its neck.

That road on the island is too narrow, too white, too straight. As night falls, I choose to walk home on the beach.

Reunion: Ricki Ann

"How are you?" Virge says, smiling. "It's been so long! Twenty-five years! I can't believe it's you."

Ricki Ann opens her mouth, but nothing comes out. Everyone is looking. Michelle squares her shoulders, about to step forward.

"Virge," Stacy Lake says, sticking her hand out, cutting Michelle off. "You probably don't remember me. Stacy Lake."

Virge moves her hand from Ricki Ann's shoulder to shake Stacy's. "Hi."

"I just loved your book," says Stacy. "It's great. Fantastic."

Virge smiles. "Thanks," she says. "I'm glad you liked it." She looks at Stacy again. "Weren't you on that Humanities trip to New York senior year?"

Stacy grins. "Yeah, that's right. You went too." She glances at Ricki Ann. "Did you go, Ricki Ann?" she asks.

Ricki Ann shakes her head. "No." She looks from Stacy to Virge. "No, that was for the smart kids." She rattles her glass. "You know, I really need to find my husband," she says, backing away.

"Wait." Virge's hand on her forearm. "Ricki Ann. I want you to meet my partner, Ruth."

The woman with the red hair and beautiful dress steps forward, extending a hand. "Hello," she says. "So good to meet you."

Ricki Ann murmurs a greeting, barely touching the woman's palm. "I, uh," she starts and stops. "Yes," she says. "Good."

"Virge told me so much about you," Ruth says.

Ricki Ann feels her face flush.

Michelle grunts. "Well, I guess we all know all about that," she says, sneering.

Virge moves a step to the side, turning her back to Michelle, a subtle snub. "What have you been up to all these years?" Virge says. "Are you married? Kids?"

Ricki Ann glances at Michelle and the few others who are still listening. "Oh yes, well. Married." She smooths her face. "And divorced. And married, and divorced and married again. And kids . . ." She pauses, just as she always does. "Well, the first two husbands certainly *acted* like children . . ."

A few people laugh and Virge grins, that old funny open smile she'd had when they'd been young. Before everything changed. "Still in Jacksonville?" she asks.

Ricki Ann nods, relieved. She knows how to handle this kind of conversation. God knows she's done it at a million cocktail parties. Maybe no one will mention that chapter in the book. "Yes," she says. "Well, I traveled around some in the Seventies. Had to get away. Tried to at least . . . California for awhile. The first husband."

Virge nods. "But something brought you back here, huh?"

"The South," Ruth says. "You Southerners can't ever seem to leave it for good."

Virge meets Ricki Ann's eyes. "It doesn't let you loose," she says. "Something in the water, I guess."

"No," Ricki Ann says, waving her glass, pretending a wry smile. "Second husband. Came back for my daddy's funeral, met this guy who was a friend of my brother's, and next thing I knew I was packing up the U-Haul and driving cross-country again." The people around them have begun to fade into their own conversations, though Ricki Ann knows they are still half-listening. The silence grows for a long minute. "I, uh, I hear you have children," she says, finally thinking of a safe topic.

Virge grins. "Two. Twins. A boy and a girl." She fishes in her jacket pocket and pulls out a small leather wallet.

The babies in the picture are redheads. Ricki Ann glances at Ruth. Definitely the mother. "They're beautiful," she says. She keeps her eyes on the photo between Virge's long fingers.

"I feel so lucky," Virge says. "I came so close to missing out on it." She puts her arm around Ruth. "Better late than never."

Sadness washes over Ricki Ann. She'd wanted kids, but the time had never been right. The guys never right, or ready. Or maybe it was her. "Yes," she says, "well." She looks up and away, scanning the crowd for Boomer. And then it's too late. "Time runs out eventually," she murmurs. "No regrets."

Virge touches her arm again. "Sorry," she says. "I didn't think . . ."

Ricki Ann shrugs. "Yeah. Sure."

"I, uh." Virge stops. "So your father died," she says.

Ricki Ann feels her spine go rigid. Don't say it, she will think. Why had Virge written that in her damned book? She will look around the room again. Where is Boomer?

"I . . ." Virge hesitates. "It must have been hard," she says. "That he's dead."

Ricki Ann swallows, still scanning the dancing couples, the bar on the far side of the room, the shadows in the corners. Where is he? Why is she bringing this up? "Umm," she says, noncommittally, nodding slightly.

Virge steps closer and lowers her voice. "Did you ever . . ." She shakes her head. "No." She looks at the floor. "I'm sorry. Never mind." She clears her throat. "I'm sorry to hear about your dad," she says.

Something twists inside Ricki Ann. Bitch, she thinks. "It wasn't true," she whispers.

Virge's body leans back, away from her. Her eyebrows shoot up, surprised.

"Why did you write that?" Ricki Ann asks. "It was a lie. How dare you say something like that about my father? I loved him. He loved me. He was just . . ." The words are getting away, growing too fast. She forces herself to stop and breathe slowly for a minute, trying to let her head clear. "I never said he . . ." No. She bites her tongue. She can't say it. "Listen," she says. "He's dead. It's over. He was just a drunk, that's all. He'd call me on the phone out in California, all slobbery and crying, and I'd just hang up on him. He died, and that's it." She risks a glance up.

Virge's eyes seem sad. "I'm sorry, Ricki Ann," she says. "I wrote a novel, fiction. I put pieces together from here and there. A thirteen-year-old girl just sees pieces, fragments. A writer makes meaning from bits and pieces. That's what a writer does. Life doesn't mean much without some writer taking it apart and rearranging it so that the gaps, the holes, seem to mean something." She reaches toward her, but Ricki Ann draws back. "It's fiction, Ricki Ann. A story. Everybody knows that. It only seems true. It only seems real."

"Liar!" Michelle Mitchell seems to shout it into Ricki Ann's ear, over her shoulder. Virge steps back, her eyes wide. Her hand flies to her shoulder, the place she was shot. "You're just a child of the devil," Michelle screams. "He's speaking through you, you pagan. You're a tool of the devil!"

Ricki Ann doesn't think, doesn't even hesitate. The sweaty glass in her right hand, the ice cooling the itch in her palm, swings up as if her elbow is an oiled hinge, a spring that has released, as if she's been straining to hold something still without knowing it. The glass arcs, the ice flying over her shoulder. She watches Virge's mouth curve into an O. She hears Michelle gasp behind her. And then Virge laughs, a loud *ha-ha-ha*, before putting a hand to her lips, her eyes shining. Ruth and the others join in out of the sudden silence, and Ricki Ann knows that her ice has been right on target.

The Snake Story, or How I Finally Lost It

In August, I went up North for the first time. In August, I became someone new, almost like I was born again. Not as a Christian but as something else. I lost everything—my accent, my virginity, my old way of thinking about God—but it felt like I found something more important. August was as mixed-up as the whole year had been, but I didn't care. I learned how to live with being mixed-up.

I am learning how to make sense of it.

Back at the end of my first year in junior high school in June, before final exams started and Ricki Ann offered me a cigarette in the girls' bathroom, Miss Williams had called on me one day in English. I had been reading a novel called *Whispering Cliff*, which I had hidden inside my textbook while the class was reading a short story about a boy and a pony. I'd finished all the stories in the literature textbook one week after school had started way back in September, and I'd quickly skimmed that one again while Randy Sims was still stumbling over "ignoramus" in the second paragraph. The cover of *Whispering Cliff* was a smoky picture of a woman in a long dress that barely contained her boobs, falling back from the grasp of a dark, troubled-looking-but-handsome man in a coat with tails. After Mel moved away, I had discovered I could buy romance novels for a nickel at the flea market in the Winn-Dixie parking lot on Saturdays. I had read so many that they had become stupid and predictable, but I still liked the way they made my palms sweat and neck burn. I kept hoping to find the one that did not end when the woman finally fell into the dark man's arms. Maybe I was trying to find one where the woman got mixed-up like me.

That day in Miss Williams's class, I was near the end of *Whispering Cliff,* and she had to call my name more than once when it was my turn to read. "Virginia?" she said. "Virginia Young!"

I sat up and squeezed my legs together, damp down there. I hoped I hadn't gotten my period. My face and neck itched. I closed the paperback, still inside my textbook, and tried to guess where the last person had left off in the pony story. "'He brought the rifle with him . . . '"

Snickers. Michelle, who sat in the row to my left and just behind me, hissed, "Virrrrgggee—" That sound again, everywhere. That was before I knew what it meant.

"No Virginia," said Miss Williams, her accent crisp and uncluttered, like that of a Yankee or someone on TV, "the next paragraph."

I swallowed and began again. "'Y'all ain't no gunners,' said Hoyt," I read, drawling out the nasal sounds like I knew the characters would. Michelle spluttered and the rest of the class giggled. I saw Ricki Ann, two rows over, curl her frosty pink lip and turn her gaze out the window. I swallowed the lump that swelled into my throat.

Miss Williams frowned. "Class!" She looked at me. "That was an excellent example of dialect."

"Cracker," hissed Michelle. Snort Mixon snorted his trademark snort, then started snuffling a series of little asthmatic honks to catch his breath, and the whole class fell apart in laughter.

I stared at the picture of the man and woman on the cover of the paperback novel nestled inside the textbook and began to pray silently. *Help me God. Help me lose it.*

I didn't know I was praying then to lose it all.

• • •

Two months later, in August, Colter's Corners, North Carolina, was sweltering, the tobacco leaves spreading wide and lush in long rows hugging the slow curves of the land, but it was no hotter than home, and I was glad to be far away from that awful first year of junior high, and from Dad.

I had escaped. After me and Lee got caught coming back from the drive-in at nearly midnight in July, Mom said she didn't want us home alone at all. Lee had to go to work for Dad, and I got sent up North to the relatives. I hoped Lee was being extra careful, on account of Dad being so mad. As for me, first Uncle Mitch (my dad's big brother who went to college and got rich) and Aunt Doris (his *Yankee liberal wife*, Dad called her) hired me to help out with their five-year-old for two weeks, "And see the sights in New Jersey." Then after those two weeks, they had brought me down to North Carolina to stay with Uncle Deke and Aunt Wil (Willa, my mama's sister) and my cousin, Lisa, for a couple more weeks. Uncle Deke and Aunt Wil would drive me home.

Green Acres had been sold. Ricki Ann wasn't my friend. I'd seen Mel in New York, but she was different, switched to Catholic and with a boyfriend, who it turned out I didn't much like. So there I was in North Carolina, free of everything.

"What the hell would you want to come to a hellhole little hick town like this for anyway?" Shane had asked.

Shane could have been one of those dark, troubled-looking-but-handsome heroes in a romance novel, if she hadn't been a girl. So I told her everything, except the part about the awful first year of junior high and being scared of my dad. "Anything's better than being trapped at home," I said.

"Oh, she's trouble," my cousin, Lisa, had said of Shane, grinning at me through the cool gloom of the empty First Baptist Church where we'd retreated after a walk through all of downtown Colter's Corners, which had taken less than fifteen minutes.

It was a hick town, especially after everything I had seen up in New Jersey and New York, but I liked the old-fashioned milkshake machines and twirly stools at the drugstore and the way all the ladies at the beauty shop looked up from their magazines and conversations to wave when we passed the big plate window. There was something comforting about knowing that they knew who you were and what you were about and that the old men on the bench outside the post office were still going to be there tomorrow unless it rained. Colter's Corners reminded me of the stories Grandma and Papa and Aunt Belle and the old folks liked to tell in the shade of a long afternoon in St. Mary's, rocking on the front porch. It reminded me of St. Mary's too, safe, and even farther from Dad. Vietnam and the hippies seemed alien, and the moon was still just a thing in the sky instead of a place to go. Lisa said there weren't any black kids in her school, which was weird because I saw more black folks than white in Colter's Corners, but I heard "integration" spat out like a bad word under the drone of the new air conditioners in the Piggly Wiggly, and "Klan," and the heat had settled down on my head like a history of lead. I'd told Aunt Wil I felt dizzy, and she'd sent us to wait in the cool, empty church while she finished shopping for our trip to the lake.

We went in through a side door of the little church, and Lisa spotted Shane, sprawling on the stoop just outside the front door, right away. "Trouble," she whispered and giggled. "Least that's what Mama and Daddy say."

Lisa was only a year younger than me, only twelve, but she seemed even younger, still shaped like a twig, short and bony and thin. With my braces off and teeth smooth, with my new contact lenses that focused everything so sharp it almost scared me, and with the breasts I'd almost stopped hunching to hide even though they were deformed, I felt pretty grown up beside my little cousin. Lisa grinned wider. "Trouble with a capital T."

Shane flipped her black hair back out of her eyes, and I saw high cheekbones and a long nose in profile. Her eyes glinted. Ricki Ann's type, I thought, if she were a boy.

"She's almost sixteen, and she hasn't got a daddy," Lisa said. "She 'most never goes to school—probably'll drop out on her birthday—and she smokes and she works full-time at the filling station." Lisa paused dramatically and her voice fell to an even lower whisper. "She rides a motorcycle."

For some reason, I thought of Great-Aunt Belle in her golf cart with the gold tassels whipping in the wind, the log trucks cussing behind her on the highway. *A funny one,* I thought.

"Let's say hi." Lisa scooted out of the pew and toward the door. I remembered what Ricki Ann called me that day in the girl's rest-room: "Goody-two-shoes" and "Virrggge-in." I took a deep breath and followed my cousin down the aisle.

After the introductions, Shane's glittering blue eyes raked up my body slowly, from my brown feet in tire-tread sandals to my smooth-shaven legs in cut-off jeans shorts to the Snoopy for President T-shirt that was just a little too small for my new breasts. The July morning after Dad had spanked me—the last time I'd ever let him touch me, I swear—I had ridden my bike to Winn-Dixie, taken a razor off the shelf and slipped it into the pocket of my shorts. I shaved my legs in the bathroom at home that night, after I learned Mrs. Rosenbaum was dead. I'd nicked my ankle. The blood trickled down my foot into the drain like a punishment. It had healed quickly. When I saw the T-shirt on a cart outside the Statue of Liberty, I remembered Ricki Ann in hers, teaching me to dance the Swim. Dad had said it was unpatriotic. I bought it with the money I got from selling the paperback romances back to the flea market dealer. I thought I might even wear it when I got home, in front of Dad.

Shane didn't blink, watching me through shaggy bangs. Something funny fluttered up my legs and jellied the backs of my knees.

"You can siddown if you want," she offered, leaning back against the granite wall. My neck flushed hot, and I sat down on the step. Lisa started to join us, but Shane said, "Say, Lisa. You wouldn't do a guy a favor and go get us some Cokes over at the station, would you?" Lisa hesitated, and then Shane's face widened into a wide, white smile. "Would'ya?" she asked. Lisa inhaled and grinned back. You would feel like doing anything for the magic of that smile.

Shane and I watched Lisa walk across the highway, the silence between us cool and thick. Blue denim hugged the calf of her leg, which is where I was looking to avoid meeting her eyes. The scuffed toe of her boot tilted up, then over to touch the side of my little toe. I smiled. "So, how old are you?" she asked.

I bit my bottom lip. Thirteen was too young, and I am tall. "Fifteen," I mumbled, still not looking up. "You?" It seemed like the most logical next question.

"Sixteen," she said with no hesitation.

Liar. I risked a glance, but she was gazing out across the blacktop and farms toward the hazy hills. "How long've you lived here?" I asked.

Her cheek flinched. She turned her head slowly to look at me. "Too long." I saw in her eyes something far away, and a chill tweaked at the top of my spine in spite of the heat. I looked down to play with the buckle on my sandal.

Shane sighed. The buzz of cicadas became heavier, and a droning semi headed north on the distant expressway shifted lower. "Sorry," she said. "I'm not much for talk." She touched my arm, and the dark fingers, smudged with grease under the nails, but long and fine, smoothed the pale white hairs just below my elbow. Her touch was slick, cool and rough, all in the same moment. Ricki Ann would have touched the back of my hand, or maybe I would have touched the back of hers, if she had been a boy, or if I had been.

My fingertips didn't shake. I watched my hand rise, then settle lightly on her skin, tracing the bones down to the hollow between her knuckles, where I felt a pulse. I inhaled and pulled my hand back to rest on the granite step. It was like the magic that flew me up and over the creek, away from the snake. Like my fingers knew what to do without me. But I wasn't really curious about it, or afraid. It just was. I looked up.

Shane smiled, the corners of her eyes crinkling in a way that seemed too old but that also made her younger than before, or like a boy's. Her teeth glowed white. She brushed back the shock of hair from her eyes and laughed at me so that I felt like I was inside her throat. She reached into her pocket. "Want a smoke?" she asked.

The New Jersey part of my August was like being reborn into some very clean, very neat version of life, even better than Rolling Hills. The Good Humor man fascinated me. In the suburb where Uncle Mitch, Aunt Doris and their five-year-old lived, the ice cream man had a title and nametag (Steve), a spotless white uniform and truck, and a clipped and proper enunciation. "Your fudge-cickle, Miss," he said, winking as he handed it over. I blushed and mumbled thanks, and grabbed my little cousin's hand to drag him out of the way. Steve-the-Good-Humor-Man's hair was dark and trimmed and his eyes blue.

"I think that boy was flirting with you," Aunt Doris sang. I cringed and glanced back. Steve gave me a little nod and grinned with teeth as white as his outfit. Compared to the ice cream man back home, whose belly oozed from between a greasy undershirt and stained cut-off polyester slacks, the faint stench of beer on his breath, a rough stubble on his chin, and a chewed cigar with which he tried to jab kids who were too grabby, Steve was an exotic creature. I never wanted to go South again.

Maybe it was the litter-free curving white sidewalks, the little trenches that edged each one, separating the thick green plush-carpet lawns from the concrete, instead of the stinging nettles and fire ants and dirt paths of home; maybe it was the glow in the sky after dark, the never-dark radiating toward the hub of New York City, where the buildings made my neck ache and my heart beat in my throat, where suits and clacking heels and smooth nylons and all shades of people speaking more languages than I'd ever heard all hurried purposefully along to museums and to Wall Street and to Broadway where magic happened in hushed cool places more beautiful than any dream; maybe it was the way that Aunt Doris and Uncle Mitch ate alone together after the children had been tucked in bed, the table huge and gleaming with candlelight and wine (*the devil's brew,* Pastor Bob would say) in crystal glasses; maybe it was the idea that the toilet in the basement family room where I was sleeping flushed up . . . *Up!* Nobody I knew in the flat land of the South even had a basement.

Maybe the dizzy, heady feeling came from the *up* of "Up North." Maybe it was just the heat of the summer, of being thirteen. I kept telling myself I was *Up North.* It was different. Or maybe I was different.

At the end of August, in North Carolina, Uncle Deke handed me the towrope in the boat. "Float on your back with your skis in the air," he said. "Hold this between your skis, and lean back. Don't try to stand up; just let the boat pull you up."

I floated in the cool water, watching as the boat puttered slowly away, the rope pulling a little tighter. Lisa watched from the stern. When the rope was almost taut, I nodded. Lisa said something to her father. A cloud of blue smoke came from the motor. The boat jumped ahead, and the rope zzzzipppped tight. I felt my body lift slowly out of the water into the air—kind of the opposite of baptism, a pull instead of a push—like when my body carried me over the stream away from the snake. I wondered if this was how the Rapture would feel, and then I didn't care. The water slapped the boards under my bare feet. I was up! I was doing it. Skiing. Magic. It was me, my body. My arms straightened out, pulling my shoulders, my back muscles gripping. The air streamed through my hair, drying it. My thighs and butt felt hard as I stood almost upright in the middle of the V wake of white foam behind the boat. I was mesmerized by the dark blue. Huge fish, dead trees, sunken treasure, even snakes might have been down there at the bottom of the lake, but I skimmed over it all, sliding on top of the water. I was up! On top of the water! The white foam V made a smooth path, a triangle around me that almost seemed sacred.

"You think you can walk on water, don't you," Ricki Ann had said that last day of exams, the last day of seventh grade. She blew smoke out through her nose, like a bull. "Little Miss Perfect. Little Virge-in," she sneered.

I didn't know what to say. I grabbed the cool porcelain of the bathroom sink. My breath was caught in my chest. I felt my throat closing, tears filling my head. Why was she being so mean to me? *God, make me go away.* I prayed. *Make me invisible again for this last month of school. Keep me safe.*

Ricki Ann swung open a stall door and tossed her cigarette into the toilet. She pulled a mascara wand out of her bag and focused on her reflection in the mirror. "Walk on water, be perfect," she muttered, jabbing the wand into the holder a few times. "Hold onto your God-stuff so you're better than everyone else." She was talking to herself, brushing the black on her lashes with short intense strokes. "What happens when you stop looking at Jesus, Virge?" Her eyes cut toward mine then back to the mirror. "Don't you just want to get rid of it? Lose it? Isn't it a lot of work to be perfect? Don't you just want to let loose and slide back down?" Ricki Ann stopped and jammed her mascara brush back into the holder hard. She met my eyes in the mirror. "What happens if you don't get saved out of the drink?" she asked. "Don't you want to learn to swim?"

I blinked. She was talking about the Bible story. Doubting Thomas. He wanted to walk on the water with Jesus, and he did, for a minute, but when he looked away from Jesus and saw the water and waves, he sank. Jesus reached out and grabbed him, saved him from drowning. I'd never thought about it that way. Why hadn't he tried to swim?

The New York Public Library was like a church. I smelled books— millions of books, zillions of words, all the stories ever made—as I stood in the entrance, hushed and reverent. I almost wanted to pray, but I didn't know what I would say to God anymore. A woman's high heels clicked. Marble gleamed with the soft light streaming in from high windows. I wished I could live there.

"Come on," Mel said. "Let's go." She pulled my arm toward the door.

Aunt Doris had brought me into "The City" to meet Mel. We had one hour on our own before we had to meet her back here again, and Mel wanted to show me everything. Mostly, I thought she wanted to show me Paco. Trotting down the steps after Mel, I touched the foot of one of the big granite lions. I'll be back, I promised.

Around the corner, Paco waited in a doorway. Mel rushed to press her chest against his, and while they kissed, long and sloppy and with lots of *ummmumm*-moaning, I watched the people walking by, all in a hurry, and looked up at the tall buildings, and listened to the accents and languages, blowing horns and construction hammers and subway screechings. "Virge," said Mel, finally breaking her lips free, "this is Paco."

He held out a hand to me, palm up. "Give me five," he said. I hesitated, then started to shake his hand. He laughed. "No, man. Give me five." He grabbed my right hand and turned it palm up, then slid his own palm over it. "Cool," he said.

Paco was not what I had expected. He was hardly tan at all, and his clothes were regular jeans and a T-shirt like everyone else's. He was shorter than me and Mel both, and he wore black horn-rimmed glasses. I had never seen a Puerto Rican person before I got to New York, except in *West Side Story*, but he really didn't look like the people in the movie. His T-shirt had a big peace sign on it. His hair hung below his collar.

Mel couldn't seem to look at anything but him. "Paco's going to a protest," she said. "Too bad your aunt won't let you alone for longer— We could go too."

I shrugged. "That's okay. I wanna see that Empire State Building anyway," I said. And I didn't want to be one of those kids lying dead on the sidewalk like at Kent State.

Paco burst out laughing. "Oh my God," he said. "What an accent!" He stuck his thumbs into his shirtsleeves, pretending he was a farmer with suspenders or overalls. "I wanna see that there Em-pire State Building," he mimicked, exaggerating my accent. "H-yuck, h-yuck, h-yuck."

My face flooded with blood. I hated him. What was Mel thinking?

"Yawl sound just like them hicks on TV," he said.

Mel shifted uncomfortably. "Hey, Paco," she said. "Be nice. She can't help it."

He snorted. "She ought'a try," he said as she tugged his hand. "Like you."

My mouth opened, but nothing came out. I swallowed. The street was suddenly very loud around me. It smelled of garbage.

"It's okay, Virge," Mel said. "Paco's just not used to Southerners." She looked at him. "He helped me lose my accent, you know."

I realized that she did talk differently than she had. I had thought it was just living up North that had done it.

"Take my word for it, man," Paco interrupted. "Lose the accent and you'll go farther. People think you're stupid if you talk like a spic or a hick."

Paco didn't have an accent either. He didn't sound like a Puerto Rican, not even the ones in *West Side Story*. He sounded like—well, like nothing. Like a TV person. Suddenly my tongue felt too big for my mouth, lying like a dead fish between my teeth. I looked at my watch, swallowing back the tears in my head. "I ought'a get back to meet my aunt," I mumbled, turning as I spoke.

Mel's hand brushed my arm, but she didn't catch me. "Wait, Virge," she called. "He didn't mean it," she said. But I was already crossing the street, losing myself in the crowd.

Later in August, half-way home in North Carolina, I lost something else while learning to water ski.

Lisa, standing in the stern of the motor boat watching me, clapped her hands together in pantomime. The white foam V curved a little as the Uncle Deke turned the boat. I saw the water, the bubbles churning underneath the surface. I was flying.

A little wave slapped the bottom of my left ski. It skidded outward. I slipped back, fast. My left leg pulled away, then my right, then both legs spread out wide. Too wide! Water slammed into my crotch. OW! Oh God. Oh, oh, oh. Water fountained up from between my thighs and into my face. OW! I choked on water. My chest emptied. OW! Pain between my legs. Water slammed into me. Water slapped the backs of my thighs. My hands were still clamped to the tow rope bar. Let go, I thought. LET GO!

• • •

The last day of school, I had watched Ricki Ann's pale orange-white lashes darken and grow longer with the mascara. I used to like the way her lashes were nearly invisible until you got close up. I remembered her breath on my neck, her face coming into focus and those pale lashes fringing her blue eyes, something you could only see when your nose almost touched hers, when you almost kissed.

"What?" She put her hands down, leaning on the sink. "What're you looking at me like that for?"

I wished Miss Williams had written two hall passes instead of one. I wanted to leave. I sucked in a breath and let my eyes meet Ricki Ann's again. "I just was thinking that I like it better without the stuff on your eyelashes," I said.

She focused again on her applicator and eyes. "Like I care what you think," she muttered. With a couple more quick strokes, she finished and jammed the brush back into its tube. "You ask me, you could do with a little covering up," she said. "Don't you have anything you want to hide, Virge? Are you really all that perfect?"

In New Jersey in August, I met the Good Humor truck almost every afternoon with my little cousin. And every day Steve-the-Good-Humor-Man in his perfect white uniform with his perfect diction winked at me. On my next-to-last day in New Jersey, I told Aunt Doris I was going for a run and followed the route I had guessed from the sound of the truck's song. I breathed the Yankee cool air and let the smooth lawns and clean lines settle into a blur, the rhythm of my sneakers slapping on the sidewalks like a song. I remembered my bike, Pegasus, and my old going-to-sleep stories. Running was better. I felt like I was almost awake. At the end of a dead-end street, I found Steve's white truck parked under a huge leafy tree.

"Hey Miss Fudge-cickle," he grinned. He was lying with his head against the trunk of the tree, his white shirt off and a can of beer resting on his flat, tanned belly. I stopped short and blushed. "Looking for something to cool you off?" he asked.

I didn't know what to say. I wasn't really sure why I was there, except that he had winked at me. That he was all white and clean and neat in his uniform, a Yankee, different.

"Come have a cool one with me, Miss Fudge-cickle," he said. He sat up and pulled another can from the pack beside him and knelt, holding it out to me.

I watched my hand take the can from him, watched my fingertip pop up the ring tab and pull it off. It was like it wasn't even my hand. But it was. It didn't shake at all.

My legs quivered, Jell-O-like, but I made it up the hill from the dock by the lake to Uncle Deke and Aunt Wil's cabin. In the bathroom I stripped off my suit and discovered that I'd gotten my period. I was bleeding. But it was too soon for my period. It was two weeks early. I sat on the edge of the bathtub and put my head between my knees to stop the pounding, the dizzy feeling that swept over me. It was as if the lake itself had pushed itself inside me, burst something.

And then I knew. I wasn't a virgin anymore. I had lost it.

"What happened to you, Ricki Ann?" I had asked that day in June in the restroom, then I gaped at myself in the bathroom mirror. I couldn't believe I had said it. The words had just come out. It was like someone on TV, saying something natural, even though it wasn't their words. I hadn't even tried, hadn't thought. My tongue, my mouth, had worked without me.

Ricki Ann's face paled, and she looked away quickly, down into her purse. "Shit," she said, fumbling stuff inside her bag. She came up with a lipstick, focusing on the tube as she slipped off the top and unscrewed it so that the slick orange point rose from its silver sleeve. She untwisted, then twisted, making the lipstick go up and down, watching it. "What makes you think it's any of your business, you goody-two-shoes?" she mumbled. I kept watching her. She blinked several times fast. "Nothing," she said. "Nothing happened to me. I—I just lost it—" Ricki Ann stopped and swallowed.

I couldn't move. I was frozen, somehow standing again on the bank of that stream in the summer heat with the snake behind me. But my mouth moved. "Who?" And this time, I was asking for me, not for Mom or Dad or God. Or maybe I was asking for Ricki Ann.

Ricki Ann shook her head, one hard little shake. "No," she said. Her eyes seemed glassy, wet maybe. She took a deep breath and let it out, then puckered and slid the lipstick across her lips. She hesitated, her hand in the air. "I grew up, that's all," she said. "So I lost it. No big deal.

Something you might want to do, Miss Perfect." She blinked at me in the mirror. "Just grow up."

"Whoa-ho," said Steve-the-Good-Humor-Man in New Jersey in August. "You're more grown up than I thought!"

I put the cool metal can to my mouth, felt the edges of the tab-hole sharp against my lips, and sipped. It was cold, but sour. The smell made me want to wretch, but I swallowed it without making a face. I smiled at Steve. "What do you mean by that?" I asked, cringing inside at the fake way the words sounded, but pleased nevertheless with their clipped, non-accented precision. It was like I was on a stage, like someone else was inside me. Steve was an idiot; that was suddenly clear to me.

He smiled back. He thought he was going to get something from me. He thought I was just a kid, just a girl. He thought he could get me drunk and kiss me. Do things to me. Maybe what Ronnie Lane did to Ricki Ann. Or somebody else. The smell of the beer reminded me of Ricki Ann's dad, his hands covering mine on the Colt .45, his body behind me. I thought of the hay dust drifting down from the loft. I remembered the tree house, that long year ago.

Steve was still grinning, his face kind of slack. He was no stranger, not all that different from any other boy. I saw that his white pants had grass stains on them, and his shirt was soaked with sweat. He reached up and touched my fingers, still curled around the beer can. "What's your name, Miss Fudge-cickle?"

The ring of the pull-tab was still in my right hand, encircling my finger. I touched it with my thumb, the tab edges sharp. "I'm Virge," I said. I took another swallow of beer and smiled the fake smile.

The tampons under Aunt Wil's sink worked, just like that, even though I had never been able to figure out that particular part of my anatomy before. After water skiing—after losing it—I got it right, just like that. And without the bulky Kotex, I could run, even with my period. Or my not-period.

While I had been staying at Grandma's in June, I had read this article in the *Reader's Digest* about this new jogging fad, about how it was good exercise and you lose weight and all, so I got Mom to buy me some sneakers. I had been running almost every day since I got away from home. It was better than my bike, slower but realler. I liked wandering the new roads.

I pounded along the shoulder of the black tar highway near Aunt Wil and Uncle Deke's house, soaked in sweat like a warm rain. The tar was soft in the sun, mirages radiating ahead, steam rising up under my feet. Wide-leafed tobacco plants grew in rows on either side of the road; orange trumpet flower vines snarled in wild clumps off the barbed wire fences. I felt funny, almost like I used to feel telling my going-to-sleep stories to myself. I was sleepy and dazed, but I was also awake and excited.

I heard the hum of the engine before I saw it. A speck came down a hill then disappeared into a low spot. The hum got louder. A buzz.

Then the buzz was close, a different buzz. Cold splashed up the nape of my neck. Rattlesnake! My legs stopped before I finished thinking the word, and then I was sliding backward through the air.

Uhhnh. I landed and backpedaled a few more steps. On the shoulder of the road, the coiled snake's triangle-shaped head was raised and its little tongue zipped out, tasting. The tail shivered its warning, buzzing. I was safe, a dozen or more paces down the hill and still backing away. The little black eyes, like dots of gleaming night, seemed to watch me.

The motorcycle roared up and over the hilltop in the opposite lane. The snake struck. The long line of it stretched up and out in a flash of brown, fangs extended. I screamed, a sound I remembered, but not ever from me. I felt it in my chest, and heard it, but far away. Was that me? Was that sound coming from me? The snake thunked onto the blacktop, barely clearing the shoulder, then essed into the brush. The motorcycle, already past me, stopped and turned, and I heard it, thrumming slow, as it pulled up behind me.

"You okay?"

I turned. Shane. The top of my head seemed to open, and my legs jellied. I opened my mouth and sucked in air. "Snake," I said.

"Do you remember that snake?" Ricki Ann had looked down into her bag, pretending not to care. She glanced up, then back down. "You know," she said. "Last summer at your farm."

I felt my mouth hanging open, so I closed it and nodded. "Uh-huh." Did I remember it. "That scared me pretty bad," she said, her hands still, not looking up from the opening of her purse.

"Yeah," I said. "Me too." My heart whammed at my chest. She looked like she was seeing something far away. My whole body zinged, trying to hear what she was about to say.

"I thought it was God," she said. "Like a miracle." She swallowed. "I thought God kept you from getting killed by that snake." She bit her lip. "I thought if I got saved like you, God might make a miracle for me too." Ricki Ann's eyes cut over to mine in the mirror. Then, as if something washed over it, her face hardened into her mask. She spoke very slowly, each syllable separated: "But. God. Is. Bull. Shit."

I couldn't look away from her eyes.

"You were lucky," she said. "Like that guy with the stick looking for water. The diviner. Bullshit. Maybe he made it happen himself, something inside of him. Maybe just luck. Like you not getting killed by that snake. Something inside you did it, made you get out of the way. Not God. You."

She slung her leather-fringed bag over her shoulder, the little bells tinkling. "And not me. I'm not lucky, not perfect, and that's the way it is. Nobody takes care of me but me. So I lost it, so I'm not a virgin, who cares? Who cares how? Nobody. It doesn't matter. I am who I am—a slut, a sinner, fast, whatever—take it or leave it." She breathed, straightening her shoulders and tilting her chin defiantly.

My former best friend turned to the door, then stopped and glanced back at me, her hand on the handle. "Stop hiding behind God, Virge," she said. "Lose the act. Stop hiding from yourself."

In New Jersey, when Steve-the-Good-Humor-Man had moved his hand, I was fast. I had let him kiss me, just to feel what it was like. His lips seemed rubbery but hard, and his face was scratchy with whiskers. He smelled of beer. His tongue pushed against my lips, insistent, like a fat wet slug. "Umm," he said.

My stomach turned and my heart beat fast, but I didn't feel all warm or dreamy like the romance novels said. It was more like I was watching a science experiment. A kind of boring one. I opened my eyes. Steve's eyelashes twitched, and sweat streaked the skin on his cheeks. He stunk. He tried to push his body closer to mine, but I leaned back. I put my hand up to his chest to push him away. "No," I said.

He grabbed my wrist, clamping down hard with his fingers. For a second, I felt trapped. My heart thunked once, slow. "No," I said, louder.

He grinned and snorted a hard laugh—*ha!*—and that made me mad. Idiot. He thought I was just a girl. Just a stupid kid. Who did he think I was? I jerked my Budweiser up and into his chin. Beer sloshed up and the can crumpled.

His eyes widened. "Uhhn." His grip on my wrist tightened. I pulled my thigh and butt muscles—strong from a summer of jogging—tight. I rammed my knee into his crotch. Mom warned me about strangers, but the *Reader's Digest,* an article called "Self-Defense for Gals," taught me what to do about them. Steve's hand released in the same instant that his face went blank and his mouth formed a perfect O. "Ye-ow!" He fell back away from me and huddled around himself on the ground.

I dropped the beer can, turned and jogged off, twirling the ring from the pull top on my finger, enjoying the sun beating into my skin, charged with adrenaline. So that was what it was like to kiss a boy.

Shane's shadow as she crouched over me on the hot tar road did not cool but it did block the sun. I could barely make out her face, the fringes of her hair tucked back behind her ears, the sun making a bright ring behind her head. "Hey," she said. "Feeling better?" She laid the back of her hand against my cheek, and my heart thunked at the chill, like water splashed up from somewhere deep.

I blinked and swallowed. Her eyes glittered, light blue, like the sun on the lake when I was skiing, in the shadow between us. I felt warm but light. My blood was a river fed by warm springs. I reached up and took her hand and held it steady against my palm. Both were ice cold.

I moved my thumb to feel the pulse in her wrist, one hard, sluggish beat. *Thunk.* And then I felt mine in my chest. *Thunk.*

I wasn't in a trance; I knew exactly what my hand, my body, were doing. I placed her palm against my mouth, watching her eyes. I felt the *thunk* of her heartbeat against my lips, then in my hand as I twined my fingers into hers. I pushed my body up from the road into hers, and lifted my mouth to her mouth. Her soft lips hesitated, then opened just a little against my own. I tasted something alive, neither dark nor bloody nor mysterious, but clear and cold and magical on my tongue.

Reunion: Ed

Ed feels someone kissing him. The lips are open and warm, soft but pressing hard onto his mouth. He has not been kissed by anyone but his wife in over forty years, and this is surely not Mary. He wants to push away, but his arms won't move. He wants to open his eyes, to see who it is, but his lids won't lift. He hears a wailing.

"Come on, Ed," he hears. His lips cool as the kiss stops. Come on where? He tries to see something in the shadows. Isn't there supposed to be a bright light? I'm trying, Lord, he thinks. What about floating up above his body and looking down? Isn't that supposed to happen at the end? "Come on, Ed," the voice repeats. Where are all his dead relatives who're supposed to come and greet him? Where is Lee? His mother. Pops. Nothing. Black.

"He's not ready," someone says. "Hang on."

I'm ready, Ed thinks. I'm ready, Lord. Come and get me. I'm ready. The wailing has stopped, but someone is singing. A radio maybe. That old hymn, "Amazing Grace."

Ed feels a hand touch his, and he slides back to that day at Green Acres again, the little hand sweaty and trembling in his. Virge had been such a good little girl. Strong. Quiet. Why hadn't she stayed little? And quiet. Good.

Just that one time, when he'd caught her and Lee sneaking in after midnight . . . He'd been so mad, so scared. Anything can happen to a girl. A boy can take care of himself. A girl needs protecting. He wishes he hadn't hit her when he was so mad. Scared. But she'd been good after that. No more trouble.

Then he'd woken up one day and she was gone. A woman, near as tall as him. Off to college, then off to *Up North*. Anything can happen to a girl off like that in the world. But she didn't listen to him, just went off on her own. Good, he'd thought. Be on your own then. Stay away.

Lee, lying on the ground, looking up at him, then him gone too. Just like that.

I should've been a better dad. Shouldn't've hit 'em when I was mad and scared. But nothin' left to do about Lee.

Ed strains to open his eyes, but his body is numb, not there. Not heavy, just not there. A rhythmic whooshing sound, like water rushing. This is his end, nothing to do in heaven but wait for the end of time. Why isn't Lee waiting for him, helping him along to heaven?

"Right here, man." The voice is deep, far away and right by his ear at the same time. Where? Again Ed strains to see into the shadows. Light seems near, shining from behind his eyelids maybe, but he can't open his eyes. Lee?

"Sorry." Ed's own voice croaks, startling him. His throat is dry. Has Lee heard him? "Sorry," he repeats.

He opens his eyes.

"Mr. Young?" A black man peers into his face. "Hey there. You're in the hospital. I'm your nurse," he says. "You're gonna be fine." He watches the monitor beside Ed's bed, then shakes his head. "You damn lucky, man," he says. "The doc'll be in in a minute. She'll tell you all about it."

Ed blinks. "Diviner?" he asks.

The man raises his eyebrows. "Huh?"

"A diviner, girl, name J.C." He licks his lips. "Water."

The nurse pours from a pitcher into a plastic cup and holds the straw between his lips. "Don't know about that," he says, shaking his head. "EMTs brought you in from way out in the middle of nowhere. Responded to a nine-one-one call, found you lying on the ground out there." He glances at the monitor again. "Six blockages," he mutters. "You damn lucky they found you."

"I was alone?" Ed asks. What happened to J.C.?

"So they said." The nurse shakes his head. "You been in surgery a good six hours, man." He points to Ed's wallet lying on the bedside table. "We left a message on your home phone, but couldn't get nobody. Only thing you said till now was "'Sorry.' Over and over again. Sorry sorry sorry." He chuckles, crossing his arms over his chest. "You want me to call someone now?"

"Sorry," Ed repeats. He closes his eyes, trying to think. "Virge," he says. "My wife's at my daughter's. Virge. She's . . ." He pauses. What should he say? "Up North."

"You know her number?" the nurse asks. "You know how to reach her?"

"Call my daughter-in-law," Ed says.

The boys will come see him. The boys love him. And Virge? Does she? Will she come here? He hasn't gone to her. He gives the nurse his daughter-in-law's name.

"It's in the book," he says. "Tell her to call my wife." He bites his tongue. "Tell her to call Virge."

At the glass window a woman in scrubs looks at a chart, about to come in. The doctor, Ed realizes. "I'll take care of it," the black man says, turning toward the door.

"She's gettin' hitched," Ed says. He inhales. "My daughter. To a woman."

What happened to the diviner? Ed tries to remember what she said. Something about her daddy. And sorry. He'd said "I'm sorry." He thought he had said it in his mind, his prayers maybe. She'd been there when he opened his eyes. He'd seen the buzzard circling in a lazy black loop against the blue sky, heard the wailing sound getting closer, and she'd said, "My daddy always said that sorry only works on the living."

He hadn't seen her, but he'd heard her voice. "Sorry's only good if you do something to fix it."

Backslide

At the top of the hill, I kill the engine of the old truck and sit in the perfect silence of whiteness. Clouds seem to bloom up from the mountains, laddering into the sky. The old white house is alive with all of you—my children, boy and girl, my partner and lover, and also with all of those other loves, friends who have become family, mothers and fathers and aunts and uncles and grands and greats, all those past and future, all those I have imagined, who have been born in my mind or heart or from the molecules that unite to form any other thing. To make you. Me. Us.

The pain in my shoulder has diffused into everythingness. I have come together, reached the destination, by the way we each must, by way of back roads, sliding this way and that, sometimes forward, sometimes back, sometimes sideways, cross-roading and bushwhacking and switchbacking and dead-ending through terrain of sin and salvation. The only map is love. We are all on this path together. I have been sinner, over and over again. I have been saved, reborn, each time I chose love.

In the next moment, I will step from this vehicle into a whole world, close the creaking door, shut the book. Remembering, I will live.

The True Story, or What Made Me Change

September 1970

I am painting my room again, white this time, during the Labor Day weekend before school starts. Eighth grade. I like the way the white rolls over the orange, covering the flowers in clean, blank bands. It's new, like me, but it's not hiding anything. The paint smells fresh; the walls seem clean and unmarked. Anything can happen.

As I paint, I slide back and forth from this story into that one, all mixed-up. From one person into another one. From here to there to somewhere else, like in a maze of dirt roads. From now to then and ahead to something yet to come. I'm trying not to be afraid.

I'll be fourteen in two weeks, and I start my job as a cashier at Winn-Dixie the day after that. I can get my driver's license in another year. Mom says I can date when I turn sixteen, but I don't think I will. I don't really like boys much. If I work hard, I can go to college—Miss Williams told me that I'm smart enough to get a scholarship, maybe even to a school up North. Five more years until I can escape for good.

The white of my walls makes me think of snow, of *Up North*. It reminds me of that season I don't really know about. It reminds me of Steve-the-Good-Humor-Man, the grass stains on his uniform. I've never seen snow, but I want to write a story about it, about being cold and frozen and about how it hides everything underneath, waiting for spring to bloom again. When I sit down to write, the paper is white like that, like a Christian soul washed clean in the blood of the Lamb, which is pretty mixed-up if you think about it. When I write down my stories, the black marks on the white paper are a kind of blood too, and it doesn't matter if it's mixed-up. It's all true because I make it true.

Before I painted, I cleared my bulletin board of the stuff I put up last year: the postcard with my homeroom assignment for seventh grade; the lock of my own long hair; the cedar Christmas tree shaving; the metal wire from my braces; the photos from the Kent State shooting; the Georgia driver's manual; the story with Miss Williams's round red writing. *What did make her change?*

While the paint dries, the walls white and empty, I put all of those things into the drawer with my old glasses. I balance the diviner's stick on my fingertips one more time, considering Miss Williams's question and watching the light glint off the metal beer can tab on my ring finger. I remember what Mrs. Rosenbaum said: "Life is about losing . . . a little here, a little there. It is what we keep, what grows from what is gone, that matters."

This year I lost Ricki Ann, Mel, Mrs. Rosenbaum. I lost my accent. We lost the farm. I lost Dad, I think. Maybe I lost my virginity, but I'm not sure water skiing counts. I think about *Up North,* about my escape plans and my mixed-up true stories. I think I've lost God too. He's not out there anymore. He's in me. He is me. But I am not lost. Maybe I'm backslid, but it doesn't feel like I'm really going backward.

I broke almost all God's official rules for Baptists this year. I dishonored my parents. I lied. I bore false witness against Ricki Ann, though I did not mean to. I coveted. I stole. When I filled out the application to work at Winn-Dixie, I requested work on Sundays so I won't have to go to church anymore. Maybe I committed adultery too, or something like it. I don't know what it means to have kissed Shane, but it didn't feel like a sin. And I'm not a virgin anymore, but I am too. I'm not pure, but I'm not evil either. The rules are mixed-up too, and they don't seem much use anyway.

Maybe what has really changed is God, not me. Maybe now the way, the truth and the life are in me, or maybe they're just down the road. Maybe that's why I feel saved, born again again, or just about to be. Backsliding seems to have made me real.

I keep my eyes on the diviner's stick, the V branches balancing on my fingertips, merging away into a Y.

When it's my time, I am going to write a book called *Sinner*, but not about being a sinner according to God and the Baptists and all, but about breaking the really important rule—loving each other and all the parts inside ourselves. About listening for each other's voices inside your own head. About sliding back into fear and hate instead of being brave and quiet enough to trust what's inside.

Now when I look at the story I wrote for Miss Williams last year, I know the true story. She didn't change. She always was who she was, but she wasn't always brave enough to hear what was inside her own heart. That's what changed. Maybe God is like whatever it is that makes birds up North wake up restless on a September morning, confused, on the edge of something, stretching their wings, sniffing the wind, thinking about heading south. Maybe just some kind of magic inside. And maybe that's why she changed, God or a kind of magic inside. Maybe that's a rule too, that thing inside, but it's a harder rule to figure out. Maybe it's just mixed-up, like a story, a true one.

Reunion: A Civil Union

Mountains unfold from our home at the top of the hill, rolling out like green waves dissolving into blue heavens. Family relax on folding chairs or stand in the semicircle, behind them a white open-sided tent with ribbons fluttering in a summer breeze. They are an island of color: party dress, Sunday best, haircuts fresh and faces scrubbed. They are a family of disparate hues and textures united not by blood but by the couple—us—standing before Justice, hands linked with those of children.

The house on the hill behind us is plain and upright and old, a place for generations and ghosts and histories—family—to merge. The village below seems an anchorage. The world embarks like a blue-green wave from these circles: a couple and children and Justice; family of mothers and fathers and children, brothers and friends, aunts and great-aunts; uncles and nephews, cousins and lovers, sisters and school friends, roommates and neighbors and teachers, witnesses and ghosts and strangers and demons and gods; home and village and mountains and valleys; the me and the others within me.

I am all of these, finally arrived or finally returned to this home on the hill, traveled by way of the backslide, the long way around. This time has not yet happened, I know. But it belongs to the times already gone, within me. Which is real? Which is true? All of them. All of us. All of me.

Mother, Father, are you here? Do you hear me in your silence? Do you see me? Imagine me? Us? You are created now in our image. How else do we exist? How do we become you, and you become me—us?

The tide turns and the wave rolls in again—from dark to light, Eden to America, South to North to West to East—back to this center. I am father, mother, brother and all the others. I am my first love and my love forever after. I am you too. The pain in my arm, my shoulder, my chest still throbs, but I have arrived somewhere bright and warm with love, with all of you. Home. This time is all times, and this place is all homes; all within me.

About the Author

Teresa Stores's first books, *Getting to the Point* (1995) and *SideTracks* (1996), were published by Naiad Press. She is Associate Professor of English and Director of Creative Writing at the University of Hartford. She lives with her partner, Susan Jarvis, and their children, James and Isabelle, in Southern Vermont.

Publications from Spinsters Ink

P.O. Box 242
Midway, Florida 32343
Phone: 800-301-6860
www.spinstersink.com

ACROSS TIME by Linda Kay Silva. If you believe in soul mates, if you know you've had a past life, then join Jessie in the first of a series of adventures that takes her *Across Time*.
ISBN 978-1883523-91-6 $14.95

SELECTIVE MEMORY by Jennifer L. Jordan. A Kristin Ashe Mystery. A classical pianist, who is experiencing profound memory loss after a near-fatal accident, hires private investigator Kristin Ashe to reconstruct her life in the months leading up to the crash.
ISBN 978-1-883523-88-6 $14.95

HARD TIMES by Blayne Cooper. Together, Kellie and Lorna navigate through an oppressive, hidden world where lines between right and wrong blur, sexual passion is forbidden but explosive, and love is the biggest risk of all.   ISBN 978-1-883523-90-9 $14.95

THE KIND OF GIRL I AM by Julia Watts. Spanning decades, *The Kind of Girl I Am* humorously depicts an extraordinary woman's experiences of triumph, heartbreak, friendship and forbidden love.
ISBN 978-1-883523-89-3 $14.95

PIPER'S SOMEDAY by Ruth Perkinson. It seemed as though life couldn't get any worse for feisty, young Piper Leigh Cliff and her three-legged dog, Someday.   ISBN 978-1-883523-87-9 $14.95

MERMAID by Michelene Esposito. When May unearths a box in her missing sister's closet she is taken on a journey through her mother's past that leads her not only to Kate but to the choices and compromises, emptiness and fullness, the beauty and jagged pain of love that all women must face. ISBN 978-1-883523-85-5 $14.95

ASSISTED LIVING by Sheila Ortiz-Taylor. Violet March, an eighty-two-year-old resident of Casa de los Sueños, finally has the opportunity to put years of mystery reading to practical use. One by one her comrades, the Bingos, are dying. Is this natural attrition, or is there a sinister plot afoot? ISBN 978-1-883523-84-2 $14.95

NIGHT DIVING by Michelene Esposito. *Night Diving* is both a young woman's coming-out story and a thirty-something coming-of-age journey that proves you can go home again.
ISBN 978-1-883523-52-7 $14.95

FURTHEST FROM THE GATE by Ann Roberts. *Furthest from the Gate* is a humorous chronicle of a woman's coming of age, her complicated relationship with her mother and the responsibilities to family that last a lifetime. ISBN 978-1-883523-81-7 $14.95

EYES OF GRAY by Dani O'Connor. Grayson Thomas was the typical college senior with typical friends, a typical job and typical insecurities about her future. One Sunday morning, Gray's life became a little less typical, she saw a man clad in black, and started doubting her own sanity. ISBN 978-1-883523-82-4 $14.95

ORDINARY FURIES by Linda Morgenstein. Tired of hiding, exhausted by her grief after her husband's death, Alexis Pope plunges into the refreshingly frantic world of restaurant resort cooking and dining in the funky chic town of Guerneville, California.
ISBN 978-1-883523-83-1 $14.95